CITY OF DARK MAGIC

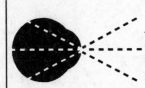

This Large Print Book carries the
Seal of Approval of N.A.V.H.

CITY OF DARK MAGIC

MAGNUS FLYTE

THORNDIKE PRESS
A part of Gale, Cengage Learning

GALE
CENGAGE Learning

Detroit • New York • San Francisco • New Haven, Conn • Waterville, Maine • London

LIBRARY OF CONGRESS CATALOGING-IN-PUBLICATION DATA

Flyte, Magnus.
  City of dark magic / by Magnus Flyte.
    pages ; cm. — (Thorndike Press large print basic)
  ISBN-13: 978-1-4104-5643-4 (hardcover)
  ISBN-10: 1-4104-5643-9 (hardcover)
    1. Music students—Fiction. 2. Prague (Czech Republic)—Fiction.
  3. Paranormal fiction. 4. Large type books. I. Title.
  PS3606.L98C58 2013
  813'.6—dc23   2012047398

Published in 2013 by arrangement with Penguin Books, a member of Penguin Group (USA) Inc.

CITY OF DARK MAGIC

The manuscript of the book you are about to read arrived in the mail one day at the original publisher, Penguin headquarters in New York, with no cover letter. It was written on stationery from the Hotel La Mamounia in Marrakech using a manual typewriter, and postmarked on the Isle of Mull. The return address was simply "Flyte, Magnus." When the editors sought details about the author, they found them to be conflicting. He may be American. He may have ties to one or more intelligence organizations, including a radical group of Antarctic separatists. He may be the author of a monograph on carnivorous butterflies. He may live in Venice, Vienna, Vladivostok, or Vermont. *City of Dark Magic* may be his first novel.

Prince! what you are, you are by circumstance and by birth. What I am, I am through myself. Of Princes there have and will be thousands — of Beethovens there is only one.

LUDWIG VAN BEETHOVEN,
in a letter to Prince Lichnowsky, 1806

It is enough for the tourist to enter the twilit little streets of ancient Prague in the evening, and the same mood will breathe on him as has been felt for centuries by those who tell of the ghosts in Prague houses. It will not seem impossible to him, as he walks the winding alleys, that some of the strange inhabitants with which fantasy has peopled Prague should emerge from the flickering shadows before him.

JAN VANIS,
A Guide to Mysterious Prague

PROLOGUE

The Save Venice fund-raiser began as these things do, with Bellinis, with tiny toast points topped with squid pate, and with swaying musicians playing the greatest hits of Italian opera beneath a fresco by Tiepolo. Sequined women and tuxedo-clad men stepped out of teak vaporetti onto the private dock at Ca' Rezzonico, where, it was hoped, strong drink and the thought of beautiful palazzi sinking into the sands below would lift wallets as easily as a child pickpocket in the Piazza San Marco.

The organizers were salivating, greeting a German fashion designer, an American hedge fund owner, and a dour British playwright. Models had been hired to improve the beauty quotient, since billionaires are not especially attractive up close.

But just after midnight, something had gone terribly wrong. That was when, as one

9

of the carabinieri put it, the *cascata dei corpi,* or human waterfall, began. It was a minor member of the Saudi royal family who went first, startling everyone around him by emitting a series of hoarse screams and then crashing through a glass window and plummeting out of sight. A billionaire American industrialist, who onlookers at first thought was rushing to save the Saudi, soon joined him. They were the first two.

A honeymooning couple from Youngstown, Ohio, being poled up the Grand Canal were startled to see a series of bodies falling from the windows of the glittering palazzo. Inside, panic was raging and it was generally felt that very few that evening distinguished themselves by bravery. By the time it was over, seven people in formal wear and one waiter were floating facedown in the Grand Canal. Dead.

The city was in a panic, though a panic in Italy means most people still stand around coffee bars drinking espresso and Prosecco. St. Mark's was still very crowded.

What had driven these people to suicide? Or were the unfortunate souls already dead when they hit the water? Despite the clamor of an army of international lawyers descending like vultures, demanding the bodies of the dead, Venetian medical examiners were dutifully dissecting and testing the remains, which, since the city's tiny morgue was full, were being housed in the Church of the Redeemer next door. Its cool marble interior was considered a more dignified choice than a nearby fruit warehouse.

Because all of the dead (except the waiter) were foreigners and very, very rich, it was headline news around the world. Camera crews had descended on the city, and the Grand Canal in front of the Ca' Rezzonico was a flotilla of press boats. The local taxi boat drivers were pocketing wads of euros. The latest arrival had been crowds of teenage fans of Hilda Swenson, an eighteen-year-old Swedish pop star whose blond hair had streamed out around her floating corpse like a halo, it was said. Her Chihuahua, who had not been found and was presumed to have survived the fall, was sought by the police.

Crime scene analysts and antiterrorism experts had already combed the building and interrogated the caterers. It wasn't a bomb, it wasn't a gas, it wasn't a deadly virus. "What did these people die of?" demanded the American president, who had lost one of his largest campaign contributors, of the Italian head of state.

It wasn't a good answer, but it would allow Il Primo Ministro to save face until he could pressure the damn scientists for a better one.

"Fear," said the Italian.

ONE

Sarah picked up the envelope and sniffed it. She had an especially sensitive nose, and something about the thick stationery was odd.

"I think it's a letter," said Bailey, with whom Sarah shared a tiny office on the top floor of Exeter Hall. They always gave the music grad students the worst offices. This one was unheated in winter, stiflingly hot in summer, and smelled faintly of mice.

"I can see it's a letter," said Sarah, moving Bailey's troubadour bobblehead an inch to the left, knowing this would drive him nuts. They enjoyed finding ways to outmaneuver each other. Bailey was an expert on madrigals, while Sarah's recent work at Thoreau College in Boston focused on the emerging field of neuromusicology. Sarah had spent most of last week wondering about the differences in the brains of musicians and non-musicians when it came to pitch perception, and whether pitch was something that non-musicians could conceptualize. She had forced Bailey to listen to her musings. It was only fair, since he had been playing a particularly annoying madrigal, "Hail the Buds of Spring," over and over on his recorder.

Sarah ripped open the heavy brown paper envelope, and slid its contents — a thick wad of paper neatly tied in brown string — onto her lap. Bailey picked the discarded envelope up off her desk.

"It's from Lobkowicz Palace, Prague, Czech Republic."

"I can *read,* Bailey," Sarah said, untying the string. "And it's pronounced: LOB-ko-witz."

The name was intriguing. In the early 1800s a Prince Lobkowicz had been a patron of Haydn and Beethoven, who had each dedicated a number of works to the prince as a thank-you. She hadn't realized that the Lobkowicz family was still around, if these were the same ones.

Sarah looked down. The wad of paper looked like . . . money. Her jaw fell open and she looked more closely.

"Czech crowns," said Bailey, leaning over her shoulder. "You know, it's illegal to send cash through the mail."

Sarah examined the inch-thick pile. A curly bearded king stared intently at something just below the left edge of the banknote.

"What's a hundred worth?" Sarah asked Bailey, who quickly googled the answer. "Five dollars and fifty-seven cents," he said.

"Oh," said Sarah, who had been hoping the crown was worth a bit more. "But there are a lot of them here." She unfolded a letter that had accompanied the currency.

"Well?" prompted Bailey. "What's it all about? Are they trying to smuggle out their money?"

"No," Sarah said, still reading. "They're offering me a job for the summer." Europe. Sarah had never been to Europe, although she had optimistically kept an up-to-date passport since she was sixteen. No one in her family had ever been to Europe, at least since they had fled the great famines of the nineteenth century. She looked up from the letter.

"This is just cab fare from the airport to the palace. They're offering me two hundred thousand crowns for the summer."

"That's almost twelve thousand dollars!" Bailey exclaimed.

Sarah blinked. Her fellowship only covered the basics, which left her in the usual state of doctoral-candidate poverty. She hadn't grown up with money; she was the first person in her family to go to college, let alone pursue a PhD. Twelve thousand dollars sounded to her like a million dollars.

A trip to Europe. To Prague.

Prague. It was too bad it wasn't Vienna, since she had mastered German as an undergrad and Vienna was where Sarah's personal and professional hero, Ludwig van Beethoven, had largely lived and worked. She might be able to finagle a side trip though.

"What do they want you to do?" asked Bailey. "Not that it matters, because you'll do it."

Sarah read further. "It's about a museum the Lobkowicz family is opening," she reported. "They have a huge collection of art, musical instruments, weapons, ceramics, books. A trove of handwritten scores: Mozart, Haydn, Beethoven. Letters and other documents to do with music. They need help sorting, deciding which things should go on display, which need restoration work." Sarah leaned forward and started typing at her computer.

"Are you looking up Lobkowicz?" Bailey asked. " 'Cause I'm already there. One of the oldest Bohemian families, princes of the Holy Roman Empire, knights of the Order of the Golden Fleece, enormous fortune, politically powerful. Joseph Franz Maximilian, 7th Prince Lobkowicz, was a patron of Haydn and Beethoven, who dedicated —"

"Yes, I know about him," Sarah interrupted.

"Hereditary titles were abolished in 1918," Bailey rattled on. "So they're not really princes anymore. That sucks."

"Maximilian Lobkowicz," Sarah said, reading, "1888 to 1967. He was a patriot and a supporter of the newly formed Czechoslovak State. He fled the Nazis in 1939 and they seized the entire family fortune."

"So they lost everything," Bailey said, picking up the story. "Until 1945, when the family returned after the war and got everything restituted back to them! And then . . . oh. Oops."

"And then the communists confiscated it all again in 1948," Sarah said. "The family was forced to flee a second time. It looks like everything stayed lost until the Velvet Revolution in 1989. The family has been gathering up the stuff since then, I guess. And now they want to open a museum."

"Well, that's all clear enough," Bailey said. "But why do they want *you*?"

Sarah didn't take offense at the question.

She knew herself to be a gifted student, exceptional even, and she had experience with archival work. But she wasn't a world-class musicologist — not yet. She had been a student of such a person, which was how she knew she wasn't at that level.

Dr. Absalom Sherbatsky's "Music Cognition" seminar was by far the hardest class to get into in Sarah's graduate program. In fact, Sherbatsky had been known to cancel his course altogether if there were no applicants he deemed worthy to receive his wisdom. (He had refused to teach at Harvard after a class there had "failed" him.) When it was announced that Dr. Sherbatsky would be leading a special series of lectures with the disarming title "Beethoven: In One Ear and Out the Other," Sarah was intrigued.

For the first class, Sherbatsky strode in with a boom box circa 1985 and popped in a tape of Beethoven's *Fidelio* Overture, op. 72.

"You've heard it before?" Sherbatsky smiled, all mock innocence. "Really? You know this one?" He folded his arms and tucked his chin into his Brooks Brothers shirt, closed his eyes. A few of the more sycophantic students copied this pose. Sarah leaned forward, intent on recognizing the recording. Hans Knappertsbusch and Munich's Bavarian State Orchestra most likely.

Sherbatsky played the overture through to the conclusion and then asked for a student to write out the French horn passage in the second theme of the allegro on the chalkboard. Several hands shot up eagerly.

"So you'll all agree?" Sherbatsky asked, when this was done. "This is correct?" Nodding all around. "This is what you heard?" More nodding.

"No," said Sarah. Sherbatsky shot a look her way. "It's what it should be," Sarah said. "But it's not what's on that recording." Sarah approached the chalkboard and made a quick adjustment to the second measure. "The second horn made kind of a silly mistake. The recording is live, obviously, but not performance. Dress rehearsal, I'm thinking."

"Obviously, the presence of the audience changes the sound," someone said. Sherbatsky turned to Sarah.

"Well, that," Sarah said. "Yeah. But also the musicians wear different shoes for rehearsal. Sounds like the first violin has on boots. A rainy day in Munich maybe?"

That had been pure invention, that thing with the boots, and she was pretty sure

19

Sherbatsky knew it, but she was right about the second French horn player making a mistake.

Many of the seminars had involved strange "empathic listening" exercises, where you had to play something of Ludwig's later period on the piano or violin while wearing giant sound deprivation headphones. Sherbatsky had made recordings of "simulated noise" as well, his attempts to guess at what Beethoven had been able to hear of his own work at different periods of his life, and different places. The composer had actually had moments, even near the end of his life, where the ability to hear had returned in brief flashes. Sarah was entranced, and became Sherbatsky's star pupil.

For their final project, Sherbatsky had simply said to the class, "Surprise me." Sarah called a friend who worked at Mass General, and the girl had snuck Sarah into her lab and done a functional magnetic resonance imaging scan of Sarah's brain while she thought through the entire Ninth Symphony. When Sarah presented the printout to Sherbatsky, he had wept.

Last winter she asked him to supervise her PhD thesis, even though he was known to loathe overseeing student work. He surprised her by agreeing eagerly, saying that he thought Sarah had exceptional sensory abilities. He actually hugged her brain, which had been awkward but flattering. But, Sherbatsky said, they would have to begin in the fall. He was off on sabbatical for the spring semester. He was vague about his destination, which was not unusual. Sarah wasn't sure if *Sherbatsky* knew where he was most of the time. She hadn't heard from him since he left in January.

So why hadn't the Lobkowiczes hired someone like him, who was recognized the world over as the man who knew Beethoven better than Beethoven knew Beethoven? Or some acknowledged expert from the Royal College of Music or someplace like that?

Why her?

At the bottom of the letter was an e-mail address. If Sarah accepted the offer, she was to send an acknowledgment at once to Miles Wolfmann, head of the Lobkowicz Museum Collection. Travel accommodations would then be made. She should be prepared to leave immediately.

Sarah decided that a brief acceptance message was best. She could have pretended that accepting meant canceling equally glamorous plans, but why bother? However, she needn't tell Miles Wolfmann that the only people she'd be disappointing by her absence this summer were the members of Boston Sports Club, where she moonlighted as a spin-class instructor.

How had the Lobkowicz family even heard of her? True, she had published, but only in academic journals. Had Sherbatsky himself recommended her? That was plausible, and Sarah decided to accept it as the most likely explanation.

She left the office and biked quickly back to the tiny Porter Square apartment she shared with a roommate. Adrenaline and excitement kicked up her pace, and she beat her best time by forty-five seconds.

Sarah knew she should call her mother and tell her the news. Actually, the person she really wanted to tell was her father. Even though it had been thirteen years since his death, she still wanted to tell him things.

Sarah felt a weird mix of dread and resentment when she thought about what her mom's reaction would be to Sarah gallivanting off to Europe for the summer. Her mom, Judy, had grown up very poor and dropped out of high school when her own mom died and she was left to take care of younger siblings. Judy was cleaning houses for a living when she met Sarah's dad, an electrician she let into a fancy mansion on

Beacon Hill so he could fix the crystal chandeliers for her employers.

Sarah's dad had been delighted that his daughter loved reading and school. Her mom said all the right things ("We're very proud of you"), but even when Sarah was very little she had the sense that with every book she read, she was somehow distancing herself from her mom. This news wasn't likely to improve matters.

Sarah sighed, stowed her bike away, and climbed the stairs to her apartment. Alessandro, her roommate, greeted her at the door, clad only in a towel and carrying two raspberry-colored cocktails. Sarah accepted one gratefully.

"Campari and pomegranate juice," Alessandro purred in his thick Italian accent. "You will adore me forever."

None of Sarah's friends could believe that Sarah wasn't sleeping with Alessandro, who was hot in both the classical Renaissance sense and in a totally cheesy vampire movie one, too. Sarah, who took a scholarly interest in her own healthy libido, could only explain it as a matter of pheromones. When it came to sex, she simply followed her nose, and her nose never led her to Alessandro. "You're spoiled," her friends said. Which was probably true, since Sarah never seemed to have any trouble finding a suitable partner for the mood, and the mood occurred frequently. "What about common interests, intimacy, trust?" other friends said. "Don't you want that?" At this point, Sarah usually had to hide a yawn.

Now she followed her roommate into their cramped but immaculate (that was Alessandro's doing) kitchen and showed him the letter from Prague.

"The first thing you must do when you get there," Alessandro said, "is visit *Il Bambino di Praga,* and say a prayer to him."

Sarah rolled her eyes. Alessandro was a scientist. He was studying yeast, although Sarah wasn't totally clear on the specifics. Mostly because the way Alessandro pronounced the word "yeast" always cracked her up. She knew his work had something to do with brain functions, but in a way that didn't seem to overlap at all with her own interest in music and the brain.

"What's a bambino of Praga?" she asked.

Alessandro shook his head in mock despair. "What kind of a nice Catholic girl are you?" he asked.

"I'm not," said Sarah. That, too, had been a showdown with her mother. The day she had decided that she wasn't going to mass anymore.

"It's an ancient statue of Gesu Bambino, the baby Jesus, that has magical powers when you pray to him."

"This from the man who stares into an electron microscope all day." It never ceased to amuse and perplex her that Alessandro, a neuroanatomist, freely switched from evil eyes and the magical abilities of saints to Einstein's unfinished unified field theory in a microsecond.

"Sarah," Alessandro said, sternly. "There is much more to this life than what we can see even through an electron microscope. You will learn, when you go to Prague. There is magic there." He crossed himself. "Dark magic. Prague is a threshold."

"Prague is a city," she said firmly. "A place where, just like here, the rules of science apply."

"Rules of science." Alessandro shrugged his elegant shoulders. "And what are those? We don't even know how this works." He pointed to his head. "Eighty-six point one billion neurons. And glial cells surround neurons — eighty-four point six billion glia. For over a century, *cento anni,* we know glia are there, but not what they do. Now we know they modulate neurotransmission. But how? We don't know. And universe? Ninety-six percent of the universe is dark matter and dark energy. What are they? *Chissá?* No one knows. I tell you, rules of science are *molto misterioso.*"

Sarah downed the rest of the Campari. The doorbell rang.

"One of your lovers?" Alessandro raised an eyebrow. "I thought you say no sex till you finish paper on pitch perception in the brain?"

Sarah shook her head. "I'll see who it is," she said, and handed Alessandro her glass. "If we're going to talk about dark matter I think I need another drink."

Two

When Sarah opened the door the hallway was empty. Then she turned her head. And then she looked down.

The man was . . . small. Was he officially, Sarah wondered, a "little person," or whatever the correct phraseology was these days? She looked at the top of his head, which was large and blocked the rest of his figure, except for a set of feet in brown shoes. The toes pointed outward, in the manner of ballet dancers. Or paper dolls.

The shoes were odd. Retro, but more so. They had buckles, not laces. Sarah blinked.

"Sarah Weston?" The man's voice was not small. It was loud, and very deep. A bassoon. Well, he was about the size of a bassoon, Sarah thought, and probably the weight.

"Can I help you?" Sarah hedged. You couldn't be too careful. Not with the kind of student loans she was carrying. A tantalizing image involving stacks of Czech crowns floated before her eyes. Did you have to declare that kind of thing to the IRS?

The little man tilted his head. Raised tiny hands to frame his eyes as if he were cutting off the glare of the hallway's fluorescent lighting. Or instigating a game of peekaboo. His eyes were large, and very dark, almost black.

"So? *Chié?*" Alessandro appeared at Sarah's elbow. The knot of his towel was on the same level as the tiny man's chin.

"You do not look like her," said the stranger, ignoring Alessandro and continuing to scrutinize Sarah.

"Maybe you've got the wrong Sarah Weston," she offered. "What is this about?"

The little man studied Sarah calmly for a moment, and then spoke softly, almost chanting, his deep voice now in a minor key:

Hitherto I thought there were only Nine
  Muses, but
now Weston makes me believe there are
  ten.
For she decants songs that are musical,
  in fact Musty as new
Wine, songs full of Cecropian
  honeycombs.

Alessandro let out a short whistle, the complicated and expressive whistle of all Italian men born south of Rome. Sarah had learned most of them. This one meant, "Oh, so I guess you like your men *pazzo,* eh, sweetie? Nice conquest." Sarah wondered how Alessandro could actually manage a sarcastic whistle. In a towel. And what the hell were Cecropian honeycombs?

"It's not mine," the stranger said, modestly. "It is the verse of one Balthasar Caminaeus, a doctor of laws. Written in praise of *Elizabeth* Weston. Whom you do not resemble. Which is very fortunate for you. She was not an attractive person, even allowing for the costume of the era."

Alessandro licked his lips. He clearly had no intention of going anywhere, or aiding Sarah in managing this absurd exchange. Or putting on pants. The tiny man appeared to be waiting for a reply. One buckled shoe tapped the carpet softly.

"Did Bailey send you?" Sarah waited for the stranger to pull a recorder out of a sleeve and serenade her with another round of "Hail the Buds of Spring."

"I'm afraid Elizabeth Weston is not widely read," the little man said. "Forgotten, like so many others. But not gone. Not quite."

"I'm sorry," Sarah said. "But I'm kind

29

of . . . in the middle of something. So, if you have something to . . . say . . . or do?"

"She has to pack for Prague," Alessandro said, making himself useful at last. "She has recently become a scholar *molto importante.*"

"You are going, then?" The little man leaned forward and touched Sarah lightly on her wrist. "I thought you would. I was hoping. I think you are needed."

Sarah was suddenly on the alert. How did this person know her business?

"Yes, I think this is very good," the man continued in his strange bassoon voice. "You have an interesting face. This man in the towel smirks at me. He thinks I am *pazzo,* but what does he know? He's looking in the wrong place, I tell you. Or rather, the right place but in the wrong way. Yeast! Bah!"

"Okay, maybe I call the cops now," Alessandro said, shrugging and turning back into the apartment. Sarah watched the back of his towel retreating, the Renaissance shoulders above it in an apparent huff .

"How did you know the Lobkowicz family invited me?" Sarah asked. "I only got the letter a few hours ago."

"I am on very intimate terms with the Lobkowicz family," the little man said.

"Indeed, I have just come from Prague."
He brought his hands up to his face again,
and this time he did cover his eyes with his
palms, then held them out to Sarah. Balanced in the center of his left palm lay a
copper pillbox.

"For you," he said, simply.

Sarah could hear her cell phone ringing in
the other room.

"I should get that," she said. She didn't
want to let the little man into her apartment, but it did seem rude to just shut the
door in his face. Especially if he was connected to her new employers in some way.

"I will wait," said the man, calmly.

Sarah half-shut the door and picked up
her phone, noting that it was the head of
the Music Department, Professor Klyme,
calling. "Hello?"

"Sarah, I have some bad news," he said.
"I'm sorry to tell you this. Professor
Sherbatsky is dead."

Sarah sat down on the forest-green sofa
she and Alessandro had scavenged from the
corner of Mass Ave and Arlington on trash
day. Her mouth suddenly felt dry.

"What?" she demanded. "When? How?"

Professor Klyme told her what he knew,
which was very little. There had been some
kind of accident. In Prague. No doubt

details would be forthcoming.

"An accident?" Sarah repeated. "Prague?"

"A terrible tragedy," Professor Klyme said, somewhat mechanically. Sherbatsky had not been particularly liked in the department, where professional jealousies ran high.

"I received the news from a Mr. Miles Wolfmann," he continued. "A colleague of Professor Sherbatsky's. He offered his condolences and then informed me that you are going to Prague yourself to assist in restoration work at the new Lobkowicz Palace Museum. He's sending a plane ticket Federal Express. I should congratulate you. This is quite an opportunity." Professor Klyme sounded miffed and more than a little skeptical. Sarah thanked him crisply and then asked if there was anyone . . . would a funeral be held? Some kind of service? Professor Klyme did not know, and after a few more conventional phrases of regret and well-wishing, he hung up.

Sarah sat on the couch, stunned, for a few minutes, before realizing she had left a strange little man standing in her hallway. She crossed the room and opened the door.

The little man was gone. The pillbox lay on the ragged carpet where his feet had been. Sarah picked it up and shut the door.

She wandered back into her apartment and looked out the window, but the little man was nowhere to be seen. She had the weird sensation that something cosmologically enormous had happened, that the orbit of the earth had shifted, and yet outside her window her neighbor was planting tomato seedlings in her garden, and a little boy was bumping his tricycle down the sidewalk while his mom walked behind him with a fat Labrador.

She went to her bedroom and clicked on her computer, entering "Sherbatsky" and "Prague" into the search engine. The first result was a page from the *Prague Post*.

American scholar dies at Lobkowicz Palace.

"Shit," Sarah said out loud. She read on in shock: "Dr. Absalom Sherbatsky was recognized as one of the world's foremost experts on Beethoven, and had come to the palace to offer his services to the Lobkowicz family. He apparently fell from a window at Lobkowicz Palace late Wednesday night. Police have ruled it a suicide."

Suicide? Sherbatsky? Sarah continued searching online but found no more information. She pulled the letter from Lobkowicz Palace out of her backpack. The invitation to come to Prague was dated *before* the (apparent) suicide. So Sherbatsky *must* have recommended her. Perhaps he wanted an assistant.

They had sent her the job offer. And then Sherbatsky threw himself out a window? It just didn't make sense. Had he simply fallen? He was not a physically strong man. It had been a joke between them. He always commented on Sarah's mental and physical toughness, on her "townie" upbringing. Thin and gangly Sherbatsky seemed to admire her combination of brains and brawn, and unlike the Professor Klymes of the world, he had never treated her like a bimbo just because she also looked good in a bikini. Sarah felt tears come to her eyes. Poor Sherbatsky. What had happened to him?

Alessandro appeared in the doorway and Sarah told him the news. She read the *Prague Post* article to him.

"Are you sure you should go?" asked Alessandro. "Look at what happened in Venice two weeks ago. People go crazy and throw themselves out window in middle of party. There is something about this, *cara . . .*"

"I'm going," said Sarah. Of course, there was the money. She'd go just for that. She'd go just to show the snobs like Professor Klyme that a girl from "Southie" could distinguish herself in academia. But she also wanted to find out the truth behind the death of her beloved mentor. The whole invitation to Prague sounded like a challenge.

And Sarah never backed down from a challenge.

THREE

"Yes, it's all coming together. It's all happening. You must find her," said Pollina, frantically poking the fire with a stick, even though the windows were wide open on this spring evening. Sarah had had a busy day, organizing herself to leave for Prague, but she would never have missed a music session with her favorite pupil. "Pupil" was the wrong word. Pollina was more of a colleague. Even though she was only eleven.

"You're sad." Pollina suddenly turned to Sarah, her eyes shining brightly in the semidarkness. "You want some ice cream?"

Sarah did not want to tell Pollina about Sherbatsky. The girl was already in fragile health, and the news that Sarah was leaving for the summer would upset her enough. Pollina was too alert to miss Sarah's mood, though. She had been thinking over the death/ suicide of the professor all day, and it still didn't make any sense.

"Chunky Monkey or Oreo Cookie?" Sarah asked, heading for the kitchen, stepping over Boris, the elderly giant mastiff who napped next to the fire.

"Both," said Pollina.

While still in high school, short on cash and wanting to avoid babysitting, Sarah answered an ad taped to the music room bulletin board for someone seeking a violin tutor. Sarah dearly hoped the person who needed the tutoring was not a horrible child, forced into the violin by crazed aspirational parents. She called the number, left hers, and received a brusque message back telling her to report to the address on Commonwealth Avenue at four p. m. on a Friday afternoon. No other details. She pedaled over on her bike and stared up at the massive mansion. *Must be divided into apartments,* she thought, but there was only one doorbell. Sarah pushed it, there was a long pause, and finally an actual uniformed butler answered the door. "Meess Weston?" he said. Sarah just stared at him, openmouthed, unable to believe that Jeeves had in fact come to life. And was Mexican. Finally, he sighed and leaned in conspiratorially.

"Okay, they're all a little crazy, but they pay really well," he said, stepping back to let her in.

Sarah nodded, wondering what Wonderland she had just tumbled into. This was the kind of wealth that her mother always talked about with resentment. The door shut behind her and the house was plunged into murky gloom. It took several seconds before Sarah's eyes adjusted to where she could see the place was chock-full of what her mother would have called "old junk."

Jeeves — Sarah would learn his name was actually Jose Nieto and that his previous job was maintaining the swan boats in Boston Common — climbed the stairs, and Sarah hurried to catch up. "There's an elevator," he said. "But it's wicked slow."

He showed Sarah into another dark room and left. She could make out some oversized stuffed animals looming in the darkness — a zebra, a giraffe, and a prostrate lion. There were creepy dolls on velvet tasseled sofas draped in huge paisley scarves — her mother would be in hives — and a grand piano. Sarah went over to the piano and ran a hand over its inlaid top.

"It's from 1795," said a small but strong voice. Sarah caught movement and turned toward it, but found herself staring at her own image in a smoky old mirror across the room. "It's unsigned, but we know it's

Viennese." The voice was coming from the sofa. Sarah turned — she hadn't seen anything there but pillows and dolls. "We bought it from the Frederick Collection. I wanted the Joseph Brodmann from 1805, but even though the moderator was missing, they felt it was too valuable to sell."

Sarah realized a child was sitting there. A child who looked to be no older than four. She was wearing a white dress with a poufy skirt and a red sash. Then the lion shifted and raised its head and Sarah realized it was a dog, a mastiff. She glanced at the giraffe, half expecting it to reach up and nibble on a drape.

"Is your, uh, mom around?" asked Sarah.

"She's in India," said the little girl, gesturing toward the piano. "Play."

"Um, well, okay," said Sarah. The kid was a little spooky, but she was excited about the idea of playing a historic piano. "What do you want to hear?" she asked.

"Dvorák. *Romanza.* Opus eleven." The girl picked up a violin off the table in front of her. Sarah had only a moment to wonder if it was a Stradivarius before the girl began to play the obscure, lilting piece, from memory, and Sarah had to hustle over to the piano, flip through a stack for the music, and catch up.

The child was incredible — she played as if she actually felt the romance of the music as strongly as Dvořák himself. How could someone feel so much, someone who had been alive for such a short time?

When they finished, the girl laid the violin down.

"It's twenty dollars an hour," said the girl. "Five days a week for two hours a day."

Sarah nodded. "I've never met a child prodigy before," she said. "Do you want me to teach you, or just accompany you?"

"My hands are too small to play what I compose on the piano," the girl said, holding them out for Sarah to see. Her eyes filled with tears. "I need someone to play the music in my head."

Though she cringed to admit it, it had taken Sarah three entire sessions to realize Pollina was blind. That day, while playing a game of fetch with Boris, Sarah had tossed the ball over to the stiffly serious little girl to try to engage her, too. The ball bounced off the child's face.

"What was that? What hit me?" cried Pollina, who suddenly lost her balance and stretched out uncomprehending arms in front of her.

"I'm so sorry," said Sarah, rushing over to put her arms around the girl.

"Stop it," said Pollina. "Write this down." She then proceeded to dictate to Sarah an entire sonata. In twelve minutes.

So it had gone for the past seven years. Pollina had composed fifteen symphonies and hundreds of other pieces of music that Sarah transcribed and played on the piano. They were beautiful, eerie, enchanting works, widely varied in emotion and complexity, often inspired by whatever book Pollina was listening to, from *Green Mansions* to *Misty of Chincoteague.*

Sarah never really got to know Pollina's parents, though they made the occasional breathless appearance as she was coming or going, and thanked her profusely for being such a good companion to their daughter. They were passionate amateur archaeologists who had met in Sicily, both searching for an ancient Greek city in a tiny village called Pollina, for which they had named their daughter. They were not themselves musical in the least, and seemed kind of clueless about her talents. When Sarah tried to talk to them, they said, "We don't want her to have the pressure of performing or being famous. Music should be fun for her. There's plenty of time for that later."

So no one in the world besides Sarah and the parents seemed to know that a baby

Mozart was living in Boston, right down the street from the Baby Gap.

In lieu of schooling, Pollina — and God help anyone who called her Polly, though Pols was acceptable in some cases — had a tutor named Matt, an English major at Harvard, who came and read aloud to her on whatever topic caught her fancy. She loved European history, and English poetry best. She would often perplex pizza delivery boys by hiding behind Jose and reciting large chunks of Spenser's *Faerie Queene.* Jose would sigh, roll his eyes, and tip the kid double.

When Sarah started college, Pollina had asked Matt to read her everything on Sarah's syllabi. At this point Pollina probably knew more about Beethoven than she did, Sarah guessed.

"Hey, I have some news," said Sarah carefully. "Something came up and I'm going to be leaving town for the summer. Just until Labor Day. But listen, it's really exciting." She explained the job, focusing on the parts she knew would interest Pols. Manuscripts in Beethoven's own hand. Priceless antique instruments.

Pollina frowned.

"You said we would work on the music together all summer." Pols hated changes to their routine.

"It's a great opportunity," said Sarah soothingly. "I'll find someone who can transcribe your music for you, I promise."

"Actually I've been using a voice-activated computer for two years now."

Sarah was surprised. "Really?"

"Yes. And my hands, they're big enough to play everything now." Sarah looked at Pollina's hands, her long slender fingers. When had they grown longer than Sarah's own?

"Why didn't you tell me?" Sarah asked.

"I didn't want you to feel useless," said Pols, sharply.

Sarah was rather touched that Pols was being so sulky. It would be nice to be missed.

"I had a dream last night," Pollina continued. "I dreamed that you were swallowed by a dragon. And you died. You were dead, and trying to talk to me."

Sarah thought of Sherbatsky with a pang.

"I'm right here. I'm not dead and don't plan to be for a long time."

"I suppose God will look after you while you search for her," said Pollina.

"Who?"

"Duh, the Immortal Beloved."

Sarah laughed. It had been one of the

great musical mysteries of the last century: the identity of the woman to whom Beethoven had written three passionate letters. He had called her his *Unsterbliche Geliebte,* or Immortal Beloved. They had even made a bad movie about it, with Gary Oldman as Beethoven.

"I am resolved to wander so long away from you until I can fly to your arms and say that I am really at home with you, and can send my soul enwrapped in you into the land of spirits," Pollina quoted with a sigh. "It's so romantic."

"Pols, I know you had Matt read you Maynard Solomon's book," said Sarah, referring to the great musical scholar who had presented a masterful and nearly incontrovertible case for the identity of the Immortal Beloved. "Antonie Brentano was the *Unsterbliche Geliebte.* And she was married, and had a few children, and it seems pretty clear that LVB really wasn't interested in taking on all that." Sarah's shorthand name for Ludwig van Beethoven usually got a smile out of Pols.

"It wasn't *her,*" burst out Pollina with passionate disgust. "Antonie Brentano. She was just another one of his silly flirtations." She started coughing, and it took a few moments for her to stop.

"Okay, okay," said Sarah gently.

As much as Sarah loved Beethoven — and it seemed to her at times that no other kind of love could possibly come close to it — she wasn't particularly interested in Beethoven's own love life. Much had been made of Ludwig's series of failed affairs, aborted attempts at marriage, passions for married ladies, etcetera, and the subject was exhausted. Sarah had done far more research on how Beethoven's intestinal troubles were reflected in his work. When it came to giving bad gas a melody, nobody did it better than LVB.

"I promise I'll keep in touch," Sarah said, but Pollina, deep in thought now, interrupted her.

"In my dream, the dragon breathed flames at you and you wouldn't ask for help. You have to ask for help. There was a dwarf there, too."

Sarah felt the hair on her arms rise up.

"And a prince, and a witch." Pols reached out to stoke the fire. "Sarah you must *promise* me that you will pray to the Infant of Prague to help you."

The one thing about Pollina that made Sarah uncomfortable even after all these years was her extreme religiosity. Sarah avoided all talk of God with Pols, but it

45

wasn't always easy to keep silent when she was talking about God's love for everyone, and how we must all labor for the glory of God, and telling Sarah not to worry, that it was all in God's hands. Sarah understood that Pollina, being blind and a musical genius, felt especially noticed by God, but couldn't quite grasp why Pols wasn't angry about some of the special attention. Still, she was glad that Pols felt there was meaning to it all, since it seemed to give her comfort.

"Alessandro went on and on about that, too," Sarah said, hoping to avoid making an actual promise to pray to a statue of baby Jesus. " *'Il Bambino di Praga,'* he called it."

"You have to pray for help. But Sarah, don't ask until you're sincere." Sarah said nothing. "Be careful," Pols added, continuing to cough in a way that worried Sarah. "Prague is a threshold."

"A threshold?"

"Yes. Between the life of good and . . . the other."

Sarah thought of Buffy the Vampire Slayer. "I'm not going to have to fight demons, am I?"

Pols did not like her teasing tone. "You can laugh, but it's true. There's a castle outside of Prague built over a hell portal.

46

Half-man, half-animal winged creatures fly out of it, and if you go near it you age thirty years in one second." Pols coughed again. "Prague is a place where the fabric of time is thin."

Sarah sighed. "Pols, are you okay? And how do you know all this about Prague?" Despite her globe-trotting parents, as far as Sarah knew, the little girl hadn't been out of Back Bay.

"I just wish I could go with you," Pols said sadly, leaning against Sarah's shoulder. "The Lobkowiczes are a great Catholic family. And Joseph Franz Maximilian Lobkowicz was my favorite of Beethoven's patrons. He was a singer and a musician, too. And he had a clubfoot, did you know that?"

"Yup. Did you know that Beethoven once freaked out over something he did and stood in the doorway of Lobkowicz Palace shouting, 'Lobkowicz is a donkey!' over and over again?"

Pollina giggled.

"Let's eat some more ice cream," Sarah said. "And then play me something, okay?"

An hour and a half later, Sarah left an almost sleeping Pollina tucked up on the sofa, covered partly by one of the many embroidered shawls in the room and partly by Boris.

Jose met her in the hallway, wearing a giant peach bathrobe. Sarah was surprised to see him still awake and, it seemed, relatively sober.

"She asleep?" Jose asked, jerking his head in the direction of the music room. Sarah nodded, attempting to thread her way between Jose, a Louis XVI commode, and a porcelain cheetah umbrella stand.

"Listen, Jose." Sarah lowered her voice. "Is she okay? I mean, all that coughing? She seems a little feverish."

Jose shrugged theatrically.

"Who knows? I tell her to let me call the doctor and she tells me that she is in God's hands. I say, God's hands are awesome, but what about a little Theraflu? Lately she no want to sleep at night and she keeps coming to my room and waking me up: Jose, I can't find Lamby; Jose, I can't reach the cereal; Jose, this can't be Otto Klemperer conducting, you messed up my CDs again."

Jose leaned forward.

"And then when she does sleep, she get the nightmares. I worry, okay? She dream of fire, all the time. And you see, she want that fire all the time, going. It's hot as hell in here."

"I'll be away for a couple of months," Sarah said. "You e-mail me, all right? Every few days. And get her to see a doctor."

"Everybody goes away," Jose said sadly. "But we stay, slowly burning up to death."

Sarah patted Jose on his fuzzy shoulder and stepped out into the Boston evening. It was already muggy and warm, though slightly less so than the interior of Pollina's mansion. Sarah was surprised to find she was shivering.

Four

Sarah's T ride home was blissfully free of the usual subway saxophonists and zealots, and gave her a few minutes to organize her thoughts. Tomorrow she should get a few books on Prague, maybe a Czech-English dictionary. A raincoat? She was going to a castle, did she need some kind of evening gown? She had never owned anything remotely like that. The last time Sarah had bought a dress was for her former roommate Andrea's wedding. It was a hot dress, but the zipper was broken. Her date, George, whom she had taken to the wedding on the theory that you should always take a wildly inappropriate person to functions where nuptials were involved, had gotten it caught in the lining. Served her right, really, having sex in a supply closet of the Boston Hyatt. But George had smelled like oranges and leather and he had bent her over one of those carts housekeeping wheeled around with soaps and shower caps and dry-cleaning request forms. That had been fun, and afterward she had pocketed some shampoo and conditioner. There probably wasn't time to get the zipper fixed.

Sarah realized she was focusing on inanities in order not to think about Sherbatsky. And leaving poor Pols.

Sarah let herself into the apartment. Alessandro was out, and she decided to take a bath. Stripping down, flinging clothes around her room, she almost tripped over something hard and sharp. Funny. Her father's toolbox was in the middle of the room. She kept it in the back of her closet. What was it doing out? Sarah glanced up and noticed something else. Her computer laptop was open. She never left it open. And Alessandro, as odd and boundary-free in many ways as he was, would not have touched her computer. Had someone been in her room? She hadn't turned on many lights when she came home. Had there been a break-in? Was she not alone in the apartment?

Sarah looked around for a weapon. Not seeing anything more threatening than her *Oxford Unabridged Dictionary,* she knelt down, opened her father's tool kit, and grabbed a hammer.

The good thing about the kind of square footage two young academics in Boston can afford is that one can conduct a thorough investigation of it in just under fifteen minutes. Sarah wondered how this previously overlooked feature of her apartment might be condensed for a real estate ad: *Must see! This easy-to-search-for-lurking-psychopath 2 bdrm charmer with orig wd floors will go fast!*

As empowering as it was to walk around her apartment like Thor, it was also tiring. Returning to her bedroom, Sarah examined her computer to see if any files had been deleted or anything looked tampered with. She searched through the papers on her desk and then examined the toolbox more closely.

Her mom had given it to her the Christmas before she went off to college, although Dad had already been gone for a decade by then. It had been a weird, startling thing to see on Christmas morning. Intensely familiar yet upsetting. And she had felt an unreasonable rush of disappointment when she opened it up and found only tools. She wondered what she had expected — a last letter from her father telling her how much he loved her? A CD of his voice? Her father himself, emerging cramped but whole from

52

this tiny hiding place? It was all she had of her father's possessions. Perhaps that was why she had added The Page to its contents, which was her own secret bittersweet talisman. The Page was just an ordinary sheet of ruled paper, covered with Sarah's fourth-grade writing.

Sally and Cindy walked around the house and counted the windows again. Sally went one way, and Cindy the other. They met up again on the sagging porch by the front door.

"Fifty-two," said Sally firmly.

"Fifty-two," said Cindy, just as firmly.

They marched back into the ancient old structure.

"I'll start at the top," said Sally. "In the attic. You start in the basement."

The two girls went from room to room, counting the windows. They were very careful, counting little round windows and big dormers. French doors onto balconies counted as one. The rules were very clear to both of them, for they had been counting for days.

Once again, they met by the front door. "Fifty-one," said Cindy.

"Fifty-one," said Sally.

There was a window missing. If they

counted fifty-two windows on the outside of the house, then the house had fifty-two windows. But they could only find fifty-one windows when searching the rooms. That meant only one thing.

"There's a secret room," said Sally.

Cindy looked at her sister and nodded. "We have to find it."

The scene did not come from Sarah's imagination. It was from a book, whose title she did not know, whose author's name she could not remember. A book that her fourth-grade teacher, Miss Hill, was reading on the day when the school's guidance counselor had come and interrupted the teacher's afternoon story session. The counselor whispered to Miss Hill, who turned to Sarah.

"Sarah, would you go with Miss Cummins, please?"

Sarah had been surprised. She could sometimes be naughty, but her father had promised her that if she continued to excel in school and music, he would buy her a violin in the spring, and so she had been especially good all winter. This promise was, of course, a secret from her mother, who would have pointed out that their car had four bald tires that needed replacing. Sarah told her dad that the violin she rented through the school was fine, but he said he was proud of her talent and wanted her to have her own. Though a trace of snow still coated the frozen ground, crocuses were beginning to appear, and Sarah lay awake every night, thinking about how smooth and scratch-free a new instrument would be. Sarah wondered if maybe this was some kind of wonderful surprise that Miss Cummins was in on. Maybe she was about to present her with the violin!

Sarah skipped down the hallway alongside Miss Cummins, who closed the office door behind them and motioned to a chair. When Sarah looked up at her, she was suddenly surprised and uncomfortable to see Miss Cummins was crying.

Sarah looked at her, wondering what was the matter with her. She slid off her chair and went over to the counselor, putting a hand on her back. The woman took a breath and looked at Sarah.

"Your father had an accident on the highway," Miss Cummins said. "I'm so sorry, Sarah. He's dead. Your daddy is dead."

Sarah never heard the end of the story about Sally and Cindy and the house with the missing window. And she could never be certain if the accident hadn't been caused by the bald tires on her father's car. Tires that might have been replaced if her daddy hadn't been saving up to buy her a violin. In some strange way, these things had gotten tangled up in her mind, and Sarah spent a lot of time in the year after her father's death trying to reconstruct the story of Cindy and Sally and the house with the secret room. But this one little scene was all she could remember. She wrote it over and over again, but it didn't change anything. Her father was gone forever.

She couldn't even ask her old teacher, Miss Hill, about the book, because after the funeral, her mother had needed time to get their lives together, and she had sent Sarah off to stay with her uncle Fred and aunt Margot. Sarah had lost touch with her classmates. Then she was selected to attend Boston Latin for high school, a long commute from the old neighborhood. By the time Sarah went back to ask about the book, Miss Hill had left the school. And no one knew which book she was talking about.

It wasn't like Sarah hadn't spent a lot of time in libraries. But it was hard to find a book when you didn't know the author or the title, and it wasn't a well-known favorite. She had asked every children's librarian she had come across, with no luck.

Sarah didn't keep a journal, didn't scrap-book, or make photo albums. But she had hung on to The Page.

Restless, Sarah prowled the apartment again but found nothing other than a bug on the ceiling of the kitchen. Well, she could at least kill the bug. It might feel good to smash something, let off a little steam. Sarah took off her shoes and, holding on to the hammer, stood on a kitchen chair, then on the table, then on top of her beloved and completely outdated seven-volume *Lives of the Romantic Composers.*

It was only then that she could see that her intended victim was not a bug. It was a symbol, written in a minute hand:

Sarah stared at the strange drawing. Someone *had* been here.

"Gesu cristo," said Alessandro, coming through the apartment door and spotting Sarah perched on the heights of musical

scholarship with a hammer in her hands.

"I think someone broke into the apartment," said Sarah, climbing down. "But I don't think they took anything."

Alessandro made a quick check of his belongings, and returned to confirm that nothing was missing, not even his stash of pot.

"Why they no take our TV?" he said, insulted. "Is very nice TV."

Sarah showed him the strange symbol, but Alessandro had no idea what it meant either.

"I think what we need is a nice grappa," he suggested. "Tomorrow you sleep on plane."

After a grappa, Sarah still had no idea what the symbol meant, who would have put it there, or why. But after two grappas, she didn't care at all.

FIVE

Of course they performed a particularly thorough search of her carry-on bag at Logan Airport. Sarah, nursing a serious hangover, stood patiently in her socks and watched the mustachioed officer calmly laying out her stuff on the metal folding table: laptop, camera, iPod, chargers, toiletries, an electrical converter, her favorite Micron pens, a couple of notebooks. Condoms.

Sarah put on her sunglasses.

The guard confiscated her toothpaste.

Sarah stopped at a newsstand to buy a new tube. Digging into her backpack for her wallet, her fingers closed around a strange object. Sarah pulled it out. It was the small copper box the little man had left on her doorstep. She must have thrown it into her bag before she had gone over to Pollina's house and forgotten about it. Well, at least it hadn't set off any security alarms. That would have been awkward, since she didn't even know what was in it. God, what if it were drugs? Her summer would have ended before it began.

Cautiously, Sarah opened the small box. Inside was a half-moon sliver of something gray. It looked like . . . a toenail clipping.

"Seriously?" Sarah laughed. She had half a mind to throw it in the nearest trash can, but she kind of liked the box. Sarah shoved it deep into her backpack.

Unexpectedly, her ticket put her in first class. Sarah had never flown first class. She hadn't done much traveling in general. Instead of watching the in-flight movies, she picked up the guidebook to Berlin, Prague, and Budapest that she had grabbed at the airport bookstore. She realized with dismay that the college-student authors had grouped the three cities in a single volume for tourists most interested in their shared culture of beer. There were many suggestions as to how to speak to the police when you were arrested for public drunkenness, but little on local history. At last she found a small section on Lobkowicz Palace at Prague Castle, with two glossy photographs: one of the exterior, and one of a grand Imperial Hall inside the palace. The building had been known by its present name since the marriage of Polyxena Pernstein to

Zdenek, 1st Prince Lobkowicz (1568-1628). And thus the dynasty began, she thought. Hard to believe the family was still around and kicking long after families like the Plantagenets and the Romanovs had disappeared from the society pages.

Sarah kept reading and learned that in 1618, in what was known as a "defenestration," Protestant rebels had thrown Catholic Imperial ministers from the windows of Prague Castle, but the ministers had survived the fall, and taken refuge in the adjoining Lobkowicz Palace, where Polyxena had hidden them under her skirts. Those must have been some seriously big skirts, Sarah thought. She flipped to the maps in the back. Prague Castle seemed to incorporate a number of buildings, including several overpriced snack bars that served Pilsner and (the writers deigned to mention) a cathedral.

Sarah shut her eyes and reclined her seat back as far as it would go, letting her mind drift.

Beethoven had lived and worked almost entirely in Vienna, but he had made three trips to Prague. The first in 1796, when, like Mozart before him, Beethoven had gone to do the eighteenth-century version of networking. According to a letter to his younger brother Johann, Beethoven was received well and enjoyed himself. Even got a little composing in, minor works mostly, like the concert aria dedicated to the Countess Josephine De Clary, a typical Beethoven romance: brief, inappropriate, probably tortured, almost certainly unconsummated. During the second trip, in 1798, Ludwig premiered his Piano Concerto No. 1 in C Major, playing the piece himself. At the time, Beethoven's prodigious gifts as a pianist were more remarked upon than his compositions. The last visit was in July of 1812, and believed to be the one where Beethoven met his Immortal Beloved, Antonie Brentano, before going to a spa in Teplitz. (The waters there were good for his gas.) *Be calm — love me — today — yesterday — what tearful longings for you — you — you — my life — my all — farewell.*

Sarah sighed. She knew the contents of the letter nearly verbatim, of course, but only because she was a quick study, and it was endlessly quoted. Ludwig's enormous, awe-inspiring genius, his productivity, his prescient modernism were all contained in music. Beside that, the letters to the Immortal Beloved looked no more impressive to her than bathroom stall graffiti: *L. V. B. luvs his I. B. Wishes she wuz here.*

Sarah began playing through in her mind the rondo from the *Waldstein* Sonata. Her left hand raced up and down her thigh in fast scales, her right hand trilling. Second theme. Triplets. Then a daring swing into A minor, then back to C major. There was nothing like Beethoven's middle period for steeling the nerves. Sarah played happily. Shortly before the last pianissimo section, she fell asleep, although her hands played on into the coda, triumphantly.

Eleven hours later, Sarah threaded her way through Prague's Ruzyne Airport. Emerging from passport control into the arrivals lobby, she was surprised to see her own name neatly printed in block letters on a small white sign. Sarah smiled weakly at the man holding it. He must have had the chauffeur's uniform custom made for him. Sarah slung her bag over her shoulder.

"We meet again," said the little man gaily, his deep bassoon voice cutting through the mixture of languages all around them. "Welcome to Prague, my dear."

SIX

There had been an awkward moment with the luggage. Sarah hadn't wanted to hand her enormous duffel over to the little man, fearing it would topple him, and in her haste to fling the bag inside the trunk had almost crushed another — a flat object about the size of a laptop, encased in bubble wrap.

"Careful," the little man had said, snatching it up. "This is actually rather valuable and I went all the way to Venice for it. And it is still not easy to get in and out of Venice after the tragedy."

Sarah nodded, although if it weren't for Alessandro, she probably wouldn't have paid much attention to the gas leak or whatever it was that had killed those people in Italy.

"So sad," the little man said. "Although Venice would be a lovely place to die." He sounded almost wistful.

Sarah settled into the backseat of the Citroën, feeling a wave of fatigue wash over her. Her eyes stayed open, taking in red ceramic roofs, tidy backyard gardens, tiny cars, but her mind went to sleep. Sarah thought vaguely that the outskirts of Prague looked grim and unpromising. Every balcony of every apartment had a satellite dish on it.

Suddenly through her foggy head a question surfaced.

"Why did you give me a box with a toenail in it?" Sarah asked, leaning forward. She was slightly alarmed to notice that as he drove, the little man was also reading a Czech newspaper. He changed lanes so fast it made Sarah's head hit the window next to her with a gentle thunk.

"I thought you might like it," the little man said. "It was in Professor Sherbatsky's pocket when we found him. If it had stayed there, then now it would be in some cardboard evidence box at police headquarters never to be seen again. I took the liberty of . . . liberating it."

"But what is it?"

He shrugged. "It must have been important to him, if he intended to take it with him to the Great Beyond."

"Why are you so sure," asked Sarah, "that it was a suicide? I knew him. It doesn't seem like something he'd do."

"You knew him, but you don't know Prague," said the little man.

"Okay, so why'd you break into my apartment and go through my stuff?" she asked, in her best South Boston tough-girl voice. Of course she wasn't sure it *had* been him, but she didn't like the feeling that the little man was sort of messing with her. Best to go on offense. "Why'd you draw a symbol on my ceiling? What's that about?"

"I'm flattered," said the little man, as the car emerged from a tunnel and a fairy-tale city appeared in front of Sarah, "that you think I could reach your ceiling."

Sarah couldn't help it. She burst out laughing. The little man joined her.

Sarah settled back in her seat and took in the pastel buildings, pointed terra-cotta roofs, narrow cobbled streets. According to the brief historical notes in her ridiculous guidebook, this was the city where people had labored to turn lead into gold, where Rabbi Loew had turned a handful of dirt into a golem, where anything was possible. Prague. *Praha.* The name actually *meant* "threshold." Pollina had said the city was a portal between the life of the good and . . . the other. *A city of dark magic,* Alessandro had called it.

They passed a kitschy ice-cream store with the words "Cream & Dream" curlicued across the front. A family posed by the doorway, all carrying tall cones and holding up their thumbs while someone took their picture.

I need coffee, she thought, closing her eyes.

After what was either five minutes or an hour, the car bumped to a stop. "We have to walk from here," said the little man. He hopped out of the car and moved to the trunk, gently lifting out the bubble-wrapped package and then swinging her huge duffel out like it was filled with feathers. Sarah looked across the street at a gilt arch over stone pillars. The pillars were topped with shocking images of sheer brutality: On one, a giant man raised a club like a huge base-ball bat, about to swing at the head of a screaming, crying victim lying on his back, defenseless. On the other, a massive caped soldier with washboard abs prepared to stab a person curled up in the fetal position.

"Welcome to Prague Castle," the little man said, smiling.

Looking at the statue's naked, muscled torso and the bulging biceps on his up-turned arm, Sarah felt a surprising surge of sexual interest. Apparently jet lag was not a deterrent to libido, nor was cold hard stone. She thought about the Supreme Court justice who said art was art and porn was porn and he knew the difference when he saw it. She was not so sure.

Sarah widened her gaze to take in the two striped guard boxes, à la Buckingham Palace, in front of which uniformed men posed with rifles.

"We are all the way at the back," explained the little man. "This building here belongs to our neighbor, the president."

A tour group of Germans in sandals and socks passed in front of them, following a guide holding an umbrella topped with a stuffed dragon.

Sarah noticed an incongruously dark-haired kid of about twelve lingering on the edges of the group. She watched as the boy sidled up to an upward-gazing tourist, saw the kid's thin hand reach into a gaping shoulder bag. Sarah had grown up in a neighborhood where this kind of thing was routine, but it still pissed her off. She wasn't about to let a snot-nosed Prague townie ruin some poor slob of a tourist's day. In two seconds she tackled the thief, grabbed the wallet, and handed it back to the startled woman as the kid fled.

"Danke schön," the woman said. The entire

crowd of Germans applauded.

Sarah returned to the little man, who had a strange, not entirely approving expression on his face. Sarah, usually quick to size people up, was having trouble with . . .

"I just realized," Sarah said, picking up her duffel bag. "I don't even know your name."

"Nicolas Pertusato," he said, with a quick, shy smile. "I thought you'd never ask."

Nicolas waved his arm to indicate the square past the gates of the Mad Batter and Sexy Stabber. "And this is called the Courtyard of Honor."

"More like the Courtyard of Dishonor," Sarah said, brushing gravel off her jeans.

"That depends on your point of view," said Nicolas Pertusato, calmly.

SEVEN

Sarah's teeth felt mossy, her eyelids were gluey, and maybe it hadn't been the greatest idea to tackle a child thief after being on a plane for eleven hours. She bent down to massage a cramp out of her calf muscle as a woman in her early fifties came rushing up to them.

"Mr. Pertusato," the woman said, a little breathlessly. "I was sent out to greet you and our new arrival."

"Then your timing is fortunate."

"Miles wants to see you immediately," the woman continued. "You're supposed to leave the car and the luggage here and our valiant Petr will take care of it. Bring the package straight to him, Miles said. The word 'immediately' was stressed. Heavily." The woman widened her eyes theatrically. Sarah had time during this speech to take in the woman's appearance. A sky-blue Pashmina wrap over a paisley tunic. Overloaded charm bracelets. Silver hair in an unmistakably Midwestern feathered bob. Brocaded Indian slippers.

The kind of woman, Sarah decided in an instant, who uses the word "marvelous." A lot.

"Well," Nicolas said, hefting the bubble-wrapped package under his arm. "Naturally I obey every command of Dr. Wolfmann's. But first I must escort Ms. Weston to the palace and show her to her room."

"Oh, but that's the other thing," the woman said, in a rush. "There was some kind of accident in Sarah's room. Something was spilled or broken or cracked or possibly *leaking.* They're cleaning out another room for her. Miles suggested I show Sarah around while they get everything ready."

"An accident?"

"Something might have fallen. There was *crashing.*"

The little man gazed thoughtfully at the woman for a moment and then appeared to make a decision.

"Ms. Weston," he said. "Your bag will be quite safe in the trunk. Petr can be trusted and you will find it cumbersome, carrying it about."

Sarah swung her duffel into the trunk but retained hold of her carry-on bag. Nothing was going to separate her and her Mac. The little man leapt nimbly into the air and managed to grasp the top of the open trunk, bringing it down shut.

"Sarah Weston," he said, turning around, "I leave you in the care of Eleanor Roland, a compatriot of yours, as you may have noticed, and a fellow scholar. Possibly *not* as foolish as she appears, although, conversely, possibly much more so. I leave you now. Immediately. As directed."

Eleanor Roland seemed not at all bothered by the little man's words and, laughing merrily, held a hand out to Sarah, who shook it. Eleanor Roland had a powerful grip.

"You didn't have any trouble with your flight?" she asked. "Considering what happened in Venice, security must have been *terrible.* They still haven't found the little dog of that poor girl. What a world."

"They took my toothpaste," Sarah said, trying to get her bearings. Little dog?

"It'll be nice to have another young person join us," Eleanor said.

"Us?" Sarah mumbled, as she watched Nicolas navigate around a clump of Goth Japanese teenagers. One of the kids whipped out a phone and aimed it at Pertusato's retreating back while his friends giggled.

"Us," Eleanor repeated, laughing again.

"The academics. We're quite a little family. I'll show you St. Vitus now. It's still early enough that the worst of the crowds haven't descended. You must start with St. Vitus. It's marvelous. Now see, this second gate dates from 1614. Note the German Imperial Eagle on top with two heads. Baroque, of course."

Sarah followed Eleanor into a second courtyard. It made sense that there would be a number of specialists gathered at Lobkowicz Palace. The collection was enormous, and varied.

"Are you a musicologist?" Sarah asked, feeling slightly anxious about meeting a lot of academics who might look down on her credentials. She hadn't really counted on having to measure pedagogic dick length with a whole tribe.

"Oh no!" Eleanor laughed. "Miles contacted me three months ago. Apparently he had read my book on seventeenth-century women artists and suggested I come and have a look at some things here."

"Oh cool," Sarah said, her eye caught by what looked like a giant iron birdcage planted in the second courtyard. "I didn't know there *were* seventeenth-century women artists, actually."

"Well, it's a very short book," Eleanor

sighed. "Which is why this is so exciting really. They've recovered a whole cache of portraits by one Princess Ernestine of Nassau-Siegen. Mother-in-law to the 3rd Prince Lobkowicz. An amateur painter, but a good one. And I've got first dibs on her, which is nice for me. But you've got the big kahuna, I hear. Beethoven. Now behind you there's the Chapel of the Holy Rood. That's really the box office now. Our fearless leader is looking into getting us free passes to all the things, but until that happens we must pay our crowns just like all the unwashed masses. That's the New Royal Palace, not open to the public. This fountain dates from 1686. All of this was built over a buried moat, if you can believe it."

"Who's the fearless leader?" Sarah asked, lagging behind Eleanor so she could check out the birdcage next to the fountain. "Do you mean the . . . um, Nicolas Pertusato?"

"Miles Wolfmann," the woman corrected. "Head of the Collection. Absolutely everything goes through him and he knows everything about . . . well, everything. He's American, too. And a darling. You'll love working with him."

Sarah peered into the iron birdcage, which loomed over an octagonal opening in the ground.

"It's a well," Eleanor instructed. "Early eighteenth century. This cage thingy is by an unknown artist. Not terribly interesting. But just wait. This will take your breath away." Sarah followed her guide across the courtyard and through an arch of the New Royal Palace. The giant Cathedral of St. Vitus loomed up before her.

"Yowsa," Sarah said.

Eleanor prattled on about the history of the cathedral, which Sarah listened to with half an ear. Sarah knew almost nothing about architecture, but it was hard not to be impressed with the size of the thing.

"The images on either side of the central arch are of Charles IV and his wife, Elizabeth of Pomerania," Eleanor was saying. "Apparently Elizabeth could bend a sword with her bare hands. Oh good. No line. We can just duck right in."

They entered the cathedral. The interior was enormous and pleasantly cool, filled with early-morning light filtering through huge stained-glass windows running down either side of the nave. Religion might be a pretty dubious gift from our ancestors, Sarah thought, gazing upward, but it did come in some fairly kick-ass wrapping paper. It was hard to focus on one thing.

"I come here nearly every day," Eleanor

said. "It just never gets old. Spectacular, isn't it? Romanesque, Gothic, neo-Gothic, Baroque, and some good old twentieth-century cash as well. The windows were sponsored by banks and insurance companies, of all things. Over here to the left is the window done by Mucha."

Sarah followed Eleanor, suppressing a desire to shout and test the acoustics. She wasn't sure what this guy Mucha was trying to depict in his window — her hagiography was a little muddled — but the blues and greens were pretty.

"How long have you been here?" Sarah murmured.

"A month," Eleanor replied. "There are enough Ernestines to devote a whole room to them for exhibition. If we can raise the money to repair them. They're in deplorable condition. I've rather fallen in love with all my ladies. Wait till you see them."

"If you've been here a month then you must have known Professor Sherbatsky," Sarah said.

"It was . . . very shocking." Eleanor lowered her voice. "Terrible. I'm sorry I didn't get a chance to know him very well. Miles spoke very highly of him. They were good friends, I believe. You were the professor's student, weren't you?"

Sarah nodded. Maybe this all-knowing Miles Wolfmann person could illuminate something about the supposed suicide of her beloved professor.

"Were you there when he . . ." Sarah hesitated.

"I was in Germany," Eleanor said quickly. "A little field trip to the place of Ernestine's death. It's proving terribly difficult to find anything about her. When I came back from Mengerskirchen I learned . . . well, everyone was very upset." Eleanor placed a hand on Sarah's shoulder. "I'm so sorry. Were you close?"

Sarah hesitated. She had felt close to Sherbatsky, but their intimacy was musical. What did she really know about his personal life?

"He was a brilliant man," Sarah said. "I'm still kind of in shock about it. So it was Nicolas Pertusato who found him?"

"Well, it was the prince who found him," Eleanor frowned. "Prince Max. The current heir. But Nicolas was there, too. The prince . . . well."

Sarah waited.

"Anyway," Eleanor chirped. "Did I tell you why the cathedral is dedicated to St. Vitus? King Wenceslas was interested in converting the local population to Christianity. And apparently he had acquired the arm of St. Vitus on his travels — a relic, you know."

Sarah nodded, wondering how she could get her enthusiastic tour guide back into the twenty-first century.

"Now over on the other side is the Chapel of St. Wenceslas," Eleanor chirped on. "It was built in 1345 and there are 1,345 jewels decorating it. On special days they display his skull!"

Sarah threaded her way through gaping tourists. The Chapel of the Good King was cordoned off and they had to wait their turn to peer in.

"Mmmm," Eleanor said. "Marvelous."

Sarah began to feel a little claustrophobic, which was odd considering the enormity of the place.

"Wenceslas was murdered by his brother, Boleslav the Cruel," Eleanor said, brightly. "And over here through this door are the Crown Jewels. We can't go in, naturally. They're said to be very unlucky. A few days after the Nazis' head honcho tried them on he was assassinated."

"Coffee," Sarah mumbled. She had only been in Prague for what felt like ten minutes and already her head was swimming with tales of dead people and murder. "I need some coffee."

"Oh, but you'll want to see the tomb of St. John of Nepomuk," Eleanor insisted. "Wenceslas IV had him flung from the Charles Bridge. It's all silver! And legend has it there's a hell portal somewhere in the cathedral —"

Sarah reached out a hand and braced herself against the nearest pillar.

"Oh, you poor thing," Eleanor cooed. "Did you fly British Airways? They stuff you with salty chips. You're probably dehydrated."

Sarah and Eleanor exited the cathedral. Sarah riffled through her bag to find her sunglasses, even though the morning was turning cloudy.

"There's a nice little spot over in front of the Schwarzenberg Palace," Eleanor said, leading Sarah back outside the castle gates. Sarah glanced up at the Sexy Stabber on the way out. He no longer seemed quite so sexy.

"Watch out!" Eleanor cried, grabbing Sarah by the arm as a glossy red vintage Alfa roadster driving way too fast swung by them, screeching to a halt next to the little man's car. Sarah half-stumbled, the muscle in her calf sending out a warning twinge.

The driver of the Alfa flung open the door

and whirled around toward the two women. Sarah had the confused impression of a tall, thin man dressed in an impeccable three-piece suit. A homburg shaded his face.

"Where's Pertusato?" he shouted, so loudly that several pigeons flew up in alarm around him.

"At the palace," Eleanor called back. "They only just arrived. Let me introduce —"

The man pounded angrily on the top of his car and then set off in a dead sprint through the gate without a backward glance.

"Who was that?" Sarah asked.

"That was Prince Max," Eleanor said. "Maximilian Lobkowicz Anderson."

"I thought Maximilian Lobkowicz died in the seventies or something," Sarah mumbled, trying to remember what she and Bailey had gleaned of the recent family history on Google.

"That was the *grandfather* of this Max," Eleanor replied. "He died without any male heirs, so it all passed to a daughter's family, the Andersons."

"Oh. He seems like kind of an asshole," Sarah said.

"He's a little strange," Eleanor said, sighing. "I'd try to stay out of his way if I were you."

EIGHT

Sarah had to hand it to the anonymous architects of this spired city — the place had a vibe. And vibe central was the Prague Castle complex, which would be her home for the summer. Even the espresso wasn't totally keeping her brain activity centered on the logical left side. That old loony right side kept saying "for a thousand years, people have lived and died on this very spot." But then she imagined that the right side of her brain was speaking in a pirate accent ("on this very spot — *argh*"), and she felt normal again. This place was just a pile of old stones. Pretty stones arranged in intriguing ways, but just old stones.

"And outdated wiring," her father would have added.

Eleanor fluttered her way past the entrance to St. George's and Golden Lane. "You can see those later," she said. "You must be dying for a shower." Sarah was desperate to brush her teeth, and to massage her aching calf muscle, which made her feel even more like a pirate, as she dragged it along like a wooden leg.

At last, as the cobbles began to descend toward the gate at the narrow end of the wedge-shaped castle complex, they came to Lobkowicz Palace. The façade was completely hidden behind scaffolding. Sarah could hardly hear Eleanor over the sounds of men wielding power tools above them. "Steam cleaning," Eleanor shouted. "Poles." Poles? Finally Sarah understood that Eleanor meant the workers themselves were Polish, and that the building had suffered years of neglect, now being remedied.

As they stepped around tarps and sheets of plastic and coils of tubing, Eleanor muttered to Sarah, "I don't think there's a licensed contractor in the whole city. Sometimes I wonder if this whole place isn't going to come down on our heads. I suspect Prince Max wouldn't even care. Secretly some of us are rooting for the cousin."

"Cousin?"

"Marchesa Elisa Lobkowicz DeBenedetti. Head of the Italian branch, and my dear, you wouldn't believe the *style*. There's been quite the kerfuffle between Max and the Italian Lobkowcizes over who is the rightful heir, but Marchesa Elisa and Max are friends. She's charming."

They made their way through rooms where men were painting and plastering. The building hadn't looked that big from the outside, but they seemed to walk and walk until finally they came to a door with a note stuck to it.

"Oh dear," said Eleanor, reading the note. "It's from Jana, the prince's assistant." She pronounced it "Yunna." "They've moved you to the basement."

In her fatigue, Sarah lost track of how many stairs she and Eleanor went down. The sound of the power tools faded away, for which Sarah was initially grateful. Eleanor pulled a tiny flashlight out of her purse as they turned down a dark corridor with a cheery, "It's best to keep one of these with you at all times here." Finally they came to a small door. Eleanor threw it open, and turned on a light.

The room had a sagging but comfy-looking small bed with a clean quilt on it. There was a side table with a lamp for reading and an old bureau for clothes. On the wall was a not bad engraving of a cow.

"The bathroom's right down the hall," Eleanor said. "And you don't have to share.

So lucky — those ceramics people are filthy."

"I don't think I've ever slept in a room without a window," Sarah said.

Eleanor looked behind the door, as if a window were suddenly going to appear. "At least you won't have to deal with the noise upstairs," she said. "I'd be lost without my earplugs. Why is it art people all have septum issues? Dinner's at eight. Pretty informal, long table, we alternate who's cooking. Sometimes the power goes out. Well, anyway, welcome!"

Eleanor's Moroccan heels clicked away into the distance until there was no sound. Sarah sat down on the bed. She was living underground. Like a mole. Like a bottle of wine. Like a corpse. Like nuclear waste. Sarah tried to tell herself that a window was not an essential part of a bedroom. Bedrooms were for sleeping. And with Prague's history of defenestrations, she should be happy there were no windows for her to be thrown out of. She sighed, lay back, and fell instantly asleep.

When Sarah awoke, she felt a moment of panic. There was not one glimmer of light anywhere. She put her hand in front of her face and saw nothing. Was she dead? Buried alive? Remembering where she was, she groped for her phone: 3:17 p.m. She had only slept for a couple of hours, then. She felt unsettled, groggy, and hungry.

Sarah found her way through the maze of corridors and up several flights of stairs. The sound of the power tools resumed, and light began to appear.

"There you are, Miles has been waiting for you," said an accented voice. Sarah turned and was greeted by a short, plump Czech woman with bristly colorless hair. Her clothing, her expression, her manner all said, "Everything will run smoothly now that I am here."

"You must be Jana," said Sarah.

Jana had Sarah holding a steaming cup of coffee and a brioche in what felt like four seconds, and suddenly she was standing in the doorway of a crowded office filled with bubble-wrapped paintings, sculptures, enormous ledgers, photographic equipment, and a large Macintosh computer.

"Here's Miss Weston," announced Jana. "And Dr. Wolfmann, the prince wants to see you as soon as possible." From her tone, Sarah could tell that Jana, at least, respected the prince. Sarah thought it was funny that people who had grown up under communism would still tingle at the thought of nobility.

"Were you able to nap in the bomb shelter?" said a handsome man in his late forties with an academic's prematurely stooped shoulders and skinny calves. He wore a giant, round, illuminated magnifying lens on his head. "Isn't it funny that only twenty years ago, they were down there cowering in terror that we trigger-happy, decadent, capitalist Americans would go nuclear on them any minute? Little did they know our secret weapon was Starbucks." They shook hands and he seated Sarah opposite his desk, removing his magnifier and then fussing somewhat self-consciously with his hair.

Sarah's eye was caught by a strange little bronze object on Miles's desk. It had a figure that looked like a Greek goddess, and others that looked like jesters.

"It's an automaton," Miles said. "Turn the handle. Gently."

Sarah did, and the crank made the jesters jump while the goddess spun around. "Cute," she said.

"It's worth about three hundred thousand dollars," said Miles calmly. Sarah withdrew her hand.

"We found it in the Austrian Fine Art Database," Miles said. "It was in a box in the basement of the Kunsthistoriches Museum in Vienna, where it had been since 1945, when the Allies found it in an SS officer's home in Munich. I admit, when you're looking for a missing Brueghel, a windup toy doesn't seem all that exciting. But any collector in the world would kill for it."

"How did you know to even look for it?"

"The 1906 inventory. It's been a godsend. If your family has any special collections, make sure they have an inventory done, and stored somewhere safe."

Not really an issue for us, thought Sarah. Miles poured them both more coffee.

"What do you know about the family background?" he asked.

"Just the general Wikipedia stuff," Sarah said, deciding brazen honesty was probably her best approach. "I know a bit more about Joseph Franz Maximilian Lobkowicz of course."

"Oh yes, the 7th. We tend to call the princes by their numbers around here, saves time." Miles continued on with more details of the Lobkowicz history. The palace had been in the family since the first Prince Lobkowicz married extremely well, to the rich widow and future defenestratee-shielder Polyxena Pernstein in 1603. While other noble families had died out or lost favor, the Lobkowiczes had always managed to both produce an heir and chart a safe course politically and financially, and thus for five hundred years had accumulated properties, books, paintings, ceramics, and all the other trappings of European nobility. By the early twentieth century, they were one of the richest families in Europe. The fairy tale began to unravel in 1938, when Hitler started making noises about annexing "German" lands in Czechoslovakia, and ended up swallowing the whole country. Maximilian Lobkowicz, who would have been the 11th prince except titles were abolished by then, barely escaped to England with his life. The Nazis seized everything and dispersed it, sending some pieces to be part of what was to be the Führer's Museum in Linz, and handing out others to key SS members.

"Including this piece," said Miles, pointing to the automaton. "Can you imagine Heydrich turning the crank as he planned the Holocaust?" Miles paused for effect.

"I can't believe how recent World War II still feels here," Sarah said. "It's come up like three times since I arrived."

Miles nodded. "It's anything but ancient history here. Anyway, when the war ended in 1945, Maximilian returned and managed to get most of his belongings back. But in 1948, there was a communist coup and he was forced to flee again, leaving everything behind. Every single item that the Lobko-wiczes owned became the property of the Czechoslovak government. And of course, ripe for plucking by higher-ups in the Communist Party all the way to Moscow. And that was the state of things when the current Prince Max, Max's grandson, got the palace back last year after a legal marathon with the Czech government over restitution, and with warring branches of his own family."

"Wow," said Sarah. "What a crazy story. So I guess the current Prince Max would be the 13th, if they bring back titles. Do you call him the 13th, or is it like with elevators and you just skip that number and call him the 14th?"

Miles laughed. "It's fine to just call him 'Max,'" he said. "But people have gotten into the habit of Prince Max, and I don't think he really minds."

"What was Prince Max doing before he got his family stuff back?"

Miles looked around as if the room might be bugged and leaned in close. "Officially, he was in banking. Really, he was the drummer in some sort of rock band in Los Angeles," whispered Miles. "But no one knows that, and I didn't tell you."

Sarah smiled. She liked Miles Wolfmann, who was clearly an expert at what he did and was treating her as someone intelligent and capable. Her brain began to focus into something like its usual acuity and she was able to form some coherent questions about what she would be doing. Miles explained that most of the work on the music collection was complete, but there were gaps, loose ends, and a certain amount of disorganization. He hoped she wouldn't be overwhelmed.

"Fortunately for us, the 10th prince had all of the family's art, ceramics, weapons, books, and papers inventoried," Miles explained. "So we work off that 1906 list, plus the Nazi records of what they took. The Nazis were bastards, but very meticulous bastards. When we find things listed in the inventory, like say, the automaton, that aren't here in the palace or in one of the castles, then we begin searching the databases of Germany, Austria, Switzerland, Italy. We try to determine if it disappeared during World War II, or after 1948, when the communists starting dispersing the collection. If it went to Moscow, it can be tricky, but we did have a sixteenth-century pillbox restituted from the Hermitage."

"Wow," said Sarah. "How did you learn to

do this?"

"I have a masters in art crime," said Miles. "After drugs and weapons, art crime is the third most lucrative illegal worldwide business."

Miles showed her how to access the computerized inventory from 1906. The original hard copy was kept in his office. He also showed her the links to the art databases of the major countries and Interpol's list of stolen artworks.

On one point, Labrador Miles became a pit bull: Every single item, as soon as it was acquired, he glowered at her, *had* to come to his office. No cleaning, no exploring, no examining. Just straight to Miles. No exceptions.

"I catalog everything," he said. "I know it sounds harsh, but you understand. We're talking thousands of objects. We have to assign them numbers and track them through the restoration and installation process. Some things are to stay here and go on display, others will go to one of the other family castles, like Roudnice or Nelahozeves, or Nela as it is known. We have a large staff and tons of workmen around. It's kind of a nightmare, frankly, so sometimes I have to be harsh with people. We can't have things disappearing after we've worked so hard to get them back." His tone had become cold, and slightly aggrieved.

"I totally get it," said Sarah soothingly. "Everything goes through you."

Miles brightened again. "I don't expect it will be a problem. Like I said, most of the music collection is complete, it just needs to be organized for display in a coherent fashion. Okay, so I'll give you the tour and show you your workspace."

He led Sarah up the stairs to the second floor.

"These were the public rooms, so they're pretty spacious," explained Miles. "They haven't been renovated yet, so forgive the water stains and don't expect working AC. Each room is dedicated to a different area of the collection. That way we try to stay out of each others' way." Something in his tone suggested that that was more of a goal than a reality.

The first room at the top of the stairs had a series of large canvases leaning against the walls, and long worktables set up with portable lights, brushes, and solvents. Some of the paintings were torn, and others had water and mold stains. Standing over one of these was a tall, very thin woman with magenta hair, wearing a pale blue lab coat.

"Sarah Weston, music, meet Daphne

Kooster, family portraits of the sixteenth and seventeenth centuries," said Miles. Daphne looked Sarah up and down and gave a provisional smile. "Did ve meet at Harvard?" asked Daphne in a thick Dutch accent, shaking Sarah's hand firmly.

"Daphne's from Amsterdam but did her masters at Harvard," explained Miles.

"I'm at Thoreau," said Sarah.

"Oh," said Daphne. "I thought ve vere all connected vith Harvard or Yale in one vay or another. Thoreau?" She struggled to pronounce the name.

"It's a couple stops from Harvard on the T," Sarah said, holding her ground.

"Sarah was a student of Professor Sherbatsky," Miles said.

"Ohhhhh," said Daphne. "I am sorry. I didn't really know him."

"Polyxena's coming along beautifully," said Miles, admiring Daphne's work. Sarah, interested, looked now at the portrait. Polyxena Lobkowicz was a pale and intelligent-looking woman standing next to a badly painted green velvet chair in which a small white dog lay curled.

"You see de white gown she wears, richly embroidered, showing de family's wealth and influence," said Daphne authoritatively. "De red rose in her hair symbolizes her

Spanish ancestry. De prayer book in her left hand to display de Catholic allegiance."

"What does the dog symbolize?" Sarah asked. Daphne blinked at her for a moment.

"De dog is just a dog," she said, finally.

"You've done an exquisite job with this," Miles said, crisply.

"You think so? I am gratified to hear you say it," Daphne replied with great formality. They did not look at each other.

Okay, Sarah thought. Clearly Miles and Daphne were sleeping together.

Sarah turned to another painting, a smaller one featuring a somewhat mischievous-looking man with a funky plumed hat.

"Rudolf II," Miles said. "The Holy Roman Emperor who moved the Imperial Court from Vienna to Prague and ennobled the 1st Prince Lobkowicz."

"I hope you play soccer," said Daphne. "I'm trying to organize a regular game for de staff, but mostly they are a bunch of bookvorms."

Sarah did not get a really good look at the Ceramics Room or the smaller intermediate room filled with packing crates and large signs saying "Do Not Touch" in about eight languages.

"This will be Weapons when the collection arrives tomorrow from Roudnice," said Miles as they entered a room with astonishingly ugly flowered wallpaper. The parquet floor was slightly buckled with water damage. Miles kept walking.

"And this is the Balcony Room."

"Because there's no balcony?" Sarah asked, looking around.

"There was," said Miles. "Before a nineteenth-century renovation."

Sarah went to the window and tried to look out, but the glass was covered with plaster dust that had been speckled by rain, making it difficult to see through. She threw the window open and leaned out, taking in the panorama of the city. For a moment, the power tools stopped and there were birds singing, and a light breeze whiffled the leaves of the trees beneath them.

Miles appeared next to her.

"Quiz me," she said, pointing to landmarks she recognized from the guidebook she'd read on the plane. "Vltava River, Charles Bridge, Malá Strana . . . and where's —" Sarah suddenly had the sensation she was leaning too far out. Her stomach fluttered and her heart raced. Vertigo? She had spent her whole life climbing trees, skateboarding off handrails, sitting on the roof to watch fireworks with her dad. The blood began to drain from her head as if she were going to faint . . .

"Careful," said Miles, grabbing her arm and pulling her back, closing the window. Heart pounding, Sarah looked through the dirty window four stories down to where a cement staircase made its zigzagging way down the steep hillside in front of the palace.

"This is the window that Professor Sherbatsky fell from?" Sarah framed it as a question, but it wasn't really. Somehow she knew it was the place.

Miles nodded.

NINE

"Eleanor told me it was Prince Max who found him?" Sarah asked, forcing herself to deal with the wave of nausea passing over her and to think logically. It just didn't seem a likely place to commit suicide. The height wasn't particularly great, and if you were going to throw yourself out a window in a torrent of despair, would you really choose an inconvenient and awkward exit onto a flight of concrete steps? Granted your last view would be pretty, but they were in the Prague Castle complex. There were at least a dozen really fabulous places to off yourself within easy walking distance.

"Well, yes," Miles said, frowning. "Yes, it was Max. And Nicolas Pertusato, whom you've met."

"How did the police conclude it was suicide?" Sarah asked, a little more sharply than she intended. "I'm sorry, but it just seems so unlikely."

"Max has had video cameras installed outside the building," Miles said, pointing out the window. "He doesn't trust the construction workers. Or anyone, really. Sadly, one of the cameras had footage of . . . apparently it was very deliberate."

Sarah shook her head in disbelief.

"And Douglas Sexton — he's working on the collection of Carl Robert Croll paintings — had a conversation with Absalom earlier that evening," Miles explained. "Douglas had gone to Sherbatsky's room to borrow some antihistamines and Sherbatsky had given him the whole bottle saying that he no longer needed them. He told Douglas, *The way across has been revealed to me, and I intend to cross over tonight.*"

"That doesn't even sound like him." Sarah frowned. "Sherbatsky was fusing traditional musicology with brain science. He definitely did not talk like Professor Dumbledore."

Miles smiled sadly.

"I met Sherbatsky about ten years ago," he said softly. "In Vienna. I liked the man, enormously. I can't help feeling responsible."

Sarah glanced quickly at Miles, who seemed unable to tear his eyes away from the window.

"I asked him to come," Miles sighed. "I

admit I knew that with his name behind it we could draw a lot of attention to the Beethoven collection, but I also wanted his company. I should have known something was wrong. He was very preoccupied. And there were complaints. I put it down to Sherbatsky's eccentricities but I feared he was making . . . enemies. In the group."

A door across the room clicked open and Miles's troubled and pensive gaze was instantly smoothed out as he smiled over Sarah's left shoulder. His hand moved from Sarah's elbow to the small of her back as he led her away from the window. "Ah, good. Here are two more of our family. Sarah Weston, meet Bernard Plummer and Miss Shuziko Oshiro."

They made an almost comically contrasting couple. Bernard Plummer was well over six feet and massively built. He sported a luxurious mustache and was clad — there was really no other word for it — in a kind of medieval cape. Shuziko Oshiro barely came up to his shoulder despite at least five inches worth of spiky heels. She was impeccably dressed in a gold suit with a green-and-gold-flowered scarf wrapped around her throat.

"They are Rococo and Weapons," Miles added. "And Miss Weston is Beethoven, of course."

Bernard Plummer barely glanced at Sarah before launching into a complicated story about a wrangle with certain imbecile customs officials. He waved enormous hands that looked more than capable of handling pikes, staves, and battering rams. Miles at once became extremely business-like and whipped out a cell phone.

"Sarah," he said, "I'm afraid we're going to have to pick up our tour later. And I need to bring you up to speed on what you'll be working with. Let's meet tomorrow morning. Get some rest today." Miles, with Bernard at his heels, left the room as Sarah turned to the delicate Japanese woman.

"So, Rococo?" Sarah said, because she couldn't think of anything else to say and her mind was still sorting through the conversation with Miles.

"Ah, shit, no," the Japanese woman said, in a thick and unmistakable Texas drawl. "Rococo is Bernie. And don't get him started, girl, because once you do I swear to Gawd it'll be hours of descriptions of funny-lookin' snuff boxes. I'm Weapons, honey. Guns, baby. Guns."

An hour later Shuziko — "call me Suzi" — and Sarah were in the cramped kitchen of

Lobkowicz Palace sipping beers from the Lobkowicz family's brewery. Here, as elsewhere in the palace, construction was in full swing, and Sarah sat on a stepladder while Suzi chopped vegetables. Sarah offered to help, but it was clear that Suzi had extremely precise ideas about slicing and dicing.

After Miles and Bernard had left them, Suzi led Sarah through a whirlwind tour of the rest of the rooms, moving at top speed despite her five-inch heels, and chattering a mile a minute.

Then they had gone to Suzi's room so Suzi could change, although first Suzi asked Sarah to take her picture — smiling primly by a window — so Suzi could send it to her mother in Dallas. "She likes to see me looking all ladylike," Suzi explained. "I had a meeting with the Minister of Culture, so I hauled out the old war paint. My mom's a real typical Texan. I think she's still hopin' I'll go back to pageants and twirling."

"Twirling?" Sarah laughed, as Suzi stripped down to a g-string, pulling out a pair of karate pants and a Pokémon T-shirt and tossing them on the bed.

"Rifles! That's where it all started for me. I was seven, eight years old and twirling these old guns: the Winchester Model 1866, British Enfield 1853, the Sharps Rifle.

People freaked out, watching this little Japanese kid hurling these big ole rifles around. Man, I loved those guns. I won every pageant I entered. They probably thought I would shoot 'em down if they didn't give me the tiara."

Now, as Suzi chopped, Sarah sipped her beer and tried steering the conversation away from firearms toward the other academics at the palace. Unfortunately, Suzi had spent most of her time at Roudnice, the massive family ancestral home fifty kilometers north of Prague where the weapons were stored. Suzi did, however, have a little bit of gossip to share about (Prince) Max.

"I had a girlfriend who knew him at Yale," Suzi said, picking up a meat cleaver, tossing it up in the air, catching it neatly by the handle, and bringing it down with a swift thunk on the chicken she was dismembering. "He was in her Dostovsky seminar. She thought he was a freaky loner type, you know, the kind who's memorized *Crime and Punishment*? I'd stay away from him if I were you."

"Not my type," said Sarah.

"Oh yeah?" Suzi asked, leering at Sarah and flipping her cleaver again. "I'm glad to hear it."

"Not my type of *guy*," Sarah amended firmly.

"C'est la fuckin' vie," Suzi sighed. "It's gonna be a long hot summer."

Sarah was glad they had gotten that cleared up. She liked that the team here at the palace was clearly a little unusual. Suzi was a force to be reckoned with. The girl had dismantled four chickens in about three minutes.

"Anyway," Suzi chattered on. "You're gonna be up to your pretty eyes in Beethoven, right? Too bad about the other guy. He was some kind of a drug addict, I heard."

"What?" Sarah almost did a spit-take with her lager. "Professor Sherbatsky a drug addict? No way."

"That's what Douglas told me." Suzi leaned over her cutting board confidentially. "The Croll paintings guy? Douglas Sexton. Or was it Daphne who told me? Anyway, I'm glad you're here, girl, even if you ain't on my team exactly." Shuziko set down her cleaver. "You're about to meet," she said dramatically, "just about the craziest group of people you can imagine. And there's something . . . going on here. Something . . . kind of *off*, if you know what I mean."

"Please don't start in on the hell portals."

"Hell portals?"

"I am so glad you have no idea what I'm talking about." Sarah was about to ask Shuziko to explain what it was she *did* mean, but Suzi grabbed an enormous copper dinner bell and informed Sarah that if she wanted to take a shower, now was the best time to grab a free bathroom. Shuziko swung the bell in a wild arc above her head.

"Half hour till chow time!" she yelled.

And it was as if the cacophony rattled something loose in Sarah's own brain, pushed through the fog and disorientation. Why had she been so slow?

There *was* something off here.

Miles Wolfmann had said that Sherbatsky had been making enemies in the group. What if someone had forced him to jump out of the window? Threatened him in some way? It was hard to imagine the professor as a drug addict. Maybe someone had drugged him? It might not have been a suicide.

It could have been murder.

It wouldn't be the first time someone got pushed out a window in Prague. It was definitely time to meet the other people staying in the palace.

TEN

While getting dressed for dinner, Sarah became aware of two very inconvenient physical facts. The first was that the slight frisson of sexual interest aroused by the Sexy Stabber at the castle gates had returned full force. She was, she had to admit, somewhat uncomfortably . . . aroused. The second was that traveling for eleven hours in a pressurized cabin had completely blocked up her sinuses. She had no sense of smell.

This was a bad combination. Sarah relied on her nose to steer her libido into appropriate waters. Without it, she couldn't really answer for the results. This was especially irritating since she was about to meet a room full of colleagues, one of whom just might be responsible for the death of her professor. She needed to be at her sharpest.

Well, Sarah thought philosophically, it

might not be so bad. After all, during her senior year of high school while working her way through the practice SAT tests in her workbook, she had scored the highest while masturbating. Though tempted to ask for a private room during the actual exam, she had restrained herself and still gotten 800s. Presumably she could make it through one dinner.

On her way back upstairs, Sarah glanced at herself in the Rococo mirror in the hallway outside the dining room. Her lips were slightly swollen and there was sweat on her upper lip. Her eyes had a glazed look. Damn it. A man had died! A man she knew and respected. Rumors were being circulated that he was a drug addict. Miles said he had made enemies in the group. She needed to find out who and why.

And she was horny as hell.

She pushed open the kitchen door. The long table was now covered with a painter's white canvas drop cloth and crazily baroque candlesticks dripped white church-candle wax down its length. The benches were almost all occupied with people digging into Suzi's roast chickens. It was like something out of a knightly engraving, tankards and revelers holding chunks of meat in their hands, while a large dog made hopeful rounds. Tiny Nicolas raised a goblet and winked at her. Only a monkey was missing. Which made her think of spanking. *Stop it,* she told herself. *Right now.*

"Sarah," called Suzi, patting space on the bench next to her. Unknown faces looked up and called out greetings and she made her way through the room, shaking hands and smiling. She nodded at Daphne, who sat protectively close to Miles, who was arguing in Czech on his cell phone, and waved at Eleanor, who was chatting with Bernie. Sarah slid into the space between Suzi and a slim, red-haired guy in a paint-stained T-shirt.

"Sarah Weston, meet Douglas Sexton," said Suzi. Douglas smiled and waved fingers glistening with chicken juices.

"Sorry, love, we can't seem to find the silverware," apologized Douglas in a cockney accent. "Or the napkins." The sight of Douglas's wet fingers, his British accent, and his pillowy lips had a distinct worsening effect on Sarah's situation. Cut off from her nose, she was forced into intense awareness of other physical stimuli.

She looked around the table. In the dim candlelight, she took in the unfamiliar faces, and one she recognized eating alone at the end of the table.

"Max," whispered Suzi. "Doesn't talk, just eats and runs."

Something underneath the table pushed against Sarah's legs, trying to nudge her knees apart.

"Jesus," Sarah said, half-jumping off the bench. An extremely large creature emerged, looking enthusiastic. It looked like a . . .

"It's a *vlčák,*" said the man across the table from Sarah, smiling at her behind giant Buddy Holly glasses. He had introduced himself as Moses Kaufman, an expert in seventeenth-century decorative arts. "A Czechoslovakian wolfhound. Very closely related to the Eurasian wolf. He's Max's dog."

"Ain't he gorgeous?" Suzi said, thumping the fearsome animal on its hindquarters. "His name is Moritz."

"After the 9th prince," said Moses, helpfully.

"The 9th had the most gorgeous crossbows made for his children with staghorn tillers," Suzi said. "Hey, Sarah, are you all right? You look a little funny."

"Jet lag," said Sarah, grabbing a piece of chicken off a platter.

"Have a cold *pivo,*" said Douglas, pouring from a dewy silver pitcher into a glass tankard. "Beer is the one thing Max doesn't stint on."

Sarah tilted her head back and let the cold beer pour down her throat. Out of the corner of her eye she saw Douglas notice the drops that fell onto her slightly moist chest. She smiled what she hoped was a professional smile at him, trying not not *not* to think about how his slim forearms would feel wrapped around her. He was quite possibly the last person to see Sherbatsky alive, and was spreading rumors that he was a drug addict. Douglas could be dangerous.

"What's your thing?" he asked her in a slightly husky, amused voice.

She met his cobalt gaze. Rather disturbingly, his eyes locked onto hers. She held his gaze for a few more seconds, just to challenge him, and then said a little coldly, looking away, "Beethoven." She made a point of turning to the right and addressing Suzi in a totally professional way:

"Suzi, if I need certain supplies, who's the best person to ask?" As Suzi turned to answer the question, Sarah felt a hand on her left knee. Light, unmoving, but present.

"Jana," said Suzi. "She's a miracle worker. But she does need time, if it's something not available here. Customs is a bitch." As Suzi talked about the availability of high-quality cotton balls and mineral oil, Sarah carefully kept her eyes on her. She debated her options. She could remove Douglas's hand. She could stand and go get something from the kitchen. She could take a fork and stab the offending paw. But there were no forks. And . . . there was another problem. She really liked the feel of his hand there. In fact, without even meaning to, she shifted her hips just slightly, so that his fingers moved up an inch, reaching the edge of her dress. Her heart rate increased. She continued, however, to keep her eyes on Suzi, who was talking about how a supply of paintbrushes had been stuck in customs for a week.

Douglas's fingertips brushed their way up her thigh like Suzi's paintbrushes, sliding under Sarah's knit dress and dropping down into the space between her legs. Sarah risked a quick glance down, just in case prying hands were visible to prying eyes. But the bulky canvas drop cloth hid their laps completely. Sarah ate her chicken and returned her gaze to Suzi.

"Tell me about your work with the weapons," she said, hoping that was enough to keep Suzi talking for several minutes. Although it might not take several minutes. As Sarah shifted her weight onto her elbows and spread her knees slightly, Douglas agilely grasped her leg closest to him and pulled it over his own, giving him the perfect leverage to slide his occupied hand under the elastic of her panties. Sarah tried not to gasp, but as a musician she approved of anyone who had mastered good fingering.

Sarah continued eating her chicken, licking her fingers and taking the opportunity to bite them a little.

"You're gonna read all about it in the Lobkowicz Collections guidebook, but the family used to have several hunting preserves," explained Suzi. "To our ears that sounds sort of cruel, keeping animals just for the purpose of killing them someday for sport, but in fact it's the only reason there's any undeveloped forest land in Europe today. And it was the way they trained young noblemen for war. Plus it meant employment for hundreds of gamekeepers, gunkeepers, woodsmen, and stable boys. And it probably saved lots of species from extinction. Godfrey's got the job of cataloging the animals still living in the Lobkowicz lands." Sarah glanced across the table at the man Suzi had indicated as Godfrey. He had dark, furry brows and a deeply lined tan face.

"Tell Sarah about the critters," Suzi said.

"There are stags, deer, wild boar, elk," Godfrey said obediently. "Hares, an ancient oryx who likes popcorn, pheasant of course, ducks, geese, swans, tons of guinea fowl, peacocks . . ." Godfrey continued to list every possible type of bird and mammal as Sarah's mind grew fuzzy. Douglas was feathering his touches, which was especially impressive, given the odd angle he had to work with. Must be the same delicate method he used to restore watercolors . . .

Sarah felt like she was about to lose it. She wanted to stand up and hoped Doug would follow her out into the hallway, but she simply could not tear herself away from his hand. She couldn't actually *come* at the table during her first dinner with her new colleagues. Could she? She glanced across the table at Daphne, who smiled at her a little tightly. Miles had left the room to finish his cell phone call. Godfrey finished his list of animals and carried his plate off to the kitchen.

Sarah forced herself to rise, hoping her dress would fall correctly down over her thighs.

"Sorry, where's the bathroom?" asked Sarah.

"Last door on the left down the hallway," said Suzi. "Are you okay?"

"Just hot," said Sarah.

She avoided eye contact with Douglas and hoped he would not follow her, even though she knew he would.

Sarah made her way down the dim hall and pushed into the bathroom, not turning on the light. Nothing killed lust faster than fluorescents. She pulled her panties down and put a hand on herself. She pulled a condom out of her purse. Best to be ready for anything. The door pushed open, and Sarah grabbed Douglas's hand as it reached for the light switch.

"You'll pay for this," she said huskily, kissing him deeply. After a moment, he grabbed her ass with his hands and pulled her close. Sarah unzipped the fly of his jeans. Quite a cock on this cockney. Douglas seemed as ready as she was, and Sarah, also a master at fingering, had the condom on him in an instant. The room was very small, with barely room to maneuver. It seemed best to keep things simple.

"Wait," she said, turning around and lifting her dress. From behind wasn't the most personal way to have first sex with someone, but in terms of maximizing space it was a winner. It was also a position in which Sarah found it easy to come quickly and this was an emergency. She reached back to offer some guidance, something she had always done ever since a sexually confused hockey player (God, his uniform had smelled great) had tried for anal. She put her hands up against the bathroom wall and thrust her backside against him. He already had her on the edge of insane ecstasy, so the slight friction sent her quickly over the edge. And as she shuddered and gasped with pleasure, so did he.

"Thanks," she said after the final tremors had faded. Spent in all senses, he rested his head against her shoulder. "Great job. I really needed that. But we better get back before people start to talk." He nodded into her shoulder, obviously still overcome.

"You go first," Sarah said, kindly. Douglas left.

Sarah splashed water on her face, pulled her panties on, and smoothed her hair, taking her time. She opened the bathroom door and started confidently back down the hallway. Now she could think straight. Bernard, the Rococo guy — what was his deal? He seemed jumpy. And she needed to meet the others. There was video footage of Sherbatsky's death. Or was there? Maybe that was a lie. Now that she had broken the ice, so to speak, with Douglas, she might get him to tell her about these ridiculous drug accusations. As she reached for the door to the dining room, it opened. And Douglas stepped out, grinning at her.

"Wanted to be discreet," he said. "Didn't miss my chance, did I?"

Sarah blanched and turned back down the hallway. *Oh, Jesus help me,* she thought. Who the hell did I just have sex with?

Before she could begin to make a list of possible suspects, there was a loud crash of breaking glass and an agonized shout from the direction of the ballroom.

She and Douglas quickly headed in that direction, followed by Suzi, Daphne, and some stragglers from the dining room. They were joined along the corridor by Miles and Godfrey, either of whom could have been her lover, she realized, along with any number of Polish workmen.

But as the crowd rounded the corner into the ballroom, she saw a figure silhouetted against the rising moon shining though the huge arched windows, and with a wrench of her gut she realized there was one more possible identity for the slim, talented swordsman who, though no doubt taken by surprise himself, had taken her to a place of ecstasy.

"Goddamn it, it's gone," shouted Prince Max, kicking a hammer that lay on the ground and smashing the remains of a glass case with his bare fist. "The cross is gone."

Sarah looked at his angry eyes, at the blood streaming down his fist as he shook it at them.

"You're scum, you're all a bunch of fucking know-it-all scum, and I consider each and every one of you guilty until proven innocent," he said, dialing what Sarah guessed was the police.

ELEVEN

Charlotte Yates read through the latest e-mail message from Miles Wolfmann again. An eleventh-century crucifix had been discovered missing from Lobkowicz Palace sometime between eight and nine p.m., the night before, Czech time. The discovery of the theft was made by Max Lobkowicz Anderson, who had immediately alerted local authorities. During the subsequent search of the palace, the crucifix had been found in the bedroom of one of the visiting academics, who had excused herself from the communal dinner table some fifteen or twenty minutes before the discovery of the theft. This person — one Sarah Weston — denied any knowledge of the article and claimed to have spent the missing time period in the lavatory. She was, in fact, seen by several people exiting the lavatory. Her demeanor was described by two people as being "flushed" and "disoriented," which

Miss Weston attributed to a combination of jet lag and alcohol consumption. Miles Wolfmann did not believe that Sarah Weston had anything to do with the attempted — if that's what it was — theft, and the fact that the crucifix had been found in plain sight on Miss Weston's pillow seemed to point to some sort of practical joke by person or persons unknown. Miles Wolfmann had gathered the entire staff together and issued an extremely stern lecture, in which he was joined by an irritated special agent of the Czech police.

It was now five p.m., Washington, D.C., time, and Charlotte Yates decided that it *was* indeed the most ridiculous thing she had heard all day. And that was saying a lot, considering that she was the senior senator from Virginia, chair of the Senate Committee on Foreign Relations, and spoke to the President of the United States on a regular basis.

Charlotte sent a terse reply to Miles. She then turned to the file on her desk to review the material she had requested on Sarah Weston. The speed at which this material had arrived, the thoroughness of its contents, and the fact that its request had not been documented, was a source of satisfaction. But then, she knew the right people.

Charlotte Yates knew a lot of the right people and she had known them for a long time, and in ways that many of them would go to some lengths to deny, should it come to that.

It wasn't going to come to that. Still, old habits died hard and some recent events — the Venice disaster — could not be repeated. Now was not the time to get careless with the details. She knew that better than anyone. So with everything else that had to get done today, at least ten minutes needed to be devoted to going over this Sarah Weston's profile.

Charlotte reached for the gold cigarette case in the bottom left-hand drawer of her desk. The case — eighteenth century and encrusted with sapphires — was too ostentatious to display, but handling such objects gave Charlotte one of the few sensual pleasures she allowed herself. (The case no longer contained cigarettes. She had quit during the campaign of '86, when a photo of her smoking had been snapped by some idiot and the headlines the next day ran, "The Next Senator from Virginia . . . *Slims?*") Charlotte selected a short plastic straw, snapped the case shut, rubbed her thumb over a sapphire, and chewed the end of the straw thoughtfully.

Charlotte ran a practiced eye over Sarah Weston's background information. Slipping into recruitment training learned long ago at the Farm, she found herself looking automatically for signs of a likely operative. From this angle, Miss Weston was not without interest. Extremely high IQ. Working-class background. Dead father. Very athletic. Personally ambitious. A looker, too. In the end, though, Charlotte would have stamped a NWV (Not Worth Vetting) on the file. No doubt Miss Weston was impressive, in her way, but a self-made musicologist wasn't really Agency material. Charlotte Yates didn't especially care for music. All that abstract mooning about. Words, that was what moved people. A good play was worth a thousand symphonies. The Greeks. Shakespeare. Schiller.

Still, a few things in Weston's file struck a chord. Charlotte Yates had been orphaned young, desperately poor, and so brilliant that pretty much everyone hated her when the Agency picked her up. Those had been heady days. She had come to the attention of no less a luminary than John Paisley, director of the CIA's Office of Security. He had been like a father to her, really. Taught her everything she knew about interrogation techniques and how to . . . get along with Russians. He got her the cushy assignment in Prague. She owed him a lot.

But Charlotte's admiration of Paisley — like her collection of precious objects — was something she kept very, very private. Of course, they had never been able to *prove* that Paisley was a spy for the KGB or link him to Kennedy's assassination. But Paisley had ended up in Chesapeake Bay with a bullet in his temple and a thoroughly discredited reputation. And Charlotte Yates ended up . . . well, she wasn't done yet. There was an office with a pleasing oval shape on the horizon.

Anyway, *she* didn't consider Sarah Weston to be a possible agent for the home team, but it was always possible the girl was a plant from one of her enemies.

Unlikely. But there had been a few odd things happening at the palace.

Charlotte tossed the mangled straw into her wastepaper basket and selected another straw from the beautiful cigarette case.

The case had once been the property of the 9th Prince Lobkowicz. She had found it under her pillow one night in Prague with a message tucked inside: *The right to own beautiful things should be reserved for the beautiful.*

A lovely present from Yuri, the first of many. Charlotte smiled. Poor silly little faux Prince Lobkowicz thought he could put his grubby little mitts all over whatever he wanted, but he'd never track this one down.

Oh, dealing with the situation at the palace would be so much easier if the cousin were in charge. Although if Venice proved anything, it was that Marchesa Elisa might possibly have a screw or two loose. This, too, was worrying.

Charlotte had met Marchesa Elisa Lobkowicz DeBenedetti at a Heritage Foundation event, years ago. The party had been a sea of beaded jackets and unflattering hairstyles, from which the young Marchesa Elisa, in a ravishing Givenchy sheath and impeccable French twist, had emerged like a finely honed stiletto. Charlotte had turned to an aide to inquire who the glamorous woman might be, and was somewhat startled to hear the name "Lobkowicz."

After the Velvet Revolution, Charlotte had kept a close eye on events unfolding in Prague. She wasn't worried that anything connected to her days there with the CIA would emerge, the Agency knew how to keep its secrets. But there had been other . . . involvements that the Agency didn't know about. Memories in that part of the world were long, and then there was the matter of some personal letters, which Charlotte knew to be concealed somewhere in Lobkowicz Palace. Someone would have to know a very great deal to be able to trace those letters directly back to her, but Charlotte didn't like the idea of ~~them~~ *their* being out there, beyond her control. A too-thorough examination of the Lobkowicz goodie bag was another concern. So far the red tape had been reassuringly thick and tangled, but Charlotte knew it was important to stay several chess moves ahead. She had turned to an aide.

"What is she doing here?" Charlotte demanded. "Who is she with? What are her affiliations?"

"I'm not sure," the aide bleated. "I'll find out of course. Apparently she's seated at your table for dinner."

By the time dessert was served, the marchesa had confided to Charlotte in charmingly Italian-accented English her perturbation at being shut out of the Lobkowicz holdings.

"The heirs," sniffed the marchesa, "are American. 'A nation of lawyers and plumbers,' my father used to say. The collection means nothing to them, they have no sense of history, of our family's position, nothing. If the restitution process goes through, these Americans could get it all back and then put everything away in banks and vaults where no one can enjoy them! Or make a museum for 'the people.' My mother always taught me that the best way to keep jewels beautiful was to wear them next to your skin. What good is something that you can only look at?"

Charlotte had nodded sympathetically. Later, on a secluded balcony, she had offered the marchesa a cigarette from her sapphire-encrusted case. It had amused Charlotte — a poor orphan from Virginia — to offer a European aristocrat a smoke from a cigarette case that had once belonged to that same European aristocrat's family. The marchesa was dying to get her hands on her family's possessions, and here Charlotte was waving one of those items in front of her. Not that the marchesa would recognize it of course. The world was full of cigarette cases.

"Beautiful," the marchesa had said, her eyes glinting.

"Picked it up at a little antiques market in Prague," Charlotte had replied, with an even smile.

"Ah, you know Prague?"

"I take an interest," Charlotte had said.

"Did you know I am on the board of the American-Czech Cultural Alliance?"

"Oh yes?" The marchesa exhaled smoke through her aquiline nose. "Then of course you might support the treasures of my family being shut away in a museum."

A photographer wandered out onto the balcony and held up his camera. The two women stopped talking and posed. The photographer moved on.

"Perhaps not *every* treasure," Charlotte had said, tucking the cigarette case away. "But these things move slowly, and a restitution process will be a very complicated affair. I assume the board would support some kind of museum. If so, I plan on being *very* involved with the administration of this. Your advice could be quite . . . valuable."

"And if there is anything I can ever assist you with, I am more than happy," Marchesa Elisa replied. "Perhaps at some point we may . . . cooperate."

And that had been that, for a while. The various wheels in Prague had churned slowly, and quietly. Charlotte knew the marchesa was doing battle with the American heirs over the property, but she bided her time, waiting.

Recently things had accelerated. The current heir, one Max Anderson, was proving to be irritatingly clever with the red tape despite his youth and inexperience. The Nazis had been one thing. The communists another. But now there were *academics* crawling all over the palace. Of course, now Charlotte was quite a powerful person in Washington, but if her reach was longer, it was that much more exposed flesh. As the first woman to chair the Senate Foreign Relations Committee, the newshawks were always watching, hoping to catch her in a crying jag, or see a tampon fall out of her purse. Always better to let others do the reaching. Safer to be the one directing the puppet. The time to cooperate with the marchesa had come.

Elisa had access to the palace, and while Miles assured Charlotte constantly that he had his eyes on everything, that meant it was important to have eyes on Miles. Charlotte had told Miles to look for love letters from a woman to a man. An American woman to a Russian man. In the 1970s. Harmless love letters. Of no historical interest whatsoever. A personal one to her only.

She wanted them back. She needed them back. Charlotte brought the cigarette case to her lips.

The right to own beautiful things should be

reserved for the beautiful.

Oh, she had loved Yuri so. And he had loved her, too. Really, it had all been done for love. She had been young, and, yes, a little foolish.

Charlotte cast another quick eye over Miles's report. Nicolas Pertusato was back at the palace. And apparently he'd been lurking in Venice at the time of the disaster. That little freak show remained the only person she couldn't get a decent background report on.

Miles needed to get things under control or she was going to have to step in. Well, she would think about it on the flight to Venice. It was time to play emissary from the president and assure the Europeans that the government of the United States was terribly concerned about the recent tragedy and our thoughts and prayers were with the blah, blah, blah.

But listen to the truth:
We will be judged by what we seem to
    be,
No one is ever tried for what they are.
My right to rule this kingdom is in doubt,
So must my part in her destruction be.
A fog best hides these good and evil acts,

The worst mistake is that which comes to light.
One cannot lose if one does not concede.

Queen Elizabeth speaking to Mortimer in Schiller's *Mary Stuart.* Elizabeth I knew her stuff. And she knew how to run a secret police. But she was too emotional, getting all bothered by Mary Stuart. Charlotte had no personal beef with anyone. Not anymore. Not even with that nincompoop over in the Oval. He simply didn't matter. It wasn't, Charlotte assured herself, *personal.* She wasn't a vengeful person, really. No, not at all.

TWELVE

Sarah put on her headphones and hit "Shuffle" on her iPod. She needed a little break, so she was taking a quick jog around the castle grounds, dodging tourists and trying to work the tension out of her shoulders. Her assigned workroom in the palace — next to Arms and Armory, and down the hall from Decorative Arts — was a bit stuffy, since it had no window. Why did they always give her the windowless rooms? Were they afraid she would jump, too? Or be pushed?

She was accompanied on her run by Moritz, Max's wolfhound, who had taken a liking to her ever since that first night.

It had been two weeks since what Sarah thought of as The Very Bad Evening. Yes, the sex in the bathroom was mind-blowing, but no one had come forward to claim ownership, so to speak. And as if that wasn't annoying enough, she had no idea who had thought it hilarious to leave the precious fucking eleventh-century cross on her bed. Was it a joke? A message? A warning? Or just an attempt to rattle her? At the very least, it was embarrassing to be singled out that way.

To Sarah's mind, further proof that Sherbatsky had not committed suicide was on his worktable. Contrary to what Miles had said, it wasn't "mostly completed," it was a mess. And the Sherbatsky that Sarah knew would never have left things half-finished and unexplained. There were copious notes about "Luigi" — Sherbatsky used the nickname for Beethoven that Beethoven himself had preferred — many of them difficult to decipher. Did the note next to "April 4, 1811, letter from Luigi to Prince L" say "Venice" or "Vienna"? Annoying. There were many notes about things to be looked up in the library at Nelahozeves, the Lobkowicz country place on the Vltava River. It was overwhelming.

Sarah felt like taking a longer run, but her iPod was now playing Beethoven's Piano Trio in C Minor, op. 1. It was as if LVB were whistling her back to work.

The Piano Trio in C Minor. Early Beethoven, in which you could hear the heights of Classicism, hints of Haydn, a glimmering foreshadow of the Fifth Symphony, and

Luigi's own stubborn don't-tell-me-how-it's-supposed-to-be inclusion of an unusual four-movement format, instead of the traditional three. Even what seemed simple and obvious about Beethoven always turned out to be complicated.

Like even his birth date. LVB was born in Bonn in 1770, but for some reason he continually denied that birth date all his life, even when copies of his birth certificate were shoved under his nose, insisting that he was born two years later. His father was undoubtedly Johann van Beethoven, but Luigi did little to contradict rumors that he was the unacknowledged son of Frederick the Great. Probably because he hated his father — an alcoholic and only middling musician — so much. Daddy Beethoven had wanted his son to be a child prodigy, another boy Mozart, and drove him relentlessly at the clavier and violin, which should have driven the music out of him but didn't. LVB became a court musician in Bonn by the age of eleven, and was composing variations, sonatas, and lieder by the age of twelve.

And then he stopped composing for almost five years. No explanation, although his mother died during this period, and teenage Ludwig was supporting the family.

Then, in 1790, a burst of activity. These lapses in work, followed by insane productivity, were to become characteristic of the composer. In 1792, the drunken father died and young Ludwig hightailed it to Vienna, making a name for himself as a keyboard virtuoso. Some thought his playing harsh and disturbing. Almost everyone thought his manners were execrable. Coming from Bonn put Beethoven firmly "from the wrong side of the Rhine" among the snobby Viennese. As a girl from South Boston, Sarah could relate. Still, despite the uncouth manners and independent streak, the musician was courted by the nobility. Prince Joseph Franz Maximilian Lobkowicz was twenty, Ludwig van Beethoven twenty-two when they met. But Prince Lobkowicz was hardly LVB's only patron. In fact, less was known about the relationship between the two men than was known about other relationships Beethoven had with different benefactors. Which made the letters that had been found and restituted back to the family sort of exciting. Puzzling, too, in some cases.

Sarah forced herself to leave the sunshine and beauty of the Prague Castle grounds and returned to her monastic cell, shooing away Moritz, who wasn't allowed in the workrooms. Today's task involved going through Luigi's Fourth Symphony orchestrations page by page and determining that each page was there, not a forgery, and in acceptable condition. In his own hand, Beethoven had carefully written out the parts for every single instrument, from flute to timpani. She used a microscope to examine each sheet of paper and the ink, as well as the shape of the letters and musical notes. Like most people's, Beethoven's writing shifted with his mood but was still basically consistent.

Beethoven's moods. It still blew her away that she was sitting here, touching (with gloves, but still) pieces of paper that Beethoven had touched. When he had written the Fourth in 1806, he was still a black-haired young man, not the white-mopped madman of later years. Looking through the microscope at the way the nib of Beethoven's pen had dug into the yellowed parchment as he wrote out the viola's part, Sarah felt a chill up her spine. She stopped for a moment and listened to make sure no one was coming, then slipped off her left glove and gently put her index fingertip against an emphatically marked quarter note. She was startled to feel a little electric zing, but chalked it up to the polyester content of the gloves, hot weather, and static electricity. That's what her father would have said. She put the glove back on.

Sarah sighed and stretched. Hours had a way of slipping by when she was working like this. Bending down, her eye was caught by a Post-it note that Sherbatsky must have stuck above the work table. In the stifling summer heat, it had come unstuck and fluttered down onto the orchestration for the bassoon. Sarah read the note: "Luigi — Prince L 12/31/06 Nelahozeves." There were two asterisks below it. (Sherbatsky never gave grades, but if one turned in exceptional work, he would return it with an asterisk marked on top. Sarah was his only pupil ever to receive two asterisks.)

Sarah flipped through the binder of xeroxed correspondence between Beethoven and Prince Lobkowicz that she had made for reference purposes. "The 7th," as he was known among the scholars at the palace, had been scrupulous in keeping copies of all his correspondence. Actually, he sometimes didn't open his correspondence and some of the letters to him had been read for the first time years after his death — but he didn't throw anything out. Neither did his heirs. Even the Nazis had left the papers alone.

There was a note from Luigi to the prince

dated December 15, 1806, expressing regret that Luigi couldn't make it to the Christmas ball. There was another on January 16 from the prince thanking Luigi for the gift of an Aztec amulet vial. Hmmm. No New Year's Eve letter. She wondered how Sherbatsky knew about the December 31 letter if there was no copy of it, and no mention of it in the other correspondence. The gift of the Aztec amulet was interesting, too. Luigi wasn't much of a gift-giver. He was pretty stingy.

Deciding to do a little detective work, Sarah obediently locked the door of the workroom behind her (Prince Max had insisted on this measure) and headed down to Miles's office. If they could find the Aztec amulet, it would make a nice part of the display.

"Yes, Huitzlipochtli," said Miles, in response to her query about the amulet. "I'm told that's the name of the figure depicted on it. We haven't found him yet, but the Nazis took a picture of him." Miles flipped through some files and produced a grainy black-and-white photo of a small ceramic vial with a bird god on it.

"Beethoven used to call Prince Lobkowicz 'Fitzliputzli' — his play on the name of the

135

Aztec god Huitzlipochtli," Sarah said.

She studied the photo for a second, then laughed out loud.

"Guess what Huitzlipochtli was famous for?"

Miles smiled and crossed his arms, waiting.

"The Aztecs believed he ate blood and hearts, so they made a human sacrifice in his honor every day."

"That's supposed to be funny?"

"To Beethoven it probably was. That was what he was teasing Prince Lobkowicz about, that he was expecting his pound of flesh. Beethoven had to tear his own heart out and put it down on paper in order to keep his patron happy. The vial is for his own blood."

"Conjecture," Miles said.

"Yeah," Sarah said. "But I bet I'm right."

"Well, if we find the amulet, we could display it with the letter," Miles said. "If you think it's of interest."

Sarah felt a satisfying rush of power and, beyond that, a feeling of pride that she had deciphered Beethoven's joke. Most people didn't get Luigi's sense of humor.

Miles turned back to his computer. "Eleanor was looking for you. She's going out to Nelahozeves tomorrow and wondered if you wanted to ride along."

"I do. There are a bunch of notes Sherbatsky left about things to look up there. Maybe I'll go dig around. See what I can find."

Miles looked sharply at her. "Whatever you find, bring it straight to me."

"Of course."

Sarah was glad for the chance to go to Nelahozeves with Eleanor. Nearly all the originals of correspondence were kept there in the library, and technically all the academics had access to them. The catch was that only Max had the key. Since the night of the crucifix debacle, he had become more surly, withdrawn, and paranoid. According to Suzi, when she had gone to Max's office to ask him a harmless question about missing hunting trophies, he had refused to let her in, and had all but accused her of spying. He spoke to no one but his dog, Moritz.

"He's a nut job," Suzi said. "You know how these Hapsburgs are all inbred. Look at him, he's the exact image of every one of his relatives going back five hundred years. That's not healthy."

Max took his meals apart from them now, and Sarah had only passed him once in the hallway. He didn't make eye contact.

Sarah made loud footsteps on the polished

terrazzo floor as she walked down the hallway to his office. She rehearsed her speech about asking for the key, and steeled herself.

But only Jana was in the office, with Moritz panting beneath her desk. He thumped his tail at the sight of Sarah. "Are you looking for Prince Max?" Jana asked politely.

Sarah nodded. "We need the key to the library," she explained.

"The prince is at Nelahozeves now," Jana said. "But the phone lines are down and his mobile is turned off. I'm not sure . . ."

"Will he be there tomorrow?" Sarah asked. "I mean, is it okay if we just show up?"

Jana hesitated.

"We won't disturb him," Sarah promised. "But we really need the time with the archives. I promise he won't even know we're there."

"I did get one message from the prince asking for his drum set," said Jana. "Petr was going to take it in the van tomorrow. Perhaps you and Eleanor can drive the van and deliver it for us?"

Drum set, thought Sarah. *That completes the picture.*

"Oh, and would you take this to him?"

Jana asked, handing Sarah a letter. "It came yesterday."

Sarah looked at the envelope. It was high-quality stationery, printed with the return address of the Hotel Gritti Palace in Venice. Fancy.

"Sure," Sarah said. It was weird how everyone assumed it was an honor to do things for aristocrats. As if they weren't already the privileged ones.

As she was turning away, she sensed Bernard Plummer, the Rococo expert, to be close by. Once Sarah's nose had cleared, she learned that Bernie tended to overdo it on Chanel No. 5. Beneath the massive chest beat the heart of a refined and accomplished French matron. He often brought embroidery to the dinner table.

"Oh, Sarah, some of us are going over to Old Town Square for dinner out," Bernie said, appearing from behind a corner. "It's Godfrey's turn to cook and I just can't face the offal." Sarah nodded.

"Plus we have to plan the costume ball," he said, as they turned into Daphne's portrait hall. Daphne, dressed as always in her impeccable lab coat, was giving instructions to two workmen who were carrying a glass case.

"Costume ball?"

"Yes, we're all dressing up like *them.*" Bernie nodded at the family portraits staring down at them. "I've already dibbed rights to Maria Manrique de Lara and I found an extraordinary shop where I can get ermine. Fake ermine! I love these kinds of things."

Sarah and Bernie paused to peer over Daphne's shoulder into the glass case. It contained a small blond, blue-eyed wax doll with pink cheeks dressed in a fancy red muumuu. The dress was trimmed with gold embroidery and sported a white lace ruff and cuffs. A cross hung from its neck.

"Somebody's dolly?" Bernard said, pulling out a pair of glasses to inspect the needlework.

"De Infant of Prague," Daphne corrected with a sniff.

"*That's* Il Bambino di Praga?" Sarah almost laughed out loud.

"It's a copy of course," Daphne said, witheringly. "De original is in de Church of Our Lady Victorious."

"Huh," Sarah said. "What's this one doing here?" Daphne sighed.

"Polyxena Lobkowicz vas given de original Holy Infant by her mother, Maria Manrique de Lara, who brought it here from Spain in 1555. When Polyxena's husband Zdeněk died, Polyxena gave it to de Carmelite

140

church. This copy vas made in the 1930s, I believe. It vas found in a trunk filled vith old shoes."

"It's *fabulous,*" breathed Bernard. "Can I carry it around at the costume ball?"

"That vould be most impious," Daphne sniff ed. "It is not a toy. And I believe Dr. Volfmann has not authorized this costume party."

"Oh, we have to do it," Bernard pleaded. "I've already made Eleanor's costume, and mine. Daphne, let me cook you up something. You could be Polyxena."

Sarah thought she detected a suppressed gleam of excitement in Daphne's eye. Even stuffy Dutch academics couldn't resist a chance to play dress-up.

THIRTEEN

Sarah left Daphne and Bernie and made her way to Eleanor Roland's domain to see about hitching a ride to Nelahozeves Castle. The Ernestine portraits were housed next to the room where Douglas Sexton was working on the Carl Robert Croll watercolor collection. Nimble of finger Doug who was also cheating bastard Doug. Somewhere between Max's tirade and the arrival of the Czech police, Sarah had noticed the wedding band on Douglas's left hand. How had she missed that? Mentally re-creating the under-table experience, Sarah realized that Doug had pulled off the pyrotechnics with the right hand alone. Sort of like Beethoven in the famous chord sequence of Piano Sonata No. 2: the one where LVB had carefully notated the fingering in the score — something he never did — knowing full well that the only person capable of playing the passage with one hand was himself. Sarah liked to imagine Luigi holding his left hand up while ripping through the sequence, so those without a view of the keyboard could watch and be amazed. It must have been quite a turn-on for the ladies of the late eighteenth century. Sarah pictured Doug waving his chicken wing around with his left hand. Not quite the same.

Now that her sinuses were clear, she had no interest in Douglas, but it was awkward explaining the truth, so she had used his wedding band as an excuse for her change of mind. He had sulked a bit, of course, but seemed content enough with provocative banter at the dinner table.

Sarah thought of trying to sneak past Douglas on her way to Eleanor, but then thought better of it. She had been so busy with the museum work that she hadn't had an opportunity yet to question him about the drug accusation and Sherbatsky. She turned toward his workroom.

Sarah had been at the palace long enough now to know that Douglas ranked somewhat low in the hierarchy of the experts — or, rather, the Carl Robert Croll watercolors did. The paintings gave a nice record of Lobkowicz family life in the mid-nineteenth century, but had been commissioned with no other aim than impressing the viewer with just how much *stuff* the family owned, and how very rich and important they all were. They didn't have a great deal of artistic merit on their own. Unlike, say, Beethoven's Fourth written out in the composer's own hand. Which Sarah had touched with *her* own hand. Really, if you could get away from the vague feeling of dread, the fact that she had been briefly accused of stealing an eleventh-century crucifix, paranoid Max, and the still unexplained death (murder?) of Sherbatsky, it was shaping up to be a kick-ass summer.

Sarah poked her head into Doug's room. The Crolls were in great shape, ready to be exhibited, so Douglas seemed to be mostly occupied with selecting the best ones and photographing them. Sarah suspected he was killing time, dragging out an all-expenses-paid summer in Prague away from the wifey.

"How's it going?" Sarah asked, stepping into the room.

"Hello, love," Douglas said. "Come and have a look."

Sarah walked over and peered at the delicate painting on Douglas's table. The picture was a view of a grand salon with two little girls in the foreground. Behind them, through a vaulted arch, three men were playing billiards.

"Just another Sunday in the lives of the rich and Austro-Hungarian," said Sarah.

She leaned in closer. Even in simplified and tiny watercolor form, the Lobkowicz features were unmistakable. It could have been Max standing there in a green waist-coat, cue stick balanced jauntily on his shoulder. If Max ever got around to removing the cue stick shoved up his ass, that is.

Douglas looked down the V of Sarah's T-shirt.

"How's it going in your world?" he asked. "Anything interesting turn up?"

"I'm still trying to make sense of Sherbatsky's notes," Sarah said, with a deliberate sigh. "There are a lot of loose ends."

"Doesn't surprise me." Douglas rolled his eyes and sat down on one of the rickety wooden swivel chairs they had all been issued. "That man was a loony. No offense."

"He could be . . . unpredictable," Sarah agreed, sending a mental note of apology to the methodical dead professor.

"Well, it was good shit, whatever he was on," Douglas laughed. "I thought about asking Max to hook me up, too, but who wants to deal with that punter?"

Sarah's ears almost literally pricked up at this.

"Huh," she said, as nonchalantly as possible. "So Max and Sherbatsky were like . . . drug buddies?" Douglas looked like he regretted his last comment, so Sarah leaned provocatively against the worktable to encourage him. "C'mon," she said, giving Doug a good angle at her cleavage. "That sounds juicy."

"Well," Douglas said, scooting forward on his swivel chair to get closer to the view. "Max and Sherbatsky were always going over to Nelahozeves, and coming back looking totally *wrecked*. Miles and Daphne and I went over on a Sunday morning, just to picnic on the grounds, and we found Max, fully dressed, asleep in the *driveway* and Sherbatsky . . ." Douglas widened his eyes theatrically and slid closer to Sarah, grabbing her knees.

"Sherbatsky?" Sarah prompted, hoping to get the story before the hands got any higher.

"Miles found him on the grounds . . . by the river. Passed out cold. With a crossbow in his hands."

"Whaaaat?!" Sarah spluttered.

"Miles demanded an explanation and you should have heard Max." Douglas rolled his eyes. "He did the princely roar and huffed off. Miles and I carried Sherbatsky back to the castle and Max wouldn't let us call a doctor. Locked himself in the room with the professor and told us all to bugger off."

"You're kidding me," Sarah said. "What the fuck?"

"I know!" Douglas laughed, tracing a line up Sarah's thigh. With his right hand, Sarah couldn't help noticing. God, married guys were persistent.

"So then what happened?"

"Well, he is the prince, sort of." Douglas shrugged. "So we all sort of slunk away and had our little picnic and later on when I nipped into the castle to use the loo, I heard them arguing. Max was yelling, 'What happened? What happened?' and Sherbatsky was crying, I think. Or laughing. It was hard to tell. I heard Max telling him that he had to stop. He was going to 'make him stop.' Well, at least the old codger's not *dead,* I thought. Although" — Douglas shrugged again — "a week later he was."

"Did anybody . . ." Sarah activated her inner thigh muscles, creating a barrier to Douglas's northward drifting hand. "Did anybody tell the police this?"

"Well, I sure as fuck didn't," Douglas said. "And I don't think Miles did either.

Sherbatsky was in a bad way. Calling it a suicide was a kindness. I think he was high as a kite and toppled over in some sort of purple haze."

Or Max figured out a way to "make him stop," Sarah thought.

She'd have to double-check Douglas's story with Miles or Daphne somehow. In the meantime, it was almost five and she had signed up to use the palace's one working bathtub at 5:10. And she still needed to check in with Eleanor about tomorrow.

"Well, I've got to dash," Sarah said. "Bathtub!"

"Need someone to scrub your back?" Douglas murmured, standing up, too, and pulling her by the hips toward him. Yep. Hard-on. Sarah thought about giving him a sharp knee jab, not so much for herself but on behalf of the current Mrs. Sexton, and controlled herself with effort. After all, she had been doing the Mata Hari act, and you couldn't blame the guy.

"Thanks, I think I've got it covered," she chirped, swinging her bag over her shoulder and heading off to Eleanor's room. "See ya later."

"Vixen," Douglas growled, turning back to his watercolor.

The door to the Ernestines was shut, as

Eleanor was vigilant about room temperature and "keeping her ladies cool." Sarah gave a warning knock, opened the door, and was assaulted by a strong wave of chemicals. Eleanor — decked out in a Mexican serape — tossed Sarah a paper facemask and motioned for her to shut the door.

"I'm just finishing up!" Eleanor shouted through her own mask. "Look at my marvelous Princesse de Ligne!" Eleanor pointed at the portrait she was working on of a woman in the signature Ernestine three-quarter pose, dressed in yellow satin with bright pink bows, holding a plumed hat.

"Awesome," Sarah said, dutifully. "Listen, I've got to get down to the bath, but Miles said you were going to Nelahozeves tomorrow?"

"*Nela* we call it, and yes, come with me!" Eleanor pleaded. "I don't want to be there with Max all by myself. And you need to go, don't you? To use the library?"

"Count me in," Sarah said. "I'll protect you."

Eleanor waved her thanks and Sarah dashed down the back stairs to her room, grabbed a towel and her bag of toiletries, then hightailed up the stairs to the bathroom. Outside, a grinning Petr informed her that the boiler was "fixing" and she would "have very nice hot bath to make feel good and nice."

This, Sarah soon discovered, was Czech-to-English for "*only* the hot water is working." She managed to get the tub filled to about three inches before the room filled with steam. Sitting down naked on the narrow toilet, waiting for the water to cool, she noticed the envelope Jana had given her sticking out of her jeans pocket. Right, the letter to Max from the Hotel Gritti Palace in Venice. Plucking it from the pocket, she saw that the steam had actually unsealed the envelope. Sarah had a two-second argument with her conscience and then pulled the letter out, unfolded it carefully, and started to read.

To: Prince Maximilian Lobkowicz
 Anderson
From: Piergiorgio Vampa, Director of
 Hotel Security,
Hotel Gritti Palace, Venice

Gentilissimo Principe,
 As requested, I write to assure you about safekeeping of the item left in our care by Sig. Pertusato. This item is now in a maximum security *cassaforte,* and will remain there until you choose to

claim it. Of this, I assure you personally. Furthermore, I beg leave to assure you that recent tragic events have in no way compromised the security of this hotel, and you can rest easy on this account. Please do not hesitate to contact me if you are in need of any further assistance.

On a personal note, I beg leave to add that I well remember our most amusing night in Paris last autumn. The jazz was le hot, and the mademoiselles were le hotter. You dog!

It pains me to add that Sig. Pertusato left our hotel without paying his bill. Naturally, I assume you will take care of this, but do not feel pressed. I know that you're much occupied. Senore Pertusato says his mission to seduce the American girl to Prague was a success. Is she from California, too? All girls from America should be from California like Sig.ra Pamela Anderson. Are you related?

As always, your obedient servant,
Piergiorgio.

As Sarah sunk into her bath two thoughts came to mind: Men were ridiculous, in all cultures and across time. And Prince Max was hiding something in Venice.

FOURTEEN

There was traffic getting out of Prague, and a certain white-knuckled tension in finding the right highway, then Eleanor overshot the exit, so it was almost noon when they finally got to the Nelahozeves turnoff. Eleanor was all apologies, but Sarah enjoyed seeing a bit more of the Czech countryside. You probably couldn't say that you had really seen a country if all you had seen was a city or two. You had to see where the food was grown, what the riverbanks looked like, and what the highway manners of the inhabitants were.

The Czech countryside between Prague and Nela was lightly rolling, and Highway 8 passed endless fields of yellow mustard flowers and hops, which felt right given the national predilection for mustard and beer. Sarah was a little disappointed not to see a cabbage farm or a sausage factory, which would pretty much complete the local diet.

When they overshot their exit, they had to get off at Roudnice, the location of another Lobkowicz castle that was still under the control of the Czech army. Max was lobbying for its return, though Sarah had to ask what on earth he was going to do with a two-hundred-room white elephant when he was having enough trouble with the properties already restituted to him. Roudnice had been a training center for the SS, which was creepy enough, and then had been bombarded by the Soviets in a show of force. Sarah had heard it was quite the wreck. It sounded like a major headache, but then again it was hard to put yourself in the shoes of someone who had taken it upon himself to reassemble his family's lost fortune.

Sarah was excited to see Nelahozeves, however. " 'One of Bohemia's finest Renaissance castles,' " Sarah read aloud from a guidebook to try to ease the tension as they rerouted themselves. "Polyxena Lobkowicz purchased it in 1623. It says here that during the 1970s and 1980s the castle was used to display socialist modern art." Eleanor shuddered in horror at the idea.

"There it is," said Eleanor at last, as they wound their way through a little village spread along the green banks of the Vltava. Eleanor was pointing up at a lovely castle that dominated the tiny village, but Sarah's eye had caught a historical marker.

"Oh, wait, there's Dvořák's birthplace," said Sarah, craning her head backward. "You know, the composer? Can we stop for just a sec?"

What happened next was not technically Sarah's fault, although she bore a certain amount of the blame. Instead of either ignoring Sarah's request or driving on until she found a safe place to turn around, Eleanor rather abruptly threw the little Skoda into reverse, and began to back up the fifty yards or so to the Dvořák birthplace sign.

BAM. That was how Sarah would later describe the sound of the tractor hitting the back of their small white van. Why a tractor was careening around a blind corner was also a good question, and might have something to do with the traditional Czech farmers' breakfast beer, but soon Sarah found herself standing in a crowd of people, all of whom were speaking Czech, gesturing and pointing at where the tractor, a fine piece of socialist-era machinery, had rather pornographically embedded itself in the hind end of the Skoda.

A man in uniform arrived on a motorbike and asked for documents, but Eleanor was acting as if she had never been in an accident before. "I don't speak Czech, I don't speak Czech," Eleanor kept repeating, her voice quavering.

"Es tut uns schrecklich leid. Wir sind Amerikaner, die Dvořák Liebe zu viel," said Sarah calmly. There was a dramatic pause where it seemed that no one spoke German even though by Sarah's calculation they were only about eighty miles from the German border. *"Wir arbeiten hier auf der Burg."* Sarah pointed up at the castle. Still no sign they were understanding any of this. Sarah wondered if she and Eleanor were about to be embroiled in a diplomatic incident. *"Für Prinz Max."* Suddenly they all smiled and looked up at the castle and said, "*Ano,* Max, Max," and someone translated into Czech for the others and they all smiled and nodded.

"What did you say?" asked Eleanor. "I didn't know you spoke Czech."

"German," said Sarah, surprised that Eleanor couldn't hear the difference between a Slavic language and a Germanic one. "I'm a Beethoven scholar, remember? Kind of goes with the territory. Dvořák wasn't opening any doors, but Prince Max seems to be popular." Sarah took a moment to wonder why the villagers would look kindly upon a young American reclaiming what had technically been their property for sixty years and locking himself inside.

A new struggle began as a tow truck appeared, and the policeman made it clear that the damaged van and its contents would be coming with him. He was extremely reluctant to let Sarah and Eleanor remove Max's drum set from the back.

Finally, the policeman gave them an incomprehensible lecture, frowned over the documents but handed them back, and the tow truck carried off the van. The villagers disappeared, leaving Sarah and Eleanor by the side of the road. Sarah wasn't perfectly clear on where the van had been taken, or when it would be ready again, or whether it was up to them to call the insurance company or whether the policeman would, though she had nodded sagely when spoken to in Czech.

Giving up on the idea of touring Dvořák's house, Eleanor and Sarah made their way up a long set of stairs to the castle, lugging Max's drum kit.

Sarah took in the five stories of windows, the sgraffito stonework in shades of beige and brown, the small windows at the top, and immediately fell in love with the place. Out of the corner of her eye, she saw a flash of light in a high dormer window. Almost as if a mirror had flashed — a signal? Perhaps someone was being held hostage in the place. Mrs. Rochester?

A cobblestoned bridge led over the old moat, which contained just a little stagnant rainwater and probably some healthy frogs.

The thing about Renaissance castles, Sarah decided while standing in the central courtyard, was that they were elegant, while medieval castles were massive. This castle felt like just the right size for a really good party. There was still the sense of being prepared for a siege and all that, but the large arched windows would, she guessed, let lots of light into the second-floor rooms, and even the two little dormers atop each wing didn't look too stuffy for one's servants. Or hostages. Eleanor knocked timidly on the fifteen-foot-high wooden door.

Nothing happened.

"What if he refuses to let us in?" said Eleanor. "We could be here all night."

Sarah decided it was time for bold action. She grabbed cymbals from Max's drum set and, doing her best impression of a toy monkey, began crashing them together. Eleanor laughed and covered her ears.

There was a distant sound of barking and the massive door swung open. Standing there was . . . a Chihuahua, tan in color, and wearing a way too large leather collar with brass medallions, as if it had once been a much larger dog left too long in the dryer. True to the breed, it was barking madly in a horrible high-pitched shriek.

"Darling," said Eleanor, leaning down to pet the thing. "You opened the door for us. How clever. Ow!" she said a moment later, standing back up with a bleeding finger. "He bit me."

They left the drum set where it was and strolled into the ground floor of the castle, which had a high, barrel-vaulted ceiling. Though the interior had been relatively well-maintained since 1948, having been used as a museum, it still showed inevitable signs of wear, with lots of water stains in the corners, and some plaster falling down.

They turned a corner into a long hallway lined with doors. Sarah reached for a light switch, but nothing happened.

"Power's out," she said. "The wiring in this place must be scary." Her father would be horrified.

"I suspect that's more about nonpayment of bills," said Eleanor. "Miles says the electric here runs to the tens of thousands. And the roof leaks."

"Well, we need to find the library," said Sarah.

"We need to find the prince," said Eleanor.

"Max?" Sarah called out. "Are you here?" Nothing. Not a sound. "Okay, you check that wing, I'll check this one." Sarah watched as the Chihuahua followed tasty Eleanor, its nails making little clicking noises on the stone floor.

Sarah climbed a long set of stone stairs to the next floor, where she was pleased to see that the arched windows did indeed let in a lot of light. Sarah continued to call out Max's name, but got no response. At the end of the hallway, she had a choice of two doors. She tried the left one, and it opened into a narrow passageway. She heard a distant voice.

"Max?" she called. "It's Sarah Weston. The Beethoven girl?"

She walked down the narrow dark passage and turned a corner into a large hall fit for a group of carousing knights. Even in the gloom she could make out peeling frescoes in pastels, a huge arched ceiling, and a massive fireplace.

Max was standing just to the left of the fireplace, staring at something.

"Max?" she said. He ignored her. Irritated, Sarah moved in front of him, nearly stepping into the empty fireplace.

Max looked at her wildly. "My God," he said. "Are you insane? The fire." He began beating at her body, as if it were in flames.

For a slender guy, he was very strong. And clearly on something . . . a hallucinogen of some kind. Sarah tried wrestling with him and then remembered her training. A woman's strength is in her legs. She kicked at Max's crotch as hard as she could.

Max collapsed to the ground. His eyes were clouded with pain, and then they suddenly cleared and he looked up at Sarah. "Sorry. That was weird," he croaked. And then he passed out.

"Eleanor!" Sarah called out. "I need a little help here!" Sarah leaned over Max. It was her first chance to study him up close. He looked remarkably like his namesake and grandfather, which was to say he looked like nearly all the Lobkowicz portraits she had seen. He had the long, aquiline nose, deep-set eyes, the fine hair, and high forehead. An aristocrat's hands: long, white, and slender.

Eleanor arrived with the dog. "My God, what happened?" she gasped, as her eyes fell on Max. "He's bleeding."

"Fainted, I think," said Sarah, not wanting to go into details of how she had drop-kicked the boss. "Maybe you could find some water or food or something?"

Eleanor nodded and scurried off. Sarah picked up Max's wrist to check his pulse, and as she did so his startlingly blue eyes popped open.

"What the . . . ," he said. "What happened?"

"You fainted," said Sarah. "Right after you tried to beat imaginary flames off me."

"It's okay. It's over. Wait. What are you doing here?" He looked accusingly at Sarah.

"Did you miss the part where I said you attacked me?"

Max sat up. He looked ill but not high, exactly. Was Max some kind of epileptic?

"Did I really attack you?" he said. "God. I'm sorry. God." He sounded genuinely horrified and anxious.

"Eleanor's coming with some water if she can find it," said Sarah. "Are you okay? Should I call a doctor?"

Max shook his head. "I'm fine."

"Did you take something?" Sarah demanded. "Are you tripping or something?"

"What? No, it's none of your business." Max frowned, the haughty arrogance returning to his voice even as he struggled to stand up. He refused to say anything more and when Eleanor returned, Max gave them the key to the library and stalked off.

"Oh dear," Eleanor sighed. "What an embarrassment. Passed out cold on the floor. Not my idea of a prince at all."

Sarah got another shock when they entered the library. She was expecting walls of shelves, which there were, but she wasn't expecting rows of cardboard boxes six or more feet high. The boxes, only some of which were labeled, had turned the library into a maze.

"What the hell?" said Sarah, pulling back the dusty curtains to let in some light.

"No sun," said Eleanor. She handed Sarah a headlamp.

Apparently there were literally thousands of boxes of family papers that no one had gone through in sixty, maybe a hundred years.

"Most of this is junk," Eleanor said. "Letters, estate papers, bills of sale, dance cards — it's insane."

"But . . ." Sarah said. "What if you're looking for one particular letter?"

Eleanor laughed. "Well, you try to read what's written on the boxes, and hope for the best," she said. "And anything you open: number it, label it, and make a record for Miles. There's a clipboard here, use these forms. Be as specific as possible."

Eleanor, having worked in the library before, had a rough sense of which boxes corresponded to the period she was studying. She moved off into the labyrinth. Meanwhile Sarah looked for anything with Sherbatsky's handwriting on it. As she walked through the narrow aisles of boxes, headlamp on, feeling like a miner, she couldn't help thinking that if there were an earthquake they would literally be buried in Lobkowicz papers. All for a fistful of dollars from that shit Max, who may have drugged Sherbatsky and convinced him to step out a window.

Feeling resentful and wondering how many hundreds of strains of mold she was breathing, Sarah picked a random box off the top of a column and took it down. The ancient tape disintegrated in her hands. The writing on the box was in German. On top was a shipping list of items that were sent to a warehouse at Prague University to be cataloged for "use of the Fuhrer reserve." A chill went up Sarah's spine. The memo was dated May 28, 1942. Sarah was holding a genuine Nazi document in her hands. She sniffed it. Dust, age, and what? Cigar smoke? Evil? She scanned the memo, but didn't find anything relevant to her search.

She put the top back on the box and labeled it as Miles had instructed: today's date, her initials, the contents of the box, and its location in the library according to numbers someone had duct-taped to the floor. The next box she grabbed had clippings from the social pages of various newspapers in several languages from 1934 to 1937. Wedding announcements, it looked like. Sarah labeled and recorded again. After a couple of hours, she finally came across a box labeled with Sherbatsky's handwriting, and marked with his signature double asterisk. Sarah opened it up. There were piles of handwritten sheet music, mostly not identified, all of which seemed to be out of order. Sarah groaned at the difficulty of the task: to read the scores, attempt to date them, figure out what music belonged to which piece, who it was composed by, and for what occasion.

Sarah squatted down and began to go through the sheet music. Most of it appeared to be nineteenth century, amateur work, not particularly important or worthy of the double asterisk. At the bottom of the pile she found a leather-bound book, badly damaged, containing woodcut drawings and crabbed text in Latin. Was this important? It didn't seem to have anything to do with music. Sarah peered at the gruesome drawings. In between two pages she found a letter in German, dated October 3, 1974. Sarah skimmed it, and caught the phrase *Aztec Amulett, ein Geschenk von Ludwig van Beethoven.* Excited, she began to read more carefully from the beginning. Maybe this was a clue to where the Aztec amulet had ended up. A scholarly thrill ran through her.

The letter, however, was frustrating. It was written by a Herr Gottlieb, who seemed to be a 1970s Miles-type equivalent at Nelahozeves. The letter was addressed to a functionary at the National Museum in Prague. It complained, with East German fastidiousness, of a number of items being removed from the Nelahozeves storage facility without proper documentation. The Aztec amulet was listed as one such item. Also a gold, sapphire-encrusted cigarette case, very valuable, which had once belonged to the 6th Prince Lobkowicz. Herr Gottlieb began the letter in a spirit of outrage, then seemed to lose heart halfway through, assuring the recipient that he did not mean to accuse their esteemed director, Herr Bespalov, of unethical practices. Herr Bespalov was a man of great integrity, etcetera, etcetera. The items — idolatrous and decadent — were not appropriate for display at Nelahozeves. The National Museum in Prague was, no doubt, a more suitable place.

The letter was yellowed but not creased. She wondered if it had ever been sent or if Herr Gottlieb had decided that he didn't want to risk annoying his superiors. She made a note to research a "Bespalov" who was connected to the National Museum. Well, she had tracked the amulet to the 1970s at least.

"Eleanor?" she called out.

"Yes?" she heard from a long way away.

"Nothing. Just checking to make sure you haven't left me here."

Sarah set the box aside and continued her search. Just before dark, the silence they had worked in all afternoon was interrupted by the sound of a car horn honking in the courtyard.

Brushing a few centuries' worth of dust from her jeans, Sarah met a cobwebbed Eleanor at the library door. From the glassed-in loggia they saw Miles, and a blue Renault, below.

"Heard you had some car trouble," said Miles when they reached the courtyard.

"I hate driving in Europe," Eleanor wailed. "It's so stressful."

"It was partly my fault," began Sarah. "I

should help pay for the damage."

Miles nodded. "That's very correct of you, but not to worry, it's been taken care of. I'm just glad neither one of you was injured. Where's Max?"

"We haven't seen much of him," Sarah said. "We've been in the library all day."

"I'm feeling rather triumphant," said Eleanor, producing a box. "Apparently the Lobkowicz family not only purchased Ernestine's paintings, they also collected some of her letters. I can't wait to read her correspondence with her dressmaker!" Miles smiled somewhat mechanically.

"What about you?" he asked Sarah, gesturing to the box she was carrying.

"I actually did find a mention of the Aztec amulet." She handed over the box. "It's in the letter on top. And there's a book, incunabulum of some kind. The rest is sheet music, nineteenth century. I'll need more time with it to see if it's interesting."

Miles opened the door of the car, and Eleanor made for the passenger side.

Sarah thought how easy it would be to get in the car, go back to Prague, and just be the Beethoven scholar she was hired to be. But what Douglas Sexton had told her of the strange goings-on at Nelahozeves was weighing on her mind. She really needed to get some answers out of Max as to what he and Sherbatsky were up to. She had chickened out earlier, which wasn't her style.

"You know what? I kind of want to keep working," she said. "I think I'll stay over and take the train back tomorrow."

"Really?" Eleanor sounded disappointed. "But I'm making fresh pesto tonight."

Miles frowned. "There's no electricity or running water."

"I'm a good camper," Sarah countered with confidence she didn't feel. "I'm not sure when I'll get a chance to come back here and I want to make use of the time."

Miles looked skeptical.

"Is Max okay with you staying over?" Miles said. "He's usually very squirrelly about people being out here."

"He said it was fine," lied Sarah. "I'll do my thing and he'll do his. I just want a few more hours to try and track down some of these things Sherbatsky mentioned in his notes."

"Bring whatever you find directly to me tomorrow," Miles reminded her. The Renault crunched over the cobbles and disappeared from sight.

"Now, if I were a prince, where would I be?" Sarah murmured, turning back to the castle.

She didn't relish the thought of searching through dark corridors for Max. But she still had the letter Jana asked her to give to him. The letter she had steamed open in a palace bathroom like some kind of Renaissance Nancy Drew. She wondered idly what it was that Max needed to keep in a maximum security safe in Venice. Was he planning on trying to quietly sell off a family heirloom? Maybe it had something to do with the drugs.

Happy to be out in the fresh air, Sarah decided to take a stroll around the garden and plan the best way to approach Max. She followed a flight of stone stairs down into a path through a grove of trees. These had finished blooming, but there were petals forming a carpet on the ground, and it was all rather magical. Sarah strolled along a walkway lined with a tall hedge. It was a lovely evening, and the weird, violent events of the day seemed less frightening in the soft light.

She rounded a corner and saw a small pond.

And Max, leaning over and kissing someone who was stretched out in the tall grass.

Max was kissing a man.

Sarah was about to turn away, smiling, when she realized that Max wasn't making out with the man lying on the ground. He was giving him CPR.

FIFTEEN

"Max," Sarah called, running. She dropped down to her knees next to the two men.

With a shock, she recognized the man Max was trying to revive. He was the policeman who had showed up at the accident earlier. Although now he wasn't wearing his cop's uniform.

Max continued to perform CPR, not stopping to acknowledge her presence. Sarah leaned over the man's face and looked into his open eyes. Her memory suddenly skipped back to childhood and how she and her father had found the neighbor's dog lying still and quiet in their backyard. Her father had knelt over Annie, testing her corneal reflex to make sure she was really gone. Sarah took her index finger and pushed it gently into one of the policeman's eyes. Her heart missed a beat.

"Max," she said, gently putting her hand on his arm to stop his frantic motion as he pumped the man's chest. "You can stop. It's too late. He's dead."

Max sat back on his heels and ran his hands through his hair. "Sarah," Max said. "I didn't do it. I swear. I didn't do it."

She looked at Max. His eyes were clear, and he seemed focused. But scared. It actually hadn't occurred to Sarah that Max had killed the man, probably because he had been performing CPR. But now she thought of Max's wild attack on her earlier.

"What happened?" Sarah asked, trying to stay calm.

"I don't know," Max shook his head. "I was trying to find that stupid Chihuahua. There're things around here that could eat that kind of dog. And instead I found . . . he was just lying here. I didn't hear him call out, I don't . . ."

"Max," Sarah said, levelly. "I have to ask . . . were you on some sort of . . ."

"No!" Max said. But he didn't sound belligerent or defensive this time. He grabbed Sarah's hand. "Look, I know what you must be thinking. I was . . . earlier . . . look it's not what you think, but I wasn't myself. I mean, I was myself, but I wasn't seeing what you were seeing. I can't explain."

"You're going to have to do better than that," Sarah said.

"I don't blame you for thinking I'm crazy," Max said, looking at the dead body bleakly. "But I swear to you I didn't freak out and kill him in some sort of LSD blackout. It's not like that. I've been totally . . . normal all afternoon." His hand was trembling in Sarah's. Something about his voice, his face . . . she realized she believed him. She looked at the body.

"Maybe he had a heart attack?" she suggested. "He seems kind of young for that. I don't see any kind of wound, or . . ." Sarah leaned forward slightly over the body, and her hand came down against something in the long grass. She pulled it up.

It was an old-fashioned film camera with a telescopic lens. And it was flecked with blood.

"Okay. Not good," she said, dropping it back in the grass.

"Oh Christ," growled Max. He flipped the man over, and they could both now see a jagged hole in the back of the man's jacket, in between the shoulder blades. Max plucked at the cloth and his hand, too, came away stained with blood. Max recoiled and the body flopped back in the grass with a wet thunk.

"What is it? Was he shot?" Sarah rubbed the grass with her hands. Max reached into his jacket pocket and with absentminded politeness offered a large snowy white handkerchief. My God, Sarah thought. Who is this person?

"I . . . think so," Max said slowly. "And he's cold. He was cold when I touched him. He's been dead for a while maybe."

"Well, not for very long," Sarah said, handing the handkerchief back. "Maybe for a couple of hours. I saw him this morning."

"You saw Andy this morning? Where?"

"Wait, you know him?" Sarah spluttered.

"I do." Max rocked back on his heels. "So do you apparently."

"Well, I recognize him," said Sarah. "He's the policeman who stopped us earlier. When Eleanor smashed the truck."

"He's not a policeman." Max stood up and looked at Sarah strangely. "What are you talking about? What policeman? Eleanor smashed the truck?"

"Who is Andy?" Sarah demanded. "What are *you* talking about?"

"Andy Blackman . . . he works at Sternberg Palace," Max said, pointing at the body.

Sarah looked at the dead man's face. Then at his uniform — a Nehru-style jacket with some sort of insignia over the right breast. Sternberg Palace, now an art museum, was located just outside Prague Castle's gates.

She hadn't been inside yet, but she had seen uniforms like this around the castle grounds.

"This man," Sarah said, trying to keep her voice calm. "This man stopped Eleanor and me earlier today. He was on a motorcyle. Eleanor backed into a tractor on our way over here, and this man came along. He was wearing a policeman's uniform. He was speaking Czech. He took the truck away." Max blinked at her.

"This man," Max said, "is installing the new security system over at the Sternberg. I've been consulting with him about ours. He is definitely *not* a policeman. He's not even Czech. He barely speaks it. He's from Philadelphia." Max looked around at the trees and hedges surrounding them.

"Sarah," Max said. "Whoever did this to him. They might still be here. You should go. Go back to Nela. Call a cab. Take a train back to Prague."

"I'm not leaving you," Sarah said firmly. "And I'm not wandering off by myself if there's a killer loose on the grounds." At this, they both scanned the hedge and the pond anxiously. It was all very quiet, absurdly pastoral and lovely.

They turned back to the body — Andy — and then looked at each other.

"I suppose we'd better call the police,"

Max said. "My cell is at the house." The sound of a branch snapping somewhere nearby startled them both. Max grabbed Sarah's hand and pulled her facedown into the long grass, covering her body with his own longer one.

"Max," hissed Sarah.

"Quiet," Max hissed back, into her ear. They lay there for several minutes, listening.

Sarah, her head crushed by Max's elbow, turned her face, which brought her nose directly into contact with Max's throat.

The scent of him was overpowering. For a moment it seemed as if the ground was tilting underneath their bodies. She forgot that there might be some sort of deranged lunatic lurking in the hedges. She inhaled greedily. Adrenaline was coursing through her body; she felt like running, like rolling over and over in the grass, like playing the piano. Playing the piano really, really loudly.

"Sarah?" Max said, his voice thick in her ear, as if he could read her thoughts. And then it seemed to come to both of them, at the same time, that they were about two feet away from a dead body and potentially in grave danger from becoming dead bodies themselves. They separated themselves.

"Let's get back to the house," Max said,

in a somewhat dazed voice. "We can call the cops from there."

Sarah nodded.

"Should we take this?" She picked up the camera.

"Leave it," Max said, and then, "No. Wait. Give it to me." They began walking quickly back to the castle.

"Here's the story," Max said, his eyes sweeping the landscape. "I will say I found him — Andy — who is known to me in his professional capacity at Sternberg Palace. I found him here, on my grounds. I attempted to perform CPR. I did not have a cell phone with me. When I realized that he was beyond medical help, I ran back to the house to call for an ambulance and to inform the police. You did not see me, or this. You were working in the library and saw nothing."

"That's ridiculous," Sarah said. "I've touched him. My fingerprints are all over him. And the camera. We should tell the police we found him while we were out walking together."

"I'm trying to protect you," Max said, frowning. "This isn't . . . you're not involved in this."

"What is *this*?" Sarah asked. "Do you know why somebody would want to kill him? Or why he would pretend to be a Czech policeman? Unless he really *is* a Czech policeman and was pretending to be an American security installation guy at the Sternberg Palace? I mean, which is it?"

Max stopped walking and Sarah, who was slightly behind him, collided with his shoulder.

"I don't know," Max said. "But I think someone is trying to frame me. I think someone dumped his body here and was going to make it look like I killed him. Or maybe someone thought he was me."

As if on cue, a heavy rain began to fall.

Sarah wasn't sure why, but she insisted Max adopt her version of finding the body for when they talked to the police.

"That way we both have an alibi," she said. She wasn't sure if she trusted him entirely, but she trusted that he wasn't a murderer. She knew that her trust was a little illogical, and probably owed a lot to the way Max smelled, but there it was.

Max called the police. When he was done, Sarah pointed to the camera still slung from his shoulder. "What are you going to do with that?" she asked.

"I want to look at the film," Max said. "God knows what's on it. Maybe it will give me some sort of a clue as to what he was doing here."

"Give *us* a clue," Sarah said firmly. "Give me the camera. I'll put it in my backpack." It was a challenge, and after a moment Max accepted it and handed the camera over. Sarah made for the stairs.

"Maybe you should hide it until the police leave," Max said.

"Hide it where?"

"Are you kidding?" Max folded his arms. "Look around you. My family's been hoarding crap for six hundred years. Where *can't* you hide it?"

It had stopped raining by the time the police finally arrived. Max explained the situation in Czech, which he seemed to speak well, to a set of dourly efficient policemen. At least, Sarah hoped that he was explaining the situation. Then the two officers, plus Max and Sarah, all trooped down with flashlights to where Max and Sarah had left Andy's body.

Only it wasn't there.

Max swore. Sarah dashed back and forth in the muddy grass, ineffectually. Andy Blackman had disappeared.

One of the officers made a call, and soon the castle grounds were being swept by half a dozen police officers while Sarah and Max were taken back inside the house. They sat on packing crates — the only furniture — and repeated their statements over and over again. Sarah heard her own voice say, "But I'm positive he was dead," and thought that she sounded like she was lying. Soon she began to doubt herself. *Had* Andy been dead? There was blood. Didn't the officers see the blood?

But of course the rain had washed that away.

The policeman interrogating Sarah received a call on his walkie-talkie and disappeared. Max and Sarah exchanged a glance but didn't speak. After a few minutes, an impressively wide and lantern-jawed female officer appeared in the doorway.

"Mr. Anderson," she said. "You have been, how you say, punked?"

"Punked?" Max repeated, faintly.

"I have been speaking with director of National Gallery. Andy Blackman was at work all day today at Sternberg Palace. He is clearly not as dead as you thought." She rolled her eyes and issued sharp orders to the officers present, one of whom began barking into a radio.

Sarah's mind raced. Was Max mistaken in identifying the man? Did Andy have a twin?

"We do not appreciate time wasting," said

the policewoman. "But I think you are not being clever. I think you are perhaps a little stupid." Sarah expected Max to begin shouting and protesting, but he was strangely silent. His face was impossible to read.

One of the cops came back in carrying something. Sarah saw it was a violin. "This was in the stables," he said gruffly. "I do not think it should be left out there."

"No," said the policewoman, obviously angered by the mistreatment of the musical instrument. "I would expect that Mr. Anderson would not want these treasures, which have been conserved for so long by others and are now in his sole care, to be treated suchly." Her voice dripped with loathing.

Sarah took the violin carefully from the cop and nodded. As the cops were leaving, Max assumed his princely role. "I'm so sorry," he said. "I am very ashamed to have wasted your time. We're having a hunt here in the fall. I hope you'll be my guest."

"Yes," said the female officer. "My father often hunted here on the grounds of the castle when it belonged to the people." Someone wasn't so excited about the fall of communism, thought Sarah.

Max and Sarah stared in silence until the last police car crunched over the gravel of the bridge.

"Okay, what happened?" Sarah asked first.

"I think Sherbatsky might have left that in the stables," Max said, nodding at the violin.

"Not *this*," Sarah could have chucked the instrument at him. "You know what I mean."

"Let's take a little walk," Max said. Sarah followed him out and down the steps into the garden, realizing too late that she was still carrying the violin. They made their way to the path by the pond and she watched Max kick at the grass where Andy's body had lain.

"There's a bench over there," he said, after a long moment. "Come and sit down with me?"

The thought entered Sarah's mind that Max had hidden the body while she was upstairs hiding the camera. He might have killed Andy, she thought, walking along beside him in the darkness, the moon just beginning to illuminate the ghostly shapes of several dead apple trees. He might be about to kill me, she added to herself. But instead of saying that, she said, "Someone is fucking with us, big time."

Max stopped. He sat down on a stone bench. He leaned over, elbows on his knees. After a moment of silence, he began talking to the ground.

"I was sitting in my apartment near Venice Beach one day. Happy," he said. "Really happy, for the first time in a long time. I just wanted a year or two off, you know? Do my own thing. I had gone to Yale to please my father, but I should have known that nothing would please him. I thought I deserved a break. I grew up in California and I didn't even know how to surf. I was always studying. So for the first time I had no responsibilities and I was good with that. Very good. So that day I was just getting stoned, about to go hang with the drum circle down at the beach, when the phone rang. It was my dad. It had been months since we'd talked. I was a disappointment to him. He had actually said that flat out, the last time we had talked: 'You're a disappointment to me.' Except this time he was all happy. He said he'd just gotten a call from my mom's family lawyer in Prague. The Czech government had declared our family to be the rightful heirs to the Lobkowicz holdings. They had been talking about it for years, but somehow I never thought it would actually happen, or that it would have anything to do with my life. But it meant a lot to my dad. See, my mom died when I was three and he never got over it.

And so I guess this was like getting a piece of my mom back, you know? Something big he could do for her memory. He had booked us tickets to go to Prague. Me and him. You'd think I would have jumped at the chance, right? Reconcile with my father. Reclaim my heritage. But there were so many times when he had made me feel like shit. My whole life, really. So that's what I did. I made him feel like shit. I looked out the window at the Pacific Ocean and told him I didn't care about the fucking castles and he could go fuck himself. Except I didn't think that would be the last thing I ever said to him. The next morning the police called. He had dropped dead of a heart attack on his way to LAX."

Max started to cry. Whatever his recent past might be, he cried like an aristocrat. Silently, with no hiccoughing or snuffling. Sarah stood over him and thought about whether she should put her hand on his back or an arm around him, but she knew that nothing in the world could make Max feel less alone in this moment.

So she picked up the violin and played.

As she gently pulled the bow across the strings, Sarah was shocked by the sound coming from the instrument — this was no villager's fiddle.

Her brain finally calmed as she lost herself in the opening of Berlioz's *Symphonie Fantastique.* It began lyrically, sadly almost, the story of a young artist who in an opium dream falls in love with a woman he cannot have. She haunts him in a beautiful melody that becomes an idée fixe, an obsession, and then begin the elements of foreboding, of danger and the occult. Sarah had always found the piece to be a little over the top, but after tonight, she felt that Berlioz was right on the money. She played on, finding solace, courage, fortitude, and a kindred spirit in a piece of music written in 1830, a series of notes scrawled on the page that sprang from the imagination of one man, who was reaching out across time, through this violin, to tell her that he knew exactly how she was feeling, how strange and frightening and intoxicating life could be.

Eyes closed, she was building to the finish of the first movement, letting all the fear and adrenaline of the day pour out of her when suddenly she felt Max's hands gently take the violin and bow. She opened her eyes to see him gazing back at her. He slowly placed his hand on her throat, and she could feel her heartbeat against his thumb. As they kissed, Berlioz's music continued in her head, driving on toward the fourth movement, "March to the Scaffold," and the last, "Witches' Sabbath."

Max, Sarah decided, may be many things, possibly even criminal things.

He was also the best kisser she had ever laid lips to.

SIXTEEN

Sarah enjoyed the early-morning high-speed ride back to Prague in Max's red Alfa Romeo convertible a lot more than the trip out to Nela in the Skoda with Eleanor. The car was incredible. Max told her it was a 1930 6C 1750 Gran Sport that his grandfather had raced as a young man. It looked like new, which gave riding in it a weird time-warp feeling. She might have enjoyed it even more if she wasn't holding a priceless violin in a blanket. In the early-morning light she had examined the instrument and found its mark: *Grancino, anno 1699.* Worth more than her mother's house. And yet another item that belonged to the man in the driver's seat.

The night before, despite the electricity generated by the kiss, Max had shown her to a cot in what he called "the Blue Room," and had discreetly disappeared to some other part of the castle. This morning in the car, he was all business, and so was she. Max said he would develop the film from the camera, and Sarah offered to pay a visit to Sternberg Palace where Andy worked, to see if she could find out anything. Max handled the interminable traffic jam that was Prague center with reckless style and Sarah clutched the Grancino to her chest.

When Max spun the sports car through the castle gates it was still early enough that the hordes of tourists had not descended. The massive verdigris bulk of St. Vitus Cathedral looked a little forlorn in the morning light.

"I'll leave you here," Max said. "Do you have my cell number?" He took out his phone and then frowned. "I know this will sound paranoid," he said. "But I think my phone is tapped."

"What, by the government or something?" Sarah raised an eyebrow.

"I have enemies," Max said, cryptically. "We'll have to do this the old-fashioned way."

"Semaphore flags?" Sarah quipped.

"Meet me in front of Powder Tower at four p.m.," Max said, seriously. "Try not to be followed."

Before Sarah could even begin to form a sassy retort to this, Max sped away. Sarah walked slowly to the palace, where she handed the violin over to an ecstatic Miles, who greeted it like a lost child. She changed clothes and stopped in the kitchen briefly to snare a croissant and some coffee. She could simply call Sternberg Palace and ask for Andy, but then she'd have to trust whatever they told her, and besides, her Czech wasn't good enough to inquire about anything more complicated than an order of potatoes. No, she would amble over to Sternberg like any other tourist, take in some paintings, and look for an opportunity to do a little covert sleuthing. The whole thing might look a little less suspicious if she took someone with her.

Suzi. Sarah didn't doubt her ability to take care of herself, but in a pinch she wouldn't mind having a lesbian who could twirl firearms watch her back. She walked up the staircase to Suzi's weaponry room and tapped on the door.

"Have you ever seen anything more bee-yoo-tee-ful in your life?" Suzi greeted her, ushering her inside.

At first Sarah thought Shuziko was referring to Nicolas Pertusato, who sat cross-legged on the floor atop a small cushion. But then she realized Suzi was indicating the table where an incredibly long gun of some sorts was displayed.

"Seventeenth-century Spanish long barrel rampart," Suzi crowed. "Doesn't it make you just wet yourself? I swear to God it makes me hot just looking at it."

"It's loaded," said Nicolas, from the floor. "So be careful."

"He's joking," Suzi giggled. "Help me move it, though? I have to clear this room for the painters. I found the most gorgeous red. It's gonna make you want to hump the guns, I swear. I'm taking over the Delft china guy's room until they finish."

"There's a Delft china guy?" asked Sarah, donning a pair of cotton gloves.

"Arrives tomorrow," Suzi explained, issuing orders as they lift ed the gun. Nicolas trailed behind them as they moved into the adjacent room. "But I'm thinking china doesn't take up much space so we can share."

"Yeah, and firearms and china make a great combo," Sarah said. "Listen, you want to do a little sightseeing with me while your room is getting painted? I thought I'd go look at the Sternberg collection. Get a little culture."

"Cool." Suzi gave the gun a final loving caress and leered at Sarah. "And afterward we could go for some Cream & Dream."

"I really hope you mean ice cream," Sarah laughed.

"I think the two of you require a chaperone," Nicolas piped up. "And I know the collection well. I'd be happy to act as your guide."

Perfect, Sarah thought. Suss out the deal with Andy and get to know the little man a little better. Plus, Shuziko did seem a little overstimulated.

"This, as you can see, depicts the Rape of Helen." Nicolas gestured at the large oil painting in front of them.

"Rape?" Suzi snorted. "She looks more like she's getting goosed."

"And over here," Nicolas continued, unperturbed, "a marvelous Last Supper by Jacopo da Montagnana. Note that the disciples and Jesus are all correctly brown-skinned."

They made a pretty odd threesome, Sarah thought. But Nicolas was a good guide. And she was grateful for Suzi's unorthodox approach to art appreciation.

"A superb portrait of Scipio Africanus," Nicolas intoned.

"Those boots are totally in now" was Suzi's comment. "Hey, Nico, how come they always show Mary with her right boob out?"

As they moved up the stairs to the second level, Sarah tried thinking of a way to discreetly inquire about Andy. The usual number of museum guards were posted about, but most of them were extremely grim-looking Czech matrons.

"I find this one a little frightening," said Nicolas, pointing to St. Sebastian suspended by his wrists. "I remember my university friends and I used to play a most amusing drinking game: Who died worse, St. Sebastian or St. Jerome?"

"Where did you go to college, Nicolas?" Sarah asked. Sebastian was pierced by an arrow and this reminded her, once again, of Andy.

"Yale," Nicolas said, smiling up at her. "Among others. But call me Nico. Everyone does."

"Is Yale where you met Max?" Sarah ran her eyes over a portrait of St. Francis, looking like hell. Religious art was pretty depressing, Mary's perky boobs aside.

"Oh, it was before Max's time." Nicolas waved a tiny hand. "It was a hundred years ago! I'm a relic, really."

Sarah hung back as Suzi wandered into

the next room, willing Nicolas to stay with her.

"I was wondering," Sarah asked softly. "About that box you gave me? Sherbatsky's box with his toenail inside?"

"It was not Sherbatsky's toenail," Nicolas said. "That would be most improper."

"I know it wasn't. Nicolas." Sarah put her hands on her hips, emphasizing his name. "I think it's a drug of some kind. What does it do? And why were Max and Professor Sherbatsky doing it?"

"You should ask Max about that," Nicolas whispered. "I haven't tried it myself. Now, in this next room, you will see a lovely Van Haarlem *Conversion of Saul, AND,* you'll notice, two dwarfs bring up the rear of this little processional. Isn't that yellow hat just divine?"

It was in the last room that Sarah found her mark. Suzi had collapsed gratefully into one of the chairs in the center of the gallery, and Nicolas perched beside her, pointing out details of the Rubens painting: St. Thomas getting whacked by various oily scoundrels, their crazed eyeballs highlighted gruesomely in white. Lounging in the corner was a young man, suited in the Sternberg Palace uniform. He locked eyes with Sarah and smiled. Bingo.

"You have enjoyed visit?" he asked in halting but serviceable English. "The Brueghels, you see? The people are so tiny. I think it funny." The young man glanced at Nicolas and turned beet red. Sarah gave him a reassuring smile.

"I was supposed to get a tour by my friend who works here," she said. "But I guess I got the date wrong or something. I haven't been able to get in touch with him."

"Oh yes?" the young man replied, as if scripted. "Who do you know working here?"

"Andy Blackman." Sarah lowered her voice. "He was in charge of installing the new security system here? An American, like me. Maybe you know him?"

"Yes!" The young man smiled broadly, clearly delighted to help. "Of course. Mr. Andy Blackman. He trained me. He is great guy. We listen to music and jam together. Old stuff. Rolling Stones, right? Classic."

"Did you see him yesterday?" Sarah asked.

"Yesterday I am not working," the guard apologized.

"Do you know how to get in touch with him?" Sarah tried to keep the urgency out of her voice. "Is there an office number I can call?"

"I check for you." The guard smiled. "I return in one moment."

194

Sarah sat down on a small chair. Shuziko had slumped down in her chair and appeared to be dozing. Nicolas swiveled around and surveyed Sarah keenly.

"Are you tired?" he asked, anxiously. "I fear I have talked too much. Some people get very sleepy in museums."

"I'm fine," said Sarah.

"You are more than fine," the little man said, his bassoon voice trembling with vibrato. "You are magnificent. I should very much like to be alone with you."

Before Sarah could respond to this somewhat alarming proposition, the young guard scurried back into the room. He handed Sarah a piece of paper.

"Mr. Andy Blackman return United States yesterday," he said. "A family emergencies. This is e-mail to be reaching him. I hope this is helpful to you."

"Thank you, yes," Sarah said, pocketing the paper.

SEVENTEEN

Charlotte Yates was not enjoying her trip to Venice. Even staying within the gilded confines of the Cipriani, she had still caught sight of the giant cruise ships that were pumping an endless stream of addictive euros into the blackened veins of the dying city. Personally, she felt the whole place should be bulldozed into the ocean. History should be studied but not worshipped. As to whether it should be exploited for profit, well, that was a matter of taste, not legislation.

Of course she was in a bad mood after the way Marchesa Elisa Lobkowicz DeBenedetti had handled what should have been a very small favor. Some months ago, in a rendezvous at the George V in Paris that did not appear on any official schedule, Charlotte had offered Elisa a present: an Aztec amulet that contained a vial filled with a nearly undetectable form of strychnine. It was darling Yuri who had given Charlotte the amulet and informed her of the poison the vial contained: a special little concoction the KGB had invented. Yuri had meant it to be protection, in case her secret was ever discovered. A gesture of love. Fortunately, she had never needed to use it. Giving it to Elisa had felt poetic — not only because the amulet had been stolen from Elisa's own family, but also because it was like Yuri was reaching out from the past to help her.

Charlotte had presented Elisa with the amulet as a pledge of their friendship, and with the promise that she would move heaven and earth to see the marchesa's rightful fortune returned to her. All Elisa had to do in return was put a drop or two of the vial's contents into the glass of a person Charlotte referred to as "a very bad man." There was no reason to tell the marchesa that the bad man was a major Republican donor who was strongly against the party choosing Charlotte as their next presidential candidate. He and Elisa would both be attending the Save Venice fundraiser; she could do it easily then. The party would be crowded, the contents of the vial untraceable, the man would die of an apparent cardiac arrest, nothing could be

197

more natural and simple.

Asking this of Elisa was standard operating procedure: If you wanted to make someone loyal, implicate them in something that could prove very sticky should it come to light.

And the marchesa had done what was requested, but she had grossly overstepped her orders and created a ridiculous clusterfuck, putting the poison in the champagne fountain, where, diluted, it apparently caused its victims to hallucinate that they were on fire before killing them. That little side effect was unexpected, but not entirely surprising. The KGB had a strange sense of humor.

Now Charlotte wondered if Elisa wouldn't be better off disposed of in some discreet way. Well, not yet. The marchesa still had her uses.

Charlotte's team had done an excellent job of mopping up the mess over at the Ca' Rezzonico. Thanks to some well-placed evidence planting, it was now clear that Al Qaeda operatives had put a form of strychnine in the champagne fountain, killing the seven guests and one tippling waiter at the Save Venice fund-raiser. One of the lovely things about operating in Italy was the culture's universal embrace of the conspiracy theory. Thus, when it was quickly uncovered that the magistrates had been bribed to leak covert Arabic chat room chatter, no one was surprised at all, and the wild accusations that followed, though they included "massive coverup by the U. S. government," and "CIA assassination," also found evidence to support Iranian, Israeli, Russian, Chinese, Mafia, German, communist, and Martian involvement. It was really too easy, Charlotte thought. Especially with Al Qaeda so delighted to accept responsibility for knocking off the American president's biggest campaign contributor and other assorted infidels. She hated giving terrorists the gift of publicity, but it couldn't be helped. Only Al Qaeda took pride in wholesale slaughter of innocents.

Now that Venice was resolved, there was the news from Prague to deal with. These researchers were so painfully slow! No wonder American universities were in such bad shape — not only were they cesspools of liberalism, but they were populated by people who couldn't even get simple tasks done. Unpack, catalog, locate, record, store — it was basic librarian stuff, for God's sake. The Nazis had cataloged every piece of Lobkowicz treasure in a couple of months. The communists had taken longer and not been as thorough, which was not surprising. But that was convenient for everyone.

Restitution was such an absurd idea, Charlotte thought. Only that *playwright* Havel would come up with such an idea. Not that Charlotte didn't love the theater, but intellectuals had no place in government. They didn't have the stomach for it. Did no one read *Hamlet* anymore? It was all spelled out in black and white: "There is nothing either good or bad, but thinking makes it so." Too much thinking had been the downfall of many American presidents, but it wasn't going to be hers.

Several problems had surfaced in the past forty-eight hours.

From Miles's latest report, the Weston girl had stumbled across a note from Friedrich Gottlieb making some noise about missing items from Nela. Gottlieb! She had forgotten about him. An odious little troglodyte. But her cigarette case and the Aztec amulet were mentioned. Charlotte was increasingly suspicious of Miles. He was such an . . . academic. He might get very uppity about the letters. Miles was her watcher inside the palace, and it would be prudent to have someone to watch him. Another job for Marchesa Elisa, perhaps. Charlotte had to admit she had redeemed herself with taking care of the Russian agent.

A Russian agent! Sniffing around Lobkowicz Palace and Nelahozeves, searching vehicles going in and out, dressing up in disguises, tapping phone lines, just like the old days. What the hell did the Russians think they were doing, planting someone like that practically under her nose. It was almost like a taunt. She barely had an appetite for the plate of *risotto alla seppia* the waiter was setting out on the table on the terrace, snapping the white linen napkin with a pleasing thwack. She allowed herself a poignant smile as he poured her a glass of Prosecco.

"The senator from Virginia ate only black food out of respect for the dead," *La Repubblica* would report the next day. "She carried out her sad task of accompanying the body of the dead American tycoon back to the United States on Air Force 2 with great dignity, in a black Valentino suit with a lovely matching hat."

EIGHTEEN

"It's an *ars moriendi*," said Miles, holding up the leather-bound book Sarah had found in the box at Nela. "In the fifteenth century, after the Black Death killed off half the population and most of the priests, the Church let secular writers produce volumes that used woodcuts to get the word out about how to die a good Christian death." He put the book down and turned back to his computer. Sarah glanced around the office.

Max had not shown up at Powder Tower yesterday as they had arranged. After some hesitation she tried his cell, but it went right to voice mail. So Sarah trudged back through Old Town Square and across Charles Bridge with an increasing feeling of dread and paranoia that was all the more strange for the happy international mélange of tourists photographing one another in front of the statues, and loading up on cheap watercolors of Prague scenes, marionettes, and "Czech It Out!" refrigerator magnets.

Today, Sarah decided to inquire about the book as a pretext for finding out if Miles had seen Max.

"Actually I was wondering if I could borrow it. I'm interested in the drawings," Sarah lied. "So was Max. Have you seen him, by the way?"

"Not since yesterday morning when you two came back from Nela," said Miles. He looked narrowly at her and Sarah tried to keep her expression blank.

"I'll bring it back," said Sarah. "But I want to learn how to die a good Christian death."

Miles laughed.

"It's not actually incunabula," he said. "It's an eighteenth-century copy and in horrible condition, not worth much, but treat it carefully anyway." Sarah promised and left his office, still anxious and unsatisfied.

After spending ten minutes staring at a single sequence of notes from the Sixth Symphony, Sarah gave up. As she went down a hallway, she could hear Eleanor and Daphne chatting about the upcoming masquerade ball, so she ducked out a side door and decided to take a walk. If she stayed in the palace she would be pulled into conversations she'd be unable to focus on, and people would ask her what was wrong. It would be hard not to answer, "Oh, you know . . . murder."

Outside, she considered walking over to Strahov Monastery to look at the famous library there, but decided she had had enough of ancient books. She turned instead toward the Royal Garden.

As she passed the old Riding School (now a contemporary art museum), she heard one of the ubiquitous tour guides addressing a group of tourists.

"This spot was once Emperor Rudolf II's private zoo," squawked the guide. "You will find a double-tailed lion on all the heraldic emblems of this country. Rudolf was particularly fond of lions. There is a story that the astronomer Tycho Brahe, who served as the emperor's private astrologer, predicted that the emperor's fate was tied to that of his favorite pet lion, Oskar. And the day after Oskar died, so did the emperor." The tourists gave a little "oooh."

She strolled through the gardens, trying to clear her head and simply be a tourist for a few minutes. The gardens, she knew, had been closed to the public during the communist era. But the commies had left their mark. Peering through a line of fir trees at the façade of Ball Game Hall, she ran her eyes over the robed allegories of Astronomy, Agriculture, Virtue, Industry, and the Elements. Carved next to Industry's head was a hammer and sickle. What would this generation add to it? A "For Sale" sign, probably.

It felt good to be moving, so Sarah kept walking, trying to focus on her surroundings and not on Max's mysterious disappearance, or Andy, or Sherbatsky. She crossed Čech Bridge, wandering into Josefov, the old Jewish section of Prague. She waved to the statue of Rabbi Loew.

"Rabbi Loew created the golem, a man out of dirt from the riverbank below," a tour guide was announcing to a group of rapt Japanese schoolgirls.

"According to *legend,*" Sarah muttered. She hated this mixing of fact and fiction, especially in talking to children. Why confuse them about what was real and what was not?

Sarah passed the high-end glass shops on Paris Street. This is what tourists do, she told herself. They stroll. They gaze. She scanned the goblets, vases, plates, and tumblers on display. They were beautiful, and she should go in and buy something for her mother. Except her mother would be too worried about how much it might have cost to ever enjoy this kind of thing.

Sarah kept going and arrived in Old Town Square just in time to catch the rays of the setting sun reflected off the golden twin spires of the Church of Our Lady Before Týn. A puppet troupe was setting up, and a portly bearded man in Elizabethan dress was explaining to a gathering group of tourists the plot of Ben Jonson's *Volpone,* while the black-clad puppeteers got their papier-mâché creations ready to begin the show.

"The action takes place in Venice," announced the man in tights. "For English audiences, Venice was synonymous with all things decadent and sinful. Corrupting wealth, greed, thievery, prostitution, disease, incest, murder . . ."

The ominous feeling was back. Where was Max? Hoping he would appear, she turned away from the puppet theater and wandered across the square to look at the Astronomical Clock, which had been drawing tourists since 1490. Sarah gazed up at a figure on the façade of the gothic stone tower: a skeleton, holding an hourglass in one hand and a bell on a rope in the other. Death at every turn, she thought.

"When the hour strikes you will see a parade of the Apostles in the little windows," said a familiar bassoon voice behind her. She turned to see Nicolas standing there in all his tiny formality. "But it is not impressive. I wouldn't wait if I were you."

"Nicolas. Are you following me?" she asked.

"Yes," he said.

"Why?" asked Sarah.

"I like to pay a visit to the master." The little man pointed across the square to the Týn church. "He is buried there. I come to make sure he hasn't gotten out. That is a joke."

Sarah frowned, trying to recall what she had read about the Týn church in the beer-soaked guidebook.

"They did exhume his body," Nicolas said. "The first time in 1901, and then just last year. It does appear that he is really, really dead."

"Tycho Brahe," said Sarah, triumphantly. "He's buried there."

The little man bowed acknowledgment.

"Why are you following me?" Sarah repeated.

"I'm your protector."

Sarah stifled a laugh. Yes, she wanted to say, you would take a bullet for me as long as it was aimed for somewhere below four-foot-six. "Why do I need protection? What do you know that you're not telling me?"

"I don't know what you know, so I don't know what you don't know. Come have an aperitif with me. They make an excellent Bellini at the Four Seasons. Best one outside of Venice."

Sarah sighed but made no move to follow him. The puppet master's words about Venice echoed in her mind. Corruption. Theft. Murder. "When you picked me up at the airport, you had just come from Venice," she said. "Why were you there?"

"To pick up a Sassoferrato that had ended up at the Doge's Palace. One of Hitler's little gifts to Mussolini. Or should I say 'regift,' since it came from the Lobkowicz's collection."

"And that's what was in the trunk?"

He nodded.

"Did Max ask you to leave something in Venice?" She continued prodding.

"Yes."

"What was it?"

"A birthday bouquet of flowers for Marchesa Elisa. She pronounced them 'dreadful' and threw them in the canal. A lover's spat, I suspect."

Lovers?

"I thought the marchesa person was his *cousin*?" Sarah frowned.

"Distant cousin, yes." Nicolas waggled his eyebrows suggestively.

"No, you left something in the safe at the Hotel Gritti Palace," Sarah said, trying to dismiss this insinuation (and how much it irritated her). "Something that Max wanted hidden. What was it?"

"What, you think I'm one of those court dwarfs from the sixteenth century?" Nicolas's voice was suddenly hostile. "Privy to all the secrets of the royal family, because they were considered to be nothing more than a talking dog?"

"No one considers you a talking dog."

"Then come with me."

Sarah sighed again. This kind of thing was exceptionally annoying. If you were not attracted to someone, they automatically assumed it was because you could not see past their physical fl aw, oddity, or anomaly, real or imaginary. "It's my freckles, isn't it?" sobbed one freshman on her doorstep. "No," she told him. "It's your personality."

But she couldn't be cruel to Nicolas. He had fashioned himself as her protector, though she felt that his feelings went a little more below the belt. And besides, she had grown out of that sort of casual cruelty. Unrequited lust was not something to exploit.

Or was it? Was Max really involved romantically with Marchesa Elisa? "Lead the way," Sarah said. "But you're buying."

NINETEEN

It was hard to feel even vaguely menaced when you were eating crostini with mushrooms, liver pâté, and pumpkin and pecorino cheese served by a gallant Czech waiter. From the terrace of the Four Seasons Hotel, even the shadowy spires of St. Vitus Cathedral looked less like Grimm and more like Disney.

And Nicolas was an excellent host, displaying a cosmopolitan masculinity as he ordered Sarah the artichoke and herb soufflé, chatted in faultless Italian with the sommelier, extracted a dark brown clove cigarette from an elegant case and lit it with a small gold lighter. Sarah caught a flash of the symbol on the case. A circle with a dot in the center. Where had she seen that before?

Sarah sipped her cocktail, not a simpering little Bellini, but a giant concoction of vodka, gooseberries, and kirsch. The waiter placed her old backpack on a satin-covered footstool. Sarah briefly wished she was wearing something other than jeans and a T-shirt, but probably nothing in her suitcase was as nice as the fabric on the footstool. Nicolas looked very much at home in the ritzy surroundings. From their seats on the terrace they could look over the river back up at the castle. A huge parchment-colored canvas balloon, tethered to a boat, lifted tourists up in the air.

"Tell me about where you grew up," she asked her host, and Nicolas launched into a monologue about a Czech mother and a Spanish father and a German nanny and summers in Forte dei Marmi.

A six-foot blonde in a Pucci sheath strolled up to their table. She leaned over, showing off enormous breasts, and gave Nicolas a kiss on the mouth. A lingering kiss.

"Oksana Dolezalova, allow me to present Sarah Weston," said Nicolas once his head had emerged from the giantess's mouth.

"Please to met you," said Oksana. Oksana's cheekbones were high, her teeth white, and her boots had six-inch spike heels. Sarah felt even more like a scruffy college girl.

"Nico," the woman purred. "I wait for you last night and you never show up."

"Emergency," said Nico. "I'll make it up to you." Oksana kissed him again, smiled at Sarah, and left.

"I have to ask," said Sarah. "Is she a hooker? Because I've heard that they hang out in fancy hotels, and I've never seen one in real life, except, you know, on street corners in New York when you're coming home from bars late, but that doesn't really count."

Nicolas frowned. "She's my wife."

Sarah laughed. Nicolas's expression did not change. "Really? Oksana is . . . your wife?"

"We were married last spring at the palace," said Nicolas coldly. "It was a lovely ceremony."

Sarah sat there in silence for a moment, then came up with, "She seems really nice."

"She is. For a hooker."

This time Sarah did not laugh. But Nicolas did. "I'm kidding," he said.

"I never thought she was your wife, okay? Nice try."

"She *is* my wife. She's just not a hooker. She's a nurse."

You could never get to the bottom of anything in Prague, Sarah thought. She now had no idea if the woman was Nicolas's wife or not. She made herself imagine him married to Oksana. It was not easy, but Sarah decided that if the evening produced nothing more fruitful than the erosion of her own shallow tendency to judge a book by its miniature cover, it was time well spent.

"Max is quite all right," said Nicolas.

All thoughts of Oksana disappeared. "Where is he?"

"He's waiting for you back at the palace."

"Why didn't you tell me?" Sarah stood up to leave.

"I wanted to clear some things up."

Sarah sat back down.

"I came to see you in Boston on Max's orders," Nicolas said. "Miles hired you because Sherbatsky asked him to, but Max sent me to vet you. It did seem an interesting . . . coincidence."

The little man reached into his jacket pocket and pulled out a photograph, handing it to Sarah. It was a picture of Sarah's fourth-grade class. Her own face was circled. It gave her chills to see it. Her gap-toothed smile. The strange yellow pantsuit with the Scottie dogs on it that had been her favorite. It was the year her father died.

"Why do you have this photo?" she asked.

"Look at it," Nicolas said.

He pointed to a boy with ears sticking out, in the third row. He looked small and shy, his face not grown into a too-prominent nose.

Sarah shrugged and shook her head.

"Max," said the little man, slightly exasperated.

"Max?" She brought the photo closer. Yes, the features were the same.

"Max and I were in fourth grade together?" she said, wonderingly. "He told me he grew up in California."

"Except for one year when his father was on sabbatical in Boston," Nicolas explained. "Max's father wanted to 'toughen him up,' so he sent him to public school. Your school, as it happened."

"He remembers me? Why didn't he say anything?"

"Max is not sure whom to trust."

He's not the only one, thought Sarah. The sight of the photo and the fact that Max had kept it from her was disturbing.

"Who killed Professor Sherbatsky?" she snapped.

Nicolas frowned. "Sherbatsky jumped."

"I'll never believe that."

"You will, soon. And Max didn't kill Andy Blackman, if that's what you're wondering."

"So Andy is dead?"

"Andy is dead."

"Who was he? Who took his body?"

Nicolas shrugged. "Sarah, these kinds of games have been played out in this country for a thousand years. Under the reign of the Czech kings, the Holy Roman emperors, the Hapsburgs, the Nazis, the communists — it's been one long invasion of the body snatchers. Who are the players this time? I honestly don't know, and to keep my own neck intact I don't ask. I would venture to guess that Andy was neither a Czech policeman nor an American security systems installer. It might not have to do with either you or Max. So please just stick to compiling the Beethoven collection. Do your job like the other researchers, have a nice summer, and go home safe and sound. That is my advice."

It was good advice, too. There was plenty of work to be done, work that would launch her career back in the States. She would publish about the relationship between Prince Lobkowicz and Beethoven, about the letters, about his notations on the symphonies. There was a lifetime of scholarship in the Nela archives alone. She could become *the* go-to Beethoven scholar for the U. S. Sarah told herself that Sherbatsky had jumped, that Andy's death had nothing to do with her, and that even if Max had once been in her class, he was a prince now (sort of) and she was from South Boston.

She sipped her drink and watched the tourists carried aloft in the balloon. Even from this distance, she could hear them scream and then laugh every time the balloon bobbed in the wind. She knew the taste in their mouths. Fear . . . and excitement.

"I don't know if I can do that," said Sarah at last.

Nicolas Pertusato held her stare.

"That's what I thought you'd say." He then raised an eyebrow and recited:

This is the wandring wood, this errours
    den,
A monster vile, whom God and man does
    hate:
Therefore I read beware.
Fly fly (quoth then The fearefull Dwarfe)
this is no place for living men.

TWENTY

Nicolas ordered another cocktail for Sarah using only a minute hand gesture. The respectfully observant waiter leapt to obey. Sarah took an orgasmic bite of crostini. The restaurant at the Four Seasons had a Michelin star, and food was one area where Sarah didn't mind a baroque sensibility. The more delicious things you can cram on a piece of toast, she felt, the better.

"A change of subject," Nicolas said, leaning forward. "Tell me about Herr Beethoven. Pretend I am one of your adoring undergraduates. Blow, as they say, my mind."

"I'm beginning to think that might be hard to do," said Sarah, wondering if the restaurant was dark enough to actually bend down and lick her plate without causing a scene.

"Most common misconception," Nicolas prompted, helpfully.

"That he spent a large part of his life totally deaf," Sarah answered. "That's kind of a big one."

"And untrue."

"Untrue. The truth is sadder, actually. The hearing loss was gradual, and intermittent. It would have been better for his mental health, probably, if it happened all at once. He kept hoping he would be cured, or that it would improve. And it did, sometimes. Can you imagine? One day you can hear the rattle of carriages beneath your window, your friend's voice, five seconds of your own playing. And then the next day, nothing."

"Better to be born into this world with your deficiencies already in place?" the little man asked. "Than lose your powers drop by drop, ever conscious of that which is being taken from you?"

"But the music got better," Sarah said. "And I think he knew it. He did his share of railing and complaining, but he knew what he was. Even all his women troubles . . . that was mostly self-created. He didn't want the Immortal Beloved."

"Ah, yes, the famous letters. Very romantic."

"Oh, give me a break," Sarah laughed. "That's misconception number two. Luigi as heartbroken lover. The Immortal Beloved letters are basically break-up notes. *'Oh God, look out into the beauties of nature and comfort your heart with that which must be —'* *'At my age I need a steady, quiet life — can that be so in our connection?'* Antonie Brentano was married with four children. She must have scared the shit out of Ludwig. All his life he had been able to safely worship these unattainable noblewomen and not lose any composing time or have to put up with PMS and diapers. An Immortal Beloved is way better than daily intimacy. *That's* what the letters are about."

"You seem very sure of this," the little man said. "And, forgive me, a little . . . cynical for such a young woman."

"Well, nobody can be sure of the letters," Sarah said, choosing to ignore the accusation of cynicism. "I mean, we can't be one hundred percent certain that Antonie is the babe in question. But it fits. She was the major woman in his life at that time. They were both here in Prague in early July 1812. It's all been totally hashed out, believe me."

"What about the 7th?" Nicolas asked. "Where was Prince Lobkowicz when Beethoven came to Prague?"

"I actually don't know where the prince was in early July," Sarah admitted. "Probably Vienna."

"But he could have been here," Nicolas suggested, tapping his spoon thoughtfully against his cup. "*Why* did Beethoven come to Prague in 1812?"

Sarah thought.

"Well, I don't actually know. On the second of July he was supposed to meet up with Karl Varnhagen von Ense, but he didn't show. Varhagen recorded this in his memoirs, along with the apology note he got from Ludwig saying that he was sorry to cancel but a 'circumstance which I could not foresee prevented me from doing so.' "

"What was the circumstance?" Nicolas asked.

"Well, presumably it was Antonie Brentano." Sarah shrugged. "Beethoven doesn't say. And then he goes to Teplitz and writes the letters. But never sends them. My guess is that he read them over and decided that he had kind of overdone it on the whole 'you're the one' stuff."

"There is always more than one explanation," Nicolas said softly. "For almost everything, my dear."

"Mind if I join you?"

Max, dressed impeccably as always in a dark three-piece suit, didn't wait for a reply. He pulled out the chair next to Sarah and sat down.

"We good?" he asked the little man.

"All clear," Nicolas responded brightly. "Oksana spotted someone from BIS earlier, but she tipped me off immediately. And I don't think he noticed us at all, actually. As Sarah correctly pointed out, a five-star hotel attracts a five-star prostitute. He left with a redhead about forty-five minutes ago. The Minister of Culture is at the far left table having dinner with, I'm fairly certain, Neil Diamond. Otherwise it's just tourists."

"You," said Sarah, "have got to be kidding me."

"No, he's right," said Max, peering. "That really is Neil Diamond."

"Okay," Sarah folded her arms. "Which one of you is Starsky and which is Hutch? And what's BIS?"

"Czech Security Information Services," Nicolas answered, ordering an espresso with a flick of his wrist. "Spies, in other words. Forgive the cloak-and-dagger theatrics, which actually I adore, but let me remind you that a man is dead and on the other side of the river is a palace filled with priceless works of art with some very shady histories. Prague is a threshold." Nicolas stood up and gave Sarah a courtly bow. "And it is steeped in blood."

"And full of hell portals," added Sarah

sarcastically, then realized they were both staring intently at her.

"You know about the hell portal?" asked Nicolas.

"Yeah, it's right under the unicorn's stable," said Sarah, laughing. "C'mon, guys."

Nicolas relaxed and smiled. "Sarah, I enjoyed our dinner enormously. Max?"

"Give Oksana my best." Max nodded. "And give me back my cigarette case, you little thief."

Nicolas sighed, took the slim gold case out of his jacket pocket, and handed it to Max. Again Sarah saw the flash of a mysterious symbol.

"And my lighter?" Max asked, patiently.

The little man slid it across the table, winked at Sarah, and disappeared into the night.

"Mmm, crostini?" Max said, reaching across the table.

"Where have you been?" Sarah tried to keep her voice neutral. She felt extraordinarily . . . relieved to see him. Yes, that's what it must be. Relief.

"Sorry. I got caught up and I didn't want to risk calling you. I've been taking care of business," Max said. He signaled for the waiter to bring him a menu. "And trying to open a museum, too, by the way. We've got the Delft china specialist coming and some dude who specializes in dog art."

"Seriously?"

"The Lobkowiczes have always loved dogs," Max said, gravely.

Your dogs lived better than my ancestors, thought Sarah.

The waiter handed Max a menu, which Max placed in his lap. After a moment, he handed it to Sarah.

"Anything else you'd like to order?" he asked, eyeing the menu significantly. Sarah sighed and opened the menu. Inside were a series of 8×10 black-and-white photographs. She pulled the menu closer to her chest to study them.

"This is what was in Andy's camera? That looks like a safe," she said.

"Yep."

Sarah slid the photograph over to look at the next one. A man's hand, reaching for the safe dial. The following two were close-ups of the dial itself; the first finger and thumb of the hand were out of focus, but the numbers were clear. In the final photograph, both the hand and the number were fuzzy.

"Eight, thirteen, something," said Sarah.

"I couldn't get it any better than that,"

Max apologized. "But it does narrow our focus significantly."

"That's the safe in Miles's office," Sarah stated, frowning.

"Visible from the scaffolding outside the far window," Max said. "If you are lying on your stomach and you have a really powerful zoom. I checked."

Sarah closed the menu and handed it back to Max.

"Andy was a spy, I'm thinking," Max said quietly. "But was he working alone or *for* someone? That's what I want to know. And I think we need to find out what Miles has in that safe."

And speaking of secrets, Sarah thought, reaching down into her backpack and pulling out the letter Jana had given her. *What's your secret, Max?*

"Sorry," she said. "What with the dead body and all, I sort of forgot to pass on your personal mail. Jana asked me to give it to you."

Max opened the letter, read it through quickly, and then stuffed it in his suit pocket.

"Just a receipt for a hotel bill," he said, dismissively.

Oh really? Sarah thought. She pulled out the fourth-grade class photograph Nicolas had given her and slapped it on the table in front of him.

"Andy was spying on Miles," Sarah said. "You were spying on me. Nicolas has been spying on everyone. And by the way, he seems *very* certain that Sherbatsky killed himself."

"Pertusato said that Sherbatsky killed himself?"

"He insists that he jumped." Sarah watched Max take the last crostini, the bastard.

"Saying he jumped is not the same as saying he committed suicide." Max's voice was hesitant.

"Well, why else would he jump?" Sarah asked sharply. But Max did not answer.

"I'm sorry about your dad," he said, after a moment. "Fourth grade was never the same after you left."

Sarah slung her backpack over her shoulder.

"I'm going to take Nicolas's advice," she said. "I'm going to go back to your stupid-ass palace and spend the rest of my summer focusing on my work. I'm going to look at manuscripts, and transcribe, and take notes, and . . . and . . . think about a five-foot-four shlub from the wrong side of the Rhine with bad gas and some serious daddy issues, who was still ten million times the man you or I or anyone else I know will *ever* be. Whatever else is going on, just leave me out of it, okay?"

Sarah stood up and walked majestically away from the table, stopping only to accept a small box of chocolates from the smiling waiter.

"Thank you for visiting the Four Seasons," he said in English. "Please come again."

Across the street from the hotel, concert-goers were spilling out of the Rudolfinum. Charles Bridge was still crowded with tourists, with lovers, with exasperated locals just trying to get home. Up and down the river, nighttime Prague glittered and blinked, beckoned and hid itself. Sarah took the long way up the hill, stumping across cobblestones, willing herself not to be entranced. Showing her security card to a guard at the castle gates, she caught the Sexy Stabber leering overhead.

Oh, fuck off, she thought.

At the palace she could hear laughter, conversation, the clinking of glasses coming from the kitchen.

That's where I should be, she thought. *That's who I should be with.* Her mother had always told her not to get taken in by rich people. "They use you," she had said.

Sarah stomped down the stairs to her windowless room, threw her backpack on her bed and herself down next to it. A spring jabbed her painfully in the ribs. She was irritated by how irritated she was. Now, Sarah thought, would be a good time to investigate a proper Christian death. But the *ars morendi* was on the table across the room and Sarah didn't feel like moving just yet.

Unzipping her backpack, she rooted around for the photograph, but her fingers closed around something else.

The little copper pillbox. Its lid was, she now noticed, in the shape of a nose.

"What would you expect to find in a pillbox?" the little man had asked.

Mysteries. Sarah was tired of them. Fuck mysteries.

Sarah picked the piece of . . . something out of the box, held it in her hand for about half a second. Then she put it in her mouth and swallowed.

TWENTY-ONE

Big whoop, thought Sarah with more than a little disappointment. She checked her watch — fifteen minutes had passed after swallowing the toenail-shaped pill, and she felt nothing except boredom. *All I ever do on drugs is fall asleep.* It had been like that every time she had tried to alter her consciousness. Sarah had come to the conclusion that she was not malleable — drugs just didn't work on her. Even at the dentist, she simply clenched her fists and told them to go ahead and drill because anything they gave her just made her groggy.

She had her nose, that was enough. And her ears.

Sarah closed her eyes for a moment, but then sat bolt upright, a feeling of panic suddenly rising in her chest. Her head was vibrating, like a cerebral earthquake, and then all of her senses felt strange. Her vision blurred, and sounds seemed far away but too close all at once. She had vertigo, and the touch of the coverlet under her hand was rough and painful. Worst of all was the onslaught of a stomach-churning stench.

Sarah stood up, but as she did, the dark room began to fill with sounds, and light, and people. *So many people.* The outlines of their bodies, faint at first, began to sharpen and solidify. She tried to push back into the corner, afraid of suffocating. How could so many people fit into a single room? She panted, terrified of the swelling noise and crowd.

It's the drug, it's the drug, she told herself, but she began to hyperventilate, and tried to push through the bodies to the door. Pushing turned out not to be necessary. The people — *there were too many* — were not corporeal — she could walk through them. But their vaporous forms crackled with sparking energy, like touching hundreds of light sockets, and now the sound of their voices all talking, shouting, crying, laughing at once was intolerable. The smell, too, was as if a thousand years of smells were condensed into one reek. Her nose was overwhelmed and this more than anything made her feel crushed, suffocated, even as she realized nothing was crushing her except her own panic. She rolled into a fetal position, closed her eyes, and covered her nose, then opened her eyes slowly. In the hurricane of overlapping people, like a hundred movies being projected in the room at once, all of which had the volume turned up high, she suddenly singled out one man, in chains, sitting on the floor next to her. He was dirty, and covered with scabs and open sores. His hair crawled with lice. She could hear screams, and she forced her eyes away from the man in chains to another man, dressed in rags, who was, Sarah realized in horror, holding down a young girl and raping her. *Jesus Christ!* Sarah leapt on him and tried to pull him off, her own shouts mixing with those of the girl, but she merely fell through him to the floor, getting an electric shock in the process, and found herself eye to eye with a small child in a pressed white shirt and shorts, holding a teddy bear and whimpering. Superimposed over the child came a lurching pair of people making love, laughing, and over them a group of Nazi soldiers, sodomizing a young boy in a torn blue shirt who screamed in agony. When his screams became too loud, they shot him, and Sarah recoiled as he fell through her open arms and landed in a tangle of bloody limbs at her feet, his eyes staring up into hers.

Though he was weightless, she could feel the energy of his body as it passed through hers, smell his urine, hear his heart stop beating.

It was hard to find the walls; the room now had strange, unfamiliar edges. She saw the rough outlines of a dungeon, the heaped-up stores of a root cellar, huge piles of wine bottles, and the smooth gray cement of a bomb shelter. She gasped as a lion wandered past, then she tripped over what must be her own bed and fell, hitting her head on the all-too-real bedpost.

Sarah sat on the floor, head throbbing, as water gushed into the room, rising quickly. She tried to swim but couldn't feel the resistance of the water, and watched in disbelief as several people drowned in front of her, their hands reaching through her chest and face, grasping for life. She felt their energy envelop her, like waves of sonar.

"Make it stop!" she screamed, as all around her people writhed, died, gave birth, had sex, suffocated, and strangled one another. It was a Hieronymus Bosch painting come to life, and she couldn't escape it.

Sarah told herself again it was the drug, but how long would this madness last? Maybe it would never wear off, and she would be trapped in this panic, this melee of humanity, forever. She tried to find the door handle to escape, but she was turning in circles, trapped in a lightning storm.

Finally she made it out into the corridor, but once there she couldn't find her way — it was as if several basements and dungeons and wine cellars and passageways and grave sites were piled up all around her. A silver casket was being lowered into a grave as a woman shrieked with grief, someone was being lashed with a whip, and a man was lying on the floor drunk. She smelled shit, and offal, and rotting flesh. She began to retch.

Her heart was pounding faster and faster and she realized she was going to die, the atoms of her being would explode, forced apart by all the energy streaming through them.

"Sarah," called a faraway voice, and suddenly Shuziko was there, looking into her face and trying to talk to her, asking her what was wrong, should she call an ambulance. Sarah tried to talk, but bodies kept imposing themselves between them, people stretched on a rack, someone being burned with a flaming iron. For a moment Sarah glimpsed someone in modern dress and, hoping it was Suzi, she reached out her hand to grab the woman and felt nothing but charged air.

"Sarah." Suzi's voice was calling her. "Are you okay? Can you hear me?"

Her brain and body overloaded with electricity, Sarah started to have a seizure. And then Max was there, pushing Suzi aside. Sarah felt a sharp, violent jolt as Max gathered her up in his arms and shouted at Suzi to open the doors, to help him get her upstairs.

"It was a dungeon," he was shouting. "It was a fucking dungeon down here. We've got to get her out."

Sarah buried her face in Max's chest. It felt good to be limp. There was a part of her that was saying, "You're Sarah Weston, no one carries you anywhere," but his smell was so good compared to the stench of the basement, a thousand years of mold and blood and pain and rot. She closed a hand around his shirt and touched the reality of the rough cotton, his muscles moving underneath. She felt like she could feel the blood flowing in his veins, the cells dividing, the neurons firing. As if she had microscopic vision and telescopic vision and X-ray vision all at the same time.

Max carried her up several flights of stairs, Suzi just ahead, opening doors, keeping Sarah's feet from banging against things.

"Why aren't we calling an ambulance?" she demanded.

"She'll be okay," said Max. "She just needs to be in a happier place."

"Where? Disneyland?" snapped Suzi. "You're a lunatic, I don't know why I'm listening to you."

"The drug," moaned Sarah.

"What drug?" said Suzi. "I've dropped acid and this is the worst acid trip I've ever seen."

"It's okay," said Max. Sarah could feel him stop moving, and once again the energy pressed on her from all sides, though it was less frantic. "You can go now," he said to Suzi. "She'll be okay."

"I am not leaving," Suzi said.

"Sarah, keep your eyes closed," Max whispered, depositing her on a low sofa. The fabric bristled under her skin. She could feel Max's breath on her cheek. After all the horrors this was such a sensual, caressing sensation that she felt she might cry, or scream, or have an orgasm.

"Before you open your eyes," Max instructed, "listen. Hear the music. Try to find the sound of a cello and then follow it."

Still keeping her eyes tightly shut, Sarah realized she could, in fact, hear several orchestras playing at once. She concentrated, trying to separate one sound from all the others.

At last she found it. A cello. Bach. The Cello Suite No. 1. She knew it like the beating of her own heart. As she focused on the familiar notes, ignoring the cacophony of other sounds, suddenly the smells, too, began to separate into distinctive threads and she could distinguish candles, and perfume. And fish. She slowly opened her eyes. It was hot, and smoky. Blurred figures swam before her, overlapping with one another. Figures seated at a table, listening.

"What do you see?" asked Max.

"People at a dinner party," Sarah muttered. "I can't . . . I can't . . ."

Sarah shut her eyes again and tried not to swoon as the energy of the music flowed through her.

"It's okay. Follow the music. And when you're ready, try focusing on the people listening to the music," said Max. Sarah imagined the energy of the Bach as a single thread, and followed it through the tangle of sound in the room. Cautiously, she opened her eyes and found herself surrounded by people wearing clothes from what she guessed was the early nineteenth century. Men in long jackets and tight satin knee pants, women in low-necked, high-waisted dresses with clusters of curls about their ears. When she focused, it didn't hurt as much to watch them. Rather than being hit with a firehose of sensation, it was like a shower. She could still see Max and Suzi, faintly. Max was watching her intently, and Suzi looked concerned.

"You okay, Sugar?" Suzi asked.

"I can see them," said Sarah. "They're having dinner." She ducked as a waiter went by with a tray of small roast birds.

Max put his arms around her and guided her toward the table. "Who's the man in the third chair?" he asked her.

Sarah carefully made her way so that she was standing behind the third chair. She realized that the same furniture was there in the past and present. In the present, where Max and Suzi were, the chair she was looking at was old, the upholstery of the seat was ripped, and the paint was flaking off. In the present of her vision, the chair was freshly painted and new-looking.

Sarah reached down and touched the back of the chair, relieved that she could feel something solid under her fingers.

"Look at the man in the chair," repeated Max.

The man had thick dark hair and was wearing a black wool coat. His high white collar was stained at the lapels. A red cravat circled his throat.

She felt strange, staring at someone who was right in front of her. The man was talking to the woman next to him, and shoveling food unceremoniously into his mouth. Suddenly he turned to quaff his wine and she came face-to-face with him.

"It's Beethoven," she said.

She could hardly say his name. It was crazy, it was impossible. But it was Ludwig van Beethoven. She'd been staring at the bust of him on her desk for years. Her stomach flipped over and it was hard to breathe again. *It's a vision,* she told herself, *it's only a vision.*

"Beethoven?" Suzi asked. "What the — ?"

Max nodded and shushed her. "What's he doing?" he asked softly.

"He's eating, and flirting. And, um . . . burping."

Beethoven. The greatest composer who had ever lived. Right in front of her. Eating — well gobbling, actually. What kind of a drug was this?

"What's happening, Sarah?" asked Max.

"It's crazy," said Sarah. "I can see him. I can see the party. It's like watching a movie — no, it's like being in a movie. It's all so real."

"What the hell is she on?" said Suzi.

Max sighed. "What we see and feel and taste is a precept. It's not what's really out there in the world, it's what our brain thinks we can handle. Her senses have been heightened, like turning up the volume. She can see the energy that people leave behind. The things that happened in this room."

"So this isn't a vision?" asked Sarah. "I can see it? I can see the past?" She was lightheaded.

"It's the traces of their energy, like the contrail of a plane or the tail of a meteor. The drug affects your glial cells, which heighten your brain's awareness past the point where time has any real meaning. Because your glial cells are on super alert, you can see the traces of high-energy moments. Moments of things that happened in the past in this room. It's not magic, it's just an expansion of our senses. Your brain is filling in the dark spaces. That's what Sherbatsky told me."

"It's so freaky," said Sarah. "I'm staring at fucking Beethoven."

"Well, you're staring at the energy he left behind in this room," clarified Max. "Normally you can't see it because your brain has evolved into thinking it doesn't need to, but we all have the capacity. The drug just lets you use the tools you already have in your toolbox."

"Sherbatsky saw this?" Sarah whispered. This was why he wanted her in Prague. He always said he thought Sarah had a special sensory awareness. He knew she'd be able to see.

Beethoven smiled at the woman next to him, who was wearing a pink dress embroidered with roses. She said something in German about a recent visit to Berlin. It was clear to Sarah that Beethoven couldn't hear her, but he nodded and said, *"Ja, ja."* The cellist finished the Bach, and people clapped. Beethoven, who was taking another drink of wine, missed the cue but quickly put his glass down and joined them.

"You must play for us, Luigi," said the woman. Beethoven turned and met the glance of a slim man at the head of the table. Sarah looked at the man. His face was friendly, but there was a struggle between them, she decided. Beethoven shook his head. But the man, his smile tightening into a frown, nodded. Beethoven sighed and removed something from his pocket.

"Indigestion," he said to the woman in the pink dress, holding up a pill.

He swallowed it.

For a few moments Beethoven continued

to eat and drink. A woman in pale green across the table asked him if he would favor them with his playing. He smiled vaguely.

"He's so difficult these days," hissed the woman to the gentleman on her right. "He used to make love to me constantly, and now he just ignores me. I am tired of him. And his music I find impenetrable."

After another moment Beethoven stood up.

"Yes, Maestro, yes, play something. Play something," the people at the table begged. The candles flickered, and smoke wafted toward the frescoed ceiling. The room was warm. Sarah's nose pricked with the odor of heavy perfumes, barely covering the smell of unwashed, or not frequently washed, bodies.

"Sarah?" asked Max. "What's happening?"

"I don't know," said Sarah. "Something changed. He . . ."

The people seemed to fade slightly, and Sarah realized the drug must be wearing off. Though she had been desperate to escape its hold on her senses earlier, now she wanted to stay in this vision forever.

The man from the head of the table came over to Beethoven, and Sarah saw that he walked with a limp. "Is it working?" the man asked Beethoven. "Can you hear me?"

The composer nodded. "It's working." But Beethoven didn't look completely happy. There was a sadness to him, Sarah could see.

The man with the limp smiled and clapped him on the back. "A toast to Brahe," he said quietly.

"It takes longer every time," growled Beethoven. "And the effect is less. I should save it for when I'm working. It's wasted on these people."

"These people include two dukes, a count, and a director of the Imperial Royal Court Theater," said the man. "And you need patrons. Play for us."

Beethoven frowned, his face turning a deep angry purple. He farted loudly.

"Really, Luigi," said the man, waving a handkerchief. Beethoven began to walk toward a harpsichord in the corner. Sarah followed him, unable to believe she was going to see Beethoven actually play. The gas she could have lived without, but the music . . . He stopped suddenly. Sarah held her breath. Her vision was fading now, becoming transparent, the actual chairs in the room almost more visible than their older selves. She wished Beethoven would hurry. Just a few moments. If she could hear him play just for a few moments . . .

He stood there in silence, and a dark expression again came over his face.

"What is it, Luigi?" asked the limping man.

Beethoven looked around him, his expression a little wild, and Sarah wondered if he was seeing the kinds of things she had witnessed in the dungeon. It was hard to imagine this pleasant room had ever been used for torture.

The composer now appeared to be listening very intently to something she couldn't hear. Beethoven turned toward Sarah, and it almost seemed as if he could see her standing there. She looked behind her, but there was only the still, dim outlines of Max and Suzi, watching her. Sarah turned back to Beethoven.

"Who is there?" he demanded loudly, in German. There was a shocked silence, then a murmur of concern through the dinner party.

"Sarah, honey, are you okay?" It was Suzi's voice.

"Sarah," said Max, reaching for her. But she pushed his arm away.

"Luigi," whispered the man with the limp. "There's no one there."

"No, no," said Beethoven. "I can feel

something. Someone is here."

Ludwig van Beethoven stared at her from one inch away, his eyes locked on hers. Sarah could smell oysters on his breath, and the warm scent of wool over his own musky odor. She was slightly taller, and Beethoven tilted his head up, assessing her with the fathomless eyes of a genius. He stood there for a long second, and then smiled and closed his eyes.

"Immortal Beloved," he said.

And with that, Sarah fainted.

TWENTY-TWO

Charlotte Yates smiled and applauded on cue, but actually she was feeling a trifle melancholy. For once this had nothing to do with the fact that she was standing behind the president. Yes, he was outlining a "three-prong strategy for increased homeland security," and of course it was maddening, on one level, to hear His Nincompoopness stumble through a policy she had designed herself, but it didn't really matter. The strategy itself was meaningless. Just a little red herring to toss to the Dems in the Senate, who would start screaming about "personal liberties" as soon as the president finished his latest malapropism. ("Assuredliness?") The results of this had already been calculated. Polk (R-La.) would champion the bill, and Davidson (D-Mass.) would organize the filibuster. The good thing about the Senate was that every member was concerned entirely and exclusively with building their own campaign chests, and stayed well out of any actual government. Fox and CNN would feast on what she fed them, and while they were busy stuffing their mouths, actual work could get done.

Charlotte shifted slightly to the president's left, so that the cameras could get a fuller view of her pantsuit — a nifty plum Elie Tahari. Polling indicated that the American people liked and trusted her more when she was wearing warm shades. Recently she had taken out a pair of reading glasses while giving a speech, and her likability had gone up ten points across three different demographics. "Humanizing" was what her aide Paula had said.

Charlotte sighed internally, smiled outwardly, and focused on the source of her uncharacteristic funk.

Now that she knew the Russians were hovering around Lobkowicz Palace, the need for the letters became a bit more urgent. The cold war was over, but all the little games persisted. It was a good thing those puppets in the Middle East had been too busy grubbing around in their deserts to play any serious role in international espionage. They were the future, but Charlotte knew she needed to dispense with the old enemies before she could take on the new. She took a calming moment to visualize the entire Arab world as a giant parking lot. Lovely.

No, it was troubling that Miles had continued to come up empty-handed, but the marchesa had recruited another agent to work the palace now. The person had no idea that they had been recruited of course. The marchesa knew how to get dirt and how to manipulate it.

Well, if she were perfectly honest there was a certain element of . . . thrill to the whole thing. It had been so long since she had inhaled that sharp sweet scent of danger. Plotting, controlling, maneuvering, making deals, these things were enjoyable, yes, and not without risk, but she had become almost *too* expert at it. Just last week she had sat down with some promisingly destabilizing African pirates, and her heart rate hadn't gone above 100. Truly, her thirty minutes of morning cardio were more challenging.

Perhaps she was simply nostalgic for the good old days?

Prague in the seventies had been a magical place to be young and a CIA operative. Her official cover was that of an art historian. As a spook, she was deployed to be a liaison between scientists and artists wishing to defect to the West. The Soviets had seen through her cover soon enough, although with typical arrogance the CIA had never known it. Yuri Bespalov had been sent as delicious bait. She had met him several times before he made his first move at a little cocktail party at the National Museum. Yuri had been so courteous, offering her a glass of champagne, inquiring about her "work." She had been genuinely surprised when he pressed a piece of paper into her palm before turning to another guest. She had stepped onto the balcony, lit a cigarette (ah, those carefree days of smoking), and read what was to be the first of the many letters he would give her —

I know who you are. You know who I am. We are both being watched. But I must find a way to escape these many eyes, so that I may look into yours. This will seem crazy to you? I can hardly believe it myself. Burn this.

It was just the sort of career-making opportunity Paisley had schooled her to watch for. Helping ballet dancers and physicists escape to the land of plenty wasn't going to get her noticed. But shagging the potential next Minister of Culture and maybe getting a bead on some inner sanctum dealings . . . bingo. Charlotte could hardly wait to pass the note on to her chief.

Except she hadn't. Because at the end of the evening, Yuri had sidled up and explained that his driver would be happy to escort her home. And she had accepted gratefully because the cobblestone streets of Prague were murder to traverse in heels, and the maintenance of her lowly cover meant she had to either walk or take the bus. She had expected another note, perhaps with a suggestion that they meet somewhere neutral, as if by accident. Maybe he was going to try to recruit her! That would be fun.

Was she surprised when the driver had taken her to Dalibor Tower on the Prague Castle grounds? Was she nervous when the driver had left her alone in the car, ambling off into the darkness, whistling? Was she startled when the door next to her opened and Yuri crawled in, pushing her backward, sliding his hands under her cheap rayon dress?

Her first thought had been that she should grin and bear it. Take one for the team. Let the commie bastard have his way with her and then see what information she could pump.

At what point had her manufactured

moans become disturbingly realistic? When he had actually ripped her panties off? When he had wrapped her thighs around his neck and licked her like a starving cat? Definitely before she straddled him like a frantic jockey.

Present-day Charlotte Yates shifted inside her Elie Tahari, mindful that too much movement played terribly on camera.

Later, much later, Yuri had confessed that while, yes, his original mission had been to recruit her to the other side, the sex had been his idea. And the love . . . well, that had just happened. Dig your nails deep enough into the back of a Soviet, and eventually you'll find a Russian.

So things had played out in Prague a little differently than everyone had anticipated. But she had *always* been a patriot. *Nothing* she had ended up doing for the Soviets constituted any threat to the United States. So a few dozen would-be defectors ended up having to stay at home? Nobody was actually hurt. Well, hurt permanently. Well, probably nobody had been killed.

But if it all got out? People could be led to see it differently. People.

There. She had at last located the source of her sadness. It was people. Charlotte Yates loved humanity with all her heart, but she really had to draw the line at individuals. For the most part they were incredibly stupid, clumsy, selfish, and criminally short-sighted. Look, for instance, at who they voted for.

Charlotte forced herself to smile at the back of the president's head. Thank goodness that for every million incompetent losers there was someone like herself ready to step forward and do what was necessary to safeguard America and the world at large.

When the president finished mangling his remarks ("Islamification?"), she would applaud. Later she would stand on the steps of the Capitol and deliver her own statements. At a designated time, Paula would step forward and hand her a piece of paper. Charlotte would smile ruefully at the members of the press corps while putting on her reading glasses, then turn and say that unfortunately she would not be able to answer any questions, that she had a very important meeting with a Girl Scout troop at the Senate. "And let's remember who we're doing all this for, people," she would say. "For the children."

She'd give the marchesa and her new sidekick in Prague a week or so to turn up something — anything. There was nothing like a time deadline to inspire people to

251

get . . . creative. She needed those letters. It was a matter of national security. And also she just really wanted to hold them again. Remind herself that in this crazy old world there were simple things to cherish. Really, if people knew that deep down, deep, deep, *deep* down, she was such a softie, she wouldn't have to wear the fucking glasses.

Twenty-Three

"He learned to play the violin in his prison cell," said Max. "If you focus on that sound, you can see him. His name was Dalibor of Kozojedy, and he was imprisoned for being too nicey-nice to some peasants. He's wearing an orange tunic, but look for the violin. That's how I know it's him, and I know it's 1948 because that's when he was executed. I always see him when I stand here. Can you find him?"

"I'm trying, but I keep getting stuck on these people humping like bunnies in the backseat of a black Lada," said Sarah. "It's like a seventies porn film. Wow, that guy is . . . talented."

Sarah and Max were standing in the moonlight in front of Dalibor Tower, which rose above Deer Moat. The drug had mostly worn off, but Sarah was getting little flashbacks as she and Max walked around the castle grounds, not a (present-day) soul in the place. Max was trying to teach her to hone her perceptions and not be over-whelmed, but Sarah was still finding it hard to breathe when layers upon layers of intense human activity suddenly swooped up around her. She tried peering through the windows of the black Lada, but couldn't make out the faces of the occupants.

And then, as a light breeze stirred the candy wrappers on the cobblestones, Sarah was suddenly staring at an empty patch of pavement.

"It's gone," she said. It made no sense that she was not relieved. The past two hours had been the most terrifying of her entire life. She had come to in Max's arms, mut-tering "everything, everything" over and over. Suzi was out of her mind with worry, but Max had convinced her to leave doctors out of it, and just get Sarah a glass of water and an aspirin.

"I don't know what you gave her," Suzi said. "But you gave her too much."

Max frowned, and asked her to please be discreet. Suzi nodded, and Sarah had thought she looked a little awed. Whether at the authority in Max's voice, or over what she had just witnessed, Sarah couldn't tell.

Once she could stand up and walk and talk on her own without hyperventilating,

Max took Sarah outside into the night air. Suzi had gone to bed muttering that she would not say anything to anyone, but that tomorrow she would be needing some explanations.

Max and Sarah had walked around the castle grounds, with flashes appearing to Sarah here and there. Max was like a little kid, leading her around by the hand excitedly, wanting to show her his great-to-the-tenth grandmother Polyxena standing up to the Protestants when they came looking for the Catholic ministers they had just thrown out the window, Tycho Brahe gazing at the sky from the palace roof, and poor depressed Kafka, hard at work on his account books in Golden Lane.

"You're my tour guide to the past," laughed Sarah. "Hey, let's go over to the Riding School. I want to try to see Emperor Rudy's lion again."

Sarah badly wanted to get a glimpse of all these famous people and events, but the problem was, with so many people having experienced moments of intense fear, pain, joy, or longing in one place for over a thousand years, it was hard to sift through it all. It reminded her of when she was a little girl and visited her mom at work at a Beacon Hill brownstone. In the cavernous basement laundry room, rows of sheets were hung on long lines to dry. She loved to close her eyes and run through them, letting the clean linen whap her in the face. Her mom had yelled at her that she would get them dirty, but she hadn't cared. Now Sarah had a hard time getting through the layers.

"What time is it?" Sarah asked. "I'm exhausted."

"Just after three," said Max. "We should go to bed."

Sarah wondered what that meant. One thing about all your senses being heightened was that . . . well, all your senses were heightened. The smell of Max himself was enough to make her hallucinate.

She took Max's hand and pulled him toward the statue of St. George in the courtyard between the Old Palace and St. Vitus Cathedral. The armor-clad saint was glowing inkily in the moonlight. Sarah could no longer see any history happening around her, but the air still felt electric. Even in the cool night breeze, her skin was hot, as if she had spent the day at the beach.

She knew that tomorrow morning she would be demanding to know why Max hadn't told her about the drug, what it was, who developed it, who knew about it, what had he seen, and a thousand other questions. But right now, she wanted to feel his skin against hers.

Sarah looked up at St. George. Rather slim and feminine, yet determined and feisty, he was looking down at her, driving his lance through the open throat of an alligator-sized winged dragon, while his well-behaved horse also stared at her appraisingly. It was as if the two of them — the saint and the horse — were reminding her that life is short, and that soon she, too, would be one of the wraiths floating around this castle. But only if she really *lived* first, otherwise there would be no trace of her at all. Only the passionate were immortal, it seemed. If you fought, screwed, screamed, laughed, or otherwise experienced life intensely, for better or for worse, you left a record. Those who lived a quiet, well-behaved, well-tempered life? Gone without a trace.

She spun around and pulled Max toward her, reaching for his belt with her hands as her mouth sought his. He had his hands under her shirt in an instant, and they were frantically all over each other, ripping their clothes in their hurry. Later, Sarah could only remember flashes of the event, Max holding her on his knees, deep inside her, his back against the statue's base, the soles of her feet against the cold bronze; her face next to the impaled dragon's, screaming in pleasure, Max's face buried between her legs; him standing and holding her upside down, his head in her as she swallowed him — was that even possible, she wondered?

One thing Sarah knew for sure. The identity of her bathroom lover was no longer in doubt. It was Max.

It was the best sex of her life, and that was saying a lot. Sarah felt about great sex the way St. George felt about slaying dragons — it may not have been the main of her life's work, but when the opportunity arose, it was a true passion. But even during great sex she always had moments when her mind broke the concentration of her body. Not this time. This time her brain was switched off, no doubt exhausted by all that it had experienced this evening, and her body was fully present, every cell given over to pleasure. When she felt her orgasm coming, she knew it would explode in every nerve ending of her entire body.

So when they were interrupted by flashlights and sirens, it was, shall we say, a bit of a downer.

The back of the patrol car smelled like vomit, and Sarah was trying with her handcuffed hands to close the buttons on her shirt, but they seemed to be missing. Max was shouting at the police officers, saying he had every right to be in the castle complex at night, and they had no right to arrest him. At one point he said angrily, "She is not a prostitute." *Wow,* thought Sarah. *I am glad my dad did not live to see this.*

Worried and clearly awakened from sleep, Jana came down to the police station on Jungmann Square to bail them out, after Sarah had sat in a detention room for three hours with two sobbing Ukrainian teenagers in go-go boots. Sarah could not even meet Jana's eyes; she just whispered a small "thank you" and followed her toward her car, a tiny blue Skoda. Sarah expected to see Max waiting by the car, but Jana told her she had secured his release earlier and he had taken a taxi home. Sarah found this slightly ungallant, but couldn't exactly be sure she wouldn't do the same. She just wanted the night to be over.

She got in the passenger seat, closed the weirdly lightweight door with a thunk, and Jana put the tinny little car in gear and backed out of the parking space. It was just before dawn, and there was no traffic in the city center, the first time Sarah had ever seen it this way. Men with brooms and little carts were the only people out, sweeping the ice-cream wrappers off the sidewalks.

As they bumped over the cobblestones and dodged the tram tracks on the Národni, the relief of being out of jail gave way to complete mortification. She knew she was fired. Jana would certainly tell Miles, and how could Max protect her this time? Word would get back to the university at home, and not only would she never get tenure, she would be the laughingstock of the entire East Coast academic establishment. They'd be telling jokes about her at Yale. At Dartmouth, they'd name a sexual position after her. At Columbia, medievalists would snicker into their lattes about how Sarah Weston learned the hard way — the very hard way — that the dragon was a symbol of lust. She'd have to move west, maybe to some small women's college in Idaho where they'd barely have heard of Prague, and Beethoven was merely Schroeder's hero. There would be no more men. She'd be like some modern-day Hester Prynne, condemned never to have sex again.

They crossed Legion Bridge, and Sarah thought about flinging open the door of the Skoda and jumping into the cold black water below. It was all so awful that she started to giggle, and when Jana shot her a look, she began to laugh uncontrollably.

"I've never been so embarrassed in my entire life," said Sarah at last. "Did you see the faces of the cops? They were *disgusted.*"

"Especially when I told them that Max really was who he said he was," agreed Jana, now starting to laugh herself.

" 'Lobkowicz? Lobkowicz? This man's name is Anderson!' " Sarah imitated the security guards and police officers who had surrounded, disentangled, and pulled them to their feet. " 'No Lobkowicz would ever defile St. George in this way! Why, the Lobkowiczes are members of the Order of the Golden Fleece! These people are like dogs!' "

"You two are terrible," said Jana, chuckling. "Love makes people so stupid."

At that, Sarah's laughter ended abruptly and she fell silent. Jana drove on, passing the Carmelite monastery that housed the Holy Infant of Prague, the sun rose, and the city began its day.

TWENTY-FOUR

"Sarah!" shouted Pols, from what sounded like the bottom of a pool. Sarah had slept for all of two hours, then been awakened by Daphne, who had rather coldly informed her that her "visitors" had pranced unannounced into Daphne's workspace.

"Visitors?" Sarah had responded groggily. "I'm not expecting any visitors. . . ." She had rolled over, hoping Daphne would go away. Quickly.

"A blind girl, a dog, and a Mexican?" snapped Daphne. "It's like a knock-knock joke." Sarah almost fell out of bed — *what the hell were Pols and Jose doing here, in Prague? And Boris?!*

"Tell them not to move! I'll be right there!" she told Daphne's retreating haughty back. She quickly splashed cold water on her face and made her way upstairs.

Last night all of her senses had been alive, and today they all felt muted and a little sore. The sunlight hurt her eyes, and sounds seemed far away, as if she had been at a rock concert. She couldn't really smell anything, and the slice of toast she shoved into her mouth to settle her stomach on her way through the kitchen tasted like wood.

"Sarah!" shouted Pols again.

"I'm here," said Sarah, hugging the little girl, who was noticeably taller and thinner. "But what on earth are you doing here?"

"We've been invited," said Pols. "Tell her, Jose."

Sarah smiled at Jose, who had chosen for his traveling costume a pair of pale blue tuxedo pants, a tailcoat, and a long, fringed scarf. Pols, it seemed, had also brought along her mastiff, Boris, who wore a jaunty orange bib around his massive rib cage that proclaimed him to be a service dog. (A clever move on Pols's part: Boris had earned his bib during a brief tenure in his youth as a K-9 Detection dog in Bosnia. He was useless as a Seeing Eye dog, but if there were any land mines in Prague he would sniff them out.)

"There's a gathering of child prodigies here in Prague," said Jose. "Organized by the Vienna Symphony and the Czech Philharmonic. We're playing at the Rudolfinum tomorrow night."

"You're performing?" Sarah asked Pols.

"Yes. It's some horrible competition."

"I thought you hated performing."

Pollina gave a little shrug and a cough. "I do, but I missed you and you needed me, so I took their invitation and came."

Sarah laughed at the idea that she needed a blind eleven-year-old, but the truth was, she was absurdly glad to see Pollina. They left Jose to enjoy the ecstasies of St. Vitus Cathedral and Sarah took Pols and Boris out to the public gardens near the old handball courts. The fresh air might help with that cough, and the gardens weren't often crowded. She thought Pols might enjoy the Singing Fountain in front of the Royal Summer Palace.

They sat on a bench facing the arching loggia of the palace.

"Something's happening, isn't it?" asked Pols.

Sarah hesitated to drag Pols into whatever was going on.

"I knew it was, and if you don't tell me, I'll hold my breath until I fall over. You'll probably be arrested for child abuse."

Sarah laughed at Pols's dry delivery of this threat. She took a deep breath and told Pols everything — well, almost everything. She left out the embarrassing sex with Max in the bathroom, and by the statue. She just said they were caught trespassing at night.

Sherbatsky's death, the cross in her bed, Sherbatsky's note about the New Year's Eve letter from Prince Lobkowicz to LVB that she still couldn't find, the Aztec amulet, the letter to Max from the concierge in Venice, the letter to Yuri Bespalov complaining about missing items, Andy's death, the fact that she and Max were in fourth grade together but he had hidden that from her and sent Nicolas to check her out. Taking another deep breath, she even told Pols about the mysterious drug that had allowed her to visit the past — or the energy of the past. She left out the gruesome visions and concentrated on the part where she had seen Beethoven, heard him speak, had almost seen him play.

"He actually said the words 'Immortal Beloved,' " she told Pols. "And it felt like he was saying them to *me.*"

That should have set Pols going, but strangely, she seemed less interested in this than she was in the letter to Yuri Bespalov and the death of Andy Blackman, who had been spying on Miles.

"I've been doing a little investigating of my own," Pols said, reaching down to pet Boris's enormous head. "Matt's teaching

265

me all about how to do historical research on my voice-activated computer." Sarah knew that Pols's tutor had orders to teach her anything she wanted to know, but Sarah sometimes worried that he should have been sticking to practical things like getting around in the world. And yet, Pols had made it to Prague, with certainly minimal help from Jose and Boris.

"After you got the job here I decided we should follow the trail of the Lobkowicz property distribution," said Pols. "I found out the Nazis kept records, but things were done kind of casually under the communists. Officially, pieces were sent to places like the Hermitage and the Pushkin on loan, but often they were handed to various high-ranking party members as gifts or bribes. The tenth-century Evangeliarium for example, went to Brezhnev and then on to his mistress, and was recovered at auction in Murmansk in 2008 and returned to the family."

Pols had a fit of coughing. Boris whined and put his head in Pollina's lap, licking her hand.

"Have you seen a doctor?" Sarah asked, when the girl had caught her breath.

"The vast majority of the collection, however," Pols continued, ignoring her, "stayed here in what was then Czechoslovakia. It was under the control of the National Museum, which was housed in the building you're now working and living in. From 1965 to 1980, the head of the National Museum was Yuri Bespalov, who was a KGB employee."

Sarah frowned. "Pols," she said. "I looked up Bespalov after I found that letter to him in the box at the Nela library. I saw that he was head of the museum. It didn't say anything about him being KGB."

"It's fairly well-known in certain circles." Pols's lower lip jutted out.

"Circles you run in?"

Pols sighed. "Sarah. Haven't you heard of the Internet?"

"Okay, okay," Sarah smiled. "Go on."

"I've been learning all about the restitution process and came across this whole article on the board of the American-Czech Cultural Alliance. The article mentioned that Charlotte Yates sits on the board, and seeing how she's a powerful senator and all I got curious. Because, you know, *why*? What's her interest in Czech culture? It's not like she just found out she's of Czech descent like Madeleine Albright or something. And then Matt found a photograph of her and Marchesa Elisa Lobkowicz De-

Benedetti together. She's from the Venice branch of the family. They thought they were the rightful heirs."

"Yes, I know about Elisa," said Sarah, not wanting to tell Pols about Nicolas's insinuations. Not after what had happened under, around, and against St. George.

"The weird thing is," Pols continued, "when Matt and I checked back two days later the photo was gone."

"Maybe you just weren't looking in the right place."

"No, it was *gone.* And you know how the Internet is — things never really disappear. But this one did. It's important, Sarah. I feel it. I don't know how, but it's important."

Sarah looked at this odd little girl, wearing a rather strange, old-fashioned party dress, her hair slightly mussed, her ribbon askew, a giant dog at her feet. The sky was blue, the tourists were passing by chatting about how *magical* the whole place was and snapping photos. The Renaissance palace was still standing where it had been since the 1600s. But the world had turned upside down more than once since then.

And yet Sarah was always skeptical about conspiracy theories. If there was a connection between Senator Charlotte Yates and Max's cousin, so what? They both ran in jet-set circles.

"I think this Marchesa Elisa person might be working some angle," Pols said. "Maybe she hasn't given up trying to get the stuff back. What's your impression of her?"

"Haven't met her," Sarah muttered.

"I keep having funny dreams," Pols said. "Dreams with fire. I feel like something is about to happen."

"Something is about to happen," Sarah said, firmly. "You're going to kick ass in this competition tomorrow and then I want Jose to take you to see a doctor for that cough. Where are your parents?"

"Excavating some temple in Nepal. Sarah. Can you trust Max or are you just in love with him?"

Sarah shot Pols a glance. Her face was unreadable. "What? Why do you say that?"

"It's obvious."

Sarah didn't answer. She had been the only little girl in the neighborhood who *hadn't* dreamed that one day her prince would come, and here was, well, a prince. It was absurd, and slightly embarrassing. But if someone shoved bamboo under her fingernails and made her tell the truth?

"Aren't you excited that I saw Beethoven?" she asked, changing the subject.

"I see him every day," Pols shrugged.

"You mean when you play his music, but I really saw him, or rather the trace of him."

"Sarah, I may not see him with my eyes, but every time I pick up my violin or sit down at the piano and play Beethoven, he's sitting there with me. I can feel him there. I guess I assumed everyone else did, too." She was not bullshitting, Sarah could tell.

"You literally feel his energy? Like he's there with you?"

"Sure. Mozart, too. All the composers, really. That's what music is, it's immortality."

Sarah sat back and blinked. Once again she was reminded that Pols experienced the world in a completely different way than she did. Despite the fact that they grew up in the same city, only — what? — fifteen years apart — they may as well have been an African villager and a twenty-sixth-century astronaut for how similarly they saw the universe.

"Do you feel him here?" asked Sarah.

"There's a lot to feel here," said Pols, raising her palms up. "I don't know what's Beethoven."

Suddenly Sarah wanted to see Max very badly. She texted him again. *Where are you?*

The next instant her phone rang. "Max?" she said.

There was an uncomfortable pause. "Sarah, it's Miles. Can you be in my office in five minutes?"

It didn't sound like a question.

"I have to go to the principal's office," Sarah told Pols, after she hung up. "I think I might be in trouble."

"If they are trying to get rid of you," Pols said, serenely. "Don't let them. Hey, I'm hungry. Is the ice cream good in Prague?"

TWENTY-FIVE

Sarah called Jose, who came to take Pols, Boris, and a pint of Cream & Dream back to the hotel. Sarah felt a stab of anxiety as the taxi drove away. She went back to the palace and made her way to Miles's office, her stomach in a knot.

Miles closed the door after her as she came in.

"I had a call from a friend at the police department this morning," said Miles.

Here it comes, thought Sarah.

"I can't have a drug addict on my staff," he said.

Sarah's mouth fell open. "I'm not a drug addict," she said. "It was a mistake. I didn't even know what I was taking."

"Ecstasy, I'm guessing, from your attack on the prince."

"Attack?"

"That's what Max told the police, and what the police told me this morning. That he was out for a smoke and saw you stumbling around and tried to convince you to come back to the palace and you practically raped him. He said you said you had taken ecstasy."

Sarah was so angry she could hardly speak.

"Where is Max? I should at least be able to face my accuser."

"I'm sure he'll deny it. He doesn't like having to do these things himself. He asked me to fire you and send you back to Boston."

Sarah's mind reeled.

"I don't have a drug problem, Miles," said Sarah, trying to sound calm. "This is all a ridiculous mistake."

"Perhaps," said Miles. "But Max is right about one thing. Lobkowicz Palace does not need this kind of embarrassment. Imagine if this got into the papers. I was just putting the finishing touches on our press release. The museum is set to open in a few weeks. We're hosting a gala opening event. The president of the Czech Republic, the prime minister, the German ambassador, the French president, all the members of the Order of the Golden Fleece. This is a serious job, Sarah, not a summer camp."

"I don't need a lecture," Sarah said, standing up. "If Max fired me then that's that."

"Sit down," Miles said. "The decision isn't entirely up to Max, although he seems to think it is. But actually the Lobkowicz Foundation — the governing board of the museum — has a say in the hiring and firing of staff."

"So who's on the Foundation, Miles? You?"

Miles shifted uncomfortably. "They are willing to defer the decision to me. With certain provisos. I've decided not to take Max's recommendation to fire you. We have a time crunch problem and so far your work has been exemplary. Also, frankly, I don't think he's the best person to be in charge of day-to-day operations here at the palace. So I am overriding Max's decision. I would advise you to focus on your work and not on your . . ." Miles coughed.

"Absolutely," said Sarah, through her teeth. "It won't happen again."

"Good," said Miles. "We need to focus on what's in front of us."

Ah, thought Sarah. *But what is in front of us, Miles? What's this all about?*

"I believe in your commitment to the material," Miles said. "But I'm afraid I'll need a signed statement from you. To cover us legally, you know."

Miles handed her a typewritten sheet. She glanced over it, then looked across at him. "'Max gave me ecstasy'? 'Max is an unstable personality'? These are the 'provisos'? I can't sign this."

"Then here." He handed her a plane ticket. "Petr has already packed your things. You'll be escorted out of the palace directly to the airport."

Sarah felt anger rise red in her face. Did he think she was so naive that she couldn't recognize the smell of a rat when he held one under her nose?

"This isn't about guaranteeing my behavior," Sarah said. "This is about the Lobkowicz Foundation wanting to throw Max under the bus. It's blackmail."

"You were caught by the Czech police having sex in a public place," Miles said grimly. "Max told me that you are unstable, violent, and possibly a drug addict."

"Which you are willing to overlook," Sarah said, taking up the paper in front of her, "as long as I sign this? And how will my indicting Max help you with your *insurance,* exactly?"

"I will send you home," Miles said, standing up now. "Immediately."

"Great." Sarah folded the paper and tucked it into her jeans pocket. "I'll just hold on to this, though. A little keepsake from the palace. I'll make sure Jana gets it back to Max, or maybe Nicolas can deliver it for me. Max hasn't been ousted yet, has he? I mean, he's the Lobkowicz around here, so I'm guessing that if he can fire me, he can fire you, too. You want me to book you a seat next to me on Delta?"

Don't move, Sarah told herself. *Don't blink. Stand your ground. Unlock the knees. Center your balance. Be prepared for a fight. Max never told Miles to fire me. This is all coming from somewhere else.*

Miles sat down in his office chair. Sarah waited.

"You misunderstand me," Miles said, after a long moment. "I'm trying to protect you, Sarah. Of course, if you feel uncomfortable signing the letter, I will do what I can to talk Max out of his decision, and see what I can settle with . . . all the rest of it. But I don't want any more . . . problems."

Sarah smiled.

"There are a lot of things to get done," she said. "Before the opening. I expect that I'll spend the rest of my time here at my little workstation, doing my job. Don't you think that's the best plan? Just forget all about this and focus on what's in front of me, like you said. This collection will make a wonderful museum. It's really such an honor."

Sarah turned and walked out of the office. She wasn't sure if she had saved her ass, or achieved only a temporary reprieve from having it handed to her. Either way, she was sick of being jerked around.

Twenty-Six

Sarah had some serious adrenaline going. It was either attend to archival work or challenge Daphne to some kickboxing. Better to work. She had outmaneuvered Miles for the moment, but it was going to be important that she actually *be* the dedicated scholar she was. She was here to work. And now that she had seen Beethoven himself, listened to his voice, heard him belch and chew and fart, she felt even more connected to the objects he had once touched. With hands that she actually — incredibly — had seen. The idea that Ludwig could have seen *her* was still too weird to really take in. And why had he whispered "Immortal Beloved"? He couldn't have been talking to her — *could he*? She shook off the thought. It was ridiculous.

Sarah headed upstairs to her workstation. She could hear Bernard singing to himself in his Rococo Room, and Suzi's laughter from the space she now shared with Delft china, but she met no one. Confront Suzi? No, Sarah was pretty sure she was right and that Miles had not spoken to her. Best not to get Suzi involved.

Her things appeared to be just as she had left them, the long tables covered with boxes and papers, filing cards, "Do Not Touch" signs. Her tools: gloves, magnifying glass, plastic slipcovers, etcetera, were all neatly laid out. The most precious objects she had already moved to the climate-controlled glass cases where they were locked up when she wasn't actually handling them. Prince Lobkowicz had purchased a good deal of sheet music in his day, and since much of it had either never been published or was long out of print, it would be a definite draw to musicologists and serious musicians. But even the unwashed masses that would eventually pass through the palace would have plenty to gawk at: Gluck's manuscript for his opera *Ezio,* Handel's *Messiah* (densely revised and orchestrated by Mozart himself), Haydn's Opus 77 String Quartets (a commission from the 7th to the composer that was never finished), and of course, the Beethovens.

Performing parts for the premieres of the Fourth and Fifth Symphonies in the master's hand, another copy of the Fifth with LVB's corrections and alterations. The Opus 18 String Quartets with LVB's notes for the first public performance. An acknowledgment from Ludwig of the stipend Prince Lobkowicz had allotted him. The 7th had provided Ludwig with more than just money. He had given the composer the use of his own private orchestra. Probably a lot of good free dinners. And, if the drug-induced vision held any truth, he had given him something else . . . for Sarah knew that the limping host of the dinner party could only have been the club-footed Joseph Franz Maximilian Lobkowicz. There had been an air of intimacy between the two men, some sort of tacit understanding.

Sarah shut her eyes and tried to remember the sequence of events. Beethoven had taken a pill, she remembered that clearly.

What had the prince said about it? He had asked Ludwig if he had taken it, if it had helped.

He had asked if Beethoven could hear.

And Beethoven had said yes.

Sarah opened her eyes.

Apparently Lobkowiczes had a long history of giving people drugs.

There was evidently more, much more, between the composer and his patron than had previously been discovered.

Sarah picked up the box that contained what had been found so far of the correspondence from Beethoven to his patron. She couldn't be totally sure, but she was fairly certain that most of it had never been properly documented before. There might be enough material for a book. If they ever let her back in the palace after the opening.

Of course, the most famous letters of Beethoven were the Immortal Beloved missives, and the so-called Heiligenstadt Testimony, the letter Ludwig had addressed to his two younger brothers in which he confessed his loss of hearing; defended his behavior; railed, raged, talked of suicide; and swore allegiance to his art. A good deal of the rest of his surviving correspondence concerned business, household affairs, petty grievances. The personal letters that had been documented weren't terribly riveting. The most common closer he used was *in der Eile* — "in haste" — and his punctuation, spelling, and handwriting were fairly atrocious. He made a lot of really bad puns. He would start off a letter calling the recipient a "rascal" and end with calling him his "dear friend."

Sarah pulled on her gloves and started going through the correspondence between

Luigi and Prince Lobkowicz again. At first glance she had not seen anything especially unusual, but now she had something to look for. Was there a reference, however oblique, to some kind of pill or drug?

Sarah paused over a letter, undated, stained a tea brown and torn at one corner.

My health is very bad but for now I will only say that I am better for knowing that your prodigious key will soon emerge from the heavy skirts of your noble house and once more sing notes of wonder.

"Prodigious key" sounded like a typical LVB jab at his patron's member. The 7th prince did have ten or eleven kids. Nothing mysterious in any of it, and yet . . . there was something . . .

The sound of the dinner gong rang loudly from the first floor. Sarah placed the letter back in the box, removed her gloves, and took a deep breath. There was a soft tap on her door.

"Yeah, come in," Sarah called.

"Oh, marvelous, you're *here*!" Eleanor Roland called out, gaily. "I felt just wretched, leaving you all alone with the dark princeling, and then, rather nervous, because I haven't seen you since. Suzi said you weren't feeling well?"

"Just a headache." Sarah shrugged. "Probably allergies or something. Who's cooking tonight?"

"Douglas," Eleanor chirped, widening her eyes. "I'm predicting bangers and mash, or fish and chips. The English, you know."

Miles was not at dinner. With his absence, and without the glowering presence of Max, the academics loosened up considerably. Sarah, self-conscious at first, was soon reassured that none of the other academics knew about her brush with the police and near firing. Evidently both Jana and Miles were keeping their own counsel. She looked around for Suzi but didn't see her. Moritz lurked under the table, feeling free to beg without his master around to rebuke him.

There was a lot of good-natured, or mostly good-natured, teasing around the table. And a new addition: Fiona Upshaw, a delicate blonde with a heart-shaped face who had come to curate the Delft china collection. Sarah was also introduced to Janek Sokol, a thin and elderly Czech scholar who spoke in perfect, if accented, English. Janek had spent the day at Nelahozeves. His interest, he told Sarah, was in the library.

"I'm using the latest technology to explore

it." He twinkled at Sarah. "A wheelbarrow. And Miles has promised me the use of a slingshot for the top shelves."

Sarah laughed and complimented him on his English.

"Ah, yes, I have been living in Washington since 1990. And before, I studied English secretly, here, with a few friends. There was a time, my dear, when even speaking Czech here could be considered a political act. Our children were forced to learn Russian."

"Janek works for the National Archives," Eleanor chimed in. "The Berlin Document Center."

"Which in 1994 was moved back to Germany," Janek explained. "But we have everything on microfilm in the States. And now German researchers have to come to the U.S. to be able to study Nazi documents, because the Fatherland limits access. Privacy laws, they say."

"Is that what you are looking for here?" Sarah asked. "Nazi documents?"

The Czech scholar laughed. "No, this is vacation for me! I'm hoping for love letters. Recipes for soup! Sixteenth-century court gossip. I have always been fascinated with the reign of Rudolf II. It is a private passion. My good friend Miles has been so kind to let an old man come and poke around."

Sarah excused herself to greet Suzi, who had just entered the kitchen. Suzi wrapped her up in a brief but bone-crunching hug.

"Are you okay, girl?" Suzi whispered in her ear.

"Just embarrassed." Sarah smiled slightly. "I'm sorry I was such a mess."

"Girl, that was a freak show." Suzi punched her lightly in the shoulder, and continued whispering. "Don't get me wrong, I'm no angel, but you can't mess with all this crap they got over here. Who knows what they lace it with? Ground-up bones or something. Anyway, I'm glad you're better, 'cause I've got news for you. You've been replaced."

Sarah's stomach took a quick dip down to her knees.

Suzi pointed with her chin at Fiona Upshaw, now giggling at something Douglas was telling her. "I'm in love," Suzi sighed. "I'm in love with a woman who loves china."

"Love is strange," Sarah agreed solemnly, although she felt almost giddy with relief. And really, love was strange. Take Max, for instance. No. She was going to try to get through the next half hour without thinking about Max. Wherever he was. Where was he?

Sarah took a seat between Eleanor and

Bernard, who were full of plans for their outfits for the planned costume party.

"Who are you going to be?" Eleanor asked Sarah. "You have to pick a painting."

"I'm thinking of going as one of the dogs," Douglas called out, setting down a huge platter of lamb curry in the middle of the table. "Sarah, love, be my Polyxena."

"Daphne is going to be Polyxena," Bernard said. "Someone should go as her husband, Zdenek, the 1st Prince Lobkowicz."

"Miles would make a good Zdenek," said Suzi, with wicked innocence. Daphne busied herself with the curry, a little smile on her cool lips.

"Did they have a happy marriage, Zdenek and Polyxena?" Eleanor wondered aloud. "Or was it one of those terrible arranged things? Does anybody know? Daphne?"

"A very happy marriage," Daphne said, her normally clipped and frosty tones softened a little. "There are many letters between de two. He called her his 'golden princess,' and she addresses him as 'my king.'"

"Polyxena was an expert politician," Janek commented. "A very clever and resourceful woman. And it was through her influence — her interest in music and art and literature — that the Lobkowicz collection began. The letters are indeed fascinating."

"There is a gift from Rudolf II to Zdenek and Polyxena," Moses Kaufman, the decorative arts expert, piped up. "An ebony altar. Lovely example of *pietra dura.*"

"Yes, Rudolf brought Florentine artists to Prague." Janek nodded. "He assembled some of the most fascinating and learned men of the day around him. Painters, alchemists, astrologers, printers, publishers, architects."

"Tycho Brahe," Sarah said suddenly.

A toast to Brahe. That's what Prince Lobkowicz had said to Beethoven, in her vision. In reference, it seemed, to the pill or drug or whatever LVB had "taken." But that was absurd. Tycho Brahe had been dead at least two hundred years before Beethoven's time.

"Indeed." The Czech scholar smiled approvingly at Sarah. "Brahe was a friend of the mathematician and numerologist John Dee, who traveled to Prague in 1583 or thereabouts. Dee sold Rudolf two mysterious collections of writing: the famous Voynich manuscript, currently at Yale University. It has never been decoded. And another, a book of alchemical formulae Dee claimed to have copied from the Aztecs. But

we have only the rumors of this book, references, allusions. No one has ever found a
copy."

"Tycho Brahe." Fiona leaned forward
across the table. "I've always found him
fascinating. Did you know he lost his nose
in a duel and made himself a new one out
of copper? And he kept tame elk? And he
had a dwarf servant with supposedly clairvoyant powers."

The mention of a little person made Sarah
think of Nicolas, and the pillbox he had
given her. A pillbox shaped like . . . a copper
nose. That was weird. Miles had said that
he had Petr pack up her things. She wanted
to make sure the box was safe, and she
excused herself, racing down the stairs to
her room.

Petr had indeed, it seemed, packed up all
her belongings. Sarah unzipped her duffel.
Yep, all her clothes, neatly stacked. Even
her thongs had been folded into tiny tri-
angles. Sarah dumped the contents of her
backpack out on the bed, frantically riffling
through them.

And there, incredibly, it still was. The little
copper nose pillbox. Tycho's pillbox? Tycho's . . . nose? She slid the nose sideways
and opened the box.

There was something in it. A piece of

paper, the size of a fortune inside a cookie. Sarah opened it and recognized Max's distinctive handwriting.

2 a.m. Be SAFE

A warning? A recommendation?

No, Sarah realized. It was an invitation. Max was planning on breaking into Miles's safe tonight, or rather tomorrow. Two a.m.

Sarah decided the best place to hide an object was somewhere really dumb and ordinary, so she tossed the pillbox into the plastic zip bag where she kept all her bathroom stuff. As she jogged up the stairs, she tore Max's note into tiny pieces. *I should switch to coffee,* she thought, entering the kitchen. It was going to be a long night.

Twenty-Seven

She had dragged dinner out as long as possible, downing espressos while encouraging everyone else to drink up the Roudnice red, so that they'd all be sound asleep when she and Max began prowling. But she was the one who felt sleepy. It had been a long day, a long week, a long summer. She was exhausted, and the walls of the windowless room hummed gently in a very lulling way. She closed her eyes for just a second, then startled — had she fallen asleep? What time was it? She looked at her phone: 12:27. Better set the alarm, just in case.

Sarah tried to think. She thought about Sherbatsky and wondered what the professor had seen when he took the drug. The drug. Where did it come from? It was dangerous. It was wonderful. Max. Max thought someone was trying to frame him, and her recent interaction with Miles offered some proof of that.

Max. The drug. What was in that drug? She had traveled back in time . . . no. She stopped herself. Max had given her a scientific explanation for what she had seen — something about glial cells. Traces of energy, like the lingering impression of a lightbulb on your retina after you close your eyes.

Sarah opened her eyes. Alessandro had talked to her about glial cells. And the dark matter of the universe. She hadn't spoken to Sandro all summer, just a few e-mail exchanges to make sure he had paid the electric bill and that no one else had broken into the apartment.

Alessandro might be able to tell her more about glial cells. It was early evening in Boston. Sarah climbed out of the sub-basement, and made her way up to the roof of the palace, the best place for cell reception. People took cigarette breaks up here, and the view was spectacular. Sarah took deep breaths of the foggy night air, admiring the scattered lights spread out across Prague. The dark spires of the innumerable churches cut into the night sky like teeth. She walked along the roof, examining the different views of the city, feeling the night air, trying to get amped up for some safe-cracking.

It was strange how much the real city

looked exactly like the insanely precise cardboard model begun as a hobby in 1826 by Antonin Lagweil that was now housed in the Prague City Museum. Sarah had hoofed it over to the exhibition in order to get a good look at the city as Beethoven had seen it. Not all that much had changed since 1826. Less horse manure to wade through now, no doubt, but probably the same number of crazy-eyed marionette vendors. Down on the banks of the river she could just pick out the Rudolfinum, where Pols would play tomorrow. She could see the walls of the old Jewish quarter, and closer below her, the big Malostranská metro station with its crazy quilt of tram tracks around it. There was a bar there where one night she had been drafted into a multilingual Ping-Pong tournament that had almost devolved into violence.

She walked to the other side of the building and looked down into the courtyards of the castle complex, which also looked sort of fake, like the cheap 3-D paper models they sold in the St. Vitus gift shop. No one about except a lone figure crossing the courtyard carrying something large. Laundry, she thought. A big bag of laundry.

Her view was suddenly obscured by a thicker bank of fog, and she shivered, and dialed Alessandro's number.

As her phone rang through, she heard a warning beep. Shit, it was almost out of battery. Why hadn't she checked that? Now she would have to quickly say, "Hi, how's your summer? Can stimulated glial cells make you see traces of energy from the past? Oh, oops, I have to go."

Damn it.

"Ciao, bella! We were just talking about you!" Sarah could hear music playing in the background. It sounded like Bailey's recorder.

Beep, said Sarah's phone.

"Bailey come over to drop off mail from your office," Alessandro said. "I make him cocktail. He play me 'Merry Wenches A-Washing Their Wimples.' Very funny madrigal."

"Ha. Listen, do you have anything you can e-mail me about glial cells?"

"What?" Alessandro laughed. "What you say. Eels? Bailey, Sarah wants to know about eels!"

Beep.

"Sarah," said Bailey, who had evidently grabbed the phone. "How's Prague?"

"It's great. Loving it. Can you put Sandro back on?"

Beep.

"You have a letter here from Professor Sherbatsky," Bailey said, with a slightly more somber tone. "I guess he must have sent it before he . . . you know."

The hair on Sarah's arms stood up. Sherbatsky had written to her! Maybe it was about the location of the missing letter between Luigi and Prince Lobkowicz. Maybe it had to do with the drug, or Max.

"My phone's about to die," Sarah shouted. "Bailey, open the letter, okay? Read it to me. Right now, be quick."

"Okay, hold on."

Sarah looked at her watch: 1:15.

"Okay," Bailey said. "Here it is. Oh. It's just a doodle."

"A doodle?" Sarah shrieked, feeling a little hysterical.

"It's like a circle, with a dot in the center, and then a line with . . . oh, Alessandro is saying it's like something that's on your ceiling. Huh. Listen, you still want me to send it or should —"

The phone went dead.

The symbol that had been drawn on the ceiling. What was that about? As last messages go, it was a totally sucky one.

Sarah bent down and tried to trace what she remembered of the symbol in the gravel

of the roof. After a few minutes, she thought
she had it.

Sarah couldn't be certain, but she thought
that was the symbol she had glimpsed on
Max's cigarette case. Or was it the symbol
on the cigarette case that she was remembering? The brain did funny things.

Sarah stepped around the skylights and
over to the door to the stairs. She turned
the handle and pulled, but it wouldn't open.
She pulled again, as hard as she could. It
didn't budge. She realized in horror that
she hadn't blocked it open when she had
come out here, and it had locked behind
her. But hadn't she blocked it? There was a
little cast-iron dog that all the researchers
used to hold the door open. It was one of
those automatic gestures, like tossing your
keys on the hall table, so she couldn't be
sure she had done it. But it would be odd if
she hadn't. Well, the point was, she was
stuck on the roof. Crap. It was getting
colder by the second, not to mention that

she was supposed to be cracking Miles's safe with Max in forty-five minutes. Forty-two minutes, now.

Sarah walked around the roof, looking for another way down. There's always Sherbatsky's way, she thought with a shiver, unwilling to look over the edge. She peered down through the skylights into the third-floor workrooms, but saw only the faint glow of security lights, no one moving below. She walked back over to the edge of the roof, and noticed with relief that the figure she had seen earlier was crossing back across the courtyard, now minus the laundry. If she got his attention, she could get him to come up and let her down.

She whistled, but the figure was running, no doubt anxious to get home after a long day's work, and didn't stop.

The fog was making her thin black T-shirt wet, and she began to shiver for real. She leaned over the south wall of the roof and considered the scaffolding. Too far to jump. She could see little red dots among the beams that she hadn't noticed before. Cameras, she thought with a start. Was there a camera in Miles's office? Would Max know that? Had Andy installed them? She was not having trouble staying awake now.

She heard a nearby sound, almost underneath her feet, and ran to the skylight, peering down. Someone moving slowly, with a mop. She knocked on the skylight. The person stopped, looked around, not sure where the knocking was coming from. The woman — Sarah could see now that it was a woman — started mopping again. Sarah knocked again. The woman looked up. Sarah waved, not sure if the woman could see her or not. But the woman waved back, and shuffled off. Sarah heaved a sigh of relief.

A few moments later, the door opened.

"Thank you!" Sarah almost shouted. Her savior was a woman in her sixties in a long ragged cardigan, hair pulled back into a sleek bun. Her shuffling gait made her look older. Sarah followed her slowly down the stairs to the third floor. She stopped and looked back. There was no cast-iron dog doorstopper. Who had moved it?

"I am slow," said the woman, going one stair at a time. "Excuse me."

"No problem. I went out to make a phone call, and the door locked behind me," Sarah explained, following the woman down the stairs. "Thank God you came along."

"I am happy I can help you," said the woman. "I am usually alone here at night. Just me and ghosts."

Sarah smiled, thinking, *You have no idea.*

"Your English is very good," said Sarah. As Janek had explained at dinner, usually anyone over thirty had not studied English, since under the communists it was strictly verboten, or whatever the Czech word was for verboten.

"Yes," sighed the woman. "I was to go to America."

Sarah hesitated. She should really go and find Max and warn him that there was someone else awake in the building. But the woman seemed so lonely, and she had saved her. Sarah checked her watch: 1:37.

"Did you ever go?" asked Sarah. "To America?"

The woman shook her head. She shuffled back to her mop and bucket. Her gait looked so painful. She must have terrible arthritis, thought Sarah.

"I was dancer," she said. "Principal ballerina in the Prague National Theater Ballet."

"Wow," said Sarah. There was something regal and dancer-like to her posture, now that she mentioned it, despite the arthritis. "That must have been exciting." Sarah didn't really know much about ballet.

"Yes. But no, how you Americans say it, artistic freedom. We were going on tour, to

New York, 1978. I had never in my life thought of defecting. But that year, I think of it. There was boy, here in Prague. Jack, an American visiting his mother's family. We were both sixteen year old. My first love."

Sarah realized with a shock that the woman was not in her sixties. She was barely fifty.

"He tell me all about America. Teach me English. One day he say he find American woman in Prague who can help me. She can arrange things. I am nervous. I never see this woman, she work for your government, but in secret intelligence, I am thinking. Your CIA. I talk to her on phone. 'I will help you,' she say. 'Thank you,' I cry. I tell her I will never forget her. Every day, every breath, I will think of her. I suppose meet her on certain night. She will have papers and a car for us. We will get to Berlin. I tell no one. Not even family. That night after performance I am coming out of Lenin metro station. Now is called Dejvická. A black car come out of nowhere. Hit me. I fall to ground, screaming. The car stop. A man come over. He look at me. He see that I am mostly okay. 'Help me up,' I say. 'Please, I am okay.' I think I can still go to meet Jack. Then man grab my arms. Hold me. The car back up. He hold me while the car back over my feet. Both ankle. All bones crushed to dust. He get in car and drive away." Sarah stared at her, but the woman did not say anything more. She picked up her mop and swabbed the parquet.

"Did you ever see the boy again?" Sarah asked. "Did he know why you didn't show up?" Did the guy spend the last thirty-plus years thinking that a fickle ballerina had changed her mind and broken his heart, or was he the one who had ratted on her?

The woman shook her head. "I am out of ballet. Not allowed even to teach. My parents lose jobs. My aunts and uncles lose jobs. No one want to talk to me. I think I will die of starvation. But Yuri Bespalov, head of National Museum, take pity on me. He give me job here. I am lucky I work here many, many years, while it is state museum. Every night I make sure it is clean for next day's visitors. I scrape all the gum. I clean toilet. But I am worried now. Museum is private. Run by Americans. I am old woman, 'insurance liability' they say. I am afraid I will lose job. I have nothing. Please ask them to let me keep job."

"I'll do what I can," said Sarah. It sounded hollow. She was intrigued though, to hear Yuri Bespalov's name. He didn't sound like a KGB agent. He gave the poor woman a job. Maybe Pols was wrong about that.

"Thank you for saving me. I'm Sarah," she added.

"Stefania," said the woman.

Sarah looked at her watch. It was 2:07.

TWENTY-EIGHT

The hallway leading to Miles's office was nearly pitch-black. Sarah felt her way, sliding her hands against the wall. It was 2:15 a.m. The door, of course, was shut.

Sarah crouched down on her heels, trying to peer through the narrow crack between the door and the floor. No light. Sarah stood up and put her ear against the door, listening intently. Nothing. She pressed her ear harder, straining, holding her breath.

One small warning creak and then she was grabbed from behind, a gloved hand clamping down over her mouth, stifling the scream she didn't have time for. Arms held her tight. For a second Sarah thought she might actually pee from fright, but then animal instinct kicked in and she reflexively prepared for a countermove. Luckily, she also inhaled.

"You're late," breathed Max, into her ear. *You're lucky I know your scent,* Sarah thought. *Or you'd be minus a testicle right now.*

Max released her and flicked on a tiny flashlight, holding it under his chin and giving himself the traditional horror movie face. He held up a key and, rather unnecessarily considering the circumstances, a gloved finger to his lips. Sarah waited tensely as Max unlocked the door, opened it just wide enough for them to slip through, and shut it behind them, sliding the bolt shut. Sarah took a deep breath.

"Are you okay?" Max hissed, before Sarah could ask him the same question.

"Later," she mouthed. They had business to do. Max handed her a pair of gloves and another tiny flashlight. These were barely adequate. The office was even darker than the hallway. Sarah couldn't see Max, or, for that matter, her own gloved hand. She tried to re-create the office in her mind as she had seen it in daylight. She swung her light to the side, and caught a glimpse of the doorknob to a closet. Right. The safe was in the opposite corner, but between it and them was a desk, a chair, stacks of papers and boxes, and potentially a shitload of things made out of glass, china, or tenth-century bones. She reached out and found Max's back. "Let's work our way around by

303

the wall," she hissed, jabbing her penlight toward the closet. Max nodded and they inched over, barely daring to lift up their feet.

"Fuck it, maybe we should hit the lights," Max whispered, but then grabbed her hand. Sarah froze. She could hear it, too, voices outside in the hallway, and footsteps. And then Miles's voice, apologetically: "My office is a bit of a mess right now."

Sarah lunged for the closet door, praying like hell it was unlocked. It was, and Sarah had just enough time to shove herself and Max through, plunging face-first into a wool coat, as she heard Miles sliding his key into the outer door. Sarah twisted, reaching up to stop the coat hanger from banging into the wall, and knocked into the handle of something (a broom? A seventeenth-century rifle? A skeleton?). She just managed to catch it before it fell. Max, bent double beside her, grabbed her hair. Miles was coming in now, snapping on the overhead light.

Sarah turned her head. She hadn't been able to fully close the closet door behind them, but it was less than a quarter inch open. Enough for a little light to filter in. Enough for Miles's voice to be fairly clear, even through the pounding of her heart.

Enough for Miles to notice it was open.

"I keep a bottle of scotch here," Miles was saying. "Join me?"

For a wild instant, Sarah thought he might somehow be addressing them, behind the door, but then there was a grumbled assent, and the sound of clinking glasses. The squeaking of chair springs.

"Please, my friend," said an accented voice, which Sarah identified as belonging to the Czech scholar, Janek something, she had met at dinner. "This light is a little harsh for my old eyes. Would you?"

"Oh certainly," Miles replied. They heard the snap of the brass desk lamp turning on, footsteps dangerously close to the closet door, and then the overhead light went off. Now only the faintest of light made its way through the door crack. Sarah could hear Max's breath beside her. Like her heartbeat, it seemed incredibly loud. Max shifted his weight and to Sarah's ears it was like thunder crackling. *All it takes is one little squeak,* she thought. *And we are absolute toast.* She'd never be able to talk her way out of this. This was an unbelievably stupid plan.

Sarah held her breath, willing Max to do the same. Her ears strained to follow the conversation.

"I apologize again for disturbing you," Miles said.

"Nonsense. I slept most comfortably on the plane, and so I am now in the white night of jet lag. I was glad you called the hotel. But, forgive me, why so much secrecy?"

Sarah could hear Miles sighing heavily.

"I have something to show you," he said. "I didn't want to leave the palace with it. And yet, I don't want it here either. I need advice."

"Ah," said the old man. "You intrigue me."

"This isn't intriguing," Miles said sharply. "It's not some scholarly puzzle, Janek. I'm in over my head."

More sounds of movement. Was that the safe being opened? Now that her eyes were adjusting to the dark, she could see Max beside her fairly well. The closet was shallow, nowhere to hide and nothing to hide behind. There were boxes at their feet, some cleaning supplies, running shoes, umbrellas, a soccer ball. The sleeve of a coat dangled in Max's face. The soccer ball lay right next to his heel. They looked like cartoon characters, caught with their hands in the cookie jar, arrested. Their glances met. Sarah found it steadying, especially when Max released her hair and took her hand. He squeezed.

Hold on. Keep still.

Sarah heard the rustling of papers.

"I want you to look at this," Miles was saying. "Don't touch it. Let me turn the pages."

What followed seemed like an eternity of silence. They could hear absolutely nothing from the office but the occasional sound of a turning page, a clinking glass. Sarah felt a cramp growing in her calf. Her gloved hand inside of Max's grew hot. Her ear itched. The smells of the closet separated themselves into distinct entities: cardboard, orange disinfectant, mold, feet. The fear of coughing, sneezing, or farting grew so intense that she had trouble *not* doing any of these things. She clenched her ass cheeks and tried to take shallow breaths, which made it all worse. Beside her, Max swayed slightly. Was he falling asleep? Finally, she heard another deep sigh and then Janek's voice.

"So. I see."

"Do you?" Miles voice was urgent, anxious. "What do you see?"

"I see that these are love letters," Janek said, slowly. "From a woman to a man. The man is Russian; the woman, American. The man is evidently being very generous with objects of value, and the woman is being very generous with her body."

"The dates —" Miles interrupted.

"Yes, the dates. Well, the dates tell us that these two did not find their passion impeded by the brutality around them. The dates tell us that it is less than a decade since the scent of the martyr Jan Palach's scorched flesh hung in the air, as these two make arrangements for candlelit dinners. The dates tell us that Prague Spring is over and that our country is plunged into a winter that will last twenty-one years, but these two are not feeling the cold, no no."

"The man, she addresses him as Yuri . . ."

"Yes, and it would seem that Yuri has access to many things. Many priceless things. And the woman, too, she has maybe access. What kind of 'list' would an American woman submit to a Russian man in 1978? Names, she is giving him names. And a man who is able to give a woman a jewel-encrusted cigarette case in Prague, in 1978, this man must be a powerful man indeed."

"Janek?"

"Yuri Bespalov, it would seem," Janek said, heavily. "Head of the National Museum. I knew him, slightly. Almost certainly KGB, of course. But Miles, you can hardly be shocked by this. You, of all people, who must riffle through the attics of Nazis, and who must search under the mattress of every grubby little communist minister and his mistress to find what has been stolen? Surely you are not shocked to discover that a Party member gave a few trinkets to a lover? What is it that disturbs you? That this American woman is almost certainly a CIA agent? And not, perhaps, the most loyal to the red, white, and blue?"

"She doesn't say anything about —"

"She does not say, 'It is so neat, I am a turncoat spook,' no, I agree. She does not. Let us return to what we know. The receiver of these letters is called Yuri and he is important and in charge of a lot of precious objects and able to move freely in high political circles and provide much caviar and champagne and he is living in Lobko-wicz Palace, which is coincidentally the same place that Yuri Bespalov resided dur-ing his tenure, but let us not make too many assumptions. We do not have a name for the writer of these letters. She signs herself in a variety of interesting ways. I like particularly the reference to her hot, wet, dripping —"

"Janek," Miles snapped. "Stop playing games."

The two men fell silent and Sarah waited tensely, trying to process what she was hear-ing. She could hear Polis's voice in her ear, telling her to concentrate. Sarah thought of the woman — Stefania — whom she had just met. Stefania had said that it was an American woman who had pledged to help her. Possibly CIA. Names. The writer of the letters Miles and Janek were discussing had been giving names.

Once again Sarah locked eyes with Max, but he looked blankly back at her, shaking his head slightly. Sarah swallowed, then almost choked. Her eyes watered. Max clenched her hand, his eyes growing wide with alarm.

"You know who is the writer of these letters?" Janek was asking softly.

"I . . . I do yes. She is a very public and very powerful woman and she has been a friend to what we're trying to accomplish here at the museum. Janek, believe me, when she first contacted me about —"

"Please," Janek said, his voice rising. "Do not tell me the identity. Do not place me in that position."

"No, no, I'm sorry. I can't . . . I won't. Really I won't. You've been through enough in your life, God knows. But I'm in over my head here, and you're the only one I can trust."

"Where did you find these letters?" Janek asked, his voice softening a little.

"I didn't," Miles said. "One of my researchers found them. Eleanor Roland. She got the mad idea that maybe the fireplace in her room was functioning and started investigating the flue. These letters fell out. She's a good soul. She brought them straight to me."

"Are you positive of this? I met this woman tonight. She is excitable, an enthusiast. Perhaps she held on to them for a few days? Read them? Discussed them with others?"

"Every person here is under strict orders to bring everything immediately to me," Miles said. "From the beginning, I have insisted. *Everything* comes straight to me."

"Really?" Janek replied, softly. "Is that so? That does seem wise, of course. Such a large collection. So much opportunity for . . . loss."

There was another long pause. Sarah could hear more drinks being poured. Which made her dry throat ache. Her legs were strong, but the cramps were getting worse. Max, too, stuck in an even more uncomfortable position, looked like he was ready to topple over.

"How long have you had these papers?" Janek was asking now.

"A few days."

"And you are going to return them? To the writer? Or is this what you want advice about? Because you feel, you *know,* that a wrong has been committed. Perhaps many wrongs. Perhaps these letters are only the beginnings of a very dark and very dirty tunnel."

"Or not." Miles sounded almost desperate.

"Or not. Perhaps they are just the love letters of two foolish people. We have all been foolish."

"Janek?"

Sarah heard the sound of chair legs being scraped back, the thump of a glass upon the desk.

"I think," the old man said, "that I have dedicated my life to the preservation of documents of evil. I think that there are crimes for which there is no proper punishment. I think — and this is an old man's thought — that the less we have to accuse ourselves with, the less frightened we are of the place that awaits us all. I think those letters must get out of your possession very soon. I think that I do not wish to be involved. And now I think that I am finally tired, and should go to bed."

"Forgive me," Miles said. "I'm ashamed of myself. We didn't . . . this conversation never happened. I don't know . . . I don't know what's come over me lately."

"Let us call it Prague," Janek said, somberly. "It is a city of secrets and dark whisperings, my friend. Even you are not immune. You must think this over very carefully, but I cannot advise you. This is a matter for your conscience."

More silence, then at last Miles's voice, tired but resigned.

"I know what you are saying. Tomorrow, I will . . . well, tomorrow." Sarah heard more chair squeaking and what sounded like the safe being shut. "I'll let you out and then I have decisions to make."

"Ah, yes. And tomorrow I will return to Nelahozeves and my hunt for the intrigues of some eminent dead people. You see, I am not immune either. But it is safer, I think, to read the love letters of those whose crimes are long forgotten. Ghosts, my friend, are very quiet."

Sarah thought she might actually pass out, the relief was so great. Miles and Janek were leaving, they were walking out of the office! She and Max had not been caught!

She thought about what she had heard. An American woman, CIA, had an affair with KGB agent Yuri Bespalov in the 1970s, and had become a double agent herself.

313

That woman, Miles had said, was now very public, very powerful, and "a friend to the museum." And she was looking for the letters Eleanor had found.

"Miles said he was coming back," Sarah whispered. "We need to get out of here."

Max was already opening the closet door and pulling her with him. They sprinted down the hallway. They heard a door slam close by. Someone called out in Czech. Someone answered. Was that Miles's voice? They ran down the stairs, almost falling, and sprinted down a passage. Max turned a corner, slipped down more steps, pulled her through an absurdly short door and into another hallway. Sarah had no clue what part of the palace they were in, until suddenly she realized they were in front of her own bedroom. Max opened her door and they fell in, shutting the door behind them and leaning against it, gasping for breath.

Sarah's windowless room was even darker than the office.

"Are you okay?" Max wheezed.

Sarah shook her head, then realized he probably couldn't see her.

"You?"

"I'm okay," Max whispered. "What do we do now?"

"My goodness, what have you been up

to?" said a familiar bassoon voice, from somewhere behind them in the room.

Sarah scrabbled around the wall till she found the light switch. Nicolas Pertusato was sitting cross-legged on Sarah's bed. Even more disturbingly, he was wearing Sarah's "Beethoven Rocks" T-shirt. Sarah shut her eyes. The little man was not wearing pants.

TWENTY-NINE

Calling him "Nicolas" felt a tad formal under the circumstances. "Nico," hissed Sarah, "for God's sake put some pants on." She averted her eyes only after noticing that the tiny man had more than tiny parts. Rather largely-out-of-proportion parts, actually. No wonder his wife looked so happy. "And then you can explain what you're doing here."

"I would be happy to clothe myself," said Nico with a grin, "except my hands are tied. Literally." He nodded over his shoulder, and Max and Sarah looked sideways at each other.

"Rock paper scissors?" said Max.

Sarah gave Max a look. She tossed a towel over Nifco's exposed lower half and Max went over to the bed and began wrestling with the ropes that bound the little man's hands to the bedstead.

"Mille grazie," said Nico, flexing his arms

and shoulders and pulling the towel around himself. "I'll be troubling you no longer."

"Uh-uh," said Sarah, cringing at the thought of Nifco's junk on her pillow. "Explanation. Now. Or we'll tie you back up again."

"I could demand the same of you two. It's almost three in the morning."

"Talk," said Sarah. Her tone made even Max sit up straighter.

"I was taking a bath," said Nico. "Rather enjoying a nice long soak. You were so kind, Max, to give me a room to sleep in here for late nights although Oksana complains —"

"Cut to the chase," said Max.

"Someone came into the bathroom. I said *'occupation,'* but before I could turn around, whoever it was knocked me over the head. Look."

Sarah and Max saw that Nico did indeed have a large purple goose egg on the back of his head. Sarah touched it and he flinched.

"It's real," he said crabbily.

"Don't you lock the door when you take a bath?" asked Sarah.

"What's the fun in that?" said Nico. "Anyway, I woke up here, naked and tied to the bed. Thanks to a summer in Siberia with a team of performing acrobats, I was able to maneuver my way into your T-shirt. I made a valiant effort to get into your pants, but they were out of reach. Now, what is *your* story?"

"We were out for a walk," said Max. "Meteor shower."

"You share so many of Tycho Brae's interests," said the little man. "Though *his* dwarf was rather a sourpuss, I understand."

"Could you tell anything about the person who hit you over the head?" asked Sarah, trying to suppress the vision of someone throwing a wet, naked, unconscious Nico over their shoulder and hauling him fireman-style all the way down here. "Male? Female?"

"Alas," Nico said. "I know nothing. It is not often that I am taken by surprise. It's actually quite thrilling. One gets so bored."

"Why grab Nico and leave him here?" asked Sarah after they had sent Pertusato on his way.

Max shrugged. "A message? A warning? A joke, like the cross? No one would hear him scream from here. But they had to know you weren't in your room."

"It doesn't make sense," Sarah agreed. "Earlier tonight *someone* locked me out on the roof. *Someone* got really tired of waiting for Nico to finish his bath and dumped him here. The same someone, or are we being invaded by a mischievous army?"

"Let's focus on the letters," said Max. "What's all that CIA stuff?"

Sarah thought about the dancer Stefania, who'd had her legs crushed. And about Andy the spy. Spying for whom? The CIA? Or someone else? If he knew the letters were in Miles's safe, then it seemed likely that his death was connected to those letters. And to whichever prominent ex-CIA agent was now hunting for them.

"Can you trust Max?" Pols had asked. *"Or are you just in love with him?"*

"Did you tell Miles to fire me?"

Max looked shocked. Really shocked? It was hard to tell.

"Of course I didn't," he said. "You don't think I would try to do that, do you?"

No. Maybe. No.

Except you lied about that letter from the Hotel Gritti Palace. And what's between you and your cousin Elisa? And how is she wrapped up in all this?

Sarah shook her head, then looked over at him. "What were you hoping to find?" she asked. "In Miles's safe?"

"Any clue as to what the hell is going on," sighed Max, heading out the door. And once again, Sarah knew he was lying.

THIRTY

Sarah's first move in the morning was to call Pols. Jose answered the phone.

"We're exhausted," he yawned. "All of a sudden, *bam.* Pols, she tell me she want to stay in hotel and practice. Me, I want the room service. But Boris no like anyone strange coming into room."

"Perfect," Sarah said. "I think Pols should rest as much as she can before the competition. We wouldn't want anything . . . anything to go wrong."

After all the talk of CIA spies roaming the palace, Sarah was now well and truly paranoid.

Is anyone listening to my phone? Do you hear me? You touch that kid and I will destroy you.

Magically, Jose seemed to pick up on her thoughts. His next words came loudly and with careful pronunciation.

"Oh yes, she want to practice and rest.

Then we go to competition. Then we go home. Her mama and papa want to make sure that she safe and sound and get back to Boston right away. And I no want to upset such powerful people, of *course.*"

Not bad, Sarah thought. Polis's parents weren't especially powerful even among the bohemian trust fund set, but at least if someone was listening they would get the idea that the girl was only here to perform and leave.

"I wish she could see a little more of Prague," Sarah sighed theatrically. "Well, not see, of course, but experience. She's so interested in all the old history. She told me she had tried to look up something online about the American-Czech Cultural Alliance but her voice-activation thingy was screwing up and sending her to random sites."

Work with me, Jose.

"Oh yes," Jose sighed. "She complain about this. We are not so good with computers, Pols and me. So we get book on Bohemia from library. Much better. Bye, Sarah. We call you later."

Her anxiety about Pols's Internet searches somewhat abated, Sarah slipped out to do a little searching of her own. She didn't want the things she was looking for to show up on her own computer, using the palace server.

"Know where I can get Wi-Fi?" she asked the Sexy Stabber. When he failed to respond, she made her way down Thunovska and eventually found a funky restaurant with Miles Davis posters on the wall and a bank of computers.

Who was a prominent and powerful American woman who was ex-CIA and would have been in Prague in the 1970s? Superspy Robert Hanssen and feminist icon Gloria Steinem showed up when she googled that. Hanssen was out by gender, and Steinem's time with the CIA was too early for 1978 hijinks.

Sarah sighed and listened to Miles Davis riff for a moment. Something else was in the back of her mind. Pols had said something about a photo of Elisa and Senator Charlotte Yates. Elisa wasn't American, and anyway she was the wrong age. But Yates was certainly prominent. Could *she* be the Spy Who Loved Yuri? Feeling slightly ridiculous, she googled "Charlotte Yates." There was the Wikipedia entry, the Senate website, and a bunch of news items. Charlotte Yates had an honorary doctorate from Virginia Tech, had been various journals'

322

and organizations' Woman of the Year (most recently the *Ladies' Home Journal* Woman of the Year for upholding family values). She was unmarried and apparently considered something of a catch, except as the most powerful woman in the Senate she intimidated all potential lovers and needed a sexier haircut, according to *Us Weekly.* God, the press was horrific.

An article in Italian about the Venice poisoning caught Sarah's eye. Charlotte Yates was mentioned in passing, something weird about black food. *Fuoco* was in the headline, which Sarah knew meant "fire." She had Google translate the article for her, which was an imperfect science. "People dead gondolier say yell fire," said the article, or rather the computerized translation. Sarah was startled to see there was a quote from someone referred to informally as *La Lobkowicz,* who was crying tears of relief that she had left the party early. Marchesa Elisa Lobkowicz DeBenedetti. Max's cousin. So she had been at the event.

Sarah clicked on another article about the poisoning, this one in English. Senator Charlotte Yates had accompanied home the body of a prominent American who had been killed in the terrorist poisoning at the fund-raiser in Venice. Al Qaeda had taken credit for the attack. Yates of course denounced their brutality and called for those on the side of right around the world to rise against them.

Sarah could find no photograph showing Charlotte Yates and Elisa together, and no connection between them at all, although she did find the same site that Pols had found, saying that the senator served on the board of the American-Czech Cultural Alliance . . . the board that had been influential in working with the Czech government during the restitution process. A board that Marchesa Elisa Lobkowicz DeBenedetti would have had a great interest in influencing.

And then there it was. Right there on the Charlotte Yates Wikipedia page. *Charlotte Yates worked at the CIA briefly in the 1970s.*

It did not give any further details.

Sarah looked around, then quickly clicked off the computer and sat back to think.

It was purely circumstantial evidence. Sarah certainly had no proof that Charlotte Yates was ever in Prague, or that she was a double agent, or even an agent at all. She might have just been a low-level policy analyst working in Washington. But in her gut, Sarah felt that Pols might have been right. Or nearly right. Pols had been trying to warn her that Marchesa Elisa was enlisting the help of the senator in order to get to the Lobkowicz fortune. But maybe it was the other way around. The senator wanted to install the marchesa as heir to the fortune in case those letters surfaced. Perhaps it was Senator Yates who was pressuring Miles to make Max seem unstable. It was unclear how much Elisa knew about her powerful friend and her motives for helping her try to regain her family's lost treasures. What Sarah felt certain of was that if Charlotte Yates had been a double agent, she would kill to get her hands on those letters.

Sarah slipped back into the palace, unable to stop herself from looking back every few steps to see if she was being followed. She tried to slow her heart rate as she shut the big door behind her. She must go to breakfast with the other academics. She must act normal. God, she was dreading Eleanor's chirpy chatter. But at least it would cover her own distracted silence.

Fortunately it was very quiet. Suzi was doing a crossword puzzle. Bernard was sewing seed pearls onto a costume for the masquerade ball. Daphne was methodically dismantling a sausage. Nicolas was fully clothed, and reading a hardbound ancient copy of *Orlando Furioso*. Fiona Upshaw the Delft expert was examining a map of Prague, and Godfrey was hanging over her, making suggestions. Moses Kaufman was forking eggs into his mouth while reading bits of the *Herald Tribune* out loud. Douglas, who never missed an opportunity to brush up against Sarah, offered her a plate with a lusty, "Sausage?"

"Coffee," she said, firmly. Suzi poured her a cup without looking up.

Max entered with Moritz and began engaging Godfrey in a conversation about wild boar. Godfrey responded enthusiastically. Max did not meet her eyes.

Sarah tried to put her thoughts into some kind of order. Who was missing this morning? Janek. Miles. Eleanor. The same three people who knew the contents of the letters.

"Anyone seen Miles?" asked Douglas. "I need to have a chat about how to hang the Crolls. I insist on being well-hung," he said with a knowing grin at Sarah. Max took a savage bite of toast.

"Miles took an early plane to Washington," said Daphne with a possessive tone. "Family emergency."

Fuck, thought Sarah, not looking at Max. Washington. Her suspicions about the senator tripled. Was Miles giving the letters back to their owner, then? And if so, was that the end of the story? Charlotte Yates would get her evidence and all would be peaceful in the palace? Was she obligated, in some moral sense, to tell what she knew? What did she know? What proof did she have?

"I hope Miles is back for the costume ball," Suzi said. "Bernie made him a Ladislav costume."

"Ladislav's the one in yellow?" asked Moses Kaufman. "The one with the key stuck in his puffy pants?

Daphne sighed as if they were all idiots. "Yes. Ladislav was Zdenek's brother. He plotted against Rudolf II and died in exile." Sarah remembered the painting now. There was something sinister about Ladislav, who had his cape tossed casually over his shoulders like a movie star, his hand on the hilt of his sword and a large medallion around his neck.

There was another question troubling Sarah. How much of what she had figured out should she share with Max? What did Max know about his cousin?

"If Miles doesn't make it back in time, I'll be Ladislav," said Max amiably.

There was a ripple of reaction around the table. They weren't used to Max being friendly to their schemes. Everyone, Sarah realized, was wondering what it meant. And so was she.

Moses turned to Max, his thick Buddy Holly glasses flashing in the morning sun just beginning to stream through the windows. "I found something yesterday. Since Miles isn't here, I suppose I should give it to you? It might interest you, if you're going to be Ladislav. I'll go get it."

Moses left the kitchen. General conversation about the costume party continued. Douglas was planning something special for the music. Godfrey wanted to know if it was okay to invite locals; he had become friendly with some members of the Czech Department of Wildlife. Fiona asked Bernie if he might help her with her costume, but Bernard shook his head, frowning over his piece of embroidery.

Moses returned with a small wooden box. He opened the box and produced a large golden key. It glimmered, and every eye in the room was drawn to it as he held it out to Max with a smile.

"I found it in a compartment in the ebony altarpiece that Rudolf gave Polyxena and Zdenek as a wedding gift," he said. "It looks like the key in Ladislav's pants, doesn't it, Daphne? From the portrait? Although I hardly think it can be the same one. You should get a replica made for your costume, Max. This one's kind of heavy, although it's not actually gold. I think it's lead, covered with gold paint."

"That," said Daphne, "should be locked in Miles's office now. Ve should all be giving vatever ve find to Jana. And you should be vearing gloves."

"I'll give it to Jana," said Nicolas. Sarah noticed his outstretched hand trembled slightly, and his eyes were glittering. Max stood up and reached for the key. He exchanged a look with the little man.

"You should be wearing *gloves,*" Daphne said, almost spitting.

Nicolas turned to her. His bassoon voice was low but unexpectedly harsh and Sarah was surprised at the anger in it.

"The key is the property of the Lobkowicz family. You will remember that everything in this palace is the property of Maximilian Lobkowicz Anderson. He can touch whatever he wants, however he wants to. You will be quiet."

Daphne stalked from the room.

The room was silent.

"What's a four letter word for 'steinbock'?" Suzi asked, after a moment.

"Ibex," said Godfrey.

They were all still watching Max.

"Thank you," he said simply to Moses. "It's probably an old house key, but I'll check the database and have it sent out for dating." He turned to address the silent academics. "If you find anything new, please bring it to Jana or myself. And for the record, I have turned the majority of my . . . my family's castles and properties over to the local governments where they are situated. Nelahozeves and Lobkowicz Palace will become museums. When Roudnice is restored it will be leased to film companies and the revenues from these may provide employment for many people, including many of the people in this room. Good morning."

He left the kitchen, with Nico close at his heels.

But he still put the key in his pocket, Sarah noticed.

"Shee-it," said Suzi.

"He is correct," Fiona said in her clipped voice. "This is a private museum, not a government one. It is all his personal property."

There was a brief silence as everyone absorbed this.

"It's hard to remember," Godfrey said, peacefully. "All of this belongs to one man."

And it doesn't seem right, Sarah thought. *And we're all thinking it.*

But she was curious about the key, and Nico's reaction to it. Every item in those family portraits was important, signified something, Daphne had told her that. What did the key signify? Or was it really just an old house key?

Nothing in Prague was that simple.

"I need some air," she said. "Anyone want to take a jog in the Deer Moat?"

A few minutes later, she found Max, as she somehow knew she would, loitering by the Toy Museum, his arms full of papers. He unclipped Moritz's leash and the dog disappeared in the direction of the Deer Moat. They started walking together. At this early hour, the castle grounds were still empty.

"The last time all the windows were glazed was when my grandfather had it done in 1937," Max said, nodding at the papers he was carrying. "It's going to be expensive."

She brushed her hand against him. Max looked at her and narrowed his eyes. Sarah wasn't sure she could trust him, but she was sure about some other things.

Max pushed her into a stone alcove.

The way his breath moved the hair around

her ear was just too much to take.

"Hopefully I've established my credentials if we get caught again," Max said.

He pulled her skirt up and shoved his hand under it. His look of triumph at how wet she was made her want to slap him. Who did Max think he was?

"They open the gates for the service workers in eight minutes," said Max. Sarah unzipped his fly. He was already as hard as she was wet. He pushed her against a bronze bas relief of St. Catherine being martyred on the wheel and put one hand under her left thigh, lifting it up and inserting himself into her in one motion. She groaned, desperate to feel his skin, running her hands under his shirt along his back, pulling him as deep inside her as she could. St. Catherine dug into her back. She felt a surge of satisfaction as Max's list of windows fluttered to the ground.

Six and a half minutes later, they were once again on their way toward the front gate. Sarah's legs were a little wobbly, but she felt amazingly refreshed and no longer irritable. Even Max's whistled rendition of "Fly Me to the Moon" didn't annoy her.

The sun was making the stained-glass windows in St. Vitus's glow as if there were a bonfire within.

"Uh-oh," said Max, looking up at the windows. "Hang on." He dashed back for his dropped list. "My windows."

When he returned, he glanced around and then started speaking quickly and quietly.

"So, I was actually waiting out here to tell you something, before you decide to jump me again."

"Oh please," Sarah said, haughtily. "You are the one who keeps shoving me up against statues at all hours of the day and night."

"Lucky for me there are a lot of statues around." Max grinned, wolfishly.

"So what were you wanting to tell me?" Sarah asked. She could see service workers at the gates now. "Is it about the key that Moses found? I thought Nico seemed kind of amped about it."

"What? Oh no." Max frowned. "Nico gets excited about anything shiny. It's about these." Max waved the drawings. "When they reglazed the windows in 1937 there were 518 of them. Now there are only 517."

They walked along in silence for a beat. *A missing window.* Like the children's book from fourth grade. For Cindy and Sally the missing window meant only one thing: a secret room. Max had been in her fourth-grade class. Would he remember the children's book? She was sure he would have no idea what she was talking about, but for some reason she couldn't bring herself to ask.

"The 6th Prince Lobkowicz walled off part of a room at Roudnice," said Max. "During the Silesian Wars. His library was walled off for thirty-six years. The occupying army never knew it was there."

"Maybe your granddad did the same," Sarah said. "Maybe he walled his library up here, before the Nazis came."

"And with the threat of the communists, he would have left it walled up even after he was back in the palace in 1945. And been glad it was walled up when he fled in 1948. And never told anyone about it. Sarah, listen. Do you remember that book, from the fourth grade?" Max said. "You probably don't. It was about —"

"Remember?!" exploded Sarah. "I've been looking for that book my whole life."

"My grandfather wrote it," said Max. "He had only a few copies printed up, just for the family. I brought it in and gave it to the teacher to read."

Sarah tried to process this.

"But the kids in the story . . . Cindy and Sally . . . they were American."

"I think . . ." Max worked it out in his

mind. "It was a message to his descendants, in case we ever got back here . . . Trying to tell us there's a hidden room in the palace."

Max was already turning back toward Lobkowicz Palace. Moritz ran up and rejoined them, tongue lolling.

Sarah grabbed Max's arm. "Do you still have a copy of the book? I never got to hear how it ended. Because, you know . . ." Sarah was horrified. Her eyes were filling with tears.

"I'll find one for you," Max said, pulling out one of his ridiculous handkerchiefs.

And then a shrill scream punctuated the quiet morning. There were shouts coming from the second courtyard.

It's not over, thought Sarah. She and Max began to run.

They came around the corner of St. Vitus and ran through the arch into the second courtyard just as the first security guards and vendors were arriving from the other direction. There was a fountain, but that wasn't what was catching the workers' attention. A few paces from the fountain was the ancient well Eleanor had pointed out that first day, with its huge ornate metal cage. Sarah had always thought the cage was large enough to hold a person, and now she had her proof.

A woman's naked body, caked with blood, hung from the hook suspended in the cage. The courtyard became a blaze of activity as security guards began shouting into their radios.

Sarah was trembling, and felt sick. Max had tried to grab her, to shield her.

But Sarah had seen the face of the woman in the cage. It was Eleanor.

THIRTY-ONE

Charlotte Yates reached for her jewel-encrusted cigarette case. She was up to a six- or seven-straw-a-day habit now. A sign of stress. Really, though, people were acting so stupidly. It was disappointing. It was dreary. And yes, it was a little stressful. She was woman enough to admit it.

Take Miles, for instance. Miles was a boor. Did he think he could stand morosely in plain sight on Charles Bridge at five-thirty in the morning with a briefcase under his arm and *not* be spotted? He was lucky her agent didn't push him into the river, a time-honored Czech tradition, as she recalled. Of course it would have been better for him if he had tossed the briefcase over, if that's what he was thinking. Instead, he added foolishness to foolishness and took himself to the airport. Her agent followed, presumably along with whomever the Russians had assigned to watch the hapless Miles. Didn't the man have a masters in art crime? You would have thought he'd have picked up a few ingenious ways to smuggle over the years. One supposed he was opting for the "hidden in plain sight" school of intrigue. Well, security at Ruzyne Airport wasn't going to blink twice at a sheaf of letters, but what exactly was he thinking, booking a flight to Amsterdam? Was he planning on hiding her letters at his little Dutch girlfriend's apartment? Clearly Miles wasn't firing on quite as many pistons as she had thought. It was a good thing the letters had been found now, before things got really complicated. The body count was still at a manageable number, but it wasn't like she could devote endless hours to this project. She had a country to covertly run, for Christ's sake.

There had been some confusion at the airport as a Russian agent had attempted to intercept Miles on his way to the KLM ticket counter. Luckily *her* agent was a former decathlete.

Miles had been gently persuaded against a flight to Amsterdam. She hoped he had enjoyed his flight to Washington. Naturally she had given her agent instructions that Miles be put in the coach section. She was a Republican, after all! First class was for friends, lobbyists, and donors, not lily-livered minions. She had given her agent instructions that Miles wasn't to have anything broken, but it can't have been too comfortable not being allowed to go to the bathroom for eleven hours. You just never knew what people might have down their pants, and she had told her agent: no mistakes. Of course, the agent could have simply relieved Miles of his briefcase back in Prague, but it was better this way. Charlotte liked to employ the personal touch.

It was irritating that Miles thought he could cross her. Her! This was what came of wearing fake glasses and eggplant-colored pantsuits. People started to think of you as unthreatening. Moderate. Empathetic. It was like during her Senate campaign, when she'd had to compromise by adding caramel highlights to her hair and getting a couple of bichons frises. Oh, it was all such crap, but you had to give the "voters" these sorts of tokens or they'd never get over your being intelligent *and* a woman. Charlotte briefly wondered what happened to those dogs. What were their names?

Miles was waiting outside her office now. He'd been waiting for two hours. They'd let him use the bathroom, poor dear, since the video surveillance in the johns here was excellent. You could even zoom in. Which is how she knew that Miles wasn't very impressively endowed, although she should be charitable and allow for some shrinkage. Fear could do that to a man, and he had had eleven hours on a plane with a gorilla-sized agent breathing pretzels in his face.

Charlotte gnawed her straw. Truth was, now that her letters were within her grasp (right outside her office!) she was feeling a little dizzy with relief. And the memories were flooding back.

Oh, Yuri. What a lover he had been. She remembered making love standing up in a shadowy corner outside the palace one night, some forgotten piece of statuary jabbing her in the back as Yuri held her by the throat, muttering Russian words of endearment. He had given her the hammer *and* the sickle, by God. Charlotte crossed her legs. They just didn't make them like that anymore. Nowadays she was lucky to get some mild flirtation from some leather-faced NRA lobbyist. Forget about doggy-style on an eighteenth-century canopied bed by a certified KGB agent who said things like "beg for it, my little Yankee poodle."

What were the names of those stupid dogs? Lucy and something? She was distracted.

All right. Time to bring the ship into port. Charlotte folded her mangled straw into a tissue and tossed it away. She picked up the phone and buzzed Madge.

"I'll see Mr. Wolfmann now," Charlotte said sweetly.

"Yes, ma'am. I will show him in." Madge sounded relieved. Miles was probably sweating all over the furniture.

"*Send* him in, Madge. Don't show him in."

"Yes, Madam Senator."

Charlotte remained seated. She picked up a folder from her desk and pretended to be absorbed.

"Shut the door behind you," Charlotte said, without looking up from her papers. She listened to the sound of the door click and Miles clearing his throat. At one end of her office was a sitting area, with a fireplace, and there were two comfortable leather chairs facing her desk. Miles was treading water on the carpet in the middle of the room, clearly uncertain as to where to go. From her peripheral vision, she caught sight of a brown briefcase clutched in his right hand. Charlotte resisted the urge to leap over her desk and snatch it away. Timing was everything. She let Miles cool his heels for a minute, then two, then three.

Finally she looked up, casually. Miles was ashen, and needed a shave. His suit was rumpled. There was a dark stain on his tie.

"Have a seat," Charlotte said, neutrally, not indicating one.

Miles shuffled back and forth on the carpet and finally decided on one of the chairs in front of her desk. Charlotte closed her folder and watched him impassively until he was seated. He held the briefcase in his lap, like a dog.

"Madam Senator," Miles began bravely. "I'm not sure what exactly is going on here but —"

"Well, Miles," Charlotte said, pleasantly. "It's lucky for you that *I* know what's going on, isn't it?"

She let him digest that for a minute. She didn't want to ask him to hand over the briefcase. She wanted him to offer it to her. She wanted him to remember that he had *given* her the letters. He would not be able to say that he had been *forced*, or any of that nonsense.

"You look a little tired." Charlotte gave him a fractional smile. "If you had informed me beforehand of your travel plans I could have arranged a more comfortable flight."

"I felt it best to act quickly," Miles began, with an admirable attempt at professional sangfroid. "I had only just come into possession of the . . . the papers. I made a quick survey of them and determined that they were the ones you had commissioned me to . . . put aside for you. I placed the documents in my safe. Certain events at the palace of late made me feel that my own computer and cell phone might be compromised. I determined that it was best if I simply delivered the documents to you in person. I did not want to risk their exposure, or misplacement."

Charlotte nodded sympathetically. She had wondered what sort of story he was going to come up with. Still, he held the briefcase in his lap. She noticed that his knuckles were white. There were beads of sweat on his upper lip.

"I thought I might have been followed," Miles continued. "To the airport. In order to throw my pursuer off, I decided to pretend to book a flight to the Netherlands. My plan was to try to lose whoever was following me in the crowd, then double back and find a flight to Washington."

"Goodness," Charlotte said, mildly. "This is all sounding like one of those spy novels. You took considerable risks."

"With all due respect, Madam Senator," Miles said softly, "I think you know more about taking risks than I do."

Charlotte narrowed her eyes.

"Is that what you think?" Charlotte drummed the nails of her right hand sharply against her desk. She didn't appreciate the implication one bit. An off-the-record joke or two about the old days with a couple of five-star generals or the Secretary of Defense (darling Todd, he ate out of her hand) was one thing, but she wasn't going to allow Miles Wolfmann that kind of latitude. Perhaps it was time to remind him of the carrot, though, before she started employing the stick.

"Well, I certainly appreciate the eagerness with which you have fulfilled your commission," Charlotte said, crisply. "I know you've been most anxious to secure a position as director of the Smithsonian, and as we discussed earlier, I think that is about to become a very real possibility. I take it you are still interested in the job? The post will be vacant in three months and will need to be filled quickly. I wouldn't want to recommend someone who wasn't interested. Especially when I know how *seriously* my recommendations are considered."

"Actually," Miles cleared his throat, "I've been offered a permanent position as head of the Lobkowicz Collection. It's a very attractive offer."

"I'm glad you think so," Charlotte smiled. "I thought you'd be pleased. I thought you would enjoy saying no. I've always found it empowering, myself."

"Oh." Miles blinked.

"Naturally" — Charlotte shuffled some papers on her desk — "if you prefer to stay in Prague that's entirely your decision. I should tell you, though, that under those circumstances I won't be able to extend your current level of . . . protection."

"Protection?" Miles swallowed and shifted in his chair.

"I'm afraid your suspicions were correct," Charlotte sighed sadly. "You were followed to the airport. Luckily my man was able to get to you first and escort you here safely. Naturally I didn't want to expose you to any unpleasantness when you've done such a thorough job of looking after the restitution of all those lovely little Czech goodies. I understand there's to be quite a glamorous unveiling of the family holdings in September. I'm attending myself, did you hear? I could use a vacation."

She could practically see the little cogs of his brain turning.

"I'm a little surprised that you are considering staying on. I should have thought the directorship of the Smithsonian was somewhat more alluring, but of course if you've changed your mind . . ." Charlotte let her words trail off.

"Protection?" Miles asked again. "But, now that you have . . . I mean . . . I thought this would be the end of it all."

"It ends when I say it ends," Charlotte said, evenly. "And not before. I think it ends with you in a corner office at the Smithsonian and a budget that would make the Lobkowiczes green with envy."

"I . . ." Miles fumbled.

"How is the little prince, by the way? Your reports seem to indicate that you've found him slightly difficult to work with. And the Sarah Weston girl, too. I suggested you find a way to get the girl away from Max, break the whole thing up. Really, it can't be that hard. The Weston person seems to have a knack for getting herself arrested."

"I tried, but she's clever," Miles said defensively. Then he looked up at Charlotte nervously. "But she's not . . . she's not dangerous. Just ambitious. I think she's hoping to make her career with some kind of breakthrough in Beethoven scholarship. And Max is probably just hoping to get hold of something he can sell off on the sly. He's looking for something. Some family possession."

"Something that's not on the list?" Charlotte found herself mildly interested in this. She thought she knew about all the really good stuff.

"He and Nicolas Pertusato have been digging around," Miles said. "And before, when Absalom Sherbatsky . . . there's . . . I think it has something to do with Beethoven. But I can't figure it out."

"Hmmmm."

"I'm sure it's nothing," Miles amended hastily, looking even more green. There was nothing like a guilty conscience. It was better than fear for making people rat out their friends and colleagues.

"Well, I assure you the position at the Smithsonian will be far less . . . sticky," Charlotte said, with a show of sympathy. "If there's one thing I understand it's how important it is to have room to do one's work properly. Can't have a bunch of amateurs looming over your shoulder. Or Russian agents, for that matter. Pesky things. They always seem to want something. Even in these days of friendship and transparency." She enjoyed watching Miles chew over this last bit.

"You said . . ." Miles's voice was shaking

and he stopped for a moment. Charlotte glanced at her wristwatch. Really, how much of her time was he going to take? The letters! They were three feet away! She was the chair of the Foreign Relations Committee. For God's sake she could start a fucking *war* if she felt like it.

"You said that they were *personal* letters," Miles said.

Charlotte really hated whiners.

"And that's what they are," Charlotte said. "They are my personal property."

"I'd like your assurance, your word," Miles bleated on, but Charlotte wasn't listening. She could see his knuckles relaxing around the briefcase. Hers. They were almost hers. All she had to do was clear up a few details and get Miles out of her office.

"You have my word," said Charlotte, once Miles stopped blathering on. "Yes."

She stood up. Miles stood up. He placed the briefcase on top of her desk. Charlotte, exerting all of her self-control, flicked it open and picked up the stack of letters. *My God,* she thought. *They're really mine. No one can touch me anymore.*

And they were all there. One letter a week for three months, although the affair had lasted longer. She had resisted committing anything to paper, but Yuri had worn her down and she had been so very much in love. He had been able to make her do anything. Charlotte had a brief vision of her twenty-three-year-old self, crawling across the floor of Yuri's bedroom in the palace wearing nothing but a garter belt, high heels, and a rope of pearls that had belonged to the 8th Princess Lobkowicz. "If you sit on my face," Yuri had said, "then you can keep the pearls." (Of course it had sounded better in Russian.)

"As a matter of interest" — Charlotte tossed the treasured packet back into the briefcase as if it was scarcely worth pursuing — "who found the letters? And where?"

"I did," Miles said. "One of my researchers turned over a piece of cabinetry and I found the letters in a false drawer."

"How interesting," Charlotte said. "What a lucky find."

"Everything goes through me," Miles squeaked. "That was the system we agreed upon. But yes, I'm surprised they were found so soon. The library at Nelahozeves is huge and it's a mess. The work of a lifetime, if not two. It was just sheer chance that I found them when I did."

"Oh, well, they're not so important really," Charlotte laughed, feeling drunk. "Just some old silliness from my youth. Sentimental value. But with the Internet and twenty-four-hour news cycles it's getting so difficult to have any kind of private life. Some things need to stay personal, don't you agree?"

Miles looked like he was ready to pass out. Well, good. She was getting anxious, too. She needed a straw. She needed to be alone with the letters.

Miles was trying to make up for his earlier cowardice by shielding Eleanor Roland. Of course she knew who had found the letters. In the flue of a fireplace! So old-fashioned of Yuri. What a romantic!

The marchesa's minion had turned out to be useful with that bit of information. Although Elisa had really overdone it with the elimination of Eleanor. Really, the marchesa was so . . . Italian.

"My cell phone?" Miles was asking, tentatively. "The . . . um . . . escort took it from me? I've been out of touch for a whole day now."

"Of course," Charlotte soothed. "Sometimes they are a little overzealous, but I understand it's all standard operating behavior. I think everything will be absolutely smooth from now on. I'll have your phone delivered to you in the car. Please allow me to have you driven back to the airport, and you'll find a comfortable seat on the next flight to Prague. First class, of course. Thank you so much for all your terrific work!"

Charlotte was especially proud of the "terrific." It struck just the right kind of chipper, down-to-earth, ordinary-gal tone that her jackass handlers were always pushing her toward. She'd have to remember that during the presidential campaign. "Terrific." Charlotte steered Miles toward the door. She'd think about what to do with him later.

She had the letters. Miles was in her pocket in ten different ways, which was reassuring. Now just a few odds and ends to clean up.

She needed to talk to her friend over at NSA. This friend had kindly alerted her when some unusual activity on a search engine site came on the grid. Apparently her name had been run along with the words "Prague," "Lobkowicz," and "CIA." Probably just another amateur conspiracy-theorist, but her NSA friend had done a routine swipe through IP addresses anyway, just to be safe. You had to do this kind of cleaning regularly, like going to the dentist. The computer used for the search was licensed to an eleven-year-old blind kid in Boston, of all things. A hacker? Well, Charlotte had asked her friend to run a background on the girl, and she should check on those results.

No, there were still things to do, but the circle was narrowing. The list was getting shorter. It was like the old days, when you could draw a line through a name and . . . poof . . . that was the end of it.

Lucy and Desi! Those were the names of those ridiculous little dogs! Success was giving her a new clarity. She patted Miles on the back and handed him over to Madge.

"Madge," she sang brightly, scaring the hell out of her secretary. "Let's make sure Mr. Wolfmann gets a souvenir pen." *God bless America,* she thought, shutting the door.

THIRTY-TWO

"Suicide?" sputtered Sarah in disbelief.

Shuziko shrugged, helplessly. "The police went through Eleanor's room and found a note." Suzi took a sip of her beer. All day long they had wandered about the palace in a blank-eyed state of shock, picking half-heartedly at their work. The Prague Castle complex had been sealed off and Eleanor's body was removed from the cage near St. Vitus Cathedral. Some sort of *CSI: Prague* crew had arrived. As Eleanor's employer, Max had gone off to talk to the police, muttering something about hoping different cops were on duty than when he had been hauled in for violating St. George two nights earlier.

As they had sat down for dinner, Godfrey suggested they have a moment of silence for Eleanor. Bernard wept noisily through this. Even Daphne looked shaken. No one knew what to say and yet it was impossible not to talk about it.

"It makes even less sense than Dr. Sherbatsky." Godfrey shook his head.

"That was the musicologist? Who was a bit off?" Fiona asked, looking at Suzi, who nodded slightly and glanced at Sarah.

"Two suicides in one summer." Moses took off his glasses and wiped them sorrowfully. "I can't believe it."

"Sherbatsky was a different case," Douglas Sexton said. "The man was a drug addict and a total nutter. Of course I sometimes thought Eleanor was a bit off, too."

"She vas a very nice, very conscientious woman," Daphne said, severely. "It vas not her fault that her subject vas insignificant."

"She didn't kill herself because her Ernestines were *insignificant,*" Suzi snapped. "She *loved* those poor old gals."

"What did the note say?" asked Sarah. She was not buying the suicide for one second and couldn't believe anyone else was. Who crawls into a cage and kills herself? Eleanor was just not that weird. But then again, none of the other academics knew what she knew. Eleanor had found the letters between Charlotte Yates and Yuri Bespalov. And someone had killed her for it.

All day Sarah's mind had been working in circles. Who knew that Eleanor had seen

354

the letters other than Max and Sarah? Miles. Janek Sokol. Anyone else? She thought about Marchesa Elisa, but she had not made an appearance at the palace since Sarah's arrival.

She thought about the lone figure she had seen hurrying across the courtyard.

And she thought about Senator Charlotte Yates.

It was nearly time to leave for the concert. She had called Pols several times during the day, and each time Jose had assured her that Pols was fine, was practicing or meditating.

Sarah had not wanted to distract her with the bizarre events at the palace. The girl was already in too deep.

A banner above the stage of the Rudolfinum pronounced the evening's event — the 32nd Annual International Youth Piano Competition — in a multitude of languages. Sarah saw in the program that the five competitors ranged in age from eight to fourteen. Besides the American Pollina, there were Russian, Japanese, and Chinese boys, and a North Korean girl.

Each year the competition focused on a single composer, and this year it was Beethoven.

Of course, thought Sarah, feeling slightly

355

persecuted by old LVB.

Seated in the orchestra section, Sarah looked at the tense faces of what she presumed were parents, extended family, coaches, mentors, and agents all around her. Clearly, there was a lot riding on this for these people. For the North Korean kid, maybe more than most.

The competition consisted of two rounds. The children would play a Beethoven piano sonata of their choosing in round one. Then they would be knocked down to two contestants. The finalists would play the same piece, for the victory.

Sarah decided that the 32nd Annual International Youth Piano Competition wasn't really all that different from *American Idol.* She felt horrible that the shy and reclusive Pols was subjecting herself to what would surely be an ordeal, just because she felt she needed an excuse to be in Prague.

Or because she was scared for her safety, too?

She wondered what Miles was doing right now. Handing the documents over to Charlotte Yates? Being strung up somewhere and pounded by CIA agents? Although she no longer trusted him, she hoped he hadn't been stabbed and left to die somewhere like poor Eleanor. Miles had gotten in over his head. And what was Eleanor? Collateral damage? Sarah shuddered. It was such a gruesome public display. Maybe that was the point. The blood and gore were a warning. *Back off or you're next.*

What could she do? Miles and Janek had both seen the letters, and it had seemed as if Miles was maybe intending on doing the right thing, but now he was in Washington. It seemed clear to Sarah that someone acting on Charlotte Yates's behalf had killed Eleanor and almost certainly Andy, too. But who would listen to her? And unless she had proof, someone would end up in prison, but it wouldn't be Yates. The task seemed impossible.

Sherbatsky was dead, too, though Sarah had trouble accepting that Sherbatsky's death was tied to the senator's search for the incriminating letters. She knew it had something to do with the drug. The drug and Max.

Max was looking for something. What was it? He seemed to trust her with certain things — like the possible existence of a secret library — and not with others.

For right now, she tried to focus on the competition. She looked at the program again. These kids had astounding résumés, and each of them had won a major competition at least once before. Pols had never even entered one. Sarah realized with a sinking heart that Pols did not stand a chance. The other children were trained, polished performers, and had been since they were three or four years old. Pols was a genius who rarely left the house, and played only to entertain herself, Sarah, and Jose.

The coordinator of the event came out and did the usual endless thank-yous, and introduced the members of the jury. The last name almost made Sarah shoot out of her seat.

Marchesa Elisa Lobkowicz DeBenedetti.

Sarah craned her head and looked up into the box where the jury members sat. The fat guy in Brooks Brothers was definitely Larry Stegner, from Juilliard. The Asians. A couple of Czechs in poorly tailored suits. That left a deeply tanned woman in a skintight satin sheath and Hermès scarf. She had the kind of unapologetically excessive glamour that only European women can pull off. Sarah saw the glint of diamonds around her neck and thought her nose could pick up the scent of the marchesa's perfume, even from her seat in the orchestra section.

Sarah riffled through her program, which merely said that Marchesa Elisa Lobkowicz DeBenedetti was an international expert on

Beethoven. Huh? An international expert on Beethoven? How come this was the first she'd heard of it? And possibly a close personal friend of Charlotte Yates. And possibly romantically involved with Max. And now here she was in Prague. On the same day that some very nasty and mysterious things had happened.

Feeling distinctly unsettled, Sarah focused in on the program, which was now beginning.

Beethoven had written thirty-two piano sonatas, all of them brilliant. Sarah was impressed by the choice of the North Korean competitor. Sonata No. 4 in E-flat Major, op. 7, was a monster of a piece, dynamic, complex, and in the first movement sort of a bitch-slap to Mozart.

It was strange to hear it played by an eight-year-old girl. Luigi had dedicated the sonata to his pupil, Countess Babette de Keglevics, and in the subtly erotic second movement Sarah had to close her eyes, to block out the fact that it was being played by a child, even a technically brilliant child.

Next up was the Russian boy, who played Sonata No. 5, op. 10, no. 1. Sarah closed her eyes and let the heavy chords of the exposition vibrate through her. The piece was full of heroism undermined by strains of fear and hesitation, which sort of worked for a little kid performing in the world's most prestigious competition. It was disturbingly good.

Finally, it was Pols's turn. Sarah leaned forward, applauding as Jose, dressed in a classic black tuxedo, led Pols, who was in red velvet, out to the Steinway. Pols settled down on the piano bench, took a deep breath, and launched into Sonata No. 23 in F Minor, op. 57. As she navigated the first of the three movements, Pols played with an increasing amount of verve that began to make Sarah nervous. People in the audience were blinking in surprise as she played as if she were possessed, her hair flying, her eyes closed. The unanswered questions Beethoven had laced the sonata with, the unstable chords, the power, grew and grew.

Sarah found herself holding her breath for the resolution, and when it finally came she leapt to her feet — along with half the audience — and applauded wildly. The other half remained seated, clapping politely, but there was a murmuring undercurrent of disapproval running through the hall. Pols had definitely gone out on a limb, although Sarah felt it was a limb of true genius.

She found Pols backstage during intermission.

"It's the way Beethoven meant it," said Pols, looking a little pale after her exertions. Boris, in his service dog capelet, leaned against the girl, offering his massive shoulder for support.

"I've never heard you play it like that before," Sarah commented.

"No," said Pols, as Jose wiped the sweat from her brow with a hankie. "I could feel him better here. That's what he was urging me to do."

Sarah did not doubt her. It made perfect sense. Beethoven went through harpsichords the way other people went through tissue, and this piece would have been unplayable on the instruments of his day. Pols had done Luigi proud.

"Well," said Sarah. "You definitely carved out some new territory for yourself. Personally I thought it kicked ass."

Sarah took Jose aside as Pols drank a glass of water.

"Go straight back to Boston tomorrow morning," she whispered. "There's been a brutal murder at the palace." Jose blanched.

"Make sure Pols doesn't talk about the Lobkowizes to anyone," Sarah said. "It's not safe. Keep a very close eye on her. Like, not out of your sight."

"No one get through me," said Jose. "But

if they do, no one get through Boris."

There was a hush in the audience when the president of the symphony came out to announce that the finalists were . . . Pols and Yevgeny Andropov. She had made the finals! The North Korean girl's supporters were flushed and angry, talking loudly among themselves and gesturing toward the jury. Sarah hoped no one would be shot when they returned home.

A hush fell over the audience. The piece that Pols and the Russian kid would both play in their duel to the death was Opus 111, Beethoven's last piano sonata, which some considered his finest. It was dedicated to the Archduke Rudolf, Beethoven's patron and pupil. Sarah thought about the three Rudolfs and their strange fates. Rudolf II, who had gone crazy and lost his empire. Beethoven's Rudolf was a distant relative in the far-flung Hapsburgs, and an epileptic. The third Rudolf, for whom the theater was named, had died at age thirty in 1889 in a bizarre incident at his hunting lodge. He was in love with a young woman who was not his wife, and rather than give her up, he shot her in the head and then turned the gun on himself.

This was Prague. Every stone here seemed to have some kind of story, and most of them involved blood or people going crazy. Maybe that's why the rest of the academics seemed willing to accept the story of Eleanor's suicide. All summer long they had been steeped in similar tales of passion and violence. And now that she had taken the drug, Sarah knew that passion and violence *were* really all around them. Flickering beneath a surface of the present that was unbelievably thin . . .

Suddenly the audience burst into applause, and Sarah realized she had zoned out during the Russian kid's entire performance. Now it was Pols's turn.

Sonata No. 32 in C Minor, op. 111 is in two parts only, an unusual enough structure that Beethoven's publisher wrote to make sure the copyist hadn't accidentally left out the third movement. As far as anyone knew, Beethoven did not deign to respond. Sarah felt a stab of grief and longing as she remembered Professor Sherbatsky lecturing on the work, quoting from Thomas Mann's *Doctor Faustus,* where the fictional music teacher explains Opus 111, stuttering and shouting that "in the end art always throws off the appearance of art."

The first part is meant to portray the world as we know it, full of struggle and hardship. The second movement is filled with unbelievably beautiful transcendence, an escape to an almost supernatural place of peace, reconciliation, love. Sarah was hearing the music with new ears, feeling its mysticism and power.

If Pols had played with verve before, now she was a whirling dervish, her hands barely visible on the keys. The tension was almost unbearable; her thin arms hardly seemed capable of the ferocity with which she was playing. And then the second movement began. Sarah's heart swelled. It was right, it was right. This was how it was supposed to be. Perhaps this was what Pols meant when she talked about God.

As she played the final chord, Pols slumped across the keyboard, apparently unconscious.

THIRTY-THREE

The doctor wanted to take Pols to the hospital for observation, and Sarah was more than happy to accommodate this, but Pols had insisted that she just needed to sleep. Sarah, not wanting to upset the girl further, agreed to take her back to the hotel if Pollina promised to see a doctor back in Boston.

"I didn't win," said Pols, sadly.

"I think you won," said Sarah.

Sarah left Pols resting at the hotel with a large bowl of chicken soup with dumplings. Jose was on guard with orders to open for no one. Apparently he had packed a bowie knife in his checked luggage. Sarah looked at the serrated edge and hoped for the best. Boris placed himself across the doorway to the little girl's bedroom.

"Show me your teeth," Sarah said.

Boris bared his fangs and gave her an understanding look.

When Sarah returned to her room at the palace, she found Max waiting for her in the hallway.

"Let's go to my office," he said, in a low voice. Sarah followed him.

Moritz, the Czech wolfhound, raised his head from a large and extremely ratty-looking dog bed in the corner. A stuffed lion, with the heraldic two tails one saw about Prague, was nestled between his enormous paws. Sarah went over to pet him. Moritz sniffed Boris on her hands, seemed to find the scent simpatico, and went back to gnawing his lion.

Sarah sat down in one of Max's leather chairs, warily.

"Eleanor was shot in the head," Max reported. "The gun was in the netting at the base of the well. Her fingerprints were on the trigger."

"You don't believe she killed herself," Sarah said. "You heard what Miles said. Eleanor found those letters that Miles and Janek were looking at."

"I have a theory," Max said. "Listen. What if the woman in those letters was Eleanor herself? She's the right age. She could've been in Prague in the 1970s. She could've been working here undercover as an art historian. She *was* an art historian. She had an affair with a KGB agent and he gave her things from the palace in exchange for information. She came back here to look for the lost letters. She was at Nela. She could've killed Andy. Maybe he was working undercover for the CIA, looking for the letters, too."

"But then why would she have turned them over to Miles?" Sarah said. She wanted to tell him about Charlotte Yates, but she hesitated.

"People do strange things," Max sighed. "Maybe she couldn't stand the guilt anymore. Maybe she was giving herself up."

For a minute Sarah wanted to believe this theory. It was certainly easier than believing that an American senator was taking hits out on people at the palace. Her mind raced back over the details of the day at Nela. Had Eleanor recognized Andy Blackman in his disguise as a Czech policeman? They had been working all afternoon in the library together, but she hadn't actually seen Eleanor during the afternoon, and they had only communicated intermittently. There were so many strange details. Sarah watched Max's dog lift his toy up in his jaws and make neck-breaking movements.

"Whose Chihuahua was that?" she asked, suddenly.

"What Chihuahua?"

"The one at Nela when Eleanor and I met you there. It bit her."

"Oh," said Max. "He belongs to Elisa."

Sarah's eyebrows went up. "Marchesa Elisa Lobkowicz DeBenedetti?"

Max nodded.

"She was at Nela the day you and I met there?"

"Yes," he admitted. "Well, she had just left, actually."

Sarah chose her words carefully, while trying to sound ten percent as emotional as she felt.

"So on the day that Andy was killed, Marchesa Elisa was at Nela and could have been responsible for any or all of that and you never felt the need to tell me about her?"

"It didn't seem that significant at the time," said Max, sounding defensive. "My cousin's not capable of killing anyone . . . unless they stole her front-row seat at a fashion show."

"So you know her very well." *Do you know that she's in Prague right now?*

Max walked over to his office wall, where

a large family tree hung. Sarah wondered what it must feel like to see your entire lineage back to the 1400s all charted out. Max pointed to the lower area of the tree.

"Her grandfather and my grandfather were brothers. Hers was the black sheep of the family. When my grandfather went to England during World War II, her grandfather went to Italy and married an Italian countess."

"And she's a Beethoven expert?"

"Expert's a stretch. She's very good at insinuating herself into any high-level gathering. She collects powerful friends. She has a historic palazzo right on the Grand Canal, and she invites people there constantly — movie stars, politicians, fashion designers. Her profession is to be fabulous." He said it with scorn, but in a way that Sarah did not find convincing.

Sarah digested all of it. It almost made sense in a very terrifying way.

But no.

Her mind clicked over names, dates, places, details. Old blood. Secrets. Power. Money. And more power. She was not crazy. For the first time since arriving in Prague, Sarah felt maybe she was ahead of the story instead of behind it.

The marchesa, with her connections in

Washington and her fondness for collecting powerful friends, was almost certainly the senator's eyes and ears — if not gun- and knife-wielding hands — in the palace. She had a bone to pick with the family itself, her grandfather having been cut out of his inheritance in favor of Max's grandfather. To the marchesa, it must be painfully clear that all this could have been hers. And much of it still could be, if she played her cards right.

Max did not seem to notice that his cousin had motive, means, and proximity to all the strange goings-on. Sarah couldn't just do the full Oprah and sit side by side with Max on the couch, starting with, "Honey, I think your cousin is trying to kill us all." She would have to think this through so as to convince him she hadn't lost her mind. She would have to prove it to him. And she needed proof about Charlotte Yates's connection to Yuri Bespalov. Just being in the CIA was not enough. The senator might have the letters, but there might be some other way to prove her involvement. Some trace . . .

"I want to take the drug again," said Sarah.

"There isn't any more," said Max, returning to his desk.

"What do you mean?"

He opened an ornate music box on his desk, slid back a false bottom, and showed her the secret compartment.

"I've been keeping it here, but someone's emptied it. Nico, maybe, but he won't say."

"That was it?" she said. "Can't we get more?"

"I don't know," Max said. "I really don't."

Sarah sunk onto a chair, realizing all the things she would do if she could have one more tiny sliver of the drug that allowed you to see the dead, to watch them going about their lives. She could have moved through time just enough to see Eleanor's murderer, or Yuri Bespalov's lover. She could have seen Beethoven.

Her father . . . if she took the drug to Boston, she could have seen her father again.

Max sat down next to her on the sofa. It made her uncomfortable, to have him so close. It fucked with her judgment.

"I found the hidden room," Max said. "It's a library. Want to see it?"

THIRTY-FOUR

"It was pretty easy," Max said, modestly, fanning a sheaf of architectural drawings out across his desk. "You remember the missing window I found? Well, I just searched around until I found earlier renderings of the palace and compared them with current ones. Here it is."

Sarah stood up and joined Max behind his desk. His finger traced rectangular lines and pointed to a tiny line of script in the middle of the rectangle. Max handed Sarah a magnifying glass and she leaned in.

$$\boxed{\textit{Library}}$$

"What's a library doing in the basement?" Sarah asked.

"Especially when there was already a library aboveground," Max agreed.

"So, how do you get to it?" Sarah asked.

Max covered the older drawing with the current architectural layout.

"You see," he explained, "the 'library' was sectioned off later into two rooms. This other one was used for storage. And maybe to help conceal the library. Like a kind of decoy. It's the only other room in the palace without a window."

Sarah looked at Max.

"My room doesn't have a window," she said.

"Bingo. Your room is the threshold into the library." Max grinned.

"Great," Sarah sighed. "So we bulldoze my room tonight? Or do the Lobkowiczes keep a couple of battering rams lying about?"

Max pulled out another sheaf of drawings and splayed them across the desk.

"Much simpler," he explained. "There's a tunnel below these rooms. Below that whole wing of the palace. I know this because we had to do a major pest control survey and it was recommended that these tunnels get sealed off." Max blinked up at her. "Rats," he said. "Rats like you would not believe. Rats the size of dogs."

"If you think I am burrowing into a rat-infested tunnel," Sarah said firmly, "you have truly lost your mind."

"The rats are gone," Max said hastily. "I think. Or I hope they're gone, anyway. We couldn't use poison. It was actually pretty disgusting. But anyway there are two un-sealed exits to the tunnels. You will have to crawl. Or, if you are Nicolas, stoop."

"You sent Nico into the tunnel?" Sarah couldn't help laughing. "Well, I guess he does have training from the summer with the Siberian acrobats. If the man can wiggle into my T-shirt while tied to my bed, he can manage a simple tunnel."

"That was my thought exactly," said Max, grinning. "Apparently there are a couple of breaks in the ceiling of the tunnel, with lad-ders leading upward. Trapdoors in the floors of the rooms above. You remember that your room was once part of the dungeon?"

Sarah shivered. She wasn't likely to forget. A wave of nausea passed through her. The smell of vomit, of shit, of fear. The scream-ing.

"Nico made a map of where the ladders are."

Max took a piece of transparent paper and smoothed it over the architectural render-ing.

"Right here. Right under where the library is, or was, is a trapdoor," Max said, trium-phantly.

"Which Nico went into?" Sarah asked, taking a deep breath and replacing the horrid smell of the dungeons with the smell of Max's skin. Sarah resisted the impulse to bury her face in his neck.

"It's locked," Max said.

"Of course it's locked," Sarah snorted impatiently. "It can't be that easy. Everything here is locked, or chained, or walled-up, or impaled or stabbed or pushed out of a window." For a moment she felt like crying. Poor Eleanor. Poor Sherbatsky. No. She didn't need to cry over Eleanor. Or her beloved professor. Or Stefania, the shuffling prematurely aged dancer who had rescued her from the roof. Or the various pawns who had been used and discarded by agents of greed and power through the years. Tears wouldn't help them. Sarah searched around for a word that would restore her to herself. Justice? Not quite powerful enough. Vengeance? Yeah, that was pretty good. But Sarah knew that deep down the thing that was driving her had nothing to do with exposing Charlotte Yates, or solving the murders, suicides, or disappearances of a rising number or people. No, it was the sense that at the end of all these dark turnings and twists there was an answer waiting for her about something else entirely. Something that Pols would understand. And maybe, if she trusted him, Max, too.

Beethoven.

"Don't look so sad," Max said, breaking into her thoughts. "Nico said the lock is old and he thinks it wouldn't take much to break it at this point. There might be something above the trapdoor, though. A piece of furniture, a bookcase. It's definitely going to be a two-person job."

"Nico's probably breaking in as we speak," Sarah said. Max shook his head.

"He's on assignment."

"Assignment?" Sarah raised an eyebrow.

"I have him keeping watch on the hotel where your little friend is staying," Max said simply. "He'll stay with her until she's safely on a flight out of Prague. Too many bad things have been happening lately. Nico understands what's at stake. He won't let anything happen to her."

This touched Sarah so deeply that she felt like it was time to come clean.

"There might be . . ." Sarah hesitated. "There might be more at stake than you realize."

Max looked at her gravely, leaning back in his chair and folding his arms, looking so much like the photograph of his grandfather Max above him that it was as if the picture had slipped out of its frame. They wore the exact same inscrutable expression.

Men with secrets, Sarah thought.

"So tonight?" she said, hedging. "Tonight we break into a secret library?"

"Tomorrow morning," Max corrected. "Nine a.m., when the construction crew gets started and there'll be a lot of noise."

"And in the meantime?"

Max waved a book at her. "I've got some reading to do. This one's about your favorite Lobkowicz: the 7th."

"When I . . . when I was on the drug. I saw him," Sarah said. "I saw his face. I heard him speak."

"I've seen him, too," Max said, quietly, shutting the book. "I went hunting with him, actually."

"I think you need to tell me about the drug," Sarah said. She looked across the room to where Max was standing. It was too dark to see his face, but she could sense him frowning, thinking.

"When my grandfather left Prague in 1948, he had nothing but the clothes on his back," Max said. "That's the official story, and it's true, as far as I know, but he wasn't absolutely destitute. Grandfather Max was a patriot, but he wasn't a fool. There were some investments, friends, connections.

Still, can you imagine? Having to leave behind a family fortune and collection that was begun in 1592. Abandon everything, totally, with no hope of ever getting it back?"

"I can't imagine it," Sarah said, honestly.

"Yeah, well, I think I'm only just beginning to," Max sighed. "I don't know. Maybe he felt sort of relieved, in a way. It's a lot of responsibility. I can't even throw away an old moth-eaten pillow because maybe it once propped up the 6th Princess Lobkowicz's head or some damned thing. Maybe it was woven by a master of the lost needlepoint style that some academic will jizz over and I need to build a special temperature sensitive display case for it."

"Heavy is the head that wears the crown," said Sarah. Max laughed softly.

"Anyway, Grandfather Max left Prague with two things. His hat and a cigarette case in his pocket."

"Is that the same cigarette case you have?" Sarah asked. "With the weird symbol on it?"

"When my dad died the lawyers gave it to me," Max said quietly. "Said my father was supposed to give it to me when I turned twenty-one. My mother's instructions. But he hadn't. He basically considered me to be a huge fuck-up. The end of the Lobkowicz line. A total disappointment to my mother's memory. And look what's been happening around here. I'm probably the laughingstock of Prague."

Sarah couldn't help it. It wasn't her style, but she reached out and found Max's hand. He laced his fingers into hers.

"Anyway, now I have the cigarette case. Grandpa Max's prized possession. He didn't smoke," Max continued. "Apparently he just carried the empty case around. Only it wasn't empty. There was an envelope inside."

Sarah found herself holding her breath, waiting.

"Toenail clippings." Max laughed. "Fucking toenail clippings. I almost threw them out. But I don't know. Something made me . . . anyway, that's where the whole thing started."

"Where what started?" Sarah asked. "I don't get it."

"Sherbatsky," Max said. "He wrote to me and asked if he could come and look at the musical collection. Of course, his credentials were impeccable. He was clearly the best man for the job. He'd been here for a few weeks and then one day he came into my office and showed me a letter he'd found. From Ludwig van Beethoven to Joseph Franz Maximilian Lobkowicz. There's the

379

usual money talk and complaints. And then a reference to his toenails."

"His toenails?"

"The infernal tricks of my body have subsided, for the moment. But strangely I find that the nails of fingers and toes grow apace. Can this be an effect of the elixir that we shall not name? I confess it frightens me. I send you some examples, which my servant with her usual clumsiness has severed from my person," Max quoted.

"Are you serious?" Sarah sat up.

"Well, that was the gist of it anyway," Max answered. "And I laughed and said, 'Oh, maybe that's what the toenails were. Grandfather Max left Prague with his hat and Ludwig van Beethoven's toenails.' "

"But . . ." Sarah sputtered. "Wouldn't they . . . be, like, totally decomposed by now? Or biodegraded or whatever?"

"Yup," Max said. "Toenails are keratin. I looked it up. They shouldn't . . . I mean it's strictly impossible. Unless whatever elixir Beethoven was taking had something in it that altered their molecular structure."

"So you're telling me the pill I swallowed shaped like a toenail . . . ?"

"Was actually one of Ludwig van Beethoven's toenails?" Max said. "Um. Yeah."

Sarah, for the first time in her life, felt

herself utterly and completely at a loss for words.

"It was Sherbatsky's idea," Max went on, hurriedly. "After I told him about the cigarette case, and the whole story, he went kind of ape-shit. Said he had been tracing all these mysterious references between LVB and the 7th prince to some kind of drug. Something the prince had given him and that Sherbatsky thought had affected Beethoven's hearing."

Sarah thought back to the strange vision she had experienced. What was it that Prince Lobkowicz had asked Beethoven?

"Is it working?" the prince had asked. *"Can you hear me?"*

"But the drug makes us move through time," Sarah argued. "And Beethoven wasn't moving through time. I saw him take the drug, or some kind of drug. I got the impression that it made him hear."

"Heightened perception." Max nodded. "Yeah, that makes sense. But we weren't taking the pure drug. We were taking, you know, toenails of someone who took the drug a couple hundred years ago. It was polluted. And we're not moving through time, you know. We're just seeing things. It's hard to know if it's all real."

There had been something else. Something the 7th prince had said to Beethoven after Beethoven took the pill. What was it?

"A toast to Brahe." Yes, that was it.

Tycho Brahe. The astronomer who had served at the court of Rudolf II. Tycho Brahe, who was, among other things, an alchemist.

"I thought it was totally ridiculous." Max was still talking. "But we did a bunch of research. First we found out the symbol on the case was some kind of alchemical thing, and Sherbatsky convinced me that there really might have been something going on. I suggested we send the toenails off to a lab, to be tested. I gave the job to Nico. Who evidently decided to keep one and pass it on to you. God knows why."

"So what did the lab results come back with?" Sarah realized that although Max was speaking calmly, he was gripping her hand very hard. Or was it hers that was clutching his?

"It was . . . strange," Max said. "Traces of keratin, like you might expect, but a whole bunch of other things. Silver. Myrrh. Elk bone, if you can believe it. And things they couldn't really identify. 'Might be this, might be that.' 'Very similar to.' 'The presence of this is quite surprising.' That kind of thing. Believe me, the last thing I thought of was to actually ingest a toenail. That was all Sherbatsky. He had talked to some neuroscientist who pointed out that certain chemicals can't be flushed from the body: They just settle into the cells. Sherbatsky had all these theories about glial cells, too, and perception. And when he told me what had happened when he took one of the things . . . the visions that he had . . . well, I decided to try it for myself."

"That's what you were doing at Nelahozeves with Sherbatsky," Sarah said. "Douglas told me that he thought you and Professor Sherbatsky were doing drugs."

"Well, he wasn't wrong," Max said. "We thought it safer to experiment there, at first. I didn't want Absalom tripping here at the palace. And also . . . I had reasons of my own for wanting to be at Nela. My mother was born there, actually."

"That's what you were hoping to see, wasn't it," Sarah said. "Sherbatsky was trying to find Beethoven, but you were looking for your mother."

"I've seen photographs of her there," Max said. "She died when I was so little. I just wanted to see . . . her face, I guess."

Sarah nodded. She knew what that felt like.

"But I never did see her," Max said. "I

saw the 7th prince a lot. Some other things. Strange things. And then Sherbatsky wasn't satisfied, he wanted to do the drug here, where Beethoven had been more often. I think that's what happened. He was tripping, wandering around the palace, but not the palace as it is now. There have been changes. There used to be a little gallery that connected one wing to the other. It's not there now. And that's how the accident happened."

"And so Professor Sherbatsky thought he was crossing a bridge," Sarah said, "and stepped out of a window instead." For a moment, grief overwhelmed her. She looked up at Max, and saw that he was grieving, too.

At least now she understood. There was some kind of closure. Sherbatsky was not murdered, had not committed suicide. His death had been an accident.

"There wasn't much left of the . . . toenail, drug, whatever, at that point," Max said, after a long moment. "And now it's all gone. Maybe it's for the best."

"What about the report that the lab sent?" Sarah asked. "Do you think that whatever was in Beethoven's toenails could be . . . recreated?"

"Not from the lab test," Max said.

"There're too many unknown variables. But I can't help thinking that somewhere . . . a formula exists. Written down somewhere. Hidden. I don't know."

"In a walled-off library?" Sarah asked, trying not to sound too eager.

"We don't have a lot of time to get our sleuthing in," Max said. "This place is going to be crawling with Secret Service in two weeks."

"Secret Service?" Sarah froze.

"For the opening of the Palace Collections on the fifteenth," Max explained. "The chair of the Senate Foreign Relations Committee is coming. Charlotte Yates."

THIRTY-FIVE

As soon as she was awake, Sarah called Jose. He told her they were stopping by the Church of Our Lady Victorious on their way to the airport. Sarah was relieved to hear Nico was with them. With Marchesa Elisa lurking in Prague, having already been in the same room with Pols, they couldn't be too careful.

She checked her watch. Plenty of time before the planned hidden library hunt. She raced out the back entrance of the castle complex and down the steps into Malá Strana.

Outside the church, she spotted Nico standing sentry by a small door, smoking a cigarette.

"Thank you for watching over her," said Sarah. Nico nodded.

"I don't like to go inside holy houses before noon," the little man said. "It upsets my stomach. But they are safe in there. My friend Sister Teresa is giving the hundred-crown tour."

Sarah stepped inside the narrow door and followed the sound of a woman's voice, clear and bell-like in the otherwise silent church. "In 1631, the monastery in Munich was destroyed and the Miraculous Infant was thrown on a trash heap where it lay forgotten for seven years . . ."

The church was decorated with typically nauseating baroque excess. The altar dedicated to the Baby Jesus was especially tricked out: gold, flowers, candles, and a special glass case for the Infant doll. It had on a snazzy blue number. Daphne had informed them all that the Carmelite nuns had a sixty-outfit wardrobe for the little guy, including a wee undershirt so the Nuns couldn't see His naughty bits when they changed His clothes.

Pols was standing with her head bent, praying. Then she handed the nun an envelope and stood back as Jose crossed himself reverently at the altar.

"Pols," Sarah said, softly.

The girl reached a hand forward and Sarah took it. They began walking up the nave. The nun, who had evidently opened the envelope and seen what Sarah was sure was a very large check, followed them murmuring thanks and blessings.

"It's not him," Pollina whispered to Sarah.

"What do you mean?" asked Sarah.

"That's not the real Infant."

Sarah blinked. "How do you know?"

Pols looked impatient. "I just know."

On the street, Sarah lingered. Pollina often resisted hugs, or physical contact, but this time she allowed Sarah to put her arms around her, gently.

"I'll pray for you," said Pols.

"Thank you," said Sarah, wondering what the rules were when the pure of heart prayed for the nonpure. Suddenly the girl gripped her tightly. Sarah was surprised at the strength in her thin arms.

"And stay close to Max," the little girl whispered.

As the car pulled away and she looked back up at the castle, there was a distant rumble of thunder. Nicely done, thought Sarah. Very theatrical. She looked at her watch, and started walking quickly up the hill.

Pollina's last words were cryptic. Did she mean stay close to Max, because Max would help and protect her? Or watch him closely because he was dangerous?

Should she come clean to him about her knowledge of Charlotte Yates? After all, the woman was coming. *HERE.* Why? The letters were now presumably in her possession. Her secrets were safe. Was it a return to the scene of the crime thing? Gloating? What was to be gained by Charlotte returning to the place of her youthful love affair with a KGB agent?

Should she tell Max about her suspicions of Marchesa Elisa?

Jana met her as she marched down the hall headed for the breakfast room. "Prince Max was called away suddenly," she said. "He sends his apologies and asks you to please wait for him before moving forward."

Sarah tried not to look as disappointed as she felt. "Of course," said Sarah. "Thank you. Do you know when he'll be back?"

"He didn't say," said Jana. "But since he flew to Venice, I expect it will be a few days at least."

Flew to Venice? Sarah wanted to shout at Jana. "Did he . . . go alone?" she asked instead, trying to be cautious.

"I believe he accompanied his cousin the marchesa," said Jana.

Sarah nodded, feeling suddenly sick. The last thing she wanted was breakfast, but she needed information, so she pushed open the door of the kitchen.

She was surprised to see that Miles was

389

back. She tried to keep her voice from betraying anything as she inquired politely after his "family emergency."

"Is the Beethoven exhibit ready to be installed?" Miles asked.

"Very close," said Sarah. "I'm working on the text for the catalog now."

"You missed meeting Marchesa Elisa," said Suzi. "She had breakfast with us. In head-to-toe Gucci. They're off to Venice to retrieve a Canova. Something urgent about an old lady on her deathbed. She got the statue during the war from a Nazi and now she wants to make it right."

"They took Elisa's private jet, to get there before the old lady croaks," added Douglas.

"She and Max make a lovely couple," Fiona said, sipping tea.

"She's a cougar," Suzi said, glancing slightly at Sarah.

"I don't know why they are called cougars," Godfrey said. "Female cougars can mate many times during the year, and when they are in heat they make a blood-curdling cry, very like that of a human. But they don't mate especially with younger males."

"Makes sense if those two got hitched," Douglas said. "Keep all the lolly in the family."

"Enough gossip," said Miles sternly. "We

all need to be in high gear to make the museum opening happen. If you need extra help or you run into a problem, let me know immediately and I'll do what I can. Also, I'm happy to report that the worst of the earsplitting construction will be finished today. We will then move on to painting, so please be aware as you move through the hallways that there will be wet paint every-where. Also, I'm sure you're all very upset about Eleanor, and so am I," said Miles. "Her suicide is very tragic. But the best thing we can do for her, for ourselves, and for the museum is to make the opening a success. That will honor her memory and the work she loved."

"You could hang a little picture of her in the Ernestine Room," said Bernard with a catch in his voice. As usual, he had a piece of sewing in his hands. A piece of red velvet trimmed with gold. Sarah noticed that his hands were shaking.

As they argued about the best way to honor Eleanor, and whether it was still ap-propriate to have a costume party for the staff, Sarah slipped out.

"Sarah, wait." It was Bernard. His eyes were red and swollen. Of course, he had really been closest to Eleanor, they had always been off gossiping together.

"I thought I'd get some flowers," he said miserably. "You know, to place in the courtyard at the well. A tribute to Eleanor."

Sarah patted his arm. "They might not let you," she said. "But that's a nice idea."

"Will you come with me?" he pleaded.

Sarah shifted uncomfortably. "I'm so sorry," she said, knowing how callous she must sound. "I'm really behind on my work. I'll come with you later this afternoon, okay? I just need to get some things . . ." Her voice trailed off.

Bernard looked as if he might argue with her, and then slumped off.

Sarah made her way back down to her room. With the construction — and its covering clamor — finishing up today, she needed to go now.

Max didn't want her going without him. And what was between him and his cousin? Was she being very stupid?

Probably. But in that case, now was no time to stop being stupid.

As she passed the place where the workmen had left their tools the night before, Sarah looked around, then casually picked up a sledgehammer and kept going.

THIRTY-SIX

Sarah changed from shorts into long pants, in case there was crawling to be done. She took the headlamp she used to examine manuscripts. It was a little bulky for spelunking, but she wanted backup in case the flashlight app on her phone failed. She also took some waterproof matches, and, at the last second, a bottle of water. It might be a long day.

As she shut her bedroom door behind her and turned right, deeper into the building rather than back to the stairway and the light, she pondered the difference between stupid and brave.

Success?

Sarah re-created in her mind the architectural drawings Max had shown her. The closest of the unsealed entries into the tunnels was in the boiler room. She found a person-sized hole beneath a sheet of corrugated metal in the corner. The sides were lined with iron rungs. She climbed down about ten feet, and then, sure enough, a tunnel opened up in front of her. Moving cautiously, she headed into it.

Almost at once, the height of the ceiling dropped. Her headlamp, better suited to scholarship than exploration, barely illuminated a few feet in front of her. She pulled out her phone and clicked on the flashlight. The compass on the app was no help — it was spinning crazily — but she didn't think she had far to go. She was still fairly close to her room, which was presumably next to the hidden library.

A junction in the tunnel opened up, with grilled gates at both openings. It seemed like the little opening to her left was the one that ran under the library. The gate wasn't locked and was only about three feet tall. She pulled it open with a creepy *eeek* of its hinges, bent over, and looked inside. It was dark, and small, and smelled fairly putrid. Sarah dropped to her hands and knees and began crawling through the passageway, telling herself she wasn't claustrophobic and that Max had said that the rats had been exterminated. At best she would only have to endure this a few feet.

But the passage twisted right and then left and then left again. The walls were hewn out of bedrock, rough to the touch. She looked up. Just above and in front of her was a small trapdoor, not much larger than she was. It had a rusty old padlock on it. This must be it. Sarah took a deep breath and pulled the sledgehammer she'd been dragging up alongside her. It was tough to really get a good swing in the narrow space — something she hadn't calculated when choosing this particular tool. On the first swing, she missed the lock entirely but gave the trapdoor a good thump. She managed to whack it the second time, but it didn't break. On the third try, the lock's hasps fell out of the wood entirely, and she realized she was through. She pushed the trapdoor up, surprised at how easily it moved. Her heart leapt up into her chest and she shoved her torso up into the dark room. She looked around the small space, her headlight flashing on pieces of furniture — a bed, a chair, some books, a pair of familiar underwear. With a disappointing groan, she realized she was back in her own room. She had never noticed this door in the floor before — she looked at the back of the trapdoor and saw how neatly it was constructed so as to be nearly invisible.

Well, it might explain how someone had snuck the cross into her room. Nico?

She could hear the faint sounds of construction up above her, which reminded her that she'd better try again quickly. She dropped back into the tunnel, the fetid air filling her lungs again. She managed to push the screws that held the hasp back together so that the lock didn't look damaged, if you didn't look too closely.

She continued crawling through the tunnel, which got smaller. She could hear water coursing through pipes. The tunnel climbed up, then down, then up again. It was too difficult to move on her hands and knees and carry her phone in front of her, so she shoved it back in her pocket. The tunnel was much darker without the flashlight and she had never longed to stand up so badly. She came to junctions with other tunnels, but it seemed impossible to determine where exactly she was. The floor became damp, which was a little alarming. If this was a storm drain and it began to rain . . . she didn't want to think about it.

She was crawling along when suddenly she felt nothing under her hands and she began to fall forward. She screamed, felt a huge uprush of cold air that seemed to come from the center of the earth, and, at the last possible second, managed to catch hold of a protruding stone and push herself back up.

She sat back on her heels, breathing for a second, her pulse racing and her mouth dry. She had almost fallen into what — a well? A drainage tunnel that went straight down? The famous hell portal? She found a small stone under her hand and dropped it. It was six seconds before she heard a faint watery *plonk* far below. Jesus. That had been a close one. If she had fallen hundreds of feet down into a well . . .

She skirted the well carefully and kept crawling along, and now there was actual water she was crawling through. She began to wonder if she should turn back, but would the water recede or get deeper? At least she was crawling slightly uphill. Sarah crept along for several more minutes before she realized she was making a huge mistake. The water was beginning to move faster and get deeper. After a few hundred yards, it was almost up to her belly. Sarah began to admit to herself that she was panicking. No one would guess she was down here except Max, and he was on his way to Venice.

Maybe he had planned this, known she wouldn't be able to resist exploring on her own and had sent her to a watery death. She could drown and her body might not be found for days, if ever. She'd be just a contrail of energy in the palace.

Why had she come here alone? Hubris. Like all the great heroes of antiquity, she was going to be brought down by her own pride and ambition.

She had to keep climbing up. Up was where the water was coming from, and if she could pass the inlet, she would be safe and dry again. If this tunnel even passed the inlet. Her knees ached, she was shivering and trying not to let her brain flood itself with cortisol, which would only increase her panic. She must think straight. She must not give up. She must keep going. A rat floated past her, squealing in distress, then caught a jutting rock and scampered up through a hole. She must move faster, look for any way out of this tunnel. The sledgehammer was slowing her down, but she would need it if she found an escape hatch.

Suddenly, with a gush and a roar, the water got deeper. She fought to keep her head above it, scraping her scalp on the roof of the tunnel. She thought about her mom, and Max, and Pols, and, somewhat absurdly, Beethoven. She braced herself against the walls, trying not to be swept away and under the deadly current.

She should pray to someone, but who? Not the fake Infant of Prague, for sure. To her father, who maybe was watching over her? No.

"Please, Luigi," she whispered. "Help me. Don't let me die in this tunnel." As she struggled to hold on, her headlight lit up something shiny on a rock sticking out of the wall at eye level.

An American penny.

She reached up to grab it, and as she did, she saw the trapdoor above her. Dustier than the last, with an older-looking lock.

With a huge effort, she raised the sledge-hammer up from under the water and tried to pry open the lock. It stuck fast.

She pushed on the trapdoor, but it didn't move. She maneuvered herself so she could put her shoulder into it, and felt some give. Hating to put her face in the water in case there was no more air when she came up again, she took a deep breath and bent over and put her back against the trapdoor, then used her thighs to crush her own body up against the door as hard as she possibly could. The choice was drown or break her back.

Her headlamp went out, dead. She was now in total darkness, underwater.

With the effort of her life, she pushed up again, her back crushed, her thighs scream-ing. The door gave. From underwater she could hear a creak, then a crash as something fell over.

With a gasp, she pulled herself up through the hole into the room.

It was completely dark, a darkness that was utterly impenetrable.

Sarah snapped her fingers and listened for the acoustics. The room was not large. She pulled out her phone, which was wet. And dead.

She remembered the matches in her pocket. They were supposed to be waterproof. This would be the test.

The tiny light caught edges of glinting corners, large objects, furniture. Sarah lit another match and felt her way around. She moved her hands lightly over things, terrified she would break something, trying to guess what she was touching. A globe. A chair. A rug. Finally, she found a table, and the heavy base of . . . yes, a candelabra. With a few candles still in it, stumpy but serviceable. She lit the wicks.

Before her was a large desk. A sort of cloak was folded neatly over the chair behind it. She held her candles over a newspaper laid out on top of the desk — an *International Herald Tribune* dated March 10, 1948. Sarah read the headline and top story: news of the death of Czechoslovak

Foreign Minister Jan Masaryk, found dead in his pajamas in the courtyard of the ministry under his bathroom window. Was this the news that prompted Max's grandfather to seal the library and leave his beloved Czechoslovakia forever?

She thought she heard a voice behind her, a whisper, but when she turned, she saw only a small wax doll dressed in a tattered piece of brocade sitting on a small table. She picked it up, reassuring herself that the thing wasn't alive. The doll was a copy of the Infant of Prague. Or was Pols right and the figure in the Carmelite church was just another copy and this was the . . . real one? It seemed unfair that she should be holding it, given that up until this moment, she had done nothing but make fun of the little guy. Pure of heart she was not. She put him down quickly.

The rushing sound of the water was lessening. She looked down through the hatch and saw that the water was indeed receding, down now to about an inch, and moving more slowly. She should leave now, in case it started up again. But there was so much to look at . . .

She opened the central drawer of the desk. There was a glinting and sharp-looking paper knife in a leather sheath. A paper knife or a weapon? Also, two small books. She pulled these out, opening the heavy leather cover of the first one and trying to make out the Latin inscription. It was dedicated to Rudolf, Holy Roman Emperor and a whole bunch of other royal titles, and was from his most humble servants, etcetera, etcetera . . . John Dee and Edward Kelley. The inside of the book was filled with diagrams in a minute hand.

Sarah picked up the second book. The frontispiece was inscribed with a single name: Tygge Ottensen Brahe. Tycho Brahe. She flipped through the pages. There were strange drawings, and lists with crabbed instructions and diagrams next to them. Recipes. Formulas.

A toast to Brahe.

Was there a formula in this book for the drug? Is that how the 7th prince had created it?

Sarah held up the candelabra and moved to the shelves behind the desk. She found a skull marked with strange symbols and ruby eyes; small, curiously shaped stones; books, books, and more books; a row of philters and vials. She squinted and tried to make out the tiny labels in Latin. *Pulvis Golem.*

Dust of the golem?

"Are you shitting me?" Sarah asked out loud.

This room was Max's rightful inheritance. A secret cache of treasures — religious, literary, scientific, and alchemical. Grandfather Max had sacrificed glittering works of art to the Nazis and communists, but not these strange secrets.

Moving around the room, she found a window frame filled in with cement blocks. The missing window from Max's map, she realized, though it must have given onto an airshaft since they were well underground, a shaft that had been filled in during some renovation. She discovered another, smaller desk and, on top of it, a leather briefcase, oddly modern in this setting. She looked at the initials on it — JP. Sarah opened it and held the candles over the papers. It took a moment to process the fact that the letters and files were in English. TOP SECRET was stamped across all of them. *How funny,* she thought. *Just like in the movies.*

Sarah glanced through the files: letters from the 1960s and 1970s. How did they get here, if the library had been sealed since 1948? She remembered the penny, and pulled it out of her pocket. It was dark with age, but she rubbed it against the cloak she was wearing until she could read the year: 1982.

Under the table, a violin case rested on a small footstool. She bent down and examined the case. Engraved on the top were three violins: two facing forward and the third one facing back. Placing the candelabra on the floor next to her, she gently removed the violin and handled it. She felt something shift inside the instrument. Something that sounded like papers.

Her hands were shaking as she carried the violin to the desk and set it gently on top, then retrieved the candelabra. She opened the desk drawer and tested the paper knife against the tip of her finger. Instantly a drop of blood appeared.

Gently, Sarah ran the knife around the perimeter of the violin, searching for weaknesses in the glue that bound front and back together. When she found a point of entry, she slid the edge around. Holding her breath, she lifted the front of the instrument off and pulled out the small sheaf of letters bound by a faded ribbon that lay within.

Unsterbliche Geliebte, read the looping familiar script, and her heart leapt into her mouth.

Immortal Beloved.

THIRTY-SEVEN

Her first thought was that she didn't have the right. Letters from Beethoven hidden in a violin and addressed to the Immortal Beloved. Letters that the world had never seen. She was only a doctoral candidate from Boston. She didn't even have the credentials to get access on her own to the Beethoven archives in Bonn.

Her second thought was that she was about to become the most famous Beethoven scholar in the world.

Her hands were sweaty, and filthy. She needed gloves. Even though she was still wet, and freezing, Sarah whipped off her T-shirt. She turned it inside out, wrapped it around her fingers, then gently smoothed the letters across the desk. There were three. Sarah moved the candelabra closer.

They were written in German, of course, in Luigi's distinct and atrocious handwriting. She turned first to the letter, which

began: *Unsterblicher Geliebten.* It was undated, although the word "Vienna" could
be made out in the upper right corner.
Authentic? (In 1911 the editor of *Die Musik*
had published a "new" letter to the Immortal Beloved, which included a song fragment. This had turned out to be a total
forgery.)

Sarah squinted, tracing the spiky and er-
ratically punctuated lines of Beethoven's
untidy scrawl.

Immortal Beloved —
Yes, I must speak once more of her to
you, L, as I can speak to no one else.
She [the handwriting became illegible]
many faces. Imagine my wretchedness
— almost to madness — when now I
turn to her and find not the restoration
— too brief always — of what was
LOST, but instead only things I do not
[again the writing was illegible]. Only
my extreme bad health drove me to her
arms last night, but it was as if I
dreamed. I heard not, saw not, what was
before me. But instead such a rushing in
my ears and then my violin sonata in
D flat — you know it — played by, if
you please, [crossed out sentence] well
you will not believe me. Perhaps the loss

of my hearing has moved even past the secret wisdom of your ancients. But what is this new gift from the Beloved? Or curse? I do not understand it. Who can we ask?

Truly she is no [illegible] woman. She is a demon in my veins. Ha, ha I must laugh though to think of the time at N and what fear in the eyes of your servant when we emerged from her arms and [illegible]. I must get a new maid and someone French who understands broth.

Your most obedient servant
and true friend,
Beethoven

So it's not to *the Immortal Beloved,* Sarah thought. *It's* about *her.* A demon in his veins. A woman that the addressee (which had to be the 7th prince) had apparently shared with Beethoven. Sarah turned to the second letter. This was written in pencil on the back of what looked like a bill from a copyist.

Vôtre Altesse!

I heartily embrace you dear donkey, Fitzliputzli, treasured friend and Doctor. You never open your letters so I feel free to write to you once more. I inquire after your wife, your children, your fortune, and your foot. Would I have that BLOCK to stop all these imbeciles at my door. Nothing but [illegible], and you know it fills me with pain to speak less than gently to any other creature. In this, as in so much else, I am not understood.

I have once again dined with that which we have sometimes called the Immortal Beloved. She is corrupted. You are too timid and too good. I am good but not timid. You [illegible] with her and go back, but I now see that she brings me forward. I go forward and I hear what I have done in the past. Ha, ha! I go forward great leaps, greater this time than ever before. Imagine if you can, a little girl, blind as I am deaf, but what a Hercules. Immortality is strange to look upon. But you should have heard — as I did, my friend, every note! — of my recently completed Sonata in F Minor. I was plunged into happiness such as I have never felt. But for this I must make payment, as always. A fall in my health, my spirits, the emptiness we have spoken of before. But for a few minutes — such joy. Such joy, my friend.

In loving haste and esteem,

L. v. B.

Sarah's hands were shaking. Pols. Pols had played the Sonata in F minor at the competition. Played, as she had said, as if Beethoven were there instructing her. The Immortal Beloved was not a woman. It was the drug. And Beethoven was moving with it, moving forward through time to hear his completed works.

When he had looked at Sarah that night and said "Immortal Beloved," he wasn't naming her, he was naming the drug that was revealing her to him.

Sarah tried to imagine how she could possibly explain any of this. Who would believe her? It was unbelievable. Unless you had taken the drug yourself, seen what it could do. What could it do? And how?

She turned to the third letter. It looked older than the other two, and unlike them was dated: July 3. Sarah smoothed the creases and folds out as best she could with the tips of her T-shirt-covered fingers.

My friend —
   Only a few words and those in haste. I leave tomorrow. Rest your mind. I will

write to A when I arrive. She heard a little, but understood NOTHING. How could she? You saw how it is between us. To [illegible] at my age — when I need a quiet, steady life, it is impossible. God give me the courage to end it. And yet how can I? To give to her what I can only give to my work? My mind is in pieces. I see them all, all at once. We must never indulge ourselves again. Destroy what you have left of it. I am suffering. But your secret is safe. I will write to A.

BEETHOVEN

Sarah put down the letter, thinking hard. On July 2 Beethoven had been in Prague. On July 4 he had taken a coach to the spa in Teplitz and on the sixth and seventh of that month he had penned the Immortal Beloved letters, almost irrefutably to Antonie Brentano. In fact, there were phrases in that letter that echoed this one: "only a few words . . . ," "at my age I need a steady, quiet life." The letter of July 6 began with "You are suffering."

She heard a little, but understood NOTHING.

A sequence of events formed in her brain. Antonie Brentano had interrupted Ludwig and Prince Lobkowicz talking about the drug, or maybe even in the midst of a drug-induced trip. Luigi had then hotfooted it to Teplitz, possibly to avoid a scene or to give himself time to think of an explanation. There he had penned the letters that effectively ended the affair with Brentano. Sarah thought through those letters. Despite their protestations of ardor and faithfulness, she had never really believed in the sincerity of Ludwig's sentiments.

Much as you love me — I love you more — But do not conceal yourself from me — good night — As I am taking the baths I must go to bed — Oh God! So near! So far!

Sarah had snorted when she had first read that sentence. *I love you but I need to get some sleep because I have a spa appointment tomorrow!*

But of course it was possible to be incredibly in love with someone and still think about ordinary things. Especially if you were ill and a genius and your girlfriend was married with four children and you had avoided getting married yourself all your life so you had time to compose the greatest music of the age and be gaseous without apology.

Sarah looked down at the letters spread across the desk. She tried reading through them as if she didn't know anything about the drug, as if she were any other musicologist. Without knowing about Tycho's secret formula, you could almost imagine that the "secret" was some sort of illicit sexual connection between Beethoven and his patron. That they had been sharing women or men, or Antonie, or having some sort of kinky three-way. That Antonie had caught them doing the nasty at the palace in Prague, and Ludwig was doing damage control with the Immortal Beloved letters.

Even what she felt sure was a reference to Pols — *a child blind as I am deaf* — could be about someone in Beethoven's own time — a pupil. Or a gifted prostitute.

There would be a firestorm of speculation.

A loud *slam* interrupted her speculations. Sarah jumped, her heart thundering. She grabbed the candelabra and turned.

The trapdoor was shut. As she moved toward it, she heard a distinct click, and something — or someone — moving in the tunnel below.

"Max?" she called cautiously. There was no sound. She set the candelabra on the floor and reached down to lift the trapdoor. It wouldn't budge.

She pulled on the door, shouting. She looked up, helplessly, for something to aid her, a tool, a wedge. She held up the candles and looked at the opposite corner of the room, which she hadn't inspected.

Perhaps this explained the 1982 penny she had picked up.

A skeleton cowered in the corner, curled in a fetal position, a pair of red wedge-heeled espadrilles still tied to the feet bones.

THIRTY-EIGHT

Sarah approached the skeleton cautiously. Whatever — whoever — this had been in life, the body was now thoroughly decomposed. The bones were not the pristine white of school science labs and doctors' offices, however. They were mottled gray and there was something . . . wrong about the angle of the neck. Fabric was twined around the neck bones. Crudely knotted, it fell in a coil around the espadrilles. Sarah glanced up at the ceiling, which was criss-crossed with a latticework of wooden beams.

She stepped back, re-creating the situation in her mind. A woman trapped in this library, in 1982 at the earliest. Accidentally? Imprisoned? How long had she survived before she had decided to take her own life? Shredding her own clothing, apparently, to make herself a noose.

Sarah shuddered. Too late to help the poor woman now. Still shirtless and shivering, she set to work on moving the trapdoor. After thirty minutes, her hands were bruised and welted and the door hadn't moved an inch.

She crawled on her hands and knees across the floor of the library, her fingers searching for a crack, a loose board, something.

Nothing.

Sarah knew that beyond one of the four walls was her own bedroom in the palace, but her twisting journey through the tunnels had displaced her normally keen sense of direction. Which wall? All of them were covered with built-in bookcases. And surely if there had been another way out, then the woman who had been trapped here before . . .

Sarah looked at the pathetic crumble of bones in the corner.

Now felt like a good time to completely fall apart. No one would blame her if she panicked, screamed, started crying.

Sarah shivered. She was freezing. She went to the desk and picked up the cloak folded over the chair. The fabric was soft against her skin as she pulled it around her shoulders. Her sensitive nose twitched. There was an odor, but not of death or decay. Something rich, strange, almost sensual. Resinous. Musky. She couldn't identify it.

The library seemed to move in and out of focus and her eyes were heavy. Was she falling asleep? She had read about situations of extreme stress sometimes causing drowsiness, the body's fight to escape the circumstances it found itself in.

Was that music? Real or imagined? Sarah started humming along.

The Diabelli Variations.

In 1819 a music publisher by the name of Anton Diabelli had composed a thirty-two-bar waltz in C major for piano and then invited fifty Viennese composers to create a variation for it. Ludwig at that time was embroiled in an epic court battle with his despised sister-in-law over the custody of his nephew Karl. His health was deplorable, his domestic situation a shambles (every other week a cook or maid departed weeping from a ramshackle series of apartments), and by all accounts he was pretty thoroughly depressed and possibly delusional. Still he managed by 1820 to have composed not just one variation on Diabelli's theme, but an astonishing twenty-two. By 1823 he handed over the final variations: thirty-three in number, a personal best for Luigi, and, perhaps not coincidentally, one more than Bach in his Goldberg Variations.

Sarah kept humming. At number 8 she felt herself dancing a little, swirling the cloak around her as she waltzed. She felt her courage grow around number 14 (*Grave e maestoso!*) and her sense of humor (*Presto! Scherzando!*) returned in number 15. By the time she hit variation 22, she was feeling almost high. In the Diabelli Variations nothing is sacred and nothing is unworthy of consideration. It is Beethoven in all his late-period glory. All risks, all invention, all extremes. Ludwig didn't revolt or rebel against the conventions of his time, the musical forms of his day. He set them on fire and sailed right through them to the other side.

By the time the variations came to an end she was shouting, singing the notes with a hysterical vigor and jumping up and down. She was warm now. Her skin prickled with heat.

She glanced over at the skeleton. She couldn't die here. She was going to set the world on fire with . . .

Sarah heard something below her, almost under her feet. A clanking, scraping noise, and then a banging. She moved quickly over to the trapdoor. Yes, someone was coming. She rushed back to the desk to conceal the Beethoven letters. They should be hidden.

But she couldn't see them. Where were they? The newspaper, too, was gone.

The pounding stopped, and the trapdoor began to creep open.

"*Hallo?*" said a voice from the darkness below. Male. Czech? American? Sarah crouched, ready.

"*Ist da jemand?*" German. *Is anyone there?* he was asking.

Sarah steadied her breathing as two gloved hands appeared, then the top of a hat. A flat tan military hat. Was she being rescued by the police?

The man hoisted himself up through the trapdoor. He was wearing a uniform: short belted jacket and boots. As he stood up to his full length, she saw he was a tall man, well-built. He looked around, and as he turned to face her, she gasped in shock. There was a swastika on his uniform.

The man stared at her for a moment, then a snarl formed on his face as he put his hands up.

"The Führer will be very angry that you tried to hide these things from him," he said in German, still staring at her. "Very angry indeed."

Sarah picked up the candelabra.

"Don't come near me," she said.

In an instant a gun was in his hand. As

Sarah heard it fire, she shut her eyes and swung the candelabra like a baseball bat, with all her strength.

She expected to feel the impact of the candelabra against his head, but with a sinking sensation instead felt it swing around, hitting nothing. She staggered.

The Nazi fell to the floor, dead. Dead?

As she stared down at him, watching a crimson stain spread over his jacket, blood spurting from a small hole, his eyes open and glassy, she felt something hot and electric pulse through her body. Had she been shot?

There was a second man in the room now. He had come from behind her. He had come *through* her. The man stared into the face of the dead Nazi.

Sarah leapt away from them, nearly tripping over her cloak. "What the hell?!" she shouted.

The man did not seem to hear her. He leaned over the Nazi, a strange and ornate antique gun in his hand with mother-of-pearl inlays.

Sarah shrank backward against a bookcase.

The man sighed. He was tall and thin, wearing a beautifully tailored gray flannel suit. He pulled a perfect square of white

419

handkerchief from his pocket.

"Max?" Sarah said. But this man was older than Max. And slightly different-looking, but just slightly. The same hawklike nose, high forehead.

Max's grandfather.

She reached out a hand and put it on his arm. He took no notice of this and her hand went right through his body, though she felt a stabbing hotness in her fingers.

Sarah nudged the dead Nazi's leg, and her foot met nothing but air, though her toes crackled with electricity.

The drug. It had to be the drug. But she hadn't eaten or drunk anything since arriving in the secret library. How else could the drug enter her system? Was she breathing it? The musky, resinous, scent she had noticed earlier? Like amber . . . Was the room itself saturated with the drug?

She watched Max study the dead Nazi, breathing heavily. His form began to fade and flicker as he began quickly stripping the uniform off the soldier.

A sense of vertigo overwhelmed her. Objects in the room began to shift, brighten, and darken. She caught a movement out of the corner of her eye, and saw another woman, very much alive, sitting at the desk, looking at the contents of the briefcase.

Wearing red espadrilles. The color was so vivid, the woman so sharply delineated, that it hurt her eyes.

"I can't believe it," the woman said.

She was dressed in the same dress the skeleton wore, but with the fabric intact. Sarah struggled to focus; she could smell the woman's hair, her shampoo, her perfume, her breath. The woman smiled excitedly over her shoulder at someone, and Sarah turned to see the faint outlines of a young man examining the contents of the bookcase. He was humming Diabelli Variation number 7.

"Me either," said the ghostly young man. "This stuff is amazing — a real treasure trove." Sarah could now make out his suit: shiny gray with wide lapels, dusty on the shoulders and damp at the cuffs.

At her feet, Max's grandfather returned. He had stripped the Nazi soldier of his uniform. "God forgive me," he said.

"No, *look* at this," cried the young woman in the red espadrilles. "Memos and cables and letters to and from John Paisley. Do you realize what this is? These are records about Paisley's involvement with the KGB. And records of the KGB's involvement . . ." The woman looked up; her eyes were huge. "The KGB's assassination of President

Kennedy." Her eyes glowed.

"This is coming with us," she said, picking it up. "This is going to make my career."

Sarah shuddered a little. She recognized herself in this woman. The ambition. It was so naked, her need. To prove herself. To prove to all of *them.*

"What if we get caught?" the young man was asking. "You know they search our luggage every time we leave the hotel. I don't want to end up in jail behind the Iron Curtain. Look, stay here. I'm going to get Joseph."

It's not safe, Sarah thought. *Wait, stop.*

Max was lowering the body of the dead Nazi down into the tunnel. A woman's voice called up to him. "I'm frightened," she said. She was English.

"Quickly," said Max. "We will drag him down to the inflow for the moat."

"They will know you did this —" the woman started to say.

"We need to leave now," said Max. "Or they will kill us. But the library will be safe. Someday this war will be over and we will come back."

Suddenly a wail went up from the other side of the room. Sarah turned to see the young woman standing with her hands against the wall.

"No no no no!" she was screaming. "Let me out! Stop it!"

Sarah could now hear terrible screams coming from the other side of the rock wall. A man — screaming in pain. Being tortured, it sounded like. It was unbearable.

The woman was pounding on the wall and crying. She tried the trapdoor again, but it was locked from the outside.

"Please!" the young woman cried. "Don't hurt him. We'll never tell anyone we were here. Please let us go."

More screaming. The woman sat down on the floor and sobbed. She put her hands over her ears, but couldn't stop the sound of the young man's screams.

The events of the room began to skid, looping back on themselves, then jumping forward. Max shot the Nazi, the woman hanged herself from the beam. Max hauled in boxes, books. He put a cigarette case in his pocket. Someone new appeared in the room. He barely glanced around the library. In his hand was the briefcase.

He said something that sounded like *"Moy strahovoy polic."* Then he set the briefcase down and picked up something wrapped in cloth on the desk. An Aztec amulet vial. Humming, he left the room with it. He was humming the Diabelli Variations.

Distraught Max read the news of Masaryk's death, left the paper open on the desk. The researcher hanged herself from the beam. Max shot the Nazi. The researcher pounded on the wall. Max shot the Nazi again and again. Flashbulbs popped. The young man screamed. The Russian set the briefcase down and picked up the Aztec amulet. It was like being forced to watch six films at once, all on fast-forward. She was trapped under layers of the past.

"Sarah?" said a familiar voice.

Sarah turned. In the midst of the chaos stood a familiar figure.

It was her mother.

THIRTY-NINE

"Mom? What are you doing here?" Sarah asked. Her mom looked so real, in her pale blue velour track-suit and white Keds.

"I came to tell you that you're a slut," said her mother matter-of-factly. "Now come get a hug."

What the — ? Sarah recoiled as her mom, suddenly holding a kitchen knife, lunged at her. Through her. And then spread wings, thick leathery wings, and flew. Sarah screamed as the birdlike beast with her mother's face pecked at her head. She fell to the floor.

It's not happening, Sarah told herself. But what kind of a vision was this? This wasn't the past.

She looked up and there was Sherbatsky, leaning over her.

"You showed such promise," he said, shaking his head. "I'm so disappointed in you. You really let me down."

Snakes, thousands of snakes dropped from the walls and began slithering through the room. Sarah screamed and writhed, willing herself not to be afraid, but failing.

Sherbatsky morphed into Beethoven, who spit in her face.

"Ausfall," he snarled in German. *Failure.*

The walls started melting, and then spinning, and she had the sense she was lying on the ceiling and not the floor, and couldn't understand why she wasn't falling.

People were walking right through her, burning her, yelling at her. As terrifying as the other drug trip had been, it was nothing like this. This was a perversion, a nightmare. Her worst fears come to life.

"Sarah? Are you there? Sarah?" She opened her eyes, and Max — her Max, was coming up through the trapdoor.

"Thank God," she said. "Help me!"

She tried to crawl toward him, but her legs were paralyzed, and he was pulling someone else up into the room behind him — Elisa. Max smiled at Sarah and then pushed Elisa amorously up against a wall. Elisa turned her head to laugh at Sarah.

"Well, the little bitch knows about us now," Elisa said.

Max kissed Elisa deeply. "It's all been a joke," he said to Sarah. "Of course it's Elisa

I love. She's family. Royalty. And you're scum."

It wasn't happening. Was it?

Grandpa Max stepped forward and shot the Nazi. The researcher screamed at the sound of her boyfriend being tortured. The skeleton stood up and danced suggestively, shaking her bones in a grotesque approximation of a striptease. The skeleton shouted at Sarah as it twitched and writhed.

Ausfall.

Slut.

The man with the briefcase appeared again and screamed, *"Moy strahovoy polic!"* as a cascade of scarlet water poured out of his mouth. Sherbatsky began babbling in Russian, then screamed and collapsed to the floor, his body a tangle of broken bones and electrical wires. Rats exploded out of his stomach, their jaws slick with blood and entrails.

Max was fucking Elisa from behind, except his penis was the head of a dragon. The dragon blinked and looked at her, then hissed.

Sarah closed her eyes, put her hands over her ears, and tried to think. She curled her body protectively inside the cloak and the resinous amber smell of it overwhelmed her.

The cloak.

The hallucinations had begun when she had put on the cloak.

Sarah flung it off her body.

It was like turning off a movie projector. Quiet. Greedily, she sucked air into her lungs. She was alone in the library again. Alone and in the dark.

Sarah lay still for several moments, trying to pull herself together and make sense of the visions. They returned briefly, in quick bursts: the thud of a fallen body, the humming of a musical phrase, a dragon's head penis. *Ausfall.* What was real, the actual past, and what was just the demons lurking in the corners of her brain?

Her emotions felt real enough. She was as furious, humiliated, disgusted, as if it had all really happened. Maybe she was a failure. Maybe she shouldn't trust Max. The way he had laughed at her . . . No. She had to pull herself together. None of it was real. It felt real because it was based — in horrible exaggeration — on her actual fears, her most hidden terrors. But she was still alive, in the here and now, and she had to forget those visions. Shakily, she pulled herself upright and lit another match. She found the candelabra amid a pile of glass and lit the candles, returned to the desk. It was as she had left it, the newspaper, the leather volumes, Beethoven letters. She picked these up and stuffed them in her jeans. So much for archival integrity. Whatever happened to her next, the letters were coming with her.

How was she going to get out of here?

A scuffling sound almost beneath her feet sent another surge of adrenaline shooting through her. Remnants of the drug? No. Someone calling her name. Obeying some primitive instinct of concealment, she blew out the candles, grabbed her T-shirt and pulled it on.

"Sarah?" The trapdoor lifted. Here and now. This was happening here and now.

"Sarah," the familiar voice called into the blackness. "Are you there? Sarah? It's Bernard."

"Bernard? Is it really you?" Sarah said.

"Are you okay? I was doing my laundry and I saw you go into the boiler room and you never came out, so I got worried and followed you."

He climbed up into the room and Sarah hugged him, hard. He was real, corporeal. He smelled like mildew and Chanel No. 5. And . . . fear.

"Wow, what is this place?" he said, pointing his flashlight around the room.

"A storeroom of sorts," Sarah said. "Thank God you showed up. The door latched behind me and I thought I'd never get out."

Sarah went to head down through the trapdoor. Bernard grabbed her roughly by the arm.

"Hey," she said. "That hurts."

"I'm sorry," he said. "But I can't let you leave." Now she could really smell the fear. It was pouring off him.

"What? What are you — ?"

And then she saw it. Bernard had a small gun in his hand. He took a step back and pointed it at her.

"Bernard? What the hell are you doing?"

"I — I can't talk about it. But you can't leave."

Bernard's hand holding the gun was shaking violently. Sarah remembered reading that nervous criminals were the most dangerous.

But this was Bernard. An expert in Rococo. A slightly odd but far from homicidal man. He had cried harder than anyone over Eleanor's death. He was sewing them all costumes for the masquerade ball.

"You want to tell me what's going on?" she said softly. Keep him calm.

"No!" yelped Bernard. He raised the gun

a little higher.

"You're not a killer," she said. "I know you."

"No, you don't," he said, trying to steady the gun with his other hand. "I messed up. She got to me, and I messed up. But I never killed anyone. And now they're going to blame it on me."

"Tell me what happened and we can figure a way out of this."

"No, we can't," said Bernard, who was starting to cry. "I locked you in. I called her and told her you were down here. Now she wants me to kill you. Or she's calling the police on me for . . ." He couldn't say the words.

Sarah scanned the room out of the corner of her eye. "Whatever it is, we can figure it out," said Sarah in as normal a tone of voice as possible. "I know some very good lawyers."

"No, I have to kill you," squeaked Bernard.

"Killing me is only going to make things worse, not better." Sarah was inching toward the letter opener. If she could distract him . . .

"I wanted to just tie you up and leave you here until she arrived." He was crying openly now.

"Much better idea," said Sarah. "Or even . . . we could go out together and I could protect you from her. It's Marchesa Elisa, isn't it?"

Bernard nodded, miserably.

"Tell me what happened," Sarah said, trying to infuse her shaking voice with all the kindness and sympathy she could muster. "We can figure out what to do together."

"She came to my workroom," Bernard said. "She was interested in my projects. She was so nice, asking questions. She collects snuffboxes, too. She said if it was up to her, a lot of the objects would be made available to serious collectors, people who would really understand and appreciate them."

"Like you," said Sarah. "I get it. Go on."

"We went to lunch," Bernard continued. "She talked about Max, about how he didn't care about the things the way we do. She made me a present, an exquisite eighteenth-century snuffbox shaped like a turtle with diamond eyes."

Sarah nodded, trying to look understanding when really she wanted to scream. *You're going to kill me over a fucking snuffbox?* But she didn't want to interrupt Bernard, who was clearly desperate to talk.

"She wanted to be kept current with what

was being discovered at the palace," Bernard said. "Just so she could keep an eye on Max, make sure he wasn't messing things up. So when I heard about things, I told her. I mean, they aren't secrets. Everything goes through Miles, too."

"Like the letters Eleanor found in the chimney," Sarah said, dully.

"Yes. And then. It was supposed to be a joke," Bernard pleaded. "I was supposed to hang it up in the cage. It was only because I was big and strong, she said. It was too heavy for her. Elisa said it was a prank to promote a nightclub for a friend of hers."

"Hang it up — ?" Sarah stuttered. "You mean . . . *Eleanor*?"

"I didn't know it was her!" Bernard started crying again. "The bag was left for me at the front gate. She told me it was a mannequin dressed like a go-go dancer. You know, like the girls they have dancing in cages at all those after-hours clubs in cellars? I was supposed to hang it up in the cage over the well. Like an advertisement. The marchesa told me not to unzip the bag until I had hung it up or the costume might fall off. So . . . So I did. And when I unzipped the bag . . . Oh God. Oh God, oh God."

Oh God, Sarah agreed.

"I'll never forget it," Bernard sobbed. "Eleanor was my *friend.* I would never have . . . I can't stop seeing her face. And the . . . blood. I ran. I ran out of the courtyard and I called the marchesa. I didn't know what had happened. I couldn't believe she would have done such a thing . . . I thought there must have been some kind of mistake. I told her that we should call the police, but she just laughed. She laughed at me. And she said that she had set up a camera in the courtyard and she had video of me hanging up Eleanor's body and running away."

"She's bluffing," Sarah said, her mind reeling. But Bernard shook his head.

"She sent me a picture. She texted it to my *phone.* Oh God, I am so fucked."

"She's not going to get away with this," Sarah said. "Bernard, listen to me —"

"No!"

"Bernard —"

"Shut up!" he screamed. "Shut up and turn around!"

"Please," said Sarah.

"Turn around!"

If she turned, she was dead. She tried to keep her eyes on his.

He grabbed her arm and spun her around. God, he was strong.

She kicked hard at him, grabbing for the gun, and he shrieked and threw her against the wall. She crashed to her knees. Bernard towered over her. Sarah covered her head with her hands.

"I'm sorry," whispered Bernard.

Sarah closed her eyes. She heard the click of the safety. Some sniffling.

Then, as she stiffened her body, a dull thunk, and then a heavy crashing noise. No. That wasn't the gun. She was still alive. She opened her eyes.

Bernard was in a heap on the ground. And standing over him was Nico. Standing on a chair. Holding something in his hands. He smiled and offered it to her.

"My dear girl," he said. "I think you dropped your sledgehammer."

FORTY

Sarah stood over Bernard's body. She nudged his stomach with her foot. Nothing. Was he breathing?

"Is he dead?" she asked Nico. She knelt down. Bernard was breathing but out cold. He had a goose egg forming on the back of his head, although his skull seemed intact.

Nico was not paying attention to her or Bernard. He was scanning the flashlight over the contents of the room.

"Nico!" Sarah said sharply. "How did you know?"

The little man turned and glanced at the pile of Bernard.

"Oh, Bernard's been following you for days," said Nico, almost absentmindedly. "And I've been following him."

Nico's eyes were jumping rapidly, greedily, from one artifact in the library to another.

"Nico!" Sarah hissed again, stamping her

436

foot. "Why didn't you tell me?"

But the little man was prowling about the room, running his hands over the objects. He picked up the Infant of Prague, laughed sardonically, sat it down, and patted the ruby-eyed skull like he was greeting a familiar dog. He picked up the leather briefcase.

"What is in here?"

"Um, I think it's documents that prove the KGB killed Kennedy," Sarah said.

"Mmph," said Nicolas, shrugging his tiny shoulders and dropping the case. "Bor-ing."

"I found a book by John Dee and Edward Kelley," said Sarah. It seemed like she should tie Bernard up somehow, in case he woke up. Or at least take his gun. Sarah picked it up, gingerly.

"I've probably read it," Nico said. "Dee was a very gifted mathematician and scientist. And a true alchemist. But Edward Kelley was a fraud. Even Tycho made fun of him. And they were friends."

"Well, I think Tycho Brahe's diary is on the desk," Sarah snapped. "If that's more your speed." Sarah crouched next to Bernard and stared into his unconscious face. "Nico, help me with —" Sarah turned to look at Nico, who was frantically flipping through the books on the desk. With a wary glance at Bernard, she joined him.

"Yes," he breathed. "Yes, yes, yes."

Sarah felt a surge of excitement.

"Can you read it?" she asked. "Nico, do you understand it?"

Nicolas was riffling through the pages, almost ripping the corners in his haste. His finger moved up and down the columns.

"No. No. No," he muttered. "It's not here. Where is it? He wrote it down. I know he wrote it down."

He continued searching frantically through the book. Sarah tried to ask him a question, but he shouted at her to be still, be quiet. She had never heard him speak so violently. At last he let the book fall to the desk and staggered backward, crashing into the desk chair. It was the first time Sarah had seen Nicolas move clumsily. She held out a hand, but he ignored it, slumping down and holding his head in his hands, groaning.

"What is it?" Sarah asked, truly frightened now. She crouched down on her heels and looked at Nico, who was rocking back and forth, his arms wrapped tightly around himself.

"Oh, it's been so long. So long." He fell out of the chair and crawled underneath the desk.

"Leave me here," he cried. "This is where I belong."

"Nicolas," Sarah said, trying to keep her voice calm, but very firm, the way you needed to with horses and student musicians. "What are you talking about? Of course I'm not going to leave you."

"That is what Sophia said," Nicolas groaned.

"Sophia?"

"The master's sister."

"Max has a sister?"

"Tycho Brahe's sister," said Nico, fiercely. "He is my master. Or was."

Sarah took her eyes off Nico long enough to look quickly over her shoulder. Bernard still wasn't moving, but did they really have enough time for a sixteenth-century history lesson? They should be figuring out how to secure the library. And what to do with Bernard. "As soon as Max gets here, we'll . . . figure out what to do with all of this," she said, hoping to get Nico back on track. "I mean, Max will figure it out. Don't worry."

"Sophia died," Nico said, his voice hollow. "And the master died. With so much work unfinished. To think he understood the heavens as he did without ever having looked through a telescope. To have learned so many secrets. But not all of them. Oh, when will it end?"

"When will what end?"

"He made me drink it," Nico whispered. "Held me down. It was a joke to him. He didn't know it would work. I should have known."

Sarah reached under the desk and grabbed the little man's arm. The contact seemed to bring him back to himself. His ravaged face cleared. He stopped rocking back and forth. He closed his eyes and took a deep breath. When he looked at Sarah again, the ghost of a smile played around a corner of his mouth.

"Dear me," he said. "Look at me. Under the table."

Sarah nodded. "You want to come out?"

She pretended to inspect Bernard's condition, in order to give Nico a moment to compose himself. When she turned back around, he was straightening the books on the desk into an orderly pile.

"Nico?"

The little man tapped the cover of Tycho's journal.

"You want to know if it's here? The formula for the drug? Your drug?"

"Is the formula there?" Sarah tried to keep the desperate hope out of her voice.

"I believe it is," Nicolas said. "It's here.

Tycho was very clever. He knew how to keep secrets." He paused. "Did you know that he kept a dwarf named Jepp?" Nico seemed very tired, but more or less sane. "Did you know that?"

"Yeah, I heard something about that," Sarah said carefully.

"Jepp sat under the table at dinner," Nicolas said. "And made many accurate predictions. He was clairvoyant, you see. Psychic. Or so people believed. He was also a fairly accomplished thief."

"Nicolas?"

The little man made a small noise, in a minor key. He shook his head, as if to clear it. "I suppose we should take care of Bernard," he said.

"Yes," said Sarah warmly, glad that Nico seemed to be focusing on twenty-first-century matters. What the hell had he been rambling about? He was talking as if . . . well, later. She'd think about it later. "The marchesa sent him, you know. To kill me."

"That does not surprise me. But I don't think he would have actually pulled the trigger."

"You let him get awfully close. But thank you for saving my life. So . . . now we call the police?"

"Heavens no," said Nico, unbuckling Bernard's belt and pulling it out. "Turn him over again?"

Sarah shoved Bernard back on his face and Nicolas pulled Bernard's wrists together behind his back, securing them with the belt.

"What now?" Sarah asked. "We can't leave him here."

"Tycho Brahe," Nicolas said, thoughtfully, retrieving Brahe's diary from the desk and tucking it into his jacket pocket, "kept tame elk. His favorite one, Albrecht, died after getting drunk and falling down the stairs."

"Elks get drunk?"

"It's a problem," Nicolas nodded. "With elks. Elk. Anyway, I suggest we stage a tumble down the stairs for our friend Bernard. A drunken slip. There will be the suggestion that poor Bernie, distraught at the loss of his dear friend Eleanor, and overwhelmed with the amount of Rococo bibelots he needed to categorize, quaffed rather more than was good for him and bumped his head."

"He'll be taken to the hospital," Sarah nodded. "And then . . ."

"And then you can leave the rest to me." The little man nodded. "Or, rather, my wife, Oksana. She is doing her internship at Na Františku Hospital. She will keep an eye on

Bernie. I believe he will require a good bit of rest."

Sarah gestured at Bernard. "Grab his feet. I'll get him under the armpits. How the hell are we going to get him through all those tunnels?"

"I think you took the long way," Nicolas said, smugly. "From this trapdoor to the one in your room is about thirty meters. And there's a handcart here we can strap him to."

Which is what they did. They lowered Bernie into the tunnel, strapped him to the cart like a refrigerator, wheeled him through the tunnel, then pulled his unconscious bulk up into Sarah's room. Nicolas stepped out into the hallway to check if the coast was clear. Sarah reflexively pulled out her phone and was surprised to see that though the screen was now cracked, it was working. Seven p.m. Her stomach growled. It was almost time for dinner. After a few minutes, Nico came back in, holding a laundry basket. Sarah recognized Bernard's fisherman's vest on top of a heap of clothes. Nico held Bernard's cell phone in his hand.

"Perfect," said Sarah. You couldn't help but admire the little man's thoroughness. Together, they dragged the body outside to the foot of the stairs and arranged him face-up in a realistically sprawled position. Nicolas pulled a tiny flask from his jacket pocket.

"Hold open his mouth," he instructed.

"You hold open his mouth."

Grimacing with distaste, Nicolas held apart Bernard's slack jaws and Sarah poured the contents of the flask (Jägermeister by the smell of it) into Bernard's mouth. This actually seemed to revive the man, who, for the first time, stirred and coughed. The alcohol spilled across his face.

"Quick." Nicolas pointed. "Make a noise like you're falling down the stairs."

Sarah dashed up the steps and then banged down the steps, loudly. Nicolas upended the laundry basket and scattered clothes.

"Oh!" shouted Nicolas, in a muffled imitation of Bernard's somewhat squeaky voice. *"Arggh!"*

Sarah couldn't help it. She started giggling.

"Calm down," Nicolas said. "And now we go upstairs and report this unfortunate accident. Quickly. I believe he's waking up."

Nico paused at the top of the stairs to look down at the feebly stirring Bernard.

"This is just how Albrecht went," he said, sighing. "God, how I hated that stupid elk."

FORTY-ONE

After Bernie had been trundled away in an ambulance, Sarah wanted to return to the secret library, but she didn't dare. Nico had said he would lock it back up again, and that nothing should be touched until Max returned. "It is his right," he said. Then he used Bernard's phone to text the marchesa that Sarah was "taken care of."

"It is better," he said, "that the marchesa believes all has gone according to plan. In her absence, we can continue to work more freely."

So, reluctantly, Sarah went back to the Music Room and tried to focus. The next couple of days passed relatively quietly. The researchers worked diligently, and the palace began to look more and more like a museum. Sarah, trying not to obsess about the Beethoven letters she had found, or Max's continued absence with the woman who sent Bernard to kill her, or the strange

445

and disturbing events in the library, sought refuge in mechanical details over the exhibition she was preparing.

But it was hard not to wonder about Nico. When he was babbling strangely in the library, it almost sounded as if he believed that he — Nico — was the same person as Tycho's own personal dwarf — the clairvoyant Jepp. Nico had always been odd, but that was just plain crazy. It would make him roughly four hundred years old. Which was absurd and defied all the laws of the universe.

She thought of Alessandro, telling her: "Ninety-six percent of the universe is dark matter and dark energy. And in that ninety-six percent, it's possible that none of the rules of science apply."

All of this made her suspicious and irritable.

As did the fact that she had heard nothing from Max.

Since Eleanor's death there had been much talk among the researchers over whether to cancel the costume ball. Eventually it was decided that it would be okay to go on, although the "ball" was now downgraded to a "party." The group was unanimously in favor of retaining the "costume" part

446

though. It was felt that Bernie's work shouldn't go to waste. Sarah was pretty sure Daphne had convinced Miles on this point. She was clearly dying to dress up as Polyxena.

"Everyone remember it is just a party," said Miles, who looked completely exhausted and wrung out. "Let's not spend too much time on this. We all know we're going to be working round the clock until the opening. I'm not canceling it only because I think we all need something to lift our spirits. But tomorrow back to work bright and early, with no hangovers. And don't bring along the seventy-five expats you've met in the bar since arriving. If you don't know the person's last name, don't invite them."

The group nodded. It was agreed that it was a shame that Bernie, who had been looking forward to this party all summer, might have to miss it because of his fall down the stairs. Sarah was a little astonished by how easily the lies had rolled off her tongue when they had "found" him.

"Poor guy. I heard a crash and got there just in time to see him at the bottom of the stairs," she said. "He must have slipped." That was certainly a skill she had learned to perfect this summer: embroidering the truth until it was completely obscured.

"Oh, and Max will be back this evening," Miles had announced. "With his cousin, who will also be attending the party. So please try to not embarrass yourselves."

Sarah had managed to get herself deputized by the rest of the team to get the costumes from Bernie's room.

Bernard may have been a spy and a potential (sniveling) assassin, but he was also a damn fine dressmaker, Sarah had to admit as she scanned the rack of costumes and capes in his room. The fabrics, the colors, the embroidery, the buttons — everything was exquisite, and as close as humanly possible to the Polaroids of the actual oil portraits from the Lobkowicz Palace collection he had meticulously pinned to each outfit. The little white feather on Rudolf II's cap, the jeweled buttons of Zdenek's black tunic, Polyxena's red sleeves, Vratislav's furlined cape, Maria Manrique de Lara's lace ruff, Vratislav Pernstein's red velvet hat . . . There was even a spray-painted copper mask of the reliquary of St. Ursula. Amazing.

Sarah reminded herself now that she was in Bernie's room not just to collect brocade and damask but to look for hard evidence on the Marchesa Elisa.

Sarah was nervous about whether Max was in danger from the marchesa, although Nico had reassured her that it was unlikely Elisa would try to do anything more for now. Sarah couldn't even text him, in case the marchesa saw his phone.

She had a brief vision of Max and Elisa toasting her death, then pushed it out of her mind. No. Max wasn't involved with his cousin.

Although he was definitely hiding something.

Bernard's room was on the fourth floor, under the rafters. Sarah wondered how many times he had bumped his head on the slanted ceiling and rough beams. It had probably been part of the servant's quarters in earlier days.

She began searching methodically through some neatly ironed and folded clothes in the dresser. She found a lot of books on Rococo and some fan magazines devoted to a teen vampire movie. She flipped open Bernard's laptop and pondered the little box that asked her for his password. She tried "Rococo." Nothing.

She stopped herself for a moment. What was she doing here, trying to find evidence of a murderer? She was a grad student in music, not a cop or a detective. She was in over her head, way over her head.

Sarah stared at herself in the mirror on Bernard's wall. She definitely looked haggard, hollow-eyed and exhausted. She should get the costumes and leave.

Sarah pulled hangers from the closet and then bent down to move a box marked HATS AND PROPS! She pulled a few items out: a fan, a crucifix, and a stuffed dog.

She fingered the costume Bernard had planned for himself. Maria Manrique de Lara, mother of Polyxena. It included a quite realistic papier-mâché mask and wig.

The marchesa never missed a party.

A plan began to form in Sarah's head.

Forty-Two

No one was sure what the proper sound track was for a costume ball, so they settled on remixing the greatest hits of Beethoven, Mozart, Dvořák, and Handel. Douglas the nimble-fingered Croll expert had spent all day on his computer adding a hip-hop or rap beat to "Für Elise," the *New World Symphony, The Marriage of Figaro,* and other masterpieces of classical music. Sarah expected to feel like she was hearing her heroes getting smacked around, but she had to admit he made it possible to actually rave to the Fifth Symphony, which was pretty rad. Moses wanted lute music, so Douglas had mixed it with some Afro-Cuban beats and it was now thumping through the seventeenth-century frescoed Balcony Room on the second floor. It was making Miles very nervous that they were holding glasses of cold *pivo* under the gaze not only of a skeptical camel frescoed on the ceiling, but also priceless oils of Vratislav III, the last Pernstein, in armor and red tights, and Caroline Schwarzenberg, whose pained look probably came from having had twelve children.

Sarah turned and Vratislav himself was standing in front of her, in remarkably realistic armor and red tights. With the mask on his face, it took her a second to detect the scent of deer musk and realize it was Godfrey.

"Bernie, I'm so glad you recovered!" he said, waving his arm at the gathering of academics, other staff, and friends who crowded the room. There were probably a hundred people there, all in costumes and masks. "Feels like we've stepped back in time. Wonderful costumes you made!"

Sarah danced away, glad that her costume rendered her impenetrable. She wore the black dress with large flaring sleeves, a golden chain at her waist, and a white lace ruff at her neck. She clutched a white hankie in one gloved hand, and the Holy Infant of Prague in the other. A black and gold necklace with a cross hung at her neck. Platform boots she had found in Old Town at a clothing store called Quasimodo Vintage Fashion raised her to nearly six feet in height. But most important, the mask of

Maria's long-nosed, aristocratic gaze covered her face, and a large amount of padding made her seem much larger than she actually was.

It was Bernard's costume, the finest he had made, correct in every detail. It was making her sweat like a racehorse, but it seemed to be doing the trick.

Daphne bounded up in her Polyxena costume.

"Bernie, you're back!" cried Daphne. "Or should I say, 'Mama'?" Daphne giggled, obviously transported by her costume into something like good humor.

There were prizes to be given by Jana for the most historically accurate costume, most inventive, and silliest. Suzi was wearing a fake set of armor assembled from the pots and pans of the kitchen, although her sword looked suspiciously authentic. She was avidly pursuing Fiona, who had attractively painted herself in the Delft china pattern. Someone had hilariously come as the archives (brown box over head and papers glued everywhere with a clipboard on his back). Petr the valet made everyone scream when he came in with an actual horse, the spitting image of one in a life-sized portrait from the early 1700s. Miles made him take the horse outside immediately and tie it in the courtyard. The beer was flowing, as were the shots of *slivovitz* when Miles's back was turned. Miles hit the breaking point and threatened to shut the whole party down when Douglas, cross-dressed as Anne of Austria, came in with a case of vodka and three giggling local girls.

"That's enough," said Miles. "We must have some respect for the place."

People were dancing, large skirts gyrating and pantaloons swaying. The room was getting warm. Miles sighed and everyone cheered when he took the bottle of vodka Douglas offered him and downed a swig.

"I'm probably dead anyway," he muttered. *Me too,* thought Sarah.

Some are born great, some achieve greatness, and some have greatness thrust upon them, Sarah repeated to herself, for courage.

She spotted Moses, dressed as one of the peasants from Brueghel's *Haymaking,* the 1565 masterpiece that was one of the showpieces of the collection. It also contained one of art's silliest jokes. Brueghel had painted one peasant with the basket on her head, another with the basket on his shoulder, and a third whose head had been replaced altogether by the basket. *Ba-da-bum.* Moses wore a rough gray tunic and his head was obscured by a giant basket of fruit. He pranced up to her.

"Bernie, I lost my head!" he joked.

Max and the marchesa had still not arrived, although Max's wolfhound, Moritz, was circling the room looking hungrily at the tables of rabbits, pheasant, and wild boar that Godfrey had harvested for the occasion from the outlying family estates.

"There hasn't been much hunting in the last twenty years," Godfrey told her, dancing up, his breath stinking of ale. "It was time for a bit of a killing spree anyway. C'mon, Bernie, you big queen. Let's dance."

It felt good — and weird — to cut loose to a hip-hip version of "For Unto Us a Child Is Born" from Handel's *Messiah*. The music was certainly beautiful, but Sarah had never quite felt like grinding her hips to it before.

She was sweating profusely inside her costume. Sarah left Godfrey on the dance floor and moved to the window to cool down. She looked down at Malá Strana and out over Charles Bridge, which was now a necklace of lights against the dark river.

She realized that this was the same window she had peered out of on her first day at the palace. The window Sherbatsky had fallen out of, convinced he was crossing a bridge. Tears sprang into her eyes. She could see him so clearly, and just as on that first day she experienced a rush of vertigo. For a moment she thought she actually *could* see him — a filmy, phantom version of himself.

"Luigi," this ghost Sherbatsky whispered. "Luigi, wait for me."

"There you are," said a voice behind her.

Sarah, her heart in her throat, turned to see the person behind her. This was no vision.

Marchesa Elisa Lobkowicz DeBenedetti wore no costume. With her burnished skin, lioness mane of blond hair, and the Lobkowicz nose, she was striking enough. Inadvertently, Sarah took a step backward.

"So," said the marchesa, raising her glass of champagne. "We celebrate."

Sarah forced herself to move closer to the woman. She held the Infant of Prague doll tightly to her chest.

"Did you get the girl's cell phone?" Elisa asked, in a soft purr.

Sarah made a gesture of assent.

"And you sent an e-mail to Miles from her saying that she was tired and needed to get out of town for a few days?"

Sarah nodded.

"Do not worry," the marchesa went on. "I will take care of the rest. Tomorrow Max will get a text message from her telling him she was too afraid and went back home. Her mother will learn she died in a taxi crash on the way to the airport. *Poverina.*"

Sarah made a gesture that she hoped signaled complicity and understanding.

"Ottimo," said the marchesa. "A little gift will be waiting for you back in Cambridge. Something lovely to reward your efforts and remind you of our special understanding. Ah, look at your little *Bambino Gesu.* So sweet. What a dreadful party. Peasants pretending to be nobles. Remember, if you breathe a word, I will release my little video to the police. Or slit your throat. *Ciao.*"

As soon as the marchesa moved off into the crowd, Sarah slipped into the hallway and ran downstairs to her room. She threw off Bernard's costume and retrieved her phone — set to record — out of the dress of the Infant of Prague. She replayed the conversation. Muffled, but it was all there.

"Thanks, Jesus," she whispered to the wax doll.

She walked back upstairs and waded back into the party. Marchesa Elisa was standing now with Max in a corner of the Balcony Room. Max looked exhausted.

"How was Venice?" she asked loudly, waving her cell in her hand. "I'm sorry I'm late.

I was checking up on Bernie, poor lamb chop. Great party, huh? If music be the food of love, play on." The marchesa dropped her glass of champagne, which was made much less dramatic by the fact it was made of plastic.

"Venice was disappointing," said Max. "The Canova was a copy. But I picked up this." He put a long-nosed Pulcinello mask up to his face and Sarah laughed out loud, watching the marchesa out of the corner of her eye, who was frantically scanning the room for Bernard, or rather Maria Manrique de Lara, no doubt preparing to give him hell.

"What on earth are we listening to?" asked Max, as a remixed Hallelujah chorus boomed through the room, stuttering "Ha-Ha-Ha-Ha-ha-ha-ha . . . ," which was Sarah's exact thought as the marchesa strode out of the room.

"Max," said Sarah, grabbing his arm. "I have to talk to you."

FORTY-THREE

Present fears are less than horrible imaginings.

For some reason, Charlotte Yates couldn't get *Macbeth* out of her head. She wished, as she sometimes did when she allowed herself a moment of self-pity, that she had someone she could swap quotations of the Bard with. Or even just show off her own acute memory skills, acquired from mastering an ancient Greek memory retrieval system during her lonely adolescence. But it was dangerous to let anyone know how good her memory was. One always needed to retain the right to credibly say "I don't remember" when questioned, and it was hard to get away with that when people knew you could recite half the First Folio by heart.

Stars, hide your fires;
Let not light see my black and deep
    desires.

The senator looked around her office. She hadn't bothered to redecorate when she moved in. Not that she didn't have strong ideas about décor, but you didn't put time and money into rentals, and that's what this office was. Just a little pied-à-terre. Once in the Oval, she would assert her taste in a more permanent way. She'd definitely return that ghastly bust of Churchill to the Smithsonian or wherever it came from. Had anyone done something attractive with Margaret Thatcher's head?

Thinking of the Smithsonian made Charlotte think of Miles Wolfmann. She had intimated that the directorship of the museum was his in return for a certain amount of discretion, and the sooner she got him installed there, the better. A favor extended, but not yet taken, could easily be mistaken for a bribe. But of course she wasn't actually bribing Miles. Charlotte Yates didn't offer bribes, or take them. She simply believed in free markets. That was American!

At least Miles's decision to grow testicles had come late enough that she had secured her letters. The letters were hers.

But too many mistakes had been made. This is how it always went, when you left things in the hands of amateurs. Mistakes got made, and then you made mistakes covering up other mistakes. Then somebody had to get killed. Or you needed to start a war, just because it was too much bother to try to unravel all the little mistakes and make amends and apologies and make sure everyone felt good about themselves, or whatever.

We have scorched the snake, not killed it.

It should have all gone quite smoothly. Making Max look unstable turned out to be something Max did very well on his own. That the Russians had shown up and planted a spy in the form of Andy Blackman had made the game more intriguing, in a way. She would have admired the marchesa's skill in framing Andy's death on her cousin and the indefatigable Weston chippy, but like most of the plans Elisa had made, it had gone badly. Furthermore, she had enlisted (again, without consulting her!) this doleful Bernard creature to be her minion and had blackmailed him with promises of snuffboxes, then made a theatrical mess of the thing.

And it had been a jolt, learning that the blind kid who had been skulking about the Internet looking for dirt on her was the pupil of the Sarah Weston person. And someone at an Internet café near Prague Castle had done a similar search. Sarah

Weston was becoming a serious pest.

Perhaps it was time for something clean and definitive. Well, soon enough she would have her boots on the ground. The opening of the museum. She had been planning on taking a lovely stroll through the scenes of her halcyon youth. Darling Yuri. So many secrets. So many memories. But now she had all these mistakes to clean up. Things that were absolutely not her fault!

There had to be some simple solution. Was there *anything,* or *anybody* left in that museum worth saving? Maybe it was time to really wipe the slate clean and give herself a fresh start. It was something to think about.

Hell is murky.

FORTY-FOUR

Sarah stared in dismay at the empty room.

They had crawled through the tunnels and pushed open the hatch, this time armed with a giant battery-powered lantern. The room was bare of every last trace of the objects that had been stored there for seventy years. Nothing remained but cobwebs.

Max came up through the hatch and looked around, confused.

"You wanted to show me an empty wine cellar?"

Sarah shone her light all over the walls and floor. There was really nothing left.

"This room was full of things," she said, her mind going a million miles an hour. "Secret things. Nico saw it. And Bernard."

Sarah had not told Max what had happened yet. She had only said, "I have something to show you." She had been planning on telling him everything once they were here.

"Where is Nico?"

"I don't know. I didn't see him at the party tonight."

"And Bernard's — where?"

"At the hospital." Sarah's heart had begun to pound. Could Bernard have regained consciousness, and double-crossed them? Called the marchesa and arranged for the room to be emptied right under their noses? But, no, the marchesa would never have compromised herself, and she had been genuinely shocked to see Sarah. So that left —

"How well do you actually know Nicolas?" Sarah asked.

"He's always been around," Max said, vaguely, running his hands over the empty shelves and walls as if they might contain clues. "My whole life. After my father died he came with me to Prague."

Sarah thought for a moment. Bernard could have killed her at any time and didn't. Nico had appeared at precisely the right moment to save her. Nico had hit Bernard and knocked him out, but what if he had only "hit" him? Was the goose egg on his head even real? What if the two of them had been in league all along, and had staged the murder attempt to scare her into getting out of there? What if Bernie and Nico were now a thousand miles away, with a truckload of treasure?

"Damn it," Max said. "What are we going to do?"

What could they do? They couldn't go to the police with stories of treasure that showed up in no catalog. It would be like reporting a missing unicorn.

And Sarah was pretty certain that if they went to the hospital, there would be no record of Bernard there. She shone her light around the room again in desperation. And then aimed it at the ceiling.

"Oh, come *ON*," she said, pointing. There was something written on a wooden beam. "How the hell does he do that?"

"You think Nico left it?" Max said, peering upward.

"It's kind of a trademark move," Sarah said. "He must have known I would check. Hoist me up?"

Max made a bridge of his hands and Sarah kicked off her shoe. Max lifted, and Sarah read the minute handwriting.

Only one who knows longing
Knows what I suffer! — Op. 83

"Fucking Nico." Max brought her down.

465

"What's Op. 83?"

"He's referring to Beethoven's Opus 83," Sarah said. "A song cycle LVB did to some poems by Goethe."

"Beethoven wrote songs?"

"He wrote the music for songs, sure," Sarah said. "He wrote the music to 'Elegy on the Death of a Poodle.' For real. It's very sad."

"It might not have been Nico. That could have been there forever. It could have nothing to do with this." Max paced around the little room, getting angrier and more frustrated by the minute. "He's the one Elisa warned me about, you know. Not you, Nico."

Elisa. Sarah needed to tell him about Elisa.

"What did she say?" Sarah asked.

"She told me he was very dangerous and that I was a fool to give him the run of the place. I knew he was a thief, but I trusted him. Goddammit, he was supposed to be helping me." Max looked ready to fall apart.

"He can't have taken it far," said Sarah, desperately hoping this was true. "I mean, it's not like you can stuff an entire room of historical curiosities into your carry-on and board a flight to Rio, can you? At the very least they'd stop you for the golem dust."

Max didn't say anything.

"He moved it, Max. To keep it safe. The poem is a clue to where." She told herself this must be true. She couldn't have been so duped. Could she?

"What's the poem again?"

Sarah recited:

Alone and cut off
From all joy,
I look into the firmament
In that direction.

Ach! he who loves and knows me
Is far away.
I am reeling,
My entrails are burning.
Only one who knows longing
Knows what I suffer!

" 'My entrails are burning' sounds better in German," Sarah said. "Well, slightly better."

"Speaking of entrails, let's get out of here," Max said. "Smells like something died in here."

You have no idea, thought Sarah.

There was something about walking and talking. Sarah had always felt that it was easier to unspool a long story while striding side by side rather than staring face-to-face, or even sitting across a table with a glass of wine. It was as if the action of moving one's legs released the words in a steady rhythm, sentence building upon sentence until the tale was told. And the lack of eye contact helped you through the rough bits.

Max and Sarah left the palace, walked through the eastern gate at the end of Jiřská Street, down the steep steps to the Malostranská tram stop, and through the streets of the darkened city.

Nico had not answered his cell phone. There was nothing to do but wait.

It was time to trust Max.

As they wove their way through Malá Strana, across Charles Bridge, through Old Town, the Old Jewish Quarter, up Paris Street, through Old Town Square, and on into Wenceslas Square, Sarah told Max everything that had happened. Her suspicions that Charlotte Yates was the author of those letters to Yuri Bespalov. How Pols discovered Marchesa Elisa's connection to Charlotte. She told him about going into the tunnels, about nearly drowning when they flooded. The discovery of the library, the briefcase with KGB secrets, Tycho Brahe's journal, the Immortal Beloved letters, and the cloak. For some reason, that brought Max up short more than anything else.

"Describe the cloak," Max said, intently. She did so.

Sarah described the bad trip she'd taken on the corrupted drug when she put on the saturated cape. How at first it had all seemed like the past: She had seen his grandfather killing the Nazi soldier, the young couple from the 1970s, the Russian man (Yuri Bespalov, surely) who had left the briefcase and taken the Aztec amulet.

"Then it got a little hairy." Sarah didn't tell him all of the terrifying things she had seen on the drug, except to say that "basically it makes your worst fears come alive."

She told him how Bernard pulled a gun on her. "Max, you need to know this. He said it was Elisa who killed Eleanor."

Max drew in a shaky breath but said nothing.

"He said Elisa sent him to kill me."

Max started walking very quickly. Half-running beside him, Sarah told how Nico had saved her life, how he had helped her get Bernard out of there, and how they had pretended to the others that he had fallen down the stairs. How she had searched Bernard's room for clues, how she knew that no one would ever believe her without proof. How she had taken Bernard's costume, padded herself up to be his size, and tricked the marchesa into believing that she was talking to Bernard himself at the party. Finally, Sarah played the recording for Max.

"Her mother will learn she died in a taxi crash on the way to the airport." The marchesa's words slithered out of the iPhone like a serpent.

Max listened, his face unreadable. They walked on in silence, under the arcades of Wenceslas Square, past the cheesy nightclubs, uphill toward the brilliantly illuminated National Museum with its impressive gold dome.

Wenceslas Square was not a bad place to ponder murder and political mayhem. The country's first proclamation of independence had been read aloud here in 1918. The Nazis had marched here, and been marched against. In January 1969, twenty-year-old Jan Palach had set himself on fire here to protest the Soviet invasion. In 1989, hundreds of thousands of people had gathered here peacefully in what would come to be called the Velvet Revolution.

Now, decades into capitalism, the square was lined with strip clubs and fast-food joints. Max sat down on the steps of the imposing museum.

"I never learned to play chess," Max said at last. "I'm not a strategist. I don't really think ahead. I just do whatever seems right in the moment."

Sarah nodded.

"Elisa asked me to marry her," said Max.

Sarah blinked.

"She made a good case for the tax advantages, and the fact that our lineages would be consolidated."

Sarah stared at a tall woman in a pink Afro and hot pants lighting a joint while standing on the curving bronze cross set into the paving stones that marked where Jan Palach had ignited himself.

"Are you . . ." asked Sarah at last, her mouth dry.

"Am I what?"

"Are you going to marry her?"

"I told her I'd have to talk to my accountant before I committed to her plan."

Sarah and Max stared at each other.

"I can't even imagine what kind of prenup you'd need," Sarah said at last.

Max laughed, although for a second Sarah thought he might be crying a little, too.

"What's upsetting is that she came really close to having me convinced," Max said. "I mean, she said that this was a marriage in the oldest sense, to unite a splintered noble house, to consolidate holdings of art and real estate for the future heirs. She acknowledged that she's older, and that she would never expect me to be a real husband to her, except for certain events and to produce children. She named lots of examples, kings in Sweden and dukes in Luxembourg. She talked about our duty to our history, to the Czech people. She made it sound like the right thing to do. And all along, she's been the only one saying that I actually have what it takes to be the head of the family. She fought with her own family and took my side. But it was all a lie."

"She's very good," said Sarah quietly. "Like, *Borgia* good."

Max nodded. "But what do we do now? We can't go to the police with any of this, can we?"

Sarah shook her head. It was the blackest moment of the night. Even the floodlights on the statue of Wenceslas barely penetrated the gloom. Somewhere nearby someone was shouting the way drunks do just before they pass out.

"You should go home, get out of here," groaned Max as if he were waking from a dream. "What if Bernard had killed you? My God."

"I'm okay," said Sarah. "I'm not leaving."

"We'll never prove she killed anyone. Your recording convinced me, but it won't hold up in court. She's too smart for that. And I bet she really does have a videotape of Bernard. God knows what else. Maybe it's better to just give in to her. You know, like in a Mafia family. Make my peace with it. I could marry Elisa and walk away from it all, let her run it, take a salary. Go back to the States, work on my music, forget any of this ever happened. It's too big a mess."

"You can pretend to yourself that you don't care about any of this," Sarah said. "But you do, and the longer you go on trying to deny that, the more time and ground you lose to people like the marchesa. You may not be a born strategist, but you need to become one. We have got to make a plan."

"Step one, keep you alive," said Max.

"Step two, you need to keep Elisa close but not too close," said Sarah, practically choking on the name. "She needs to think you heard some wild accusations from me that you didn't believe. That it's driven us apart. Don't turn down her marriage idea. Tell her you're exploring it. It will help keep both of us alive."

Max looked at her admiringly. "Yes. And step three is to gather something we can take to the police to stop her."

"I'm worried about the opening," said Sarah. "Both the marchesa and Charlotte Yates will be there."

"Along with ninety-seven different kinds of security and hundreds of other dignitaries. If Charlotte wants to keep her past hidden, the last thing she's going to do is make a scene here, of all places."

Sarah nodded but still felt uneasy. "Max, there's something else, isn't there? I know you've been keeping something from me."

Max looked at her.

She had trusted him. But to work it had to be mutual.

"I know what Sherbatsky was looking for when he took the drug," said Sarah. "But what were you? I know it can't have just been your mom. Why did you and Nico act so squirrelly when I mentioned hell portals? Why were you so interested in the cape I found in the library? What did you really hide in a safe in Venice? Why did you keep taking the drug even when you knew it was dangerous to do it by yourself?"

Max sighed. "It will sound kind of stupid," he said.

"Try me."

"Okay." Max looked her dead in the eye. "I'm looking for the Golden Fleece."

FORTY-FIVE

Sarah tried not to laugh, although she felt pretty close to it.

"What are we talking about here?" she said. "The Golden Fleece like: Jason and the Argonauts?" She thought about a Japanese cartoon she saw as a kid that followed Jason's many adventures aboard the *Argo* as he traveled the Aegean looking for the Golden Fleece. There were sea monsters, and skeleton soldiers that sprang up from the ground. She remembered equally well or better the Cap'n Crunch and Count Chocula commercials that punctuated the cartoon. Wait, there had been a theme song.

"Go, go Jason, now don't be scared! You gotta keep looking for that ram of gold!" Sarah started to sing.

"Sarah, I'm being serious."

"This is real?" Sarah felt like she had swallowed a lot of tales since coming to Prague, but this seemed excessive.

"To be honest, I don't know what it is," Max said. "Who knows if there ever was a Golden Fleece, or an Ark of the Covenant, or a Holy Grail? I only know that the Secret Order of the Golden Fleece was set up in Rudolf II's time to protect something very specific. And I'm supposed to be the head of the Secret Order now, and I have no idea what I'm guarding, or where it is."

"Well, if there's an Order, then there must be other members?" asked Sarah. Although she could see how it might be embarrassing for Max at the meetings, especially if he was supposed to be the head guy. "Hey, so, like, our Order? Like, what's our secret again?"

"There is an Order of the Golden Fleece, but it's just an honorary title," Max explained. "There's a Spanish branch and an Austrian one. There aren't any meetings or anything. And some people think the Spanish branch was discredited because Juan Carlos made King Abdullah of Saudi Arabia a member and the origins of the whole deal are all about saving Christendom from the Muslims. I think it's a totally bogus operation, although they give you a nice necklace when you're in it. I'm supposed to be officially inducted next month. I'm not talking about *that*. I'm talking about the *Secret* Order of the Golden Fleece."

Sarah waited.

"This." Max pulled out his cigarette case and handed it to her. She ran her fingers over the symbol inscribed on the front.

"It's the symbol Nico — at least I think it was Nico — left on my ceiling in Cambridge," said Sarah.

"It's an alchemical symbol," Max said. "Made by John Dee when he was court alchemist to Rudolf II. It's meant to stand for the unity of everything . . . knowledge, all material things, you name it. The circle with the dot is the sun and the earth, and that's the crescent moon crowning it. Then coming down from the sun: the cross, which rests upon the zodiacal sign of Aries. Aries, the ram. The golden ram is a symbol of the sun, of the way the sun illuminates all, which is knowledge."

"Max." Sarah's mind was whirling. "What did Professor Sherbatsky know about this? He sent me a letter, before he died, with just the symbol on it."

"Sherbatsky was taking the drug to look for Beethoven," Max said. "At that point all either of us knew was that the drug was some chemical that Ludwig had taken. Something that the 7th had given him. I was looking for my ancestors, trying to tie together all these clues that kept popping up. References in letters to something secret, something that had been lost and must be found, something that must be found before others found it. The Golden Fleece. Puzzles, codes, and over and over again, this symbol. One night I was stumbling around in Golden Lane — you know that row of little houses in the castle built in the sixteenth century — when I saw something really strange." Max bit his lip.

"I saw . . . Nico."

"Nico."

"I wasn't entirely sure about the date," Max said. "Because I was never good at controlling the drug and I skipped around in time a lot, but it was definitely Nico and it seemed to be early seventeenth century. He was with a man. The man had a piece of copper across the bridge of his nose."

"Tycho Brahe," Sarah said. "Nico called him *Master*. And he said that Tycho had given him something, a potion of some kind . . ." Sarah realized what Nico had told her was true. He hadn't just been relating historical anecdotes.

Nico was Jepp.

"On the night that I saw them," Max said, "Tycho was telling Nico, whom he called Jepp, that he was supposed to steal something from Rudolf II. 'You will know it when you see it,' he kept saying. And Jepp was scared out of his mind, that's the emotion I was following, I think. Nico's fear. He kept saying, 'No, Master, I cannot touch the Fleece. I am unworthy.' But in the end he promised to try."

"And you think he succeeded?" Sarah said. "That Jepp — Nico — stole it?"

"He bribed Rudolf's lover and says he was too frightened to even look in the bag he got from him. Just handed the thing over to his master — Brahe. Nico says he doesn't know if what he got was the Golden Fleece, or what the Golden Fleece really was. They had it — whatever it was — for one night, then gave it back. Rudolf never knew. But according to Nico, Rudolf was obsessed with keeping the object secret, not letting it fall into the wrong hands. His brother's hands in particular."

What did Rudolf bring the alchemists to court for? Gold. Immortality. Knowledge. Sarah blinked. History had said they failed.

479

But history was wrong. Whatever the Fleece was — a book, a crystal ball, a philosopher's stone, a golden ram's hide? — one night with it had led Tycho to some breathtaking pharmaceutical discoveries . . .

"And you think your family . . ."

"I think my family has been looking for whatever the Fleece is for all these years. That's what the Secret Order is all about. But I'm just guessing. I don't really know. Tycho made the drug from it, or because of it, and the formula he wrote down has been in my family. But there's more than one version. Sounds like that cloak you found in the library is one of his mistakes. The original thing . . . it would be hugely powerful. Maybe a way to move not just backward in time but forward as well. To see everything, understand everything. The unity of all things. All the clues I've found so far seem to point to the Fleece being hidden somewhere on the castle grounds. Nico thinks so, too, but I can't tell if he's trying to help me or not. He said that some things were better left hidden. And if he is Jepp . . ."

Sarah and Max stared at each other.

Sarah thought about Nico frantically riffling through Tycho Brahe's book of formulas. Crawling under the table.

"Only one who knows longing knows what I suffer," she quoted.

"Wait, you said that's from a poem by Goethe?" Max asked, his tone sharpening. "The same Goethe that wrote *Faust,* right? Not some other musical poet Goethe that I've never heard of?"

"No, the *Faust* Goethe. Why?"

"Maybe Nico *was* leaving us a clue," Max said. "There's a Faust House here in Prague. Faustuv dum. It's under construction right now. Might be a good place to hide the contents of a secret library."

"Faust," said Sarah. "The original Man Who Knew Too Much."

FORTY-SIX

Charles Square was too far to walk. They jumped in a taxi, which promptly got stuck in traffic.

"Traffic at two a.m.?" asked Max in annoyance.

The driver was talking on his cell phone in rapid Czech.

"I'm sorry," whispered Sarah. "I shouldn't have gone to look for the library without you."

Max took her hand.

"It's okay," he said. "It's my responsibility and I'm going to take care of it."

"Nice," said Sarah. "That's the kind of Sworn Protector of the Realm talk we like to hear."

The driver got off the cell phone. "Where you go again?" he asked.

"We're meeting some friends near Faust House," Sarah said. "You know where that is?"

"You American tourists? Charles Square not safe at night," he said.

"We'll be okay," said Sarah.

"Faust House closed till December. No tourists now."

"We'll definitely visit it next trip," Sarah assured him.

"In 1300s house owned by Vaclav of Opava. Alchemist. You know alchemist?"

"Yes, alchemist," said Sarah, feeling ridiculous. Max spoke perfect Czech but he seemed content to let Sarah do the pidgin English thing.

"Yah. Then Rudolf II, you know Rudolf II?"

"Yes," said Sarah. "Uh-huh. Rudolf II."

"His astrologer Jakub Krucinek live there. Younger son kill older son for treasure. Very famous Prague murder."

"Treasure?" Sarah almost shouted. Max grabbed her hand.

"Yah. Never find treasure. Then Edward Kelley live there. Also alchemist. He kill a man. Also famous Prague murder."

Kelley. Those alchemists were truly ubiquitous. And deadly.

"Then the wizard Mladota. He blow big hole in roof. His son make crazy mechanicals, like flying staircase and electric doorknobs. Then later student find alchemy book. They say devil take him up through hole in ceiling. Why through ceiling I don't know, because everyone know there is hell portal in the basement. Much easier for devil to use, no? Then Karl Jaenig, crazy guy who paint walls with requiems, sleep in coffin."

"Is there a faster way to get there?" asked Max.

"You know a lot about Faustuv dum," said Sarah to the driver.

"I am tour guide, too. Famous Prague murders. Now there's new one. You hear? Lobkowicz Palace? Lady kill herself in cage. Very bloody."

He handed Sarah a business card. "Night tours of Prague's most famous murder scenes."

They jumped out in front of the baroque salmon-and-white façade of Faust House, and Sarah paid the driver, who sped off, and turned to Max. "The place has quite a history," she said. "Mladota the wizard? And its own hell portal."

"I guess it's a pharmacy now," said Max, waving at the green cross near the door.

The building, it turned out, was currently owned by the medical school of Charles University. Everything was shut and locked up for the night.

"Hey, Jepp!" Max called up at the dark building. "Open up, you crazy dwarf bastard!"

"Shhh . . ." Sarah clamped a hand over his mouth.

Max looked up at the building in front of them.

"Something is here," Max said, more soberly now. "I can feel it, can't you?"

Sarah was about to argue when she realized she could feel . . . something.

"We need to find Nico," she said. "He has Tycho's diary, and I think the formula for the drug is in there. If he can make some . . ."

"What do you want to see?" Max asked her.

Everything, she thought. She wanted to see history unfold around her. Beethoven. She could watch him compose every day. She looked at Max. "What do you want to see?"

"Where the Fleece is hidden. What the hell it is. What's in Tycho's book would be a purer form of the drug than LVB's toenails. It might be the ride of our lives. If Nico can make it."

"Do you trust Nico?" Sarah asked. "I mean, what does he really want? Wealth? Art? Women?"

"Oh, Nico?" Max said. "He just wants to find a way to die."

FORTY-SEVEN

"Have you seen my fleece?"

The question made Sarah jump slightly, which wasn't a good thing, since she had an early eighteenth-century violin by Johann Georg Helmer in her hands.

After standing outside Faust House for an hour, coming up with and then rejecting an increasingly ridiculous set of break-in plans, Max had taken her back to the palace and then left in search of Nico or any trace of the missing treasure.

"I had it at breakfast," Suzi explained, coming forward into the exhibition room. "Now that we've got temperature control, my ass is freezing. I didn't leave it in here, did I?"

Sarah shook her head.

"Very tasteful," Suzi commented, pointing to the subtle light blue paint that Sarah had chosen for the walls of the Music Room.

"Thanks." Sarah hung the violin carefully

on a wall bracket and stepped back to scrutinize the effect.

"What time is it?" Sarah asked. "Noon already?"

"Girl, it's four in the afternoon," Suzi drawled. "You've been in the zone."

The palace had been uncharacteristically quiet all morning. At breakfast, the assembled scholars had greeted one another with hangover-inflected monosyllables. With a faint air of contrition, they had all grabbed coffee, fruit, rolls, and then hustled off to their rooms. Sarah had, in fact, been priding herself that she had spent the morning carefully conducting her work and *not* obsessing over every detail of the past forty-eight hours.

The marchesa had jetted back to Italy for a couture fitting, or so she had told Max. *Work,* Sarah had told herself, before falling asleep. *Focus on your work.*

Although truthfully, while she methodically cataloged, arranged, and organized, a second narrative had been running underneath her working thoughts as busily as the CNN news ticker.

Her primary concern was not the whereabouts of the Golden Fleece, nor the relative trustworthiness of Nicolas Pertusato. Neither was she, for the moment anyway, fretting over the arrival of Charlotte Yates or what new devious machinations Marchesa Elisa might be concocting. These things would be enough to thoroughly freak a person out for a lifetime, but Sarah wasn't thinking about them.

Sarah was thinking about the letters from Beethoven she had found in the violin. She was thinking about the Immortal Beloved.

It would change the face of musical scholarship, certainly, if it were revealed that the Immortal Beloved was *not* Antonie Brentano nor any other woman, but a nickname for a *drug* that Ludwig and his patron, the eccentric Joseph Franz Maximilian, had been experimenting with. A drug that allowed a composer with rapidly degenerating hearing to move around in time so that he might hear his own music. A drug that was, in some way, derived or extracted from an alchemical secret that held unprecedented power.

Okay, fuck musical scholarship. These revelations would change . . . well, everything.

Was that a good thing?

Sarah was identifying very strongly with Beethoven today. Luigi had also been pulled into the path of alchemy by friendship with a Lobkowicz. Sarah looked around the room, which was slowly coming together to be recognizable as a *museum* room. It was elegant, it was serene, it was appropriate, but Sarah couldn't help feeling that the display cases diminished the pulsing glory of what they contained. Tourists would pass these objects, perhaps lean in and read the explanatory notes, be guided by the inevitable audio recordings. But would they get a sense of the life they contained? These things were real, they were alive. They had been held, caressed, played by actual people. They had been tossed over shoulders, perhaps struck with impatience or irritation by their performers. From these fragile strings, soon to be protected under glass, had come heart-stopping music, passion, pain, envy, longing.

Sarah picked up a letter from LVB — an acknowledgment of the stipend he received from the Lobkowicz family, dated June 30, 1821. Even after the death of Beethoven's friend and champion in 1816, the stipend had continued to be paid by the 7th prince's son. There was no way this document could convey what she knew about the relationship between Beethoven and his patron. Important musicologists, composers, musicians of note would travel to look at these things. They would be given special access.

A pair of white gloves so they could handle the papers. A photographer would take their picture, perhaps with Max standing by smiling. But they wouldn't know . . .

"Girl," Shuziko drawled. "You need a break, honey. You look fried. Come to the gun show."

Sarah let herself be led. The horrible old flowered wallpaper had been stripped away, and now the armory rooms were fiery red, and Suzi had arranged the weapons with a dramatic flair. A huge pinwheel of rifles decorated one wall.

"Like a gun flower," said Suzi proudly. "A goddammed gun daisy!"

A suit of armor stood in the middle of one room, surrounded by a gate of upright guns and flags. There were portraits of hunting Lobkowiczes on the walls. Suzi led Sarah around her domain, pointing out interesting features to Sarah.

"These aristocrats —" She shook her head. "Hunting was like an art for them. That's what I was trying to convey. It was political, it was social, it was theatrical. It was in their blood. They knew that power was beautiful. They had respect for power. That's why I wanted something sumptuous and sexy. Power is an aphrodisiac."

"I think you've really captured it," Sarah

commented, looking around. "It's like if Ted Nugent had a *Masterpiece Theatre* porn fantasy."

"Awesome," said Shuziko. "That's kind of what I was going for. Class with ass."

The two wandered into other rooms. Moses Kaufmann was working with two local Czech researchers at arranging a sort of all-purpose Decorative Arts collection. Moses chatted with Suzi while Sarah leaned over cabinets filled with jewelry boxes, caskets, miniature flasks, tankards, shagreen notebooks, bells, locks, keys, model figurines of animals, reliquaries. It was baffling to think that although these things were being housed in this newly created museum, they were all essentially personal property. If Max wanted to, he could probably shut the doors and spend all day playing with his things by himself. Pour Diet Coke in Meissen teacups. Pluck out "Smoke on the Water" on an eighteenth-century viola.

"Nicolas brought me this from Nelahozeves," said Moses, pointing to a large cabinet in the corner. "Lovely. Augsburg, late seventeenth century. It's a traveling medicine and toilet chest. See this copper panel? It depicts an apothecary's shop."

"Nicolas?" Sarah asked, trying not to

sound too eager. "When? Is he around? I needed to ask him something."

"Haven't seen him in a few days," Moses said absently, lost in admiration of the chest. "But I think he called Daphne earlier."

As she dashed through Fiona's room, shining with the immense collection of Delft china, Fiona herself, clad in a spotless apron and bent over a cabinet, called out, "Is there a glare? The Golden Fleece is terribly tricky to light properly."

Sarah stopped in her tracks, looked over the plates, jars, and flasks. "The 1556 dinner service," Fiona said, in her high, fluting voice. "Commissioned to celebrate Polyxena's father being awarded the Order of the Golden Fleece." They were emblazoned with Polyxena's family's crest: a black bull, his nose pierced with a golden ring, and a badly painted yellow lamb tied to, or suspended from, some heraldic trim, almost like a pendant on a necklace.

Sarah made her excuses and hurried into the portrait rooms, where she found Daphne in front of a large oil painting.

"De frame is very correct," Daphne said, in her usual crisp and humorless way. "Do you not agree?"

Sarah looked up at the portrait of handsome Ladislav, brother of the 1st Prince

Lobkowicz, in his nifty white-and-gold outfit, with the large key tucked into his pants. She remembered that Daphne had told them that Ladislav had plotted against Rudolf II, and had been sent into exile. "A traitor," Daphne had called him. And yet the family had kept his portrait.

"It looks great," said Sarah. "Hey, have you heard from Nicolas?"

"Miles," said Daphne, as Miles came in, "I vould like to display that key Moses found, here vith the portrait."

Sarah remembered how Nico had been fixated on the key when Moses first produced it. "What does it open?" she asked.

"No one knows," said Miles. "It's very mysterious, because Rudolf made a big deal out of it. I mean, a key in a box was their whole wedding present from the emperor. Little bit like getting a car key for graduation, no? You kind of expect there to be a car outside. But in this case, where's the car?"

Sarah's phone beeped. It was a text from Max. *Meet me outside. Now.* "I need your sign-off on the final catalog copy," said Miles to Sarah.

"Absolutely," said Sarah. "But you know I was hoping to get over to the library at some point today. To find some household receipts there from the dates that concern Beethoven. I thought it might be nice to have a few more things to round out the general picture of the patronage of the 7th to Ludwig. Fees to the musicians that were hired for the private performances. That kind of thing."

"Okay, but by tomorrow at the latest."

Sarah came bounding out of the palace to find Max, resplendent in a perfectly pressed Brooks Brothers suit and gray fedora, revving his red 1930 Alfa convertible. Moritz sat in the back, lacking only a pair of goggles to complete the picture.

"You know where Nico is?" asked Sarah, jumping in.

"Someone at Nela just ordered a pizza with my credit card," said Max as the little car sailed through the castle gate.

FORTY-EIGHT

"Friends don't let friends do drugs," said Max as they strode into the Knight's Hall. "Not by themselves, anyway."

They hadn't needed Moritz's help to follow the trail of pizza boxes up the stairs to the second floor of Nelahozeves Castle. It seemed the Knight's Hall had become Nico's improvised laboratory. He was cooking something over a Bunsen burner placed in the enormous stone Renaissance fireplace. In front of this was a modern foldout table (horribly incongruous with the larger-than-life frescoes in delicate tints on the walls) covered in vials, boxes, and scribbled-on pieces of paper.

"Hej god dag," said Nico in what sounded like Danish, barely glancing up at them. "I think there are a couple of slices of pepperoni left. But the Czechs really don't do a great pizza."

Sarah grabbed the little man by his shirt

and lifted him off the ground. "Where is it?"

"Where is what?"

"Don't give me that. Is it in Faust House or not?"

Nico smiled in an aggrieved way. "Your tone — why, you didn't suspect that I would — Sarah. Really." Nico sounded terribly disappointed, and Sarah felt ashamed for half a second. Then, less so.

"You disappeared. And so did everything else. What was I supposed to think?"

Max stepped forward and Nico gave him a courtly bow.

"It is all safe and sound in Faust House. Where Marchesa Elisa will not think to prowl and where the conditions are . . . sympathetic." He brushed himself off and turned back to his Bunsen burner. "I believe I may have found the recipe you have been looking for," Nico said, evenly. "We might do a little cautious experimenting."

"We?"

"Tycho called it 'Westonia,' after Edward Kelley's stepdaughter, Elizabeth Weston. I find that very appropriate, Miss Sarah Weston. I don't know if I've got the formula correct. There may be . . . impurities."

Sarah could already feel her heart pounding in anticipation.

"Remember, it is not really about moving through time," Nicolas instructed her. "It is about *perception.* And about releasing the notion of linear time, which turns out to be a very difficult task for most people. Impossible, really. Like contemplating infinity. You really need to be on drugs to do it. LSD works fairly well. Psychotropic mushrooms. Which are child's play to what we have here."

"What *do* we have here, Nico?" Max sounded concerned.

"The master's journal is a palimpsest," the little man explained. "There are markings that have been erased and written over. It's difficult for me to know exactly what does what. I did not often assist in the laboratory, although I collected many of the materials."

"You mean stole." Max arched an eyebrow. "I bet you did."

"And toward the end," Nicolas continued smoothly, "the master became very secretive. Dee left Prague, he was frightened of what was happening. Kelley, in his foolishness, tried to warn the emperor against Tycho and nearly lost his life for it, too."

"But this Westonia," Sarah insisted, struggling with the odd fact of sharing her name not just with a long-dead poet, but also . . .

"This is really the drug?"

"Yes, I believe it is. Unfortunately, making just the small amount I did completely exhausted our supply of several key ingredients. I have used up the last measure of golem's dust, for instance. Which is not an easy thing to replace."

Sarah watched him work, the reality sinking in that the person she was looking at was over four hundred years old. Nico appeared to be in his forties, with a slight salt-and-pepper effect in his hair. What must it be like, to be alive for so long, to have seen so much?

The little man picked up the iron tongs and reached into the pan over the Bunsen burner, extracting a small square, about the size of a sugar cube. He placed it on a tiny plate.

"Is that it?" Sarah sniffed. Musky, resinous. Amber. Her body began trembling. *God,* she thought, *I'm like an addict.*

"This is it," Nico agreed. "But it's only enough for one person."

Sarah looked at Max.

"If it's not safe, then it should be me," he said.

"Your life is more valuable," she said. "You have a lot of stuff to look after. I don't even have a cat."

"Your lives are equally valuable, and equally insignificant," Nicolas interjected, fussily. "This is merely a matter of maximizing our potential. Sarah is particularly suited for the drug, and I believe it was Professor Sherbatsky's wish that she follow in his footsteps."

Max shot the little man a dark look.

"Oh, you know what I mean." Nico stamped his small foot. "Sarah, I believe you are better at navigating on the drug than Max, and we might only have this one chance until I am able to locate a corrupt rabbi in Josefov who can get his hands on some more *pulvis golem* and I manage to track down sixteenth-century elk bones, etcetera. You can't just order these things on Amazon, children. And yes, to be frank, Sarah, if *you* die your death will be much easier to clean up than Max's, so there you have it."

"What we need to discuss next," Max said, "is focus. The Golden Fleece."

"I haven't heard it spoken of since Tycho's time," said Nico.

"If we can find it, then we don't have to worry about Tycho's formulas. If we can find that Fleece . . ."

"We'll know everything," said Sarah. "But it's like a needle in a haystack. We don't even know what we're looking for."

"You'll feel it when you're close," said Nico. "The energy of it. For the few moments I carried the bag it was in . . ." He shook his head, still shaken by the memory, four centuries later. "Think of what you'll experience today as an enormous orchestra score," Nico continued. "You are listening in for one instrument among thousands. Well, tens of millions really."

"Golden Fleece," Max said. "That's the instrument we're looking for. We'll start here, and then if nothing turns up, and you're . . . okay . . . we'll head back to Prague Castle."

"Okay," Sarah said.

"There isn't much time," said Max. "So you can't let yourself get distracted. You're only looking for the Fleece."

Sarah nodded.

"It will not have a pleasant taste." The little man indicated the sugar cube. "I could add a little vanilla extract maybe."

Sarah picked up the cube.

"If I die, look after Pols," she said to Max. "And give her my backpack."

Pollina should have the Immortal Beloved letters. She should know that Ludwig van Beethoven had heard her play and had been moved.

"I will," said Max. "You're not going to die."

"A toast to Brahe," Sarah said, and swallowed the drug.

FORTY-NINE

Sarah's father had kept an old radio in the garage. He had taught her to spin the dial slowly to find the different radio stations. It was perhaps the first time that her keen aural perception had been noted. She had always been able to hear the music beyond the white fuzz. Tuning. That's what she was doing. Tuning.

She could still see Max and Nico quite clearly. She could hear them asking her if she was okay. It was hard to answer them at first, because forming the words seemed to activate some part of her brain that felt numb, or sleepy, but she managed to say, "I'm okay." She wasn't entirely sure what language she was speaking. Words came more quickly if she didn't worry about it. "I want to go outside," she said.

It was raining when she stood in the courtyard of Nelahozeves, but she wasn't getting wet, which was how she knew it was raining then, not now. Not now. Earlier. Raining. She heard the sound of horse's feet upon gravel, and a carriage pulled up in front of her. No. Not the right one. Another time. Yes. She waited, trying to block out the strains of music coming at her from all sides, listening, reaching. New Year's Eve 1806, she repeated to herself.

She had lied to Max and Nico. She would look for the Fleece. But first, she wanted to see Beethoven one last time. She wanted to know why Sherbatsky had left her the note marked 12/31/06. What had he seen? What did he want her to see? Whatever it was, it was here at Nela.

So she was standing outside, where she would see Beethoven come into the castle.

And then there he was, stocky form encased in a leather coat, mud-splattered knee breeches, waistcoat, disheveled hair, climbing out of a carriage in front of her. He was so small! She took a deep breath, memorizing his scent, and followed him inside.

"What do you see?" asked Max. His voice was far away.

"Nothing yet," said Sarah. "Or rather lots, but nothing about the Fleece."

Back inside Nela, it was more difficult. The castle was crowded, and she lost the scent.

Then somewhere, from another century, she heard the word "Fleece." It was hazy, whispered, distant. She was trying to find it when she heard the notes of a pianoforte. The Fleece was gone. She moved toward the music.

A room, cold, with a fire flickering in the fireplace, and candles fighting off the December gloom. Luigi, seated at a small instrument. The 7th Prince Lobkowicz stretched out in a low armchair, two whippets at his feet. In his hands he held a small lute.

Beethoven stopped playing and said something to the prince in German. Sarah was startled at the loudness of his voice. It took her a moment to accustom her ear to the tenor and the German they were speaking.

"We are trying to keep the theater open, Luigi," said Prince Lobkowicz. "You act as if we are stealing something from you."

"It is absurd that I should have to beg," said Beethoven. "I have been waiting now for three months to hear back from that pig-faced imbecile and you princely rabble."

"You wouldn't hear a thing, would you?" shouted the prince. "You're deaf."

Luigi laughed. "If you were a horse, you would have been shot at birth," he hollered back.

This seemed to amuse the two men greatly.

"Have a drink, it's a new year tomorrow," said the prince, setting aside the lute and moving to a decanter and glasses upon a marble table. "Maybe something good will happen this year."

Nico and Max were trying to talk to her, but she tuned them out. Just a few more minutes, then she would look for the Fleece.

Sarah did the math. In 1807 Beethoven had petitioned for an annual fixed income from the Imperial Royal Court Theater, and threatened to leave Vienna if he didn't get it. In 1808 he would not get it, but would stay in Vienna, finishing the Fifth and Sixth Symphonies, as well as the Mass in C Major and Piano Concerto in G, to name just a few. A superhuman outpouring of brilliance without equal. His personal life in 1808 would be the usual train wreck. Antonie Brentano was still to come.

"Sarah?" said Max. "You just said the word 'Beethoven.'"

With great effort, Sarah turned her head to look at Max.

"Yes," she said. "You look just like him," she said. "The 7th."

"Sarah, no," said Max. "You have to focus. We don't have much time."

Beethoven played a few notes, reached for a scrap of paper on top of the pianoforte, made a notation.

"Shall we?" the prince asked, coming forward with a small pillbox in his hands. Sarah leaned in to look. Inside were what looked like two communion wafers.

"What will you do?" asked Ludwig. "Will you go hunting now, your nose as keen as your dogs? Will you go looking for your lost *Fleece* with your sharp eyes?"

Max and Nico were fighting with each other about how to focus her.

"They're talking about the Fleece," said Sarah. "Shut up."

"Stop bellowing," said the prince. "You don't know what you're talking about."

"No? Perhaps not," said Luigi. "But I think you should stop looking."

"I will never stop looking," said the prince.

"No," said Beethoven, more softly now. "I suppose you will not. Can you hear me?"

"I can hear you."

"I cannot hear you, my friend. I am reading your lips. Today, I hear nothing."

Mutely, the 7th held out the pillbox and the two men swallowed the wafers.

Ludwig went back to the pianoforte. Prince Lobkowicz poured himself a glass of claret and, calling to his dogs, left the room.

Sarah and Beethoven were alone together. She could hear Max and now Nico, faintly calling to her, but she ignored them, moving toward the piano.

Ludwig began playing softly, the Piano Trio in D. *He will finish this next year,* she thought, as Beethoven began to hum the part for cello.

Sarah swallowed and hummed the violin for him. *Largo assai ed espressivo.* Not in Beethoven's time, but later, this would come to be known as the "Ghost" trio. Sarah reached out a hand to place it on Ludwig's shoulder. Her hand did not move through his body though, as she expected. Indeed she felt cloth beneath her fingers, and, under that, muscle and bone. She snatched her hand back. No, she had imagined it. She hadn't actually touched him, had she? Her hand felt like it was in flames.

Beethoven turned and looked straight at her.

"Wie viel Zeit habe ich?" he whispered. *How much time do I have?*

Sarah shook her head. Somewhere she could feel Max's hands on her wrists. She could hear Max's voice, coaxing her back into some form of the twenty-first century.

"Wie viel Zeit habe ich?" Beethoven shouted. He pointed to his ears. *"Wird es*

508

noch schlimmer werden?" Will it get worse?
There were tears in his eyes.

"It doesn't matter," Sarah shouted. "The music will get better! You are immortal!"

"Play for her," said a voice beside her. "Luigi, play for her."

Sherbatsky. He was standing right beside her, faintly outlined, snapping with energy.

And now it all made sense. Sherbatsky had known she would come to Prague, he had known she would find the note with this date. He had known because he had visited this time and he had *seen* her here. Had he also known that he was going to die? Sarah felt tears come to her eyes. Sherbatsky, too, she saw, was weeping. But with joy, with awe and wonder.

And Beethoven played.

FIFTY

Sarah felt something cool against her forehead. A cloth? Ice? She brushed it away impatiently. When she straightened, the scene in the room had shifted somehow, and Beethoven and Sherbatsky were gone. How long had she stood there listening? Hours? A few seconds? There was something she was supposed to be looking for. What was it?

Sarah flicked away Max's hands. She could hear music. She wanted to get back to Ludwig. She squinted, brushing aside mothlike ghosts battering at her peripheral vision. She felt a hand tugging hers back, clamped tight across her wrist.

"The Fleece," said Nico. "Focus, Sarah. Find the Golden Fleece."

Sarah closed her eyes, trying to breathe into it, but suddenly she felt as if she were falling, not just down but sideways, diagonally, up, back. She was being shoved and jerked through time. Not Alice falling down a hole. Alice in the Hadron collider. Sarah opened her eyes.

A young woman was staring straight at her. Someone she knew she should recognize. She was so familiar, but somehow different. . . . The eyes were filled with such naked greed and desire, such venomous passion that Sarah took a step backward. But the woman wasn't looking at her. She was looking at the object she held in her hands. A golden key.

"And where is the door that this unlocks?" the woman was asking. Her voice, despite the intensity of her eyes, sounded curiously light and casual, but her fingers worked the ridges of the key greedily. Sarah caught the blurred image of a man beyond the woman's shoulder. There was no longer a piano in the room. It was almost bare: a few pieces of furniture shrouded in sheets, packing crates, plastic sheeting. Plastic. So it must be nearly the present then. Yes, the clothes and hairstyle of the woman were contemporary, the seventies maybe.

"I cannot say," said a low voice, thickly accented. Russian. "Exactly. Maybe I find out. Maybe we search together."

"That would be fun," the woman purred softly, while her eyes blazed. The intensity of the woman made her energy surreally vivid.

"Superstition," the man's voice grumbled. "Religious mania and fantasy. You should forget I told you this silly fairy tale."

The woman began unbuttoning her blouse. Her eyes narrowed.

"I don't believe you," she murmured. "I think you know more secrets. Why don't you whisper them in my ear?"

Suddenly the man's face loomed up beside hers. It was the man Sarah had seen in the hidden library, the one who had left the briefcase and taken the amulet. Yuri Bespalov. He pressed his lips against the woman's ear.

"Charlotte, Charlotte," he murmured. "What am I going to do with you?"

"Holy shit," Sarah said, so loudly that she clamped a hand over her mouth. But neither one of the couple seemed to hear her. The couple. Charlotte Yates and Yuri Bespalov.

"It all sounds so romantic." Charlotte shrugged off her blouse and offered her neck to Yuri's mouth. "The Order of the Golden Fleece. A special gold key that unlocks the Door That Must Never Be Opened. What's behind the door, I wonder? The Fleece itself? If it's as powerful as you say —"

Yuri laughed. "There is no such thing," he scoffed. "We think maybe treasure of some kind. But is just a key, maybe. Just old key and old story."

"But the Order has been looking for *something* all this time." Charlotte laced her fingers in Bespalov's hair. "Something big. You know how I hate mysteries." Charlotte guided the Russian down into her cleavage.

"You know what I am going to do?" Charlotte smiled, stepping back and unzipping her skirt. Sarah scurried out of the way as the future senator crossed to a chair and sank into it, caressing her own legs as she pulled off her skirt and kicked it playfully into the air like a chorus girl. She brought her knees together and smiled up at Yuri, who sank with a groan to his knees in front of her.

"I'm going to keep this key," purred Charlotte, leaning forward and unzipping the Russian's pants. "Until I know exactly what it opens." She leaned back in the chair and slid her knees apart. But Sarah saw that Yuri deliberately took the golden key out of Charlotte's hands, even as he buried his face between her legs. And she saw the look of lust and rage on the woman's face.

"Sarah!" Max shouted.

Sarah blinked and yes, there was Max,

gripping her wrists. And behind him, Nicolas Pertusato, wearing an incongruously large pair of spectacles and clutching Tycho's journal.

"Charlotte Yates," Sarah spluttered. "Max, Charlotte Yates knows about the Golden Fleece."

"Knows what?" Max was pressing something cool against her forehead. "You saw her? In the past, I mean? She was here?"

Sarah nodded. She found if she focused on discreet physical sensations — the feel of Max's hands, the callus of his thumb, the slight ache in her left calf muscle, the trickle of cold water on her forehead, a mote of dust in her eye — that she could stay more or less in the present. It was a monumental effort, though, and not one she was sure she could sustain.

"The key that unlocks the Door. The Door that must not be opened. Does that make sense? It's connected to the Fleece. The Fleece is behind the Door, I think."

"Nico?" Max snapped. "What is she talking about?"

"Yes, the key," the little man said. "Tycho made it for the emperor. Tell Sarah to find Tycho. I think the key might lead us to the location of the Fleece."

"The key," mumbled Sarah, trying to stay

upright. She was slipping through time again. There was something on the floor. Blood? Someone was crying, a child. When? Where?

"Take me to Prague," said Sarah. "Hurry!"

"I will get the car," said Nicolas. "Max, keep her calm. Physical stimulation seems to work best."

Max propped her up against a wall and pulled one of her legs up and around his waist. With his other hand he reached under her shirt.

"Well," she heard the little man say, "that seems to be . . . helpful. Although crude in execution. Max, there are a number of books I could lend you that would —"

"Get the car!" Max shouted.

FIFTY-ONE

Nicolas drove the roadster at top speed, while Max held Sarah and Moritz panted anxiously. The little man was driving fast enough that the pockets of emotion they were driving through existed only as blurry wavy lines of colored light. Sarah went from feeling slightly sick to feeling definitely aroused, and then amused. "This . . ." she tried to say, "is fun!" And except for the vertigo and the occasional sounds of screaming in different languages, it was actually fun. Max was being a trouper. You had to give the man points for stamina.

Anyone else would be mumbling something about carpal tunnel syndrome by now. Well, he was a musician. Sarah was finding it easier now to divide her attention: part of it with Max and Nico, and part of it with searching and listening through the maze of energies.

"It's like cables," she tried to explain to

Max. "Lines. All around. Colors. Music. Strings."

Nico mumbled out loud to himself.

"Are we going to Golden Lane?" Max asked. "I saw you there with Tycho, Nico. You were arranging to 'borrow' the Fleece."

"They moved it right after that," said Nico. "I think they suspected. And Rudolf's poor lover was beheaded."

They were in the city now. Sarah could see Charles Bridge, tourists, the lights of nighttime Prague glittering. She could also see another Prague, much blacker, with a cloudy moon, rank and putrid smells, torches, horses.

"Turn here," Sarah ordered. Nicolas made a sharp turn.

"Charles Bridge," Sarah said. "He's there. Tycho. I can see his . . . strand or whatever now. He's moving though. Wait. Stop." The car pulled to a stop at a light. Sarah pressed her face against the glass window and gasped.

A man, dressed in a rough dark cloak. His face was covered by a hood, but underneath it she saw a gleam of copper. Her attention swiveled and locked into the energy of the man, and his outline became sharper, more focused.

"Tycho," she said, and opened the car

door. She heard Max behind her calling her name, but she pushed against an obstacle in front of her — a body? a cart? — and followed the shrouded figure onto the bridge. A part of her knew the bridge was crowded with tourists carrying cameras and backpacks and jabbering in a mixture of languages, but she shoved this aside to find the moonlit night, the dark figure, the deserted bridge.

"Sarah, what is it?" Max, behind her, holding her hand now, guiding her around the people in her path she couldn't see. Tycho paused in the middle of the bridge, grasped the railing, and looked into the glittering water below. No, he wasn't alone. There was another man, wearing a long brown cape over a high stiff collar. His curly beard was tucked into his cape; a soft four-cornered cap was drawn low over his forehead. His eyes were worried. Sarah felt his fear.

"You are not thinking of drowning yourself," said Tycho. Sarah wasn't sure if she could hear his voice or his thoughts; it was strange. And difficult because Tycho's tone was mocking and casual, but his emotions were taut, almost manic.

The man with the curly beard responded,

"I came to tell you that I am leaving Prague, Brahe."

"Leaving? Whatever for? Things are only now becoming interesting."

"I am going back to England."

"It is that ass, Kelley," Tycho laughed harshly. "I told you he was after your wife, Dee."

John Dee, Sarah thought, looking at the man in the brown cloak.

"I have also come to tell you, to plead with you, to stop," said Dee.

"I will never stop."

"My friend, we have come too far —"

"Yes," Tycho said, pulling the man closer to him, almost in an embrace. "We have come too far. Think of what we are close to, my friend. Think of what we can understand. Only everything."

"We are not meant to know everything," Dee said, his voice trembling. "I was wrong to bring it here."

"You are a coward," said Brahe, bitterly.

"Yes, I am a coward," Dee agreed. "But I can only see darkness ahead on the path you are choosing."

"And you think you will find light in England?" Tycho sneered. "With Elizabeth? The queen is a viper, she will sink her fangs in your flesh soon enough. And what of our work?"

"It is not my work anymore," Dee said. "I am a mathematician."

"And what am I? We are men of science, not necromancers. Let Kelley fill the emperor's ears with angelic babble and potions from his own urine. God is speaking to us in the true language. The language of the elements. The earth, the moon. He is showing us his secrets."

"It is not God that is speaking," Dee cried. "It is the Devil!"

"There is no difference at all between them," laughed Tycho. "I am late to meet Baron Kurz." He strode off.

"Sarah?"

She turned and saw Max beside her, Nico panting at his side. Moritz was guarding the car. Behind them she could make out a group of Korean tourists. When she turned back, Brahe and Dee were gone.

"Dee," she whispered.

"John Dee?" Nicolas said. "It can't be later than 1589, then. I think you need to move ahead a few years."

"They were arguing," Sarah explained. "And saying goodbye."

"Did he have the key?" Max asked. "Did he say anything about the Fleece?"

"It wasn't clear. He said something about Baron Kurz."

"Kurz Summer Palace." Nico nodded. "Yes. A good place to look. Rudolf had brought us from Benátky because he wanted us closer. But the master needed more room and privacy. We need to go to Kurz Summer Palace. This was our last residence in Prague before the master died."

"I've never heard of Kurz Summer Palace," Max said doubtfully.

"At Pohorelec," Nicolas said. "Just behind Cernin Palace."

It was very dark now. Sarah knew roughly where they were in the city: west of the castle grounds, near the Loreto and Cernin Palace. With concentration she could make out what Max and Nico were looking at, but there wasn't much to see. Streetlights illuminated tram tracks and what seemed like, especially for Prague, some very ordinary industrial buildings. A row of parking spaces. A giant monument in front of them. Two men standing on a stone plinth, one of them with the bulging forehead, long mustache, and lace ruff that characterized all depictions of the Danish astrologer. Tycho Brahe carried a giant sextant. Next to him, Johannes Kepler, a scroll tucked under his arm, gazed at the heavens.

"Where's this summer palace?" Max asked.

"It was torn down quite a long time ago," Nico said. "They built this on top of it. Another palimpsest, of sorts. This is a grammar school. The Gymnázium Jana Keplera. Their motto is: *Per aspera ad astra.* I think the master would be a little annoyed it's not the Gymnázium Tycho Brahe, but he does have the very nice tomb at Týn and —"

Per aspera ad astra. From hardship to the stars.

"I see a palace," Sarah said, pointing.

"Excellent," said Nico. "Let us proceed. I will have to pick a lock or two."

FIFTY-TWO

For Max and Nico it was just a school —
there were children's drawings pinned to
the walls, and the usual rows of lockers.
Lockers that Sarah immediately slammed
into, since she was operating on a completely different floor plan.

"A little help here," she called out. As she
oriented on the energy of the palace, the
functionalist four-story white school building with blue window frames disappeared
and she saw only a lovely Renaissance
palace, freshly constructed and beautifully
furnished. And here was Baron Kurz himself, talking to masons and artists who were
working on a series of frescos.

"Baron Kurz," she said to Max and Nico.

"Oh, we needn't bother with him," the
little man said. "He was a very nice man,
incredibly generous, but not so precise in
his mathematics. He sent the master a drawing of an alidade that was clever but errone-

ous. But he managed to procure figs just for me even in winter, so I will forever remember him fondly."

Max and Nico helped her climb a set of stairs she couldn't see, which made it feel like flying, and she found herself in a waiting room with large, graciously arched windows. Outside the street scene was bizarre. The lanes were thronged with people. It was a winter day, and she could hear the wind rattling the windowpanes. Soldiers on horseback in strange uniforms with breastplates and pikes galloped through the streets, where people were setting fire to buildings and throwing rocks. And yet the people were also wearing masks and costumes, and drinking, as if a party had gone horribly wrong.

Sarah could hear screams. She watched a priest run under the window, chased by a man in full harlequin costume carrying an ax.

"Something very weird." Sarah did her best to explain what she was seeing.

"Ah yes," said Nico. "You need to go back another decade. That sounds like February 1611. That old crank the Bishop of Passau decided to invade the city on Mardi Gras. It was confusing even if you weren't on drugs."

Sarah shook her head to clear the vision

524

and replaced it with the image of Tycho Brahe. *Where are you?* she thought. Suddenly she was moving quickly, Nico and Max helping when the current utilitarian design of the building impeded her progress. But here it was, a lavishly decorated bedroom, a blond man with a bushy russet beard and long mustache seated in a chair. A piece of copper was fixed across the bridge of his nose, though Sarah couldn't tell how it was attached exactly, and at his feet . . .

The little man at Brahe's feet was wearing yellow stockings and bright green slippers. A pink smock shirt decorated with bells and ribbons. A skull cap in blue covered his head. But he was unmistakable.

"I found you, Nico," said Sarah. "And you look spiffy."

"Jepp," Nicolas corrected. "That was my name then."

"So tell me," Tycho demanded of the dwarf. "What is the news at court?"

The little man — Jepp — poured a glass of beer from a pitcher on the floor and handed it to his master. He retained the pitcher for himself, drinking deeply from it. Tycho chuckled indulgently.

"The Hungarians are exhausted by this war. They no longer care about fighting the

Turks, they just want to be left alone. Can you blame them? Almost eight years they've been fighting a war they don't even understand." The bassoon voice was the same. Sarah had to fight between the urge to do nothing but compare the two little men.

"What about Mattias?" Brahe inquired. "Is Rudolf's brother stirring the pot?"

"He is." Jepp nodded. "Mattias is telling the foreign courtiers that Rudolf is losing his mind, that this war is costing too much, that he buys too much art, that he needs to focus on matters closer to home, the Jews, the Protestants, the merchants, the guilds, the sparring nobles."

"Those old vultures. And?"

"Rabbi Loew came to plead with the emperor about protection for his people. There is talk of the golem again. People say that a monster lives in the Jewish quarter."

"Mmph," Tycho snorted. "And?"

"Apparently the emperor's new painting is quite scandalous. A nun fainted when it was unveiled."

"And you saw it?"

Jepp looked insulted. "Of course."

"Describe it, man!"

"It's Italian. Someone named Correggio. *Portrait of Danae* it is called. The Italian has painted a woman unclothed with the sheet pulled down to here —" Jepp indicated his crotch and splayed back on his cushion in imitation of the pose, his legs wide open. "Boobies in all directions. Everyone got stiff just looking! And here's the best part. Jupiter is showing her how much he loves her . . . with a golden rain." Jepp laughed into his pitcher.

"A golden rain? You mean he's pissing on her?!" Tycho laughed out loud and clapped Jepp on the back.

"So, Nico, you've always been kind of twisted, I see," Sarah commented.

"What am I missing?" said Max.

"One of the world's most famous astronomers is talking about golden shower porn," she said.

"Really? What's he saying? Can you see it?"

Sarah rolled her eyes. Some things were truly eternal.

Jepp/Nico continued, quaffing his beer. "The court chamberlain von Rumpf is in a snit because Rudy spent the night with that hateful valet Philip Lang again last night."

"And Rudy's gay," said Sarah.

"Oh yes," said Nico. "Big time."

"Okay," said Max. "Not that I'm not enjoying 'Real World: Rockin' Prague,' but the drug won't last forever and we need to find some clues here. Sarah, do you see a golden key anywhere?"

"I don't."

"We're not far off," Nicolas said. "A few days. I remember the painting. Soon after that the master gave me the key and told me to take it to the emperor. Rudolf wanted to lock the Fleece away in some kind of safe. The master had designed a special lock that could never be picked and would answer to only one key. But Rudolf didn't tell the master where he put the safe."

"And you think Rudolf wanted the key to lock up the Fleece?" Max asked.

"I think it likely. I was bringing the key to the emperor when I was attacked on the way to the castle and the key was stolen. If Sarah can go to this time, perhaps we can trace the key to the Fleece."

"Just a little bit further," Max urged Sarah. "Or wait, is that backward for you?"

Sarah took a deep breath, shifted her focus to the window, where she could now see a giant red swastika banner hanging off Cernin Palace.

"Shit, I see Nazis," she sighed. "I just jumped about four hundred years."

"Cernin Palace was the headquarters for the SS," said Max. "My grandfather's friend Masaryk was defenestrated there."

A woman with a 1940s updo walked past the window carrying a paper heart. "Valentine's Day," Sarah said.

"Oh dear," said Nico.

A bomb hit the building. Sarah screamed and dropped to the floor.

"It's not happening," said Max, grabbing her arm. She could barely see him through the smoke. "Sarah, listen to me, you're okay, it's not happening now."

"February 14, 1945," said Nico. "Not the best Valentine's I've ever had. But then again, not the worst."

"I thought the Allies didn't bomb Prague." People were screaming, air-raid sirens blaring.

"A couple of American pilots got lost on the way to Dresden."

"Jesus!" said Sarah as the building collapsed around her. People screamed. The woman with the Valentine reached a bloody hand out of the wreckage. Sarah reached for it, but she was just energy, energy visible across more than sixty years of time. And suddenly the building re-formed underneath her and she was back with Tycho.

But it was fading. "We have to hurry," said Sarah. "The drug is wearing off."

Bits of modernity were creeping into the vision. A school desk. A trash can. She must focus. Max was counting on her.

"He's writing," said Sarah. "He has . . . I think it's the journal in his lap. And the key! I see the key!"

"Am I there?" Nico leaned in to see, as if he, too, could see across time.

"You are," Sarah reported. "He's giving you the key. Shut up a second."

"The emperor is becoming paranoid about his treasures," Tycho was saying. "Deliver this key to him. Assure him that I destroyed the mold to the key. He will not believe you, and he will be right, but where he is wrong is in thinking that I do not suspect where he intends to hide his precious Fleece. I have marked the spot."

"The master is very clever," said Jepp.

"You will then return to me. Kepler is coming this afternoon and we will be in the laboratory."

"Yes, Master," said Jepp. "I will come to you there."

"Not *there,*" thundered Brahe. "You make Johannes nervous. Wait for me here, later. I have a little something I want you to taste. Something I need to try. An experiment."

Uh-oh, thought Sarah. The potion.

Jepp tucked the golden key into his sleeve.

"Nico," she said. "It happened that night. Tycho poisoned you that night."

530

"There's nothing you can do," the little man said, sadly. "It is four hundred years too late."

Getting out of the palace/grammar school was a nightmare, with Sarah running and colliding into walls and Max and Nico shouting at her while Sarah struggled to stay on the heels of the quick-moving Jepp. On the street it was Max and Nico who struggled, as it was now very dark in their Prague, and a brilliant afternoon in Jepp's.

Sarah watched as the little man was loaded by a servant into the back of a hay cart. "We're going to have to run," she shouted.

But the cart had traveled only a few narrow streets when it turned a corner into a tiny alley and stopped. Jepp leapt down from the cart.

"What is this?" he called out. "Your orders were to take me to the castle!"

The driver was very tall and lean. He wore a ragged burlap cloak and a roughly made cap that covered most of his face. He came swiftly around the cart and pulled a large white handkerchief out from his cape and shoved it against the little man's face. Jepp struggled for a moment, and then fell forward, unconscious. The driver placed Jepp's body back into the cart with surprising gentleness and began searching his clothes until he found the key, which he tucked under his cape.

"Do you remember this?" Sarah asked Nico, in a whisper.

"Have we stopped in the alley?" Nico asked. "I remember that. Nothing more. Can you describe the driver?"

"Tall and thin, but I can't see his face," said Sarah, watching as the man reached under a stack of hay and retrieved a large iron casket. He lifted the lid just slightly and Sarah jumped back. The energy coming from inside the box was like nothing she had ever experienced. The blood raced through her veins, her throat closed up, her eyes swam. She saw her father, an icy road, her mother's face, her first violin, an explosion in deep space, a star, Beethoven's hands on the piano, Pols's arms around her tightly, and through it all, a sudden understanding of how it all *worked,* a system of grids, overlapping, energy transferred; there was no such thing as *time.* She fell to her knees.

The driver slammed the lid shut and slumped over it, breathing hard.

"Yes! Yes! The Fleece! He has it in the cart! I can feel it. He's leaving you in the alley," Sarah reported, panting. "He's getting back in the cart."

"I didn't tell the master," whispered Nico. "I was ashamed at my failure."

"Max," Sarah said. "I don't think we should . . . I think it's better if we . . ."

Maybe John Dee was right. Maybe there were some things we weren't meant to know. Sarah thought of Mephistopheles's lament: *Why, this is hell, nor am I out of it.*

"Follow the cart," Max said grimly. "Sarah, we have to finish this."

They were crossing the river on Jiraskuv Bridge. The cart was just ahead of them. Max and Nico were on either side of her, murmuring in her ear. *There's a step here. We can't turn left, we'll have to walk around. Wait, there's a car.*

Sarah tried to block out the sights and smells of all that was happening around her and concentrate on the cart. At the same time every nerve in her body was fighting to stop, turn back, get away from the power inside that casket. They ran on. They were in Josefov now, and the energy of a population so long persecuted was nearly choking her.

"He's stopping at the synagogue up ahead," she said, hoping that it was still standing in Max and Nico's time.

"Of course," Nico breathed. "The Old-New Synagogue. It was rumored that Rabbi Loew placed the body of the golem in the attic in an iron casket. No one's been in that room for four centuries. They say the rabbi cursed it so that no one would ever disturb the golem's slumbers. A perfect hiding place."

"Someone must have been up there at some point," Max said. "A cleaning woman?"

Nico shook his head. "One Nazi soldier went up on a dare. Said it was a stupid Jewish superstition and he wanted to get whatever gold was hidden up there."

"What happened?" Max demanded

"He died an agonizing death. That scared the rest of 'em off. The Old-New was the only synagogue the Nazis left untouched."

"He's taking the casket inside the synagogue," Sarah said. "Can we follow him?"

"It's closed now," Max said. "And there are masses of tourists still on the streets."

"You think the driver was Rabbi Loew?" Sarah asked. "Shit, we have to follow him."

"The stairs to the *genizah,* or attic storeroom, are around back," said Nico.

They hurried around the back of the synagogue. There were so many strands of emotion surrounding the synagogue, she had trouble breathing.

"Lots of tourists," said Max again. "Try to act normal."

"We could climb up these stairs," Nico said.

"Stairs?" said Max and Sarah together. They were, it seemed, looking at the same thing: a series of metal rungs set into the rear wall. The rungs began about fifteen feet above-ground, and were only about six inches across. It would take an acrobat or a telephone lineman to climb them. The door to the *genizah* was about forty feet up and made of what looked like very sturdy wood with no lock or handle on it.

"Boost me up," said Nico. "Quick, before a cop or a rabbi comes by."

Sarah watched as Max leaned over and Nico climbed on his shoulders, trying unsuccessfully to reach the bottom rung. Finally, under Nico's precise instructions and on the count of three, Max actually heaved Nico up in the air, and on the third try the little man managed to catch the ladder.

Nico quickly scaled the rungs and began ramming his shoulder against the *genizah* door. A group of tourists gathered.

"What is he doing?" someone asked Sarah.

"It's part of a historical reenactment,"

called Nico. "Feel free to tip my partner."

"It's him!" Sarah shouted. The tall, thin figure was exiting the synagogue, and as he passed her he flung off his cloak and hat and threw them away. Underneath the rough fabric he wore a rich gold and white doublet and jerkin, a matching cape over his shoulders. His long, thin legs were encased in white hose. His brown beard and mustache were closely trimmed, as was his hair. The golden key was tucked into a panel of his hose. The man was young, he was handsome. He was . . .

"That's no rabbi," Sarah said. "That's Ladislav. Brother of the 1st Prince Lobkowicz. A traitor to his country."

FIFTY-THREE

Max, Nico, and Sarah walked slowly down Paris Street; across Old Town Square; past Týn church, where Tycho, who had seemed so alive and well this morning, had been buried for 410 years; and up Celetna. They had been up all night and even Moritz was exhausted, but Sarah kept walking. When they passed under Powder Tower, she was fairly certain she saw Mozart in a powdered wig, giggling. She had the urge to wave.

Max's phone beeped. Something about the way he reacted made Sarah look at him.

"It's from Elisa," he said. "She booked us a cruise for our honeymoon. On some French actor's yacht."

"Text her back," said Sarah. "Tell her you can't wait."

Nico had reported that the Old-New Synagogue's attic had not contained anything like an iron casket, and nothing that a key would fit into. It was empty. The Fleece had been moved. Ladislav was nowhere to be seen. She tried concentrating on an iron casket and caught glimpses of it. This had drawn them on an exhausting ramble across the city, zigzagging, doubling back, hitting dead ends.

They trudged up Hybernska, passing under Wilson Highway, where the road began climbing uphill. The drug was definitely wearing off now. Max and Nico followed her in silence. Moritz panted. From Seifertova she turned slowly right into Nejedlo, then right into Mahler Gardens. Finally Sarah halted abruptly.

"What's happening?" asked Max.

The drug was almost out of her system. Sarah was fighting to see what was happening.

"I'm at a cemetery. Two men are putting an iron casket in a freshly dug grave. Right over there." She pointed and tried to walk to where two robed men were burying a metal box, but she felt herself physically blocked, grabbed by Max and Nico.

"What is it?" she said. "What's here?" She put her hands out and felt something cold, hard, and impermeable.

Sarah shook her head and moved from the past to the present. She was facing a cement wall. She looked up. She and Max and

Nico were standing at the base of a giant spaceship-shaped television tower with what appeared to be enormous black babies crawling up it.

"What the fuck?" asked Sarah.

"Žižkov Tower," said Max. "Begun in 1985. Voted the second ugliest building in the entire world."

Sarah moved back to the past.

"It's not the Fleece casket," she said. "It's much smaller and a different shape. And it doesn't . . . feel the same. I'm sorry."

It was all fading away. The end. The last of the drug. Her last time seeing the past. She strained to see more . . .

"There are rumors that the golem's body was moved to Žižkov cemetery," said Nico. "You got your iron caskets mixed up. Oh, that Rabbi Loew. He was a sly one."

Sarah kicked the concrete base of the seven-hundred-foot-high building.

"I'm sorry. I didn't find the Fleece." She felt sick, exhausted, and disappointed.

"At least we know where to dig for more golem dust," said Nicolas.

"And," said Max. "We know the key opens the place where the Fleece is hidden."

"I suspect it is somewhere on the castle grounds," Nico said.

"Well, that narrows it down," Max sighed.

Everyone sounded exhausted and depressed.

"Nico," Sarah said. "Tycho told you that he had made a copy of the key. Do you know what happened to it?"

"The master died a month after that night," Nicolas said. "I never found the copy of the key. I had troubles of my own at that point."

She sat down on the sidewalk in front of the TV tower, her head swimming with visions, with history, with secrets. She looked across the street to where a building was being renovated, just like hundreds of others all over Prague. The city was constantly erasing and writing over itself, an architectural palimpsest in action.

"I'm so tired," said Sarah. Her eyes scanned the graffiti. More mysteries, more riddles, more stories. What was important in all this mess of history and scholarship and magic and more history? Letters and paintings and music and treasures and books and words and secrets and lies and *lives*. So many lives. What had meaning and what was just chatter? Maybe none of it had any meaning, she thought. Maybe all scholarship was a wild-goose chase. We could never really know the past, even if (as in her case) you could see it right in front of you.

Maybe it was a mistake to even try.

Time. Time didn't really exist.

"Sarah?" whispered Max in her ear. "Sarah? Are you okay?"

And with that, it all went black.

FIFTY-FOUR

Charlotte Yates leaned forward in her seat. Someone shouted "Shame!" and from the opposite side of the gilded neo-Renaissance theater came "Disgrace!"

Charlotte Yates did not turn a single hair of her caramel-sprinkled-with-silver bob. She knew the words were not directed toward her, although she had glimpsed anti-American-style banners here and there as her motorcade had wended its way through Prague today. No, the complaints were directed at the orchestra. Or, rather, where the orchestra should be. The stage was empty. The concert was to begin at 7:30 p.m. and it was 7:32 p.m. In Prague this counted as an almost unbelievably egregious delay, practically cause for rioting. Charlotte expected the delay was due to her own Secret Service corps, but it was nice to see the locals hadn't lost their notions of punctuality.

Yes, here she was, back in Prague. Since announcing her intention to make a three-city sweep through Eastern Europe (Warsaw, Bucharest, Prague) to "discuss strengthening our shared global security agendas," Charlotte's sense of anticipation had reached an almost unbearable point. She had barely registered her stays in Poland and Romania, so intent was she on this last leg of the visit. The global security agenda had all been an excuse, anyway. As if Poland or Romania were going to help keep the world safe for democracy! Although it was sometimes good to make other countries feel like they were relevant.

But Prague was the key. Everything came down to the next twenty-four hours and a plan so perfect that she really wished she could tell someone about it. Brag a little. If only her father could have lived to see this.

Really, she had known from the start that getting the letters back wouldn't be quite enough. Charlotte Yates was a doer. She didn't shrink from the bold stroke.

She wished she could get away from everyone and savor the moment. Normally she didn't mind traveling with her entourage — staff, security, journalists — but if there was ever a moment when a girl needed a little personal time it was now. And of course, she assumed there was a great deal of local scrutiny concerning her visit. If Americans (most of whom probably thought this country was still called Czechoslovakia and would not even be in guessing range of its location on a map) seemed indifferent to her past activities here, the same could not be guaranteed of the natives. Memories were long in this part of the world, and you never knew who might turn up where. Luckily everyone had more or less the same agenda, in which global security took a backseat to one's own personal security. Still, she wouldn't be absolutely certain of anyone's fear of offending her until she was president. Fear made people so sweet, it was almost possible to love them.

Today's schedule had run smoothly. Jauntily dressed in a lightweight coral Ralph Lauren pantsuit (there was something satisfyingly *fuck you* about discussing terrorism while wearing pink), the caramel-silver bob sprayed into wind-resistant sleekness, Dr. Scholl's inserts discreetly cushioning her Anne Klein pumps, Charlotte had controlled the meetings expertly. Of course, it was all really token "relationship building," nothing historic, no real power to be brokered. She didn't want to step on any toes at State — Todd was such a dear little lamb chop. Though when she returned as president, things would be different.

The orchestra was on stage now, and a few members of the audience continued to reprimand them happily as they quickly tuned up. The Minister of Culture, apoplectic with embarrassment over the dishonor of starting four minutes late, lost his presence of mind and offered Charlotte a mint. Her favorite Secret Service agent, Tad, leaned forward slightly and the Minister of Culture recovered himself in time.

"I think you will enjoy this program," the minister said earnestly, pocketing the mint. "Of course, of the nine symphonies, the fourth is the least celebrated, and really more in sequence thematically with the second, but I think it a very great work. Complicated, almost perverse at times, yes, but rich and very profound."

"I very much look forward to it," Charlotte said. What the hell was he talking about? Oh, the music. She glanced down at her program. Beethoven's Fourth Symphony. Christ, she was in for a boring hour or two. A line from the program notes caught her eye. The Fourth had premiered in 1807 at Lobkowicz Palace, in Vienna.

Lobkowiczes, Lobkowiczes, everywhere

Lobkowiczes. Charlotte was sick to death of the name.

And tomorrow night she would be attending the opening of Lobkowicz Palace Museum. The last time she had set foot in that place had been the day Yuri was murdered.

Charlotte half-shut her eyes, permissible since she was ostensibly listening to the racket on stage, and shifted through her memories.

She remembered the last night they had made love. She hadn't known then it would be the last time, obviously, or she wouldn't have elected to do it in a chair covered in cheesecloth at Nelahozeves Castle. They had argued that night, too. Yuri had deliberately incensed her, in his maddeningly Russian way, by lording over some secret knowledge that he had. He had dangled a trinket in front of her, a golden key that was presumed to unlock a treasure. She had immediately assumed he was presenting her with one of the seven keys that unlocked the chamber of the Crown Jewels of Bohemia. This chamber, located in St. Vitus Cathedral, was famous for its door, which had seven different locks requiring seven different keys. The Crown Jewels included the actual crown of St. Wenceslas, a royal scepter, a fabulous jeweled apple, a crucifix, and royal vestments, including a belt and some kind of cloak. The jewels were almost never seen, and legends had grown up around them, the usual bad-luck-and-curses type of thing.

But Yuri had insisted the key had nothing to do with the Crown Jewels. He had even tried to throw her off the scent by insisting the key opened something entirely different, and gabbled on about the Order of the Golden Fleece and a door that must never be opened. Their lovemaking had been more violent than usual, and they had parted almost angrily.

A few days later she had received a strange phone call from him, using one of their many secret codes, asking to meet "as if by accident" in the middle of the day. When he gave the location as St. Vitus Cathedral, she felt sure that she had been right about the Crown Jewels. She was hoping he had managed to collect all seven of the keys. Superstition be damned, she wanted to get her hands on the Crown Jewels. Not to steal them, of course. That wouldn't be ethical. But would anyone really miss a golden apple that only a handful of people had seen in the course of six hundred years?

It was winter, bitterly cold, and with her cover as a humble art historian she had only a thin coat. In Prague, in the 1970s, practically everyone had only a thin coat, although at certain kinds of parties women would display their furs. She arrived at the cathedral half-frozen and irritable, and Yuri was nowhere in sight. She loitered about for fifteen minutes, then stepped inside. Out of the corner of her eye, she saw a dark shape darting up from the steps that led to the Royal Vault. She walked quickly over to investigate. She thought she could smell Yuri's cologne.

She peered down the nave and caught sight of the figure. Yes, it was Yuri. Charlotte caught up with him at the south doorway. He pulled her into sunlight and kissed her fiercely, although anyone could have seen them.

"I need to see you," he said, into her ear. "Go to the palace and wait for me. It's important."

She opened her mouth to reply, but he shook his head, frowning, and stepped back into the cathedral, where the gloom seemed to swallow him whole.

And Charlotte had gone to the palace, and waited for her lover for hours, but he never came. The next day's paper included an announcement that the director of the National Museum, Yuri Bespalov, had returned to important work in Moscow and his successor would be named shortly. Her division chief at the CIA was the one who showed her the photographs of Yuri's lifeless body being pulled from the Vltava River.

"Suicide," sniffed the chief. "They're trying to cover it up, of course. Not only is he an embarrassment to the Party, we now think he is pretty high-ranking KGB."

"Was," Charlotte corrected, stonily. "Was KGB."

"Right. Well, I guess we'll never know for sure now."

"No, I guess not."

She waited for someone from the KGB to get in touch with her, but no one ever did. She left Prague a few months later, covered in commendations from her chief. She was a credit to the Agency, an exemplary agent. They predicted she might go far.

They were right about that. She had gone very far.

Not far enough. Not yet.

After the concert, Charlotte returned to her suite at the Four Seasons Hotel. She paced, unable to sleep, and made lists, chewing viciously on the straws Madge had thoughtfully packed, and reviewed tomorrow night's timeline. Not the official version, of course.

That was simple enough. She was attending a private event, honoring Czech national heritage by gracing a museum opening with her presence. She would go, pose for pictures, and come home.

Unofficially, of course, things were going to go quite a bit differently.

How many birds could you kill with one stone? Quite a few. One little bomb planted in one little museum and you not only destroyed dozens of annoying loose ends, sent what were probably some not very nice people to whatever afterlife God in His wisdom had reserved for them, but reminded the world of the perils of terrorism and the need to devote large amounts of the budget to fighting it. You could spend a lot of time making fancy plans and mucking about with subtle twists and turns, or you could blow something up. Sometimes it was just better to blow shit up.

There was something romantic, too, about destroying the place where she had waited for her murdered lover. That day she had waited with fear in her heart, but now the fear was gone. Soon she was going to be beyond fear. And then, perhaps, everyone would see what a caring and compassionate person she really was. Brave, brilliant, steadfast, patriotic, and decisive. A true American. A true American hero.

FIFTY-FIVE

"Imagine a mansion with a secret room — the perfect setting for a mystery. Now imagine that the room is vastly bigger than the mansion itself — and contains more mansions."

A dirge was playing, and soft Latin chanting floated on the air.

The voice was so familiar. . . . When Sarah opened her eyes, the first thing she saw was an apple-cheeked woman in a white wimple. *Great,* she thought, *I'm back in the Middle Ages.*

A man she couldn't see was speaking Latin. *"Aperi Domine os meum ad benedicendum nomen sanctum tuum."*

Nico was sitting cross-legged on the end of her bed reading a newspaper. Or was it Jepp? It wasn't clear to Sarah if this was a vision, a dream, or . . . something worse.

" 'That would make the mystery pretty bizarre. But it's very much like a story that many scientists are beginning to tell about the universe. In what amounts to a real-life episode of *The Twilight Zone,* physicists have realized that nature may be concealing extra dimensions — not of sight or sound, but of space itself.' "

Sarah looked around. She was in a white-washed high-ceilinged room with a large window that looked out over trees. She could see telephone poles and electric streetlights, which was somewhat reassuring. She felt, well, *hungover.*

"Where am I?" she tried to ask, but only a croak came out. Nico/Jepp looked up and smiled at her.

"She speaks!" he said.

Wimple Woman held a glass of water to her lips and she drank. *That's odd,* she thought. *Am I drinking water from the Middle Ages or is she holding water from now?* Thinking made her brain hurt.

"Pater noster, qui es in cælis, sanctificetur nomen tuum. Adveniat regnum tuum. Fiat voluntas tua, sicut in caelo et in terra . . . ," intoned a male voice.

She shook her head a little to clear the cobwebs, which made it feel like her brain was rattling inside her skull.

"What is that sound?" Sarah asked as the Latin chanting resumed.

"Ave, Maria, gratia plena; Dominus

tecum . . ."

Wimple reached up and turned a dial and the chanting stopped abruptly.

"What time is it?" Sarah asked.

"Noon," said Nico. "How do you feel?"

"I've been asleep all day?" Sarah said. "I have to get back. The museum opening . . ."

"You've been asleep all *week,*" said Nico. "And I'm not sure you're ready to get up now. Why don't you just lie there and I'll read to you about dark matter. Did you know that according to current calculations, dark matter and energy account for ninety-six percent of the universe, while atomic matter accounts for only four percent?"

Sarah just looked at him. Trying to remember. Why did that sound so familiar?

Wimple spoke. "You were in a partial coma," she said. "It was quite serious. We'd like to do some more tests now that you're awake." She looked into Sarah's eyes and felt her pulse. "I'll get the doctor."

Sarah realized that Wimple was some kind of nurse. A time-traveling nurse who came with her own Latin sound track? Was that going to involve bloodletting and leeches?

Wimple left the room and Nico picked up the newspaper again. " 'If so, the known universe may be just one of many "mansions" residing in the secret room — space's hidden dimensions.' " Sarah saw it was the *Dallas Morning News.* " 'It's just really frighteningly weird,' says cosmologist Rocky Kolb. 'It strikingly flies in the face of everything we thought was true.' "

"Wait a second," Sarah interrupted. "Did you say I was asleep for a *week*?"

"We had to feed you intravenously. Now rest. Don't you just love all this talk of dark matter? When Tycho talked about it, they called him a heretic, but now it's science."

"Tycho knew about dark matter?"

"And black holes and parallel universes. Sure. But we called them 'hell portals.' " Nico read something about gravitational lensing and branes, but Sarah was not paying attention. She had slept for an entire week? How was that possible?

"Jesus," she said, sitting up and swinging her legs over the side of the bed. "What day is it?"

"Saturday," said Nico, looking up from the paper.

"Saturday? The museum opening is *TONIGHT*?!"

Sarah leapt out of bed, and almost fell over. Wobbly was an understatement. "Where are my clothes?"

Nico pointed to a pair of jeans and a T-shirt on the side table. Sarah noticed flowers, beautiful flowers. Vases and vases of them.

"Max," said Nico.

Sarah disappeared into the bathroom to get dressed. Max. The marchesa. Charlotte Yates. She splashed cold water on her face. Her tongue felt like steel wool, but she emerged from the bathroom feeling somewhat steadier.

"Welcome back, milady," Nico said with a bow.

"Cut the crap. What happened?"

"You passed out in Žižkov and Max had you brought here."

"Where's here?"

"Sisters of Mercy Hospital. Three blocks from the castle. It's privately run, so Max was able to secure you your own room, which under the circumstances seemed preferable."

"Am I okay?"

"Do you feel okay?" he asked cautiously.

"I don't know. I'm hearing Latin. Was Wimple Woman really here or not?"

Nico laughed. "The hospital is run by nuns. That is Sister Berta. And —" He flicked a switch and the Latin resumed. "There's a live feed from the mass next door."

"Of course there is," Sarah sighed.

"I have been a bit worried," the little man said. "As you have learned from my current condition . . . Tycho's formulae were not always accurate. And he did hold to his theory that the sun revolved around the earth. But," he tapped the paper, "it seems like he nailed the whole hell portal thing."

Sarah looked at a clock on the wall.

"Is it really noon? I have to get out of here. What's happening with the opening?"

"Everything is on schedule. Max finished your display himself according to your notes. The caterers and florists are at the palace now setting up."

"My backpack," said Sarah, her thoughts flying to the Beethoven letters.

Nico pointed to a chair in the corner.

"Did you look through it?"

"My dear," said Nico with dignity. "Of course I did."

Sarah heard sirens and looked out the window to see a huge motorcade going by.

"The senator from Virginia," said Nico quietly.

Sarah felt a surge of anxiety. Charlotte Yates was here. Sarah had seen in the vision at Nela that Charlotte knew about the key. Did she somehow know where the Golden Fleece was hidden? And if Charlotte Yates and Marchesa Elisa were working together . . . between them they had killed Andy, Eleanor, and nearly herself.

Sarah shuddered. She'd have to be on her game tonight. Well, at least she was well-rested. A little weak and wobbly and, she realized, *starving.* But alive.

"What did you tell everyone?" Sarah asked.

"Food poisoning from some bad chicken you had in Old Town. Fortunately, everyone has been so occupied with preparing for the opening that your absence has caused less notice than it might have a few weeks ago."

"Did you stay with me this whole time, Nico?"

He gave her a half-smile.

Sarah was somehow not surprised to be discharged from the hospital by Oksana, Nico's wife, who made the filling out of forms and the signing of release papers a very smooth process.

"How is Bernard?" Sarah asked.

"I would say he is very repentant," Nicolas smiled. "Would you not agree, my darling?"

"Will he tell the police that the marchesa killed Eleanor and tried to blackmail him into killing me?"

"I fear he is not the most reliable witness," said Nico, staring at a distant spot on the ceiling. "He will be discharged from the hospital after the museum opening and sent home."

Sarah was not sure she wanted to know why Bernard was not a reliable witness. Oksana looked quite capable of removing large parts of people's brains, or bodies.

As Sarah and Nico passed through the main gate to the castle, hurrying back to the museum, she glanced up at the massive stone figures who had greeted her upon her arrival in Prague. The naked colossus she had dubbed the Sexy Stabber, with his sword poised over a wretch with bowed head, and the Mad Batter who was clubbing a man to death. She had had no idea that day what they actually portended, what violence she would witness in this century and previous ones. And it wasn't over yet.

She had arrived in this very spot with Nico, and it had been Eleanor who rushed out to greet her. Sarah averted her eyes as she followed Nico through the arch into the second courtyard. She did not want to see the cage where poor Eleanor's body had been stuffed.

As they passed out of the second courtyard, she glanced up at the spiky ornamentation of St. Vitus, a porcupine among churches. Nico must have seen it when it was half-finished. She turned to him.

"What's it like, to have been alive for so long?"

"Let's cut through here," said Nico, avoiding her gaze.

She blinked in the gloom as the door shut behind them. Tourists moved around the aisles, heads craned up to see the stained glass. Everyone murmured out of respect, and shuffled along the stone floor. Sarah could smell incense, suntan lotion, and body odor.

"If you're not seeing ghosts in here, then you are cured," said Nico.

Sarah looked around. No ghosts. And yet, her perception had been altered by the drug. Her consciousness had changed and it couldn't be unchanged now. Nico had the formula for the drug. If they could find the necessary ingredients, they could in theory make more. With small doses, she could visit Beethoven anytime she liked. She could take the drug back to America and see her father. She could go anywhere, see anything.

I see only darkness ahead on the path you are choosing.

That's what John Dee had said.

Max emerged from a carved wooden side door in the church, followed by a man in scarlet robes and several bodyguards. Max was wearing a gray suit that made him look exactly like his grandfather, a fedora under his arm. Her heart leapt and she longed to kiss him. But was that — ?

It was. Marchesa Elisa, impressive in stiletto heels and a linen suit, appeared at Max's side and took his arm.

"Miss Weston, I am glad to see you are better," said Max. "We'll need you to discuss the Music Room exhibit this evening with the patrons and our honored guests." His tone was cold and formal, but his eyes were alive with things to say.

"Please let us know if you do not have suitable attire," said the marchesa, looking Sarah up and down.

"Oh, and Sarah," Max said. "There is a copy of *Atalanta Fugiens* from Nela that I have included in the music exhibition. Please make an appropriate card for it."

The marchesa pulled Max firmly along with her, but Sarah caught Max's meaningful quick glance.

"Atalanta Fugiens?" she said to Nico, when they had gone.

"It was published in 1617 by Michael Maier, an alchemist at Rudolf's court. We rather liked him. It's what you might call the first multimedia book ever. Fifty woodcuts, or emblems, each illustrating an aspect of alchemy, with an epigram and a discourse

561

for each, plus a piece of music created from the mathematics of the symbols."

"Alchemical music," said Sarah.

"There are alchemical symbols everywhere in Prague." Nico nodded. "I should give tours." They were hurrying past the entrance to the crypt at the north end of the cathedral and the little man pointed to a symbol etched into the stone floor before it. Sarah stopped abruptly, bent down, and traced it with her finger. A triangle.

"The alchemical symbol for fire," said Nico. "And Tycho's favorite symbol. He used to leave it everywhere, as a warning. I have a tattoo of it, actually. If you'd care to . . ."

"Why did you draw that alchemical symbol on the ceiling of my apartment in Boston?" she asked, standing up again and rushing off, Nico in her wake. "John Dee's symbol for everything. No more riddles, Jepp. Just tell me."

"I don't know," the little man said simply. "Maybe it was a warning. Knowing everything can be very dangerous."

FIFTY-SIX

As Sarah and Nico rushed down Jirska she wondered what Max's cryptic message meant.

The scaffolding that had hidden the palace for the entire time Sarah had worked there was gone. The building was like a bearded man who suddenly shaves — exciting and clean and kind of naked. Sarah and Nico had to produce several forms of ID to get in. There would be dignitaries from all over the world, and Czech security — BIS — was not taking any chances. Catering staff swarmed everywhere setting up chairs and tables and linens and glassware. Florists were hauling in huge arrangements of every shape and color. Everything was freshly painted and dusted. It was nice to see the palace looking so beautiful, she thought, amazed that only a few weeks ago it had been filled with Polish workmen and had seemed a hulking, dusty wreck of a place.

"Sarah!" shouted Suzi, enfolding her in a huge hug. "I came to see you, but you were like Sleeping Beauty, only with more drool. Food poisoning sucks!"

"It was bad timing," she said. "I'm a little freaked that the opening is tonight."

Specifically about the fact that at least one woman who wanted her dead would be there.

"We all are," whispered Suzi, on the move. "My crossbows need to be an inch higher and no one can seem to be able to tell me where my little Silesian pistol is. Miles is going to be thrilled to see you. He's losing his mind, of course."

Sarah was impressed at how much had been done. She ran up the stairs to the second floor, passing a beautiful photograph of Grandpa Max with an inscription that told the story of his marriage to Gillian, their narrow escape to England in March 1939, his work in the Underground during the war, their return to Prague in 1945, and their flight to America in 1948. Sarah wondered if the part of her vision had been accurate, when Max shot the Nazi. She realized she would never know. *The dead will keep their secrets from now on.*

Unless they were able to make more of the drug. *Westonia.*

At the top of the stairs she met an anxious Daphne, armed with a giant feather duster. Sarah made her way into the second portrait room, passing the large family tree, and the altarpiece that was a wedding gift to Polyxena and Zdenek from Rudy II in 1603. The large gold key glittered inside a glass display case. She studied the portrait of Ladislav. The thin legs and arms were exaggerated, but it was uncannily like the real thing.

A glance at her watch and she was moving again.

Turning right she passed through ceramics, and the Golden Fleece dinner set with its rather sinister-looking bull.

In Decorative Arts, Moses was practically in tears trying to get the reliquary of the head of St. Ursula to sit up straight.

"It's not funny," he said as Sarah stifled a nervous laugh. "We're two hours from showtime!"

Sarah stopped to help him and read the display card. "Did it really turn up in a box of theatrical costumes in the 1930s or did you make that up?" she asked.

"Who could make any of this up?" said Moses. "It's been a fun summer, but I'm looking forward to getting back to New York."

Sarah realized that when the museum officially opened tomorrow, most of the academics would head back to their universities, their work done. Curators would continue to oversee the collection, of course, but the task of assembling and verifying the Lobkowicz holdings and getting them on display was largely finished. They had felt like they owned the place, each academic ruling over his or her own little fiefdom of precious art and objects, but in truth they owned nothing. She would be leaving Prague herself. How could she leave now? It all felt so unfinished. How could she live her life knowing what she knew . . . with all these stories half finished . . . Beethoven . . . the Fleece . . . Max.

She thought of Absalom Sherbatsky, her beloved professor and mentor, who was the reason she was here at all. Sherbatsky who had loved music history the way she did, who had taught her how to listen. Sherbatsky should have been here tonight, to see the collection assembled. The Helmer violin. The Mozart annotations on Handel's *Messiah*. The Sellas guitar. The Guttler lute. The *Eroica*.

Sherbatsky had asked Luigi to play for her. It was his final gift.

But there was something she needed to find, something Max had alerted her to.

Back in her room now, Sarah hurried to the glass case where the music manuscripts were, but as she did, she heard footsteps behind her.

A man appeared in a belted tunic and leggings carrying a lute.

"Seriously?" asked Sarah. Another flashback?

"Is this bad time?" asked the young man, in a heavy Czech accent. "They tell me I am to play in here, but I need to use toilet. Also, this linen is very scratchy."

Sarah showed him where the bathroom was. Returning to her room, she searched the shelves. Max had carried out her unfinished work perfectly; everything was just as she had planned it. On the second shelf in the corner she spotted an unfamiliar book and pulled it out. *Atalanta Fugiens.* She unlocked the case and gently removed the book, began flipping through it slowly, glancing at the woodcuts and the large Latin letters.

On the page dedicated to the making of the Philosopher's Stone she found a slip of paper in Max's handwriting.

Because I love you.

The musician returned from the bathroom and began tuning his lute.

Max loved her?

Slightly dazed, she moved to the supply cupboard and pulled out a piece of the thick paper they used for display case notations. She would have to say something about the manuscript. What? She studied the engraving of the Philosopher's Stone. An alchemist figure held a giant sextant against a brick wall, seeming to have just finished tracing a large circle. Within the circle was a triangle, within that a square, within that another circle. Inside the circle were the figures of a man and a woman.

A man and a woman, caught in an alchemist's symbol.

She printed the name of the book, the date, and the author on her display card.

"Who was Atalanta?" she asked vaguely, pulling out her phone. Wikipedia to the rescue.

"Atalanta," said the Czech musician from his corner. "She was abandoned by parents in forest and raised by wolves. She came to live with peoples, but she no wish to marry and always she beat the men at hunting and show of strength. She promise to marry man who could win in race with her, because no man fast enough. So one man toss golden apples in her path and she pick the apples up and he run past her so he win race."

"I guess she really liked apples," joked

Sarah weakly. Max loved her. Was his love a golden apple in her path? Should she stop to pick it up?

"Atalanta was only woman to go with Jason on voyage to find Golden Fleece."

Sarah shook her head and took a deep breath. She replaced the book in the display case. "I better go get changed for the party," she said.

Miles was having a small nervous breakdown in the Imperial Hall. Sarah went over to tell him that she was here, she was fine, and she would be in the Music Room that evening to tell donors and patrons and dignitaries from all over the world about the wonderful treasures they were looking at.

"Concentrate on the rich Americans," Miles said. "The Europeans are inured to 'save our treasures,' but Americans still swoon and pull out their checkbooks at the sight of anything more than fifty years old. And we're going to need lots more funding to keep the place going. The wife of Chevron will be here tonight, and she is an amateur musician so be particularly charming to her. Let her hold something. Carefully. Oh yes, what is it?" Miles turned distractedly to a gray-haired woman in a black dress and white apron who was hobbling toward them.

"Problem with plumbing," she said. It was Stefania, the woman who had saved her on the roof. The dancer whose ankles had been broken when a KGB agent intentionally ran her over as she tried to leave the country with her American lover back in the seventies.

"Sarah," called Miles over his shoulder. "The senator will be here right at six, and will take a private tour of the palace and then leave."

Miles looked slightly paler as he said this.

Sarah nodded, her mouth suddenly dry.

FIFTY-SEVEN

Sarah sat on her bed in the windowless room and tried to focus. She was doing her job, she told herself. Her job was to bring history to light. To make ancient music and musicians comprehensible and meaningful so that they lived on in the hearts of subsequent generations. She was part of the army of the learned that kept culture and civilization alive so that we didn't sink into another Dark Ages.

She glanced at the little leather-covered *ars moriendi* that she had found in the library at Nela. The medieval book on how to die a good Christian death. That might come in handy. She flipped through it absently.

Were they just going to let Charlotte Yates get away with it all? She had betrayed her country. Killed people. Stolen and threatened and murdered. Marchesa Elisa was dangerous. She wanted Max out, had wanted Sarah dead. She might still. Sarah knew too much.

She glanced down at the book in her hands. An engraving showed a man opening a trapdoor on which was inscribed a triangle. Fire surged forth.

"Ostium quod ducit ad inferos," the caption read. *The door that leads to Hell.*

She took out the piece of paper from her pocket. *Because I love you.*

Was that real? More real than alchemy and poisoned dwarfs and an iron casket that carried the secret Golden . . . wait a sec.

She looked more closely at the woodcut. The man opening the trapdoor was holding a large golden key. Another man stood nearby, playing a violin. *A large golden key.* Maybe Rudolf II hadn't used the key to lock up the Golden Fleece. Maybe he had used it to seal off a hell portal.

But there weren't actual hell portals. Except Nico had said that "hell portal" was simply the phrase Brahe used instead of "black hole" or "dark matter," which weren't things anyone knew about in 1601.

Which weren't things anyone had named yet. She asked herself if she, Sarah Weston, Bostonian, atheist, scholar, believed in the existence of a hell portal, an actual physical door to another world. Certainly when she had arrived in Prague she didn't, but things had changed . . . she had changed. The things that one could know . . . the laws of science.

The things Nico had read to her while she was asleep were floating at the edge of her consciousness. Alessandro had once told her that many scientists now believed in a multiverse, an infinite series of possible worlds, looped around like string. And if time had no meaning, and the past was all around us, if our physical world was saturated with traces of everything that had happened in time . . .

So what was a hell portal? Dark matter? A place in the physical world where you could access another dimension?

Prague is a threshold.

She had seen the dead. She had passed over the threshold. She could not go back, like John Dee, and hide from the knowledge. At the very least she would refuse to hide from what she knew about Charlotte Yates and Marchesa Elisa Lobkowicz DeBenedetti. There had to be some way to stop them.

She needed to arm herself for battle. A shower, a black sheath that was only moderately wrinkled, hair up, a necklace her father had given her protecting her jugular.

Atalanta fleeing? No way. This time Atalanta was walking right into the fire. In heels.

FIFTY-EIGHT

Every detail was perfect. Uniformed waiters were ready with trays of hors d'oeuvres. Champagne was chilled and ready to be poured. A table of crisp white gift bags stenciled in gold with "Lobkowicz Palace Museum" contained a Brueghel puzzle, Croll watercolor stationery, a Polyxena bookmark, and a pair of earrings copied from those worn by Maria Manrique de Lara. Plus a handy envelope for making donations to the museum. In the reception rooms, musicians were poised to play. In each display room, an academic was ready to give the guests an up-close and personal take on the treasures within. It was elegant and yet intimate at the same time, although the presence of the U.S. Secret Service slightly marred the effect. Sarah hung her credentials around her neck and made her way through the ground-floor rooms. Some children and adults milled about and she stopped, turned back. There was something familiar about the man with his back to her in the toreador outfit . . .

"Jose?" she said, aghast.

He turned, and suddenly she saw that Pols was there, too, a violin case in her hand.

Oh my God, she thought. *This is not good.*

Pols was wearing an off-white full-skirted dress trimmed with pearls and red ribbons. She looked like she had stepped out of one of the paintings on the museum walls. This made Jose's toreador outfit look both appropriate and stylish. Boris the mastiff was also present, in his service bib to which a jaunty red bow had been added.

Sarah hugged the little girl tightly. Boris licked Sarah's ear. "I hate physical contact," said Pols.

"I know," said Sarah, hugging her again. "What are you doing here?"

"The board of the museum invited the finalists from the competition back to play at the opening. We arrived this morning. I wanted to surprise you." Pols leaned in close. "I keep having dreams of fire," she whispered.

Sarah looked at Jose, her eyes saying, *How could you let this happen?*

Jose shrugged. "She is unstoppable force," he said.

"It's not safe," Sarah hissed at him.

"Don't worry, Sarah," said Pols. "The Holy Infant will protect me."

Sarah groaned inwardly as Jana came into the room with a headset on.

"The senator is on her way," she announced. "Places, everyone!"

Pols and the little Russian, Japanese, Chinese, and North Korean prodigies took their seats and began to play a fugue.

"I'm right upstairs," said Sarah to Jose as Jana pulled her away.

Nicolas met her on the stairs. He pulled her into a curtained recess and pressed something into her palm.

"I lied to you," said the little man, "when I told you that I did not know what happened to the second key that the master made. I did know what happened to it. I took it." He pulled a gold key out of his suit pocket. It hung from a thin gold chain.

"The master melted down a crucifix and made these two keys. They are identical. I should like you to have this one."

"I can't take that," Sarah said. "It belongs —"

"To whom?" the little man asked. "To Max? He already has one. It's downstairs on display. To me? It was not made for me.

To history? History will not miss it. I would like you to have it. Remember that I am a little psychic and if I think you should take it, you should take it."

He pressed it into her palm.

"I admit that despite Oksana, up till now this century has been a little dull. Forgive me for not falling into a frenzy of excitement over Facebook and *American Idol*. I admit iTunes is very useful. And Oksana is good at sexting. My point is that you have reinvigorated me. And I feel a certain . . . protectiveness toward Max. I think he will make a very good Prince Lobkowicz. Most of them started out a little strange, too."

"Thank you for the key," Sarah said. She hung the chain around her neck and tucked the key out of sight into her cleavage. Nicolas smiled.

A large man in a black suit with an earpiece disappearing into his collar was stationed in her room.

"Hiya," said Sarah. The man smiled in a friendly way. Sarah showed him her credentials and he produced a flat wand like the ones used in airports.

"A matter of routine," he said calmly, waving it over her body. The wand buzzed over Sarah's watch, and the gold key. As the man bent over, Sarah saw the gun in his holster. She swallowed. *Charlotte Yates could have me killed tonight,* she thought. *She's done it before. She could do it again.*

"Guess you drew the short straw," said Sarah. "I bet you'd rather hang out in the Gun Room."

The man smiled politely but said nothing.

Sarah looked at the lute player.

"Play now?" he asked.

"Yeah, go for it," Sarah said.

They waited.

Sarah trained her hearing to the rooms behind her. She listened to Suzi jabbering away, then a sudden silence. Then a cluster of voices, a woman's laugh. Miles's voice. Suzi's again. The Secret Service agent stepped forward toward the door. The lute player fumbled a note, then started again. A rustle of silk, and then Sarah turned to greet the most powerful American senator.

Charlotte Yates did have presence, Sarah had to give her that. The off-white Valentino gown was utterly elegant, the hair was perfect, her smile could break glass. She exuded a sense of control, of power, of authority. She held a glass of champagne in one ringed hand, and a Lobkowicz Museum goodie bag in the other. An emerald bracelet glittered. Her teeth were perfect.

Three more black-suited men followed her in. And Miles.

"Sarah Weston, allow me to introduce —"

"Hello, I'm Charlotte Yates," she said to Sarah. She turned to the Secret Service agent who had been guarding Sarah's room. "Oh hello, Tad." She handed the goodie bag off to Tad. He seemed used to this.

Her handshake was firm.

"Madam Senator, we're honored to have you," said Sarah, making good eye contact. It was important to stand up to your enemies, her father had always said. Look them in the eye. Do not be cowed by bullies.

"Sarah is a musicologist from Boston who joined us this summer," said Miles.

"How nice for you," said the senator. "Tell me about all these lovely things."

Sarah couldn't believe the woman's cool. But she could match it.

"Of course. This is the centerpiece of our — the Lobkowicz — collection. The 1806 score of the *Eroica* Symphony, which Beethoven dedicated to his patron, Joseph Franz Maximilian, the 7th Prince Lobkowicz. The story is that the composer had originally meant to dedicate the work to Napoleon, but after Napoleon crowned himself emperor, Beethoven was so disgusted that he scratched out the dedication. Whether this is true is a matter of debate, but certainly Beethoven was never a man to accept the domination of authority figures."

"How interesting," said Charlotte. "I don't suppose Napoleon was too bothered by the feelings of a musician though."

"There is a story," said Sarah, "that after Napoleon's victory at Jena, Beethoven remarked, 'It's a pity I do not understand the art of war as well as I do the art of music. I would conquer him!'"

"How funny," the senator said. "It would seem the only ego larger than a politician's is a musician's!"

Everyone in the room chuckled. Charlotte's eyes remained locked on Sarah.

At that moment Max and Marchesa Elisa walked in. In black tie and tails, Max looked like a prince from the 1930s. Like his grandfather. The marchesa shimmered in red. She looked like a flame.

"Senator Yates, I am so sorry we were not here to greet you," cooed the marchesa. "A little problem with your security. I am mortified. Please forgive us. My name is Elisa Lobkowicz DeBenedetti."

"Of course," said the senator smoothly. "You may not remember, but we actually met years ago, I think."

"I'm charmed *you* remember," Elisa said. "And please let me introduce you to my fiancé, Max. He is also a Lobkowicz, but we are from different branches of the family, so it's all quite correct." The marchesa smiled and then, very deliberately, turned her smile to Sarah.

"Welcome to the Lobkowicz Palace Museum," said Max very stiffly.

"You are both to be congratulated," said Charlotte. Sarah's nose alerted her. Envy. The senator was simmering in envy. But even more than that, Sarah thought she detected a kind of recklessness in the woman, madness even.

"What a wonderful thing you have created here," the senator said.

"We have managed to bring many things back to their rightful place here in Prague," Max said. "But of course some things disappeared forever during the Nazi occupation. And under communism as well. A researcher like Miss Weston here has had many obstacles. The Nazis kept records. The communists simply stole."

Max's eyes were steely.

Your father would be proud of you, Sarah thought. *Your grandfather, too.*

Charlotte's eyes narrowed perhaps a fraction of an inch.

"Luckily, all that is behind us now," Max said. "We can leave the past behind, *all of it,* and start fresh. I confess the task has at times . . . overwhelmed us . . . this summer in particular, but now we look forward to sharing the collection with the Czech people, and I personally am determined to devote my attention *entirely* to the preservation of these wonderful works of art. We are all honored by your presence here tonight, Madam Senator. I hope in some small way, our museum will serve as a cultural bridge between the Czech Republic and the United States. Perhaps in the future we might lend certain things to American museums and institutions."

What are you doing? Sarah thought. *You're telling her that it's over. That she has nothing to fear from you. That all you want is to keep your precious museum open.*

He's doing what his family has always done, a voice inside her head answered her. *He's keeping what he values most safe. He's doing it for you.*

Because I love you.

"What a charming speech," said Charlotte. "I can imagine you will not find fundraising difficult with that level of eloquence. But if you do, you and Elisa must call upon me. I would be pleased to be of some help in your endeavor. Now please, let us continue our tour. I am quite enchanted with it all."

And with that, she was gone, sweeping out Miles, the marchesa, and the Secret Service with her. Max gave Sarah one swift look over his shoulder.

"Should I stop playing now?" the musician asked. Sarah nodded. The senator's perfume lingered in the air, nauseating and threatening.

But it's over, she thought.

Then why did she feel danger all around her?

Sarah ducked into the bathroom in the corridor to splash water on her face. Stefania was there, holding a stack of linen hand towels. Sarah took one and said thank you to her in Czech, but Stefania just stared straight ahead.

"Stefania? Are you okay? You look like you've just seen a ghost."

"No," said Stefania after a beat. "I *hear* a ghost. And now I know what she look like." And with that the woman handed the stack of towels to Sarah and walked out of the bathroom. Sarah put them down and followed her out, but she was gone.

Sarah walked to the long window facing

the courtyard and leaned her head against the cool pane. From there she was able to watch the senator's departure. The white silk column of her dress disappearing into the waiting car.

But she still felt Charlotte Yates's presence in the air. Her nose wrinkled. Something wasn't right. Her nerves were jangling. Danger. She smelled danger.

It wasn't over.

The doors were opened to the rest of the invited guests, and a mob of Czechs, French, Spaniards, Italians, and wealthy Americans poured in.

Sarah stood in the Music Room and greeted guest after guest, pointing out the treasures, telling anecdotes, explaining the restoration process. She tried to seem professional, calm, and engaging, but her senses were on high alert. Images of fire flitted through her brain.

Jana appeared and informed Sarah that guests should now start being directed to the first floor. In a short while, there would be a series of speeches and an appeal to donors in the Balcony Room. Jana wanted to make sure everyone had imbibed plenty of champagne at that point. The researchers were to gather in the Moritz Room just before. Max and Marchesa Elisa wished to thank them for their efforts personally.

Sarah was grateful for an opportunity to leave the Music Room and check in on Pols. To assure herself that her anxiety was all in her head.

But as she made her way downstairs to where the child musicians were still playing, the lingering scent of Charlotte Yates only grew stronger. It wasn't perfume. It was . . . evil. And it was still here.

A crowd hovered around the young performers. Pols looked so regal, violin tucked under chin, and utterly absorbed. Beethoven. String Quartet no. 10, op. 74, a work that Luigi had dedicated to Prince Lobkowicz. But the moment Sarah appeared the little girl immediately looked up and directly at her. And Sarah knew that Pols felt it, too, the disturbance in the air. Their faces were briefly mirror images of each other.

Jose appeared at her side, with Boris on a leash.

"I think he has to make business," Jose said. "I no want to leave Pollina now, though. Can you take him?"

"Of course," said Sarah automatically, reaching for the mastiff's leash. "I'll be right back. She turned to make her way toward the back exit. She would take the dog out through the kitchen. No need to subject the mastiff to a public display of his needs on the red carpet out front. They passed the Moritz Room.

Boris stopped. He was getting a little old, and stubborn. Although actually right now he didn't look old. He looked . . . transformed. His ears were up, his eyes fixed, his carriage alert and tense, his hackles raised. Boris began tugging on the leash, pulling her into the Moritz Room, which was empty. Sarah struggled with him for a moment, and then all of a sudden, she knew. She could smell it. Boris could smell it.

"Find it," she whispered to the dog. "Show me where."

FIFTY-NINE

Boris was doing a kind of canine dance, inching forward and back in front of the elegant white ceramic stove in a corner niche of the Moritz Room. He growled.

"Good dog," she whispered. "Good dog."

Sarah moved cautiously to the stove. Boris whimpered.

"Sarah?"

It was Max.

"I think there's a bomb in here," she said quietly. Max was at her side in two long strides. Together they opened the stove door.

Inside was a Lobkowicz Palace Museum goodie bag. Sarah would bet her life that this was the one Charlotte Yates had handed off to her Secret Service agent. Sarah reached for it and, barely breathing, looked inside.

She could see a wire, and something blinking.

"Go," said Max. "Go now. Tell Jana to get

everyone out." He reached inside and withdrew the bag.

"Max," she said. "What are you doing?"

"Everyone was supposed to gather in this room in fifteen minutes. If it goes off then, a bomb squad will be too late. I'll take it down to the tunnels. The walls are six feet thick."

"Are you *insane*?"

Max straightened. Above him hung the portrait of Moritz, 9th Prince Lobkowicz, dressed in full regalia of the Order of the Golden Fleece.

"Please go now," he said, and began running from the room with the bag.

"Go get Pols," she said to the dog. "Go to *POLS.*" Would he understand? She let go of the leash and Boris took off like a streak of lightning toward the Concert Hall.

Sarah raced back to the Balcony Room, where Jana was arranging some folding chairs.

"Jana, we have a bomb scare. We need to get everyone out and away from the palace as fast as possible but without a panic." Jana blinked once and then immediately turned to the guests in the room.

"Ladies and gentlemen," she announced loudly. "I must ask you to please make your way to the terrace and continue down the steps to the courtyard at once. Please move quickly but with consideration. We have an emergency." She ran across the room toward the Concert Hall. "Ladies and gentlemen . . ."

Sarah was paralyzed with adrenaline. Would Max run until he hit the end or until the bomb blew up in his face? She should make sure Pols got out okay. She could get crushed, trampled. She might have to shove her way through people to get to her. Sarah could hear Jana shouting instructions in three languages with martial calmness.

Then Sarah remembered the well. She had almost fallen into it, looking for the secret library. It was the perfect place to safely dispose of the bomb. But what if Max fell into it first?

Sarah made her decision. She kicked off her heels and ran toward the stairs and the entrance to the tunnels.

SIXTY

Sarah could hear Max ahead of her as she half-ran, half-stumbled, crouching through the dank tunnel, holding her cell phone before her for the beam of flashlight.

"Max!"

"Get out of here!" Max yelled. "Sarah, go back."

"There's a well!" she called. "In one of the tunnels. I saw it. The ground was damp, it came up out of nowhere. Be careful. It just appears." Suddenly, she was almost on top of him. Max was cradling the bag to his ribs like a football.

"Go," said Max hoarsely. "There are some stairs here. I'll go as deep as I can. I don't even know what's above us right now, but I'm not going to be known as the prince who blew up Prague Castle. There's no time."

He turned away and moved forward out of the light. She heard him grunt, and then

591

the sound of his feet skidding. Was he falling down the well? She inched forward and suddenly found herself skidding as well. Sarah reached out to brace herself against the tunnel walls.

The tunnel was slick as ice and she felt herself sliding out of control, unable to hold on. She could hear Max grunting and sliding below her. The tunnel curved and she was falling straight down. Sarah hit the bottom of something with a thunk, curled herself automatically into a ball and rolled. To her surprise, the darkness of the tunnel was alleviated here; she could see Max's body outlined thinly, in a heap just ahead of her. The source of light came from a narrow sliver, about three feet across, somewhere around the region of Max's ankles.

"Max?"

"Sarah?"

The tunnel ended here, clearly. There were no other branches. They were essentially at the bottom of a well. But where was the light coming from? Not her phone, which was only emitting a tiny point light now. She groped forward. Her fingers encountered a smooth groove cut into the stone.

"We can leave the bomb here," Max said. "But can we get back up?"

Sarah turned and tried to see up the tunnel. "No," she said.

Sarah moved back to the groove in the stone, her fingers working around the edges.

"Max, I think this is a door."

Sarah pushed with all her strength against the stone. She wedged her fingers into the groove and pulled. Nothing.

Max set the bag gently down on the ground. They huddled at the entrance of the tunnel, peering up.

"Shit."

Suddenly a burst of music came flooding through the tunnel. It was so loud that for a moment Sarah thought the bomb had actually gone off. Max pulled her to him and wrapped his arms around her.

But they were still alive and the music . . .

Beethoven's Adagio in F Major for mechanical clock. Being played by a really big organ.

Sarah wriggled out of Max's arms and moved back to the door, stepping carefully over the bomb. "It's coming from behind here!" she shouted, over the music. The panicked feeling was back, stronger now.

"Hey!" Max shouted into the crack of the door. "Can anyone hear me? There's a bomb here that's going to go off! Can you let us out? Hello? Who's there?"

Sarah slid her hands frantically up and

down the stone. All doors had to be opened somehow. A latch, a knob, a hinge. Her hand met a small square depression in the stone. Was this some kind of . . . she shoved her palm against it and heard something click and slide.

Max, unprepared, stumbled as the door swung open. Sarah, also unprepared, fell on top of him. They landed in an awkward tangle of arms and legs, Max holding the white paper goodie bag aloft like an outfielder holding up a caught baseball after a dramatic dive. All around them things were shimmering and glowing even in the pale illumination coming from Sarah's phone. Sarah found a narrow stairway and climbed it, and came to a door. A door with seven locks.

She came back down the stairs and shone her failing phone flashlight around the large underground space that had been hacked out of rock. Squared-off shapes loomed. Tombs.

"This is not good," said Max. He removed something from his jacket pocket.

"Is that Suzi's dueling pistol?" Sarah asked.

"I didn't know what was going to go down tonight and I couldn't bring a gun into the palace," Max answered. "So I grabbed one I already owned." He set it carefully down on a tomb. "But I don't think it's going to help us now."

Sarah, face-to-face with what she was pretty sure was the Crown of St. Wenceslas, had to agree.

SIXTY-ONE

They had escorted the senator through the subterranean service entrance of the Four Seasons. The lobby, of course, was a much pleasanter entrée, but for security reasons one got used to seeing the machinations behind five-star elegance. Employees pushing laundry carts and room service trolleys stepped aside and lowered their heads almost like Victorian servants, Charlotte noted approvingly. She could hear the sound of cutlery banging. She was hungry. She did not enjoy eating publicly anymore. She thought it made her seem weak. At dinner with the prime minister Charlotte had allowed herself only a few discreet forkfuls. Perhaps she should order some room service right away. After the bomb went off, there were liable to be delays, and it would be annoying to have to wait for dinner. The hotel's restaurant was Italian and boasted a Michelin star. Pasta. Yes, a nice dish of ziti.

She would eat in her pajamas and relax. She could probably get a good view of the burning palace from her hotel room window. It would be like watching one of those cute Bourne movies.

Charlotte Yates looked at her watch. Tad should be in place now, outside St. Vitus Cathedral, a safe enough distance from ground zero. Really the bomb should only take out the main floor of Lobkowicz Palace. Of course all the key victims would be gathered to hear Prince Max and the marchesa make their gracious speeches, but a few people might actually survive the thing. Anyone lingering on the second floor would probably be either burned or suffocated by the resulting fires or collapsing building structure, but you never knew. The important thing was that the marchesa was snuffed, and everyone who might have seen the letters or known about them would soon be ash.

Smuggling the bomb in under the skirt of her Valentino had been child's play. No one was going to dare pat down a senator's thighs. And then the museum had provided that handy little paper sack. A trip to the restroom, a handoff to Tad, and it was done. She would have liked to keep the earrings, but some things couldn't be helped. The headlines tomorrow would be terrific. In case anyone was slow on the uptake (and you could never count on journalists to write a story correctly), she had prepared a statement from Al Qaeda taking responsibility for the bomb. "Although we did not achieve our objective in annihilating our prime target, Senator Charlotte Yates, we still celebrate the deaths of the unholy, blah, blah, blah." This would go viral in about four hours. In the morning, she would be on site to comfort the "victims'" families, despite the threat to her own safety. Who wouldn't admire her after that? There would be no humiliating primary battles, just a smooth path to the presidency.

In her room now, she drew back the curtains. How nice. The hotel had champagne ready. Prague Castle was framed almost perfectly in her window, the spires of St. Vitus Cathedral etched blackly into the night sky. So pretty. There had always been a certain magic in Prague. Her private line phone beeped. A message from Tad in their special code.

They were evacuating the palace. A bomb squad had been called. Tad had tracked the Weston girl's GPS on her phone. She was in St. Vitus.

No. No. No.

Charlotte was furious. But Charlotte Yates was a doer. She would finish this thing herself.

She began texting instructions.

SIXTY-TWO

"These are the Crown Jewels of Bohemia," said Sarah, peering at an orb that glittered in the pale light from her dying phone. "So that means . . ."

"We're in St. Vitus Cathedral," Max groaned. "Sarah. We're trapped in the *Crown Chamber,* the most heavily fortified spot in the whole *nation.*" Sarah looked at the bag in his hands. The bomb inside would blow any second.

Sarah began quickly searching the room for something to use as a tool to get them out of there. She picked up and then tossed aside a golden apple. A jeweled scepter. A magnificent furred cloak. All priceless, all useless.

At least they were deep underground and the walls were thick. All the people down here were already dead. At least when they died they wouldn't take anyone else with them.

They scrambled among the massive tombs in the cold and dark, hoping to find another way out. Blind, Sarah slammed into a sarcophagus. As she hit it, she was wrenched backward and a tiny wrought-iron gargoyle's hand caught the chain that held the gold key Nico had given her. For a moment, she was strangled by the chain, then it snapped and the key clattered across the marble floor.

Max dropped down beside her. "Sarah," he said as she gasped for breath, feeling her throat. "Sarah, I —" He stopped suddenly.

What do you say when you have moments to live? "Max." But he wasn't looking at her. He was staring at the floor.

The key was moving.

It was sliding across the stone floor as if pulled by some invisible thread.

It was more than a key.

It was a magnet.

Wordlessly, spellbound, Sarah and Max followed the snaking line of the key, which came to rest on top of a small triangle-shaped piece of marble, the corner of a larger rectangular pattern on the floor.

The triangle. Tycho Brahe's favorite symbol.

Prague is a threshold. Fire.

Dark matter and energy make up ninety-six

percent of the universe.

"What are you doing?" Max yelled.

"I think there's a hell portal here," said Sarah.

Her fingers dug frantically around the edges of the mosaic piece but found nothing. No break in the stone. No way to pull it up or push it down. Max leaned over her and wrapped his hand around the key, wrenching it up.

And the piece of marble came with it, seemingly pulled by the key's magnetic force. Max stumbled backward, staggering under the heavy weight. Sarah leaned forward. In the shallow hollow left by the stone she could make out the edges of a keyhole.

"The key!" she screamed at Max. "Give me the key!"

SIXTY-THREE

Getting out of the hotel would have been a pleasant refresher course in old skills of deception, if it weren't for the urgency of the matter at hand. Charlotte had told her agents she was going to bed with a headache, hidden herself in the room service cart, and, once in the bowels of the hotel, stolen a maid's uniform. Too easy, really. The only imperfect moment had been outside the hotel, when an old woman seemed to recognize her. She limped toward Charlotte, arm upraised, and Charlotte immersed herself in a group of tourists.

Tad was waiting for her near the south doorway of St. Vitus. Charlotte glanced behind her to make sure the old woman was no longer on her tail. Despite her age the woman had managed to hobble along behind Charlotte for blocks. It was like the old days, when every babushka was an informer.

"I have the marchesa," Tad said calmly, "but she got a little feisty, so I had to be persuasive."

He had, in fact, used the bottom portion of the marchesa's own evening gown to tie her to a pew in the nave. It actually looked like Elisa was deep in prayer, which surely was a first. Tad had also stuffed a fragment of the dress in the marchesa's mouth.

"You can untie her," Charlotte said to Tad. She pulled the gag free.

"What is happening?" Elisa hissed. "You betray me? You put a bomb in my palace?"

"Shhhh." Charlotte held a finger to her lips and then pointed to a small doorway in the corner of the Chapel of St. Wenceslas. She grabbed Elisa's arm and pulled her along. Tad followed closely.

"This is what is happening," Charlotte said in a friendly way to the marchesa. "I didn't plant a bomb anywhere. But you did. And then you came and shot your fiancé, and the girl your fiancé was fucking. And then you shot yourself. Tad?"

Tad handed her his service weapon with the silencer tightly screwed on and Senator Charlotte Yates shot Marchesa Elisa Lobkowicz DeBenedetti in the head. "Shoot open the locks," she said, pointing to the door to the Crown Chamber.

As Tad centered his pistol to blow apart the seventh lock, Charlotte centered her pistol on Tad. Her bullet went right through the back of his skull and pierced the lock. He dropped to the floor and the door swung silently open.

How economical, she thought. No sense wasting taxpayers' money on an extra bullet.

Sixty-Four

Max pried the key away from the marble piece, and once it was free it flew in the air toward the opening in the floor. Sarah snatched it, guiding it into the lock, her hands burning from the now blazingly hot metal. As she turned the key the ground beneath her hands and knees began vibrating, almost undulating. Sarah fought for purchase on the cold marble. Max grabbed hold of her legs, hauling Sarah backward as the larger rectangle set in the floor flew upward, like some kind of Satanic jack-in-the-box. A jet of brilliant red-gold light shot out of the hole, seemed to hover in the air above their heads for a moment, and then rushed back down into the portal. The chamber was flooded with a powerful scent of amber. The stone rectangle hit the floor with a tremendous thud that jolted Sarah's spine and brought tears to her eyes. She heard Max shouting her name.

"Throw it in!" she screamed. "Max! Throw it in!"

And Sarah saw the white paper Lobkowicz Palace Museum goodie bag sail over her head and disappear into the portal.

For a moment there was total silence and then Sarah heard a small *pop*. She turned to look at Max and saw his head jerk up. His eyes went wide, and a spot of red appeared on his pristine white flat-pleated tuxedo shirt just below his collarbone. He looked terribly *surprised.* Sarah had a microsecond of confusion — *The hell portal shot Max?* — then threw herself at him as she heard the second *pop*.

They tumbled behind a tomb and the bullet ricocheted off the marble.

Someone was here. Someone was shooting at them.

Max was underneath her, wounded, but still breathing. He motioned with his right arm and then stifled a scream. Sarah pressed her hand against the blood pooling on his shoulder.

Think, she told herself. *Think fast.*

Max had brought a pistol. Where did he leave the pistol?

Cautiously, Sarah inched her body over Max's to the side of the tomb. If she could just see . . . With a *ping* another bullet ricocheted off the floor, inches from her head.

The pistol was where Max had set it down when they came in. On the other side of the hell portal.

They were trapped. Sitting ducks.

Still trying to stanch Max's wound, Sarah scrabbled around for something — anything — she could use as a weapon and felt Max pressing something hard and round into her hand. He pulled her close and whispered, "Atalanta."

She looked down at the object he had given her.

And then Sarah took a deep breath and burst into action. She launched herself from behind the tomb, took a running leap up onto the sarcophagus, crossed it in two steps, and vaulted across the room toward the tomb where the pistol lay. As she jumped headfirst, she twisted midflight and threw the object in her hand as hard as she could in the direction of the gunman, willing her body to replicate the move she and her father had watched countless outfielders for the Red Sox make.

Good arm, her dad always said. And he would circle her skinny bicep in his large hand and shake it while she giggled. *That's a good arm.*

The gun went *pop* again.

As her body continued to fly through the air, she suddenly felt the grip of the portal below her, pulling her into its force. Time seemed to stop. She could see galaxies, universes, cosmos. Voices and music and sound. Time and space and history and life over aeons compressed into one small doorway. *Everything,* she thought.

Then *smash,* she hit the stone floor and was scrambling for cover, her ears ringing from the ricochet of the bullet. And through that she heard the *clink clink* of something rolling back toward her along the floor. The missile she had thrown. Her knee stung with a fiery pain.

Sarah reached up, felt along the top of the sarcophagus. Her fingers closed over the pistol.

There was silence in the room, then footsteps and a low chuckle.

"Nice move," said a woman's voice.

Sarah glanced down at the ancient gun between her knees, not certain exactly how to operate it. You cocked a pistol, didn't you? She pulled a lever and something made a quiet click. *Just point,* she told herself. *Point and shoot.*

The footsteps came closer, then stopped again. Another chuckle.

"So that's what you threw at me. A golden apple. *The* golden apple. You know, I always wanted it."

Sarah peeked over the top of the sarcophagus, trying to get the woman in the sights of the tiny weapon. In the glow from the portal, she saw her. The woman wore a maid's uniform under a trench coat. But even if she hadn't known her from her voice, the face was unmistakable. It was Charlotte Yates.

The senator stopped a few feet from the portal. "A furnace," she said. "What a convenient way of getting rid of dead bodies. I love a crypt with a built-in crematorium."

The apple hovered on the edge of the portal, still spinning slightly.

Sarah steadied her breath. She remembered Suzi telling her once that you were supposed to fire a gun in between heartbeats. That was when your hand was stillest.

Eyes glittering, Charlotte leaned over and picked up the apple. "Exquisite," she said, holding it up and admiring it. A single drop of blood sat on her cheek like a ruby.

Sarah realized she would have to step out from behind the sarcophagus to fire. She would have one chance. The light from the portal bounced off the gems and lit up Charlotte's face in shades of emerald and sapphire.

Sarah waited for the space between heartbeats, stood up, stepped out, and pulled the trigger. *Ffffft.* It sounded exactly like when her dad would set off firecrackers on the beach. Some of them were always duds. This was a dud.

Charlotte looked at Sarah and began to laugh. Sarah stood there, knowing it was over. With the apple still in her hand, Charlotte raised her gun and pointed it at Sarah.

So this was her end.

And at the end it was Pols's voice she heard: *You have to pray for help. But Sarah, don't ask until you're sincere.*

Sarah closed her eyes. "Help me," she said.

Whoosh.

All at once Sarah heard running footsteps and the sound of bodies colliding and a scream.

She opened her eyes to see the apple flying through the air.

And Charlotte Yates going headfirst into the hell portal.

The massive marble lid to the portal slid across the floor and slammed into place with a resounding crash.

Sarah looked at the person now standing where Charlotte had been. She was also wearing a maid's uniform. The woman staggered a little.

"Stefania?" said Sarah.

"I do not care if they throw me in jail," said Stefania, straightening her shoulders with the ghost of her former ballerina's grace. "She steal my life. Now I take hers."

Sarah turned to see Max pulling himself up from behind the tomb. She tried to run to him, but her knees buckled under her.

"Sarah," called Max. "Sarah, are you all right?"

"He is losing blood," said Stefania, looking at Max. "And so are you."

Sarah looked down at her bare feet, one of which was now covered in blood.

"You saved our lives," said Max to Stefania. "Now I want you to go upstairs and find Nicolas Pertusato. Tell him where we are. An ambulance. Nicolas Pertusato . . ."

"The little man," Stefania said. "Yes. I . . . I will. Prince Lobkowicz." She tucked one foot behind another and bent slowly to the ground in a curtsy.

"Really, I'm just Max Anderson," said Max.

SIXTY-FIVE

The Secret Service did not like admitting that they had lost the senator, but when they went in to wake Boss Lady at five a.m., she was not in the hotel room.

"Well, where the hell is she?" demanded the head of the CIA, awakened from sleep back in Virginia by a panicked agent using the red phone.

"We think she snuck out," said the head of her detail. "Do you want us to notify the president she's AWOL?"

"No!" he snapped. "I'll alert our people. The last thing we need out there is the news that the most powerful United States senator is loose in the world, unprotected. You better hope she went for a fucking jog."

Except the head of the CIA was pretty sure she hadn't gone for a fucking jog, because while he was talking to the idiot Secret Service agent, he was getting a text message that one of his own agents in

Prague had found a briefcase sitting on his doorstep that morning, right on top of the *Financial Times* and the *Prague Post*. A briefcase full of documents linking Charlotte Yates — *Charlotte Yates!* — to the KGB. Had no one kept their nose clean during the cold war? The briefcase had belonged to John Paisley, the former head of the CIA who had been linked to both the Kennedy assassination and Watergate, and who'd been found dead in 1978, having committed suicide by jumping off his sailboat. Except that when most people commit suicide, they don't tie their bodies down with diving weights *after* shooting themselves in the head. And their briefcases don't mysteriously disappear. The Agency had always suspected that the KGB had offed Paisley, but frankly, with his disgusting swinging seventies lifestyle and his Russian connections, he had become an embarrassment to the Agency anyway. No one cared who had done the deed.

Now, more than thirty years later, the briefcase had resurfaced on the same night Charlotte Yates had disappeared. There was going to be major damage control to do. No way in hell did anyone want the news to come out that the chair of the Senate Foreign Relations Committee had been —

wait for it — *a KGB agent.* The list of people who would be embarrassed by that would be pretty much the entire Washington phone book. And where the hell was the bitch? *Probably sitting on a cruise ship along the Volga, drinking vodka and eating caviar,* thought the head of the CIA bitterly. The Russians knew how to take care of their people. As he popped a Bromo-Seltzer and tied his tie, his phone beeped again with the news that a Secret Service agent had been found dead in St. Vitus Cathedral, just down the pew from a dead Italian socialite.

It's enough to make you vote Democratic, thought the head of the CIA, texting the agent to get a cleanup going.

Sarah and Max, lying in bed at Nela under the supervision of Nico's wife, Oksana, who had had them admitted to Na Frantisku Hospital and then released without any record of their having been there at all, much less treated for gunshot wounds, were amazed to hear the news blazing from every TV, news website, and newspaper that Charlotte Yates had had a massive heart attack on an Air Force Gulfstream V C-37A while returning from her trip to Europe. A defibrillator and a doctor were onboard, but nothing could be done. It was hotly debated on every channel that despite heart disease being the number one killer of women, women's cardiac health never got enough attention or research dollars. In the days after the quietly elegant funeral, insurance companies felt pressured to pay for mandatory echocardiograms for women over fifty.

"It was all for nothing," Max sighed.

"What?" Sarah turned to him and gently straightened the collar of his pajamas. "Don't say that."

"Miles told me everything he knew about the letters between Charlotte Yates and Yuri Bespalov. I e-mailed it all to some reporter friends. But without the actual letters . . . it's like Reagan. Now that she's dead, people only want to hear nice things about her."

"I'm glad Miles came clean," Sarah said. "It wasn't for nothing. *We* know the truth." There were a lot of victims whose deaths had been avenged that night in the cathedral.

Sarah did wish Nico had copied the contents of the Paisley briefcase. He claimed there hadn't been time. *Moy strahovoy polic,* Yuri Bespalov had called the briefcase when Sarah had encountered him in the library. Sarah had looked the phrase up. *My insurance policy.* Although it hadn't been for

Yuri, in the end.

At least the items Nico had stored at Faust House were safely back in the palace, stored in a secret workroom. Max planned to go over them personally when he was back on his feet. He hoped to find some clue there about the Fleece.

Max's Czech wolfhound entered the room, with what looked like a small chew toy in his mouth.

"Moritz, put that down," Max ordered, and the dog opened his maw obediently. The damp Chihuahua yelped and skittered under the bed.

"Will you be attending Elisa's funeral?" Sarah asked, as Max turned and began kissing her shoulder.

"Too distraught," he said. "Oh, that reminds me. The police turned over Elisa's personal effects to me, and there was something I wanted to give you." Max turned to the bedside table and began rummaging in the drawer.

"I don't want anything that belonged to that woman," Sarah said.

"It didn't belong to her," Max said. "It belonged to the 7th." He put something small but heavy in Sarah's hand. She looked down.

It was an Aztec amulet vial on a thin gold

chain, with a strange warlike figure on it. Beethoven's gift to his Lobkowicz patron. And now a Lobkowicz was giving it to her.

"How . . . ?" Sarah began to ask.

Max shrugged. "Elisa must have stolen it."

"It belongs in a museum," Sarah said, tracing the pattern of the Aztec god on its surface. "It belongs in *your* museum."

"Yeah, well, there wouldn't be a museum or a me," Max said, fastening the chain around her neck where it glowed darkly, "if it weren't for you."

"Max, can I ask you something?"

"Mmmhmm."

"What did you have Nico take to Venice? You had something put in the safe at the Hotel Gritti Palace. I read the letter, actually. Remember? Jana gave it to me to give to you . . . ?"

"My little Nancy Drew," growled Max, diving below the covers.

"What was it?" Sarah sighed happily. "No, really, Max. Tell me."

He popped up from under the sheet.

"A book," he said. "By one Zosimos of Panopolis. He wrote the oldest known books on alchemy around AD 330."

"No more alchemy," groaned Sarah.

"This one's not about alchemy, it's about

618

the Golden Fleece," said Max.

"Really?" Sarah sat up. "What does it say?"

"I don't know yet. I haven't found anyone who speaks the language it's written in."

"What language is it?"

"No one can figure that out. There's someone in Venice I want to show it to, but he's away for the summer. For now it's sitting in a hotel safe."

"So the quest for the Fleece isn't over?"

"It's my sworn duty to protect the Fleece," said Max gravely. "Whatever it is. Which means I need to find it."

Max's assumption of the mantle of duty coincided with Sarah's finally letting go of hers. For the first time in her life she felt free. Free of the sadness and the confused guilt over her father's death. Free of the need to prove herself, rise above her background, show the world she was just as smart, smarter. Free of the little compartments she had put people and things in: work, ambition, sex, love.

"But you don't have to find it today," she said, firmly shoving Max's head back down under the covers.

Because after all, time didn't really exist.

A few days later, tearfully, the governor of Virginia picked a close friend of the president's to replace Charlotte Yates until the next election. The creation of a Charlotte Yates Library was announced. The nation's period of mourning for its groundbreaking feminist hero ended as the World Series began.

Sixty-Six

Sarah picked up the envelope and sniffed it.

"It's from Lobkowicz Palace," said Bailey, grinning.

They had offered her a new office, but she had preferred to stay in the attic with Bailey, even though, since falling in love with a Korean harpist, his madrigals had gotten unbearably cloying.

It had been a busy year.

Max had offered her a position at his museum, of course. And of course she had said no. That wasn't how she rolled, and she was determined to finish her PhD, anyway. Although if he wanted to offer her unlimited access to the archives . . .

She had come back to Boston and written a paper on the unpublished correspondence of Joseph Franz Maximilian Lobkowicz and Ludwig van Beethoven. She had *not* included the letters she had found in the violin. She hadn't quite figured out how to explain it all. Yet. Still, she managed to make a pretty interesting thing of the relationship, and her paper had been widely talked about. *The New Yorker* had even printed an excerpt.

To everyone's surprise, Pols had announced she was staying in Prague. Her parents bought a large apartment on Prokopova, and *she* accepted a job at the museum. Apparently she had developed quite a fondness for the city, and even taken, in her odd way, to performing. Max had hired her to play in the daily concerts that took place at noon in the Concert Hall for the tourists. She was proving to be quite the little tyrant in terms of music selection, additional musician hiring, and her salary. Max called her his "little LVB" and she called him "Fitzliputzli." They both enjoyed the historical precedence for this kind of thing, and Max said he hoped Pollina would dedicate a symphony to him one day. Boris and Jose had adapted to life in the Czech Republic very well. Jose was dating a fireman. Max had commissioned a portrait of Boris to hang in the Dog Room, in a place of honor. Boris and Moritz enjoyed long walks together in the Deer Moat, while the Chihuahua cleared the squirrels from their path.

Pollina had insisted that the Holy Infant of Prague be restored to its rightful place with the Carmelite nuns at the Church of Our Lady Victorious. Nico had arranged the transfer. Pols attributed her return to perfect health and a three-inch growth spurt to this act of piety, but Sarah thought it might have more to do with the extensive regimen of vitamins Oksana had prescribed.

Max had offered to help Stefania find her former lover, the American she had been separated from in the 1970s, but she had refused. Sarah suspected that Stefania, with typical Slavic pessimism, was certain that any meeting would be a disappointment. Perhaps she was right, although the new, begrudgingly romantic Sarah kind of hoped she would change her mind. At least Max had convinced her to let him pay for some orthopedic surgery and given her a generous pension. He was trying to arrange a position for her as a teacher at the Czech National Ballet. It wasn't enough to be alive. Everyone needed something to live for.

Or die for. Sarah hadn't heard from Nico in a while. Max had found the ancient Italian scholar who seemed to be able to partially translate the mysterious book about the Fleece. Nico had been immediately dispatched to follow up on clues.

Max. He was an old-fashioned guy. He liked sending her handwritten letters. He sent flowers. He made a surprise visit to Boston and had gone down on her right here in her office. . . .

Sarah coughed and opened the letter. The first thing that fell out was a page from a book. Sarah smiled. Ever since she had parted from Max, he had been sending her one page a day from the children's book his grandfather had written, the one about the house with the secret room. He could have just sent her the whole book, of course, but that was not Max. He was tantalizing her. Sarah read the page, on which Sally and Cindy find a mysterious hidden door behind an old bookcase. And then they take a break for a peanut butter and jelly sandwich.

Sarah smiled to herself. She was putting the page back into the envelope when she noticed something else inside. She shook the envelope and it fell onto her desk.

"Hey," said Bailey, grabbing for it. "An airplane ticket!"

"Give it to me," she said, snatching up his bobblehead. "Or I will decapitate this troubadour."

Bailey meekly handed her the envelope.

Stuck to the ticket was a Post-it note. *Think*

we found another Door That Should Not Be Opened. Bring the key!

Sarah looked at the ticket and smiled. Her nose was already twitching.

ACKNOWLEDGMENTS

Magnus Flyte would like to thank the following for their invaluable assistance, counsel, donated services, patience, fortitude, and sense of humor:

Charlotte Sommer, whose passion for Prague and mysteries inspired this volume. Bruce Walker, master of the alchemy of wine and conversation. John and Jennifer Brancato, experts in burrata *and* action sequences. Loren Segan, who masterminds a vast conspiracy of kindness. Art Streiber, who waited twenty-three years to take the picture. Mark Ganem, Web wizard and keeper of the passwords. Travis Tanner, who made horses and humans feel like supermodels. Danielle Belen, who knows her way around a violin. Kathleen McCleary, cheerleader extraordinaire. Betty Luceigh, whose courses nourish the imagination. Claudia Cross and Sally Brady, without whom this book would still be a work in progress. And Carolyn Carlson, who knows no fear.

EDITOR'S NOTE

Because Magnus Flyte can be quite elusive and shuns the public eye, we would like to thank Mr. Flyte's representatives for their cooperation in the publication of this book:

Meg Howrey is the author of the novels *Blind Sight* and *The Cranes Dance.*

Christina Lynch is a television writer and journalist.

— C. C.